THE
TANGLE
OF
AWFUL

USA TODAY BESTSELLING AUTHOR
K WEBSTER

The Tangle of Awful

Copyright © 2023 K Webster

Editor: Emily A. Lawrence
Formatting: Champagne Book Design
Photographer: Wander Aguiar

DEDICATION

To Matt—my heart will forever be tangled with yours.

*From USA Today Bestselling Author K Webster comes
a new steamy age-gap, enemies-to-lovers "why choose"
forbidden romance!*

**He's a successful attorney with a secret craving for his
too-young stepdaughter.
He wants her badly. But his wicked son wants her too…**

Love is an illusion.
In my world, collecting the shiniest trophies is what I do.
Beautiful wife. Swanky home. Expensive cars. Successful firm.
Future attorney general.
Add in the Park family name and I'm the envy of
every man in town.
True love, however, was never attainable, no matter
how much I secretly wanted it.

The desire to be loved isn't my only secret.
My wife is missing.
With my life under scrutiny as I run for office, I'm finding it
difficult to lie away her whereabouts. People are starting to
notice. My political opponent. Her best friend. And worst of all,
my wife's daughter, Aubrey.

Aubrey is finally back home after two long years with her dad, but she's asking questions I don't have answers to. Yet, that's not all she's doing…

She's invading my thoughts and my heart, driving me insane with her beauty and vulnerability.

I want her.
She's barely legal and my wife's daughter.
Forbidden and morally wrong.
I can't have her. I can't.

My son, though, doesn't live by the same code I do.
He wants her too.
But not to love…*to destroy.*

I'll risk everything to keep him from her.
Even if this tangle of awful costs me my reputation, my campaign, *and* my son.

***This is a complete mfm standalone novel with a happily ever after. Characters are of legal age and there is no romantic involvement between blood relations. ***

CHAPTER ONE

Aubrey

T HERE'S ONLY ONE PERSON IN THE ENTIRE WORLD I
hate.

Spencer Park.

He's vile. A monster. Awful.

I vowed two years ago I'd never look at or speak to him again. It was a promise I'd been able to keep until recently.

And, because of my mother, I'm once again going to be subjected to the misery he creates. This time, not because I'm being forced to but by choice.

I'm choosing this for myself.

I don't suddenly like Spencer. Far from it. I just know something is going on with Mom and I will get to the bottom of it.

"Here?" the Uber driver asks as he slows to a stop in front of the massive structure I once called home.

"This is it," I say with a shaky sigh. "Thanks."

I climb out, pull on my backpack, and grab my overstuffed suitcase before slamming the car door shut. The home looms over me, cold and mocking. Every single detail of this house screams money. From the perfectly trimmed hedges and yard to the shiny black luxury vehicle in the driveway.

And then there's me.

The leech.

At least, that's what he took to calling me seemingly out of the blue. One day, we were friends and the next, everything was ruined.

Old memories of Spencer's cruelty simmer to the surface of my mind, but I don't let them consume me. I'm no longer the sixteen-year-old girl I once was. I've changed. I'm stronger, smarter, and a freaking adult. Spencer Park holds no power over me.

I'm back now and I refuse to let him get to me.

Slowly, I wheel my dented suitcase up the front walkway toward the pristine charcoal gray door that will welcome me into a cold hell. My hands slightly shake as I reach it. Since Spencer used to always steal my house key, I kept one hidden outside. Leaving my suitcase, I walk over to the gutter spout at the corner of the house. I crouch in front of it and lift the biggest of the smooth stones on the ground in front of it.

The key is there.

My stomach twists.

It's all wrong. The metal teeth no longer sharp and jagged. It's as if it's been melted smooth. Words have been carved into the metal.

Not welcome, leech.

I curl the useless key into my palm and rise to my feet. He may have intimidated me two years ago, but I'm no longer that girl. I've been living in Los Angeles with Dad ever since I left, going to school with a whole bunch of assholes rather than just one. I've learned how to survive.

With newfound fury burning up inside of me, I storm back over to the front door. Of course, when I try the knob, it's locked. I beat my fist on the solid door, anger churning in my gut.

No answer.

I glare up at the camera pointed at the stoop and flip it off. If I know Spencer, I know he always has to have the last word.

As predicted, the snap of the deadbolt unengaging echoes its way through my bones. Gritting my teeth together, I lift my chin, preparing to face off with my enemy. The door swings open and his familiar scent—expensive cologne he's worn probably since birth—swirls around me.

Spencer steps out. Taller than I remember. Stronger, too. Every single part of him perfect as usual. His dark hair is styled a little differently—less boyish and something more manly. The eyes, though, bright blue and intelligent, are icier than ever. Two windows into an arctic hellish soul. It's his mouth that sends a chill down my spine. A cruel slant of a smile, probably charming to most, but sinister to those who truly know him.

"Hello, brother," I say in a tone dripping with acid. "Seems my key stopped working."

I toss the key onto the cement and it clatters between us.

His dark eyebrow lifts, unimpressed with my attitude toward him. *Newsflash, buddy, I'm not that girl you ran off once before.* He doesn't answer, instead perusing his gaze up and down my body, lingering on my chest. Since the material of my shirt is thin, I know he can see through it, judging my old black Walmart bra and nipples that are hard from the coldness rippling from the open front door where the icy asshole looms.

"You don't live here anymore, leech."

I refuse to shudder at the name, choosing to glower at him instead. "Where's Mom?"

His blue eyes narrow, hard gaze boring into me. "How the fuck should I know?"

"I want to talk to her," I snip. "Now."

He smirks at me. "Still a bossy princess. Go back home to your daddy. You're no longer welcome here." He fists his hand and pretends to wipe a tear from his cheek. "Mommy doesn't love you anymore."

His words are a spike in my heart. How he always manages to find my weakness is a surprise to me. I give him nothing, but he peels back my insecurities without me ever muttering a word. Two years and he's exactly the same. Still lording his power over me.

"I want to tell her I'm sorry," I mutter, trying a different approach. "She deserves that."

The last time I spoke to my mom, I screamed at her for loving the Parks more than her own daughter. Told her I was going to live with Dad. I'd wanted her to fight for me. Instead, she looked away and let me walk out that door.

"Do you really think Neena sits around like some pathetic loser wishing for her only daughter to make amends?" He laughs, a vicious glint in his eyes. "She continues to spend Dad's money so she can live a privileged life, one where she's free of her bratty kid."

The truth hurts.

"Please," I whisper. "I only want to talk to her."

Begging is more painful than hearing the truth. Pleading with a monster means I'm offering my neck to him—being vulnerable with a man whose teeth are much sharper as an adult.

"She's gone." His nostrils flare. "Now you have no reason to ever come back."

Gone?

Unease roils in my belly. "What do you mean?"

"She took off, leech. Probably fucking her plastic surgeon. How the hell should I know?"

"Where did she go?" I croak out. "Spencer, please, give me something."

He sneers at me. "Such a needy, needy leech. Always wanting something from us Parks."

Anger swells up inside me again. I want to shove him and make him fall flat on his ass. Or, maybe I should spit on his handsome face instead.

His eyes flash with something so dark and sinister I barely suppress a shudder. He raises a hand, which makes me flinch. God, I hate him. His long finger points to the road.

"Don't be a scaredy cat," he rumbles. "You know I don't hit little girls."

Not with his fists.

His tongue, though, is something far more powerful. Each lash of his mean words leaves a bruise that lasts for years to come.

Since he's still pointing, I follow where his finger is gesturing. To nothing. An empty road. Confused, I turn to ask him what he means.

The door slams in my face.

That's it.

That's all I get.

"Asshole!" I yell through the door.

Defeat surges through me and my eyes prickle with tears. I swallow down the emotion, refusing to allow him to get to me. I'm tougher now. His insults and behavior toward me don't affect me like they used to.

With a huff, I squat to pick up my key, inspecting it once more. His message mocks me. Typical for Spencer Park.

Treating everyone, especially me, like we're beneath him. All the ideas for revenge I've had over the years come flooding through me. I had an opportunity and failed to do anything to ruffle his feathers.

I glance over at his shiny car. I don't know what kind it is, nor do I care. All I know is next time he looks at it, he'll think of me.

I'm not going away this time.

Not without answers. Not without speaking to Mom. He won't chase me away.

I grab my suitcase and stalk over to his car. The key in my grip pinks against the metal as I forcefully bump it. Then, I take great satisfaction in the scraping sound as I run it over the paint, gouging a silvery line as I walk, making sure to hit the front panel, door, and back panel. When I reach the trunk, I set the key on top.

I'm not scared of you anymore, Spencer.

With vengeance on my mind, I happily walk down the road, pulling up an Uber on my app along the way. When I reach the end of the street, I sit down on my suitcase, waiting for my ride. Just as the vehicle approaches, I hear Spencer yelling out, "Fucking bitch!"

A crazed giggle escapes me. I've just started a war with the devil himself. And, for the first time, I'm not intimidated. He's just a spoiled, rich shithead. Spencer is nothing like the actual pricks I went to school with when I lived with Dad. He's all awful, terrible talk. A dog with bark, but no bite.

I climb into the Uber, attempting to reassure myself. My gut feels hollow. Despite my pep talk, I don't believe it, deep down.

"Where to?" the driver asks.

Fumbling with my phone, I show him the address. The place where I can find the one person who holds power over Spencer. My only ally and someone who can give me real answers.

Hugo Park.

My stepdad.

CHAPTER TWO

Spencer

U NBELIEVABLE.

Fury, so violent and chaotic, lashes inside of me like a sea storm. My thoughts are thrust back and forth, some of which threaten to flip me overboard altogether.

Breathe, man.

The little girl who used to drive me crazy is back. She's got some balls, too. A new fire lights up her green eyes, making promises of misery and trouble—which awakens a dormant, dark part of me.

Bring it, little girl.

Oh, she's brought it. That's for damn sure.

Scrubbing my palm down over my face, I peek through my fingers, hoping the hideous gouge in my sleek, midnight-black BMW 8 Series will miraculously be gone.

Nope.

Still. Fucking. There.

I can't believe she keyed my car. If she hadn't left her evidence on the trunk, I wouldn't have believed Aubrey even had it in her.

She's a princess.

Fragile, delicate, weak.

Not vindictive. That's more her mother.

Apparently, she's changed, which means I'm dealing with

a whole new enemy here. And while I've always been able to outsmart her, she's persistent. That is, until she reaches her breaking point. Two years ago, I pushed her to that point, happily not having to speak to her until now.

Based on the fiery indignation I was met with moments ago and the fact she keyed my car, I think it's safe to assume she's far from running back home with her tail tucked between her legs.

Time to up my game.

I take a few pictures of my car before sending them to my grandfather. Nathan Park is the powerful, throbbing vein that connects the Park family. Our influence over this town is solely because of him. His own father, though still a force, didn't compare to how my pops rules Park Mountain, Washington.

We are kings and everyone else exists to serve us in some capacity.

Pops: Someone vandalized your car?

Me: Yup.

Pops: At home? Did you pull the camera footage?

I could easily tattle to him that it was my bratty stepsister, but that would take all the fun out of making her pay for what she did.

Me: Bad connection. Wi-Fi wasn't working. It's fixed now, but I can't drive around with my car looking like shit, Pops.

Pops: I know a guy. Let me give him a call.

When Pops says he "knows a guy," it means someone owes him and he's ready to cash in. The long, ugly gouge in the paint of my car will be erased from existence within a few days. There are many, many perks to being a Park.

Satisfied that Pops will take care of it, I shove my phone in my pocket and stalk across the yard to his house. My gaze scans Park Mountain Lane, but Aubrey is long gone. I'm not sure where she went, nor do I care. All I do know is she'll be back, and when she returns, I'll be ready for her. Today, she got the element of surprise. Starting tomorrow, I'll be doing all the surprising.

Dempsey, technically my uncle, but who feels more like a cousin, is home. He's more than just family or a neighbor, he's my best friend. Though we couldn't be more different, we get each other like no one else does. Both him and his twin sister, Gemma, are some of the few people I actually trust.

I let myself in the front door and listen for any signs of life. Usually, Gemma, or her mom, Jamie, are yapping, their cheerful voices echoing all around. Considering the silence, they must be out shopping or some shit.

Good.

I need to plan with Dempsey without Gemma throwing her two cents in. She'll try and make me feel bad or side with Aubrey. I don't need that shit right now.

As I take the stairs, I hear the soft thump of bass coming from Dempsey's room. If he's jerking off, he's going to be in for a rude interruption. Thankfully, when I push open his bedroom door, he doesn't have his dick in his hand. He sits at his desk that faces the window, back to me and hunched over, as he feverishly draws on a sketchpad.

"Thought I was fucking my hand, huh?" he asks, sensing my quiet entry.

I chuff and prowl forward, stepping over discarded

clothes and shoes along the way. "Nah. I knew you were doing something much worse. Drawing."

He tenses but continues with his art. This particular topic is a point of contention between Dempsey and Pops. My grandfather views drawing as pointless. And while I agree, I don't see why he can't drop it. Dempsey would probably be more pleasant to be around if he didn't have to fight for every damn thing he wanted to do in this life.

"Who's that?" I ask, narrowing my eyes as I try to place where I know the eyes from.

Dempsey grunts out something under his breath before slamming his sketchpad closed, away from my prying eyes. He spins around in his desk chair to face me. His dark hair is in disarray as though he's been running his fingers through it all day. Smudges from his charcoal pencil dust his prominent cheekbone on one side.

"Do you ever shower?" I flick my fingers toward his gray T-shirt that's rumpled and stained with something pink. "Have you even left this bedroom since school let out?"

His lips curl into a taunting grin. "Someone's pissy today and looking for a shoulder to cry on. Do tell, cuz, what has your panties crawling up your tight ass?"

My teeth clench together and I straighten my spine. Sometimes I hate how easily Dempsey can read me.

"She's back," I grit out.

Dempsey's eyes widen comically. "Neena? Where the hell was she?"

Scowling, I give a sharp shake of my head. "Not Neena. My stepsister."

"No shit?" He starts laughing so hard his stupid ass nearly falls out of his desk chair. "This is good. Too good."

I glower at him before casting my gaze over to his bed. Energy thrums through me and I have the urge to pace, but in his messy room, I'm likely to break an ankle. The bed, however, unmade and probably crusted over with jizz, doesn't look all that inviting either.

"Come on," Dempsey says, rising from his chair. "Let's play a game of pool before you have an aneurism."

A rush of relieved breath escapes past my lips. I give him a clipped nod and then stalk out of his room toward the game room. Dempsey ambles behind me, humming a familiar song. Once we're in the immaculate game room, I can breathe a little easier. Jamie, Dempsey's mom and technically my grandmother through marriage—though there's no way in hell I'd ever call her that—makes sure the rest of the house is showroom ready. Dempsey is the smear of imperfection in this household.

While he racks the balls, I grab a cue stick and roll my neck over my shoulders in an attempt to release the tension. Dempsey, who's never been tense a day in his life, makes the first shot, knocking two of his balls into the corner pocket.

"So," he urges. "What's Aubrey done now?"

His placating tone grates on my nerves. I know he and Gemma like Aubrey. Neither of them understands my grudge against her.

"She exists."

A bark of laughter makes him miss his next shot. "Need help killing her?"

He's teasing, but I bristle at the thought. I don't want to kill her. What fun would that be? I'd much rather watch her squirm, suffer, and cry—all because of me.

"She keyed my car, Demps."

His smile fades. "Are you fucking for real right now?"

"And she's back, asking questions about Neena."

Dempsey rebels against his father any chance he gets, but when it comes to protecting the Park family name, he always gets in line as he should. Aubrey, opening up the whole Neena fiasco, means pointing a light at *my* father.

Hugo Park, soon-to-be attorney general, doesn't need a spotlight on the fact his wife is missing. It'll kill his campaign and open up a bunch of fucking worm cans. All of which, I'm not about to deal with.

"Want me to talk to her?" His head cocks to the side as he studies me. "She likes me. I can find out what her agenda is."

"We already know what her agenda is," I grind out. "She wants to know where Neena is and, based on her fucking attitude problem that she took out on my car, I don't think she's going to stop until she gets what she wants."

Dempsey's phone rings, interrupting our conversation. I pinch the bridge of my nose and squeeze my eyes shut.

"Hey, nerd," he says in greeting. "Buy me something pretty?"

Gemma snorts. "You wish."

"What do you want?"

"I was thinking me, you, Spencer, and Willa could go see a movie. Callum didn't take his claws out of her long enough to go shopping with me and Mom, but he has a meeting tonight with Jude. We can kidnap her."

My uncle, Callum, is obsessed with his child bride. Technically she isn't a child, nor his bride, but it's fun watching the vein pop on his forehead anytime I call her that.

"Can't," Dempsey says with a grin. "Have plans to crush thy bones of a mortal enemy."

"Ew. Who is Spencer trying to destroy now? Don't you two morons get bored with these games?"

"Nope," me and Dempsey say at once.

"Whatever," Gemma grumbles. "Do I know him?"

"Her," Dempsey says, chuckling. "And you totally do."

I glower at him, hoping he'll shut his mouth. Of course, he doesn't have to say much more. His twin can probably read his goddamn mind for all I know because she always seems to figure out what he's thinking anyway.

"Aubrey's here?" Gemma shrieks. "Oh my God, that ho didn't tell me she was coming!"

"Don't get too excited," Dempsey tells her. "She won't stick around long."

"We'll see about that."

She ends the call and Dempsey shrugs at me, a brow lifted in question. "So, what's the plan, cuz?"

I meet Dempsey's gaze, a menacing grin curling my lips up. "We break her down piece by piece until she runs away, yet again, like the weak little girl she is. We'll make sure she doesn't come back ever again."

Gemma won't be able to save her.

No one can save her.

CHAPTER THREE

Hugo

I DRUM MY FINGERS ON MY DESK, GLARING AT MY LAPTOP screen. The charges from Neena's card mock me. All her favorite shops see her consistently, but I can't even get a response. If she'd actually keep her phone on and return my texts, I could demand a divorce, my campaign be damned.

My wife is a manipulative, crazy bitch.

These mind games she plays—and has played them well since the day we started dating—are beyond fucked-up. In the past, I put up with her because she was the partner I needed. Not true love, like my first wife, but a companion. Someone to attend functions with and to show off at social events.

Neena is flawless.

Platinum-blond hair. Perfect, paid-for tits. A slender body kept in shape from a lifetime of eating healthy and obsessive yoga sessions.

When she enters a room, every damn eye—both male and female—is drawn to her. She can schmooze just as well as I can, which makes those around us view us as a powerhouse couple.

Very few see the woman beneath all the shiny perfection.

A vindictive, cruel woman who toys with the hearts of the ones she loves. I've seen her do it with her family, her friends, me, and her daughter.

Like now…

Pulling a disappearing act, knowing how important her presence is to my campaign.

With a heavy sigh, I forward the newest charges to Jude's email. My little brother is a genius when it comes to digging up dirt on people. But Neena has managed to evade him. All of his usual investigation tactics have come up empty.

Neena will reveal herself when she chooses.

And, knowing her, she'll pick impeccable timing. Like the eve of poll day. I have this sinking feeling she'll toss around threats of divorce in order for me to bend to her will. I wish she'd just demand what she wants so I could give it to her, avoiding all this uncertainty altogether.

If she'd answer her goddamn phone, I could get to the bottom of this whole tantrum she's throwing.

My desk phone chirps to life and for a split second, I think it's Neena. A quick glance at the caller ID and I deflate to see it's my assistant, Karla, instead.

As soon as I answer, she announces I have a visitor waiting in the lobby. I affirm I'll see the visitor, needing a break from my inner Neena-related turmoil. Seconds later, the door opens, revealing the woman who's come to see me.

At first, all I see are long, bare, tanned legs that shimmer in the sunlight pouring in from the window behind me. An intricate tattoo covers her whole right thigh, disappearing beneath frayed, cutoff shorts. From this distance, I can't see what it is, but my dick twitches at the idea of inspecting it up close. Slowly, I peruse my gaze over a pierced bellybutton peeking between her denim shorts and beige cropped top. The shirt is thin, revealing a black bra underneath. I continue my trek to her plump, glossy lips and then to her nose piercing. When I land on the eyes, I freeze.

"Hey." She waves, jangly bracelets clinging against one another. "Long time, no see."

For half a second, I think it's Neena—tattooed and pierced, rebelling against the version I know—but all the pieces snap together in an instant, revealing who it is I'm actually looking at.

Aubrey.

Little Aubrey all grown up.

My stepdaughter.

I inwardly cringe at the fact I'm sporting a chub in my slacks, still hung up on the tattoo on her thigh. This day just keeps getting better and better.

"Aubrey," I greet, voice tight with unease. "How've you been, Love?"

She saunters toward me, hips moving in a way I've never seen from her before, and stops in front of my desk. From this close, I can smell her.

Sunshine and fresh peaches.

The scent that was so innocent and sweet just a couple of years ago now awakens dormant parts of me. Parts that have no business slinking their way out of the dark corners of my mind. The sweet innocence is now a smell that taunts and teases.

"I've been better," she says, voice soft.

The defeat in her tone, though barely perceptible, has me snapping into action. All sick, twisted stirrings are shoved away as concern courses through me. I rise to my feet and stride around my desk. Grabbing her shoulders, I tug her to me, folding her into my arms.

She's tense at first and then relaxes into my hug, resting her cheek against my chest. I rub my palm up and down her spine, offering any comfort I can.

"You've been a stranger, kid," I say, voice gruff. "Never come to visit us anymore."

"I'm not exactly welcome around here."

I scoff at that statement. "Nonsense. You know we all love you."

She pulls back, the comfortable familiarity between us dissipating and making room for this new awkwardness. Her brow furls and she sits down in the chair on the other side of my desk. Rather than returning to my seat, I take the one beside her.

"Try telling Spencer that." Her green eyes dart toward mine, hurt shining in them. "He wouldn't even let me in the house."

That little shit.

I still, to this day, can't understand why he despises her.

"Spencer's name isn't on the deed," I say, smirking at her. "You know you're always welcome. Your room is still there as it was."

I certainly don't tell her that her mother was adamant about turning it into a personal yoga studio. So adamant, it took me changing the lock on the door and hiding the key so she wouldn't do it one day while I was at work. Naturally, I'm not about to tell Aubrey her mother was all too eager to wipe her existence from the house.

"Is everything okay?" I ask slowly, knowing we can only dance around the reason she's here for so long. "You're a long way from LA."

Her lips press together and her head bows as she looks

down at her hands on her thighs. Long, sunny-blond, beach-wavy hair tickles over the ink. I have the urge to push it away so I can inspect the ink more closely without her hair in the way.

"Where's Mom?"

My blood runs cold. "That's a good question."

"You don't know?" Her head jerks up and she bores her stare into me. "How can you not know?"

That's a loaded question. Does Aubrey have all afternoon to listen to me count the ways her mother is a puppet master in this town mindfucking everyone—especially me?

"Your mother," I say, carefully choosing my words, "can be cold sometimes."

She nods. "Tell me about it."

Two years ago, rather than being the mother Aubrey needed, Neena turned her back on her. Told her to grow up or go live with her dad. Even I wasn't able to smooth things over between them. I'm not sure exactly what caused the big blowup, but I do know my son didn't help matters by being an antagonistic prick.

"How long has she been gone?" Aubrey asks. "Are you two separated?"

I rub at my temple with my index finger, wondering the best way to navigate this answer. "Months. About eight or nine maybe? I don't know, but it feels like forever."

She sucks in a sharp breath. "That's about how long it's been since I've spoken to her."

"I'm assuming we're separated, but you know how your mother is. She'll show up one day acting as if nothing happened just to fuck with me."

I cringe at my oversharing. I've always been able to say

the right things in life, avoiding pure honesty for the sake of my image and career. Somehow, though, Aubrey has thrown me off my game.

"So you two were on the outs?" Her body turns toward me more and she pulls on her knee, tucking her leg beneath her on the chair.

I note that her tattoo is swirling ocean waves, designed so intricately in different shades of blue that it almost seems as though it's actually moving. It's mesmerizing and distracting. The urge to cover it up with my large palm thrums through me like electricity. Instead, I fist my hand, keeping it firmly planted in my lap.

"We've been on the outs for years," I admit with a resigned sigh. "She usually makes an effort, though, for the public. Now, she has us covering for her. With my campaign—"

"Campaign?"

"I'm running for attorney general. The competition is weak, so I'll likely win, but her timing of this stunt won't make things easy on me."

She studies my face for a long beat, glances at my mouth, and then darts her eyes back to her tattoo. "What if…What if something happened to her, Hugo?" Her voice trembles and her next words barely rasp out. "What if she's dead?"

It'd be so much easier on us all if that were the case. Being a widower would ensure my win, no doubt. Furthermore, the stress and anxiety Neena causes me on a daily basis would disappear completely. As far as the feeling of abandonment that Aubrey certainly deals with, would also be explained away. Her mother could be remembered as just that, her mom. Not someone who doesn't give two shits about her.

"She's not dead," I assure her.

"How do you know?"

"I'm tracking her purchases and phone activity whenever she decides to turn it on."

"Someone could have her card," she croaks out.

Only Neena makes weekly trips to Michael Kors or Kate Spade for new handbags and accessories. Only Neena eats at Wild Eats several times a month. Only Neena buys hair products on the regular at the high-end salons around town.

"She has her card." I scrub my palm over my face. "Her card activity is the same as it always is. If anything, she's spending more." I pause to frown. "Enough for two people."

"Have you tried her car?" Aubrey offers. "It's high tech. Don't you have access to the app?"

"It's in the garage, untouched."

"Why is she doing this?" she asks. "Making us all worry?"

Because your mother is a bitch of epic proportions when she wants to be.

"I don't know," I say instead. "I'm working on it. I can't exactly call her favorite shops and restaurants to ask where my wife is without rousing suspicion. You know how this town talks."

She nods, all too aware of small-town living and the rumor mill everyone is connected to.

"Now why are you really here?" I lift a brow at her. "This could have been a phone call. What else is going on?"

Aubrey shifts in her seat. Her cheeks slowly tinge pink. Whatever has her quietly evading the question is embarrassing to her.

"Aubrey Love," I urge, using her first and middle name. "Tell me so I can help."

Relief floods through her, taking some of the tension

with it. Did she really think I'd mock her or send her away? I reach over and hook a finger under her chin, lifting her head so that she's forced to look at me.

"Me and Dad..." She trails off, nostrils flaring. "We had a fight."

"And you decided to come stay with us?"

"I didn't have a choice," she says icily. "Dad kicked me out."

A hot burst of anger surges up my spine and straight to my head. "He what?"

"Apparently, I'm out of control." She scoffs, shaking her head. "If I can't find Mom, I don't know where I'm supposed to go."

I grab hold of her hand, enveloping it between both of mine. The pink on her cheeks turns a deeper shade of crimson and causes her neck to turn splotchy in the same color.

"You come home," I tell her in a fierce tone. "With me."

"But—"

"I'll talk to Spencer. He can get in line or he can get out. The boy doesn't have his trust fund yet. We both know he's not going to take option two, at least until he turns twenty-one."

"I'll need a new key. Mine is, uh, ruined."

I squeeze her hand between mine, hoping to offer comfort. "I'm going to take care of you, Love. Whether I'm married to your mother or not. That's a promise."

Her smile is breathtaking. "I didn't miss much about Park Mountain," she murmurs and then eyes my mouth again, "but I did miss you."

Words that should be sweet and benign are anything but. They tease at the shadowed parts of my mind, molding them and mutating them into something they're not. Something they can't ever be.

She's my stepdaughter.

Young. Gorgeous. A rebellious little angel.

Certainly not anyone my cock should even think about reacting to. I clear my throat and release her warm hand, opting to clasp my fingers together, hiding my thickening cock that's beginning to push against the zipper of my slacks.

"I missed you too, Love."

Her glossy pillow lips part like she might say something more, but then she bites down on the bottom one, stopping her words. Finally, she says, "Is it okay if I hang out here until you get off work?"

Having her in my office while I try to do anything will prove to be impossible.

"Nah," I say with a smile. "I'm taking the rest of the day off to spend time with my girl. When's the last time you had that shitty pizza from that place near PMU?"

She groans happily. "Two years, Hugo. Two long years. Can we really go to Gerri's Pizzeria?"

I wink at her. "Anything for you, Love."

Her blush is back, and this time, I let the blood flow straight to my cock, selfishly stealing a moment of forbidden bliss... *just this once.*

CHAPTER FOUR

Aubrey

DAD WAS RIGHT.

I'm a beacon for trouble.

That's the only explanation for how I've behaved since stepping foot into Park Mountain not even two hours ago.

Antagonize stepbrother. *Check.*

Vandalize a luxury vehicle. *Check.*

Flirt with stepfather. *Check.*

I'd come here for a fresh start. Find Mom. Make amends. Try and finish my last year of high school with at least Cs rather than the Fs I was pulling in last year in LA. Stay far, far away from tattooed men with fast cars and dirty mouths.

I may have left the trouble I was knee-deep in, but I've already landed myself into a new heap of trouble.

"What have you been up to the past couple of years?" Hugo asks before sipping his soda. "I feel like there's so much to catch up on."

I try not to let my stare linger on his lips, but in my defense, it's difficult. Hugo has a mouth that's often curled into a genuine, welcoming smile. His teeth are white, perfect, and probably cost a fortune. I can't help but fixate on his lips— light red and full. They look so soft and kissable.

A burst of heat burns down my spine, coiling in the pit

of my core. Why am I this way? I'm forever lusting over what I shouldn't have. It's a personality trait I'm not proud of.

"Not much," I say, choosing to turn my focus on a breadstick, dipping it into the homemade marinara sauce I've been dreaming about for far too long. "Trying and failing to stay out of trouble according to Dad."

Hugo chuckles, his voice deep and warm. It sends a buzz tickling over my flesh. My skin feels hot and I hope like hell I'm not blushing. "You're a good girl, Love. At least you always were for me."

My eyes lift to his and I meet his smile with one of my own. Hugo was definitely one of the things I missed about Park Mountain. He always said the right things to make me feel better about myself. When Mom was being her usual distant self or when Spencer was being a dick, it was Hugo who easily cheered me up.

Is that why I'm suddenly crushing on him?

I blame hormones. Not long after I left to go live with Dad, it's like my hormones went wild. It felt great to be wanted and adored, even if only for a night or a weekend. The men in LA didn't care about my age or the fact I lived in a shitty apartment with my dad or that my grades were a nightmare.

They just wanted to fuck.

To whisper all the right things as they touched me in all the right places.

"I'm not the same girl who left," I admit, hating the quaver of shame in my voice. "I, uh, was kind of out of control in LA."

Hugo's eyebrows furl together, concern etching lines at the corners of his eyes, his perfect lips pursing together. "Out of control how?"

I shift in my seat, unable to meet his stare. "Bad grades."

Shoving my breadstick into my mouth, I take an enormous bite, hoping to avoid any more digging into my past. The intensity rippling from Hugo is hard to ignore. As if he's silently commanding me to look at him, I'm forced to meet his gaze.

"Are you okay, Aubrey? Like really okay?"

My heart flutters. "I'm at the best pizza place in the world with my favorite guy. I'm better than okay."

"Favorite guy?" He smirks. "I'll take it."

He's flirting with me.

This isn't one-sided.

Right?

I thought I'd imagined it in his office, but now I'm not so sure. Right now, the way he watches me, blue eyes electric and penetrating, I'm beginning to think he might be.

All awkward thoughts vanish the moment the server brings our pizza. It's a deep dish piled high with sausage, bell peppers, mushrooms, and onions. The heavenly aroma makes my mouth water. God, I've missed this place.

Hugo, ever the gentleman, serves a slice up on my plate and then one for himself. I dig in, eagerly listening to him update me on what's going on with the rest of the Park family.

"Wait, so Callum hooked up with a student?" I gape at him, interrupting his most recent nugget of information. "For real?"

Hugo scans the restaurant with a quick glance before darting his eyes back my way. He lowers his voice as he says, "Yes, but it's not exactly public information."

"Sorry," I whisper. "That just took me by surprise."

Callum is one of Hugo's younger brothers and he's not

just a grump, but he's distant too. I'd seen him around when I attended Park Mountain High School, but never had him as a teacher since I wasn't an upperclassman. My only interactions with him were at Sunday dinners where he spent his time glowering at his dad and stepmom.

"You'll like Willa," Hugo assures me. "Even Spencer likes Willa and he's not one to accept outsiders very willingly."

I bristle at the mention of Spencer.

"How are the twins?" I ask, needing to stop thinking about him altogether.

"Dempsey is Dempsey. A little shit, of course." Hugo laughs. "And Gemma is on the verge of giving Dad all kinds of hell. Call it a sixth sense. He's kept her pinned under his thumb, but it's only a matter of time before she rebels against him."

The thought of Gemma, the princess of Park Mountain, rebelling is comical. She's perfect in every sense of the word. Her idea of rebelling might be to sneak out of the house to go swim in Spencer's pool. I seriously doubt her level of rebellion is anywhere close to mine.

Knowing Gemma, she's probably still a virgin.

Meanwhile, I've slept with more men than I can count, been tattooing my body long before I was legal, and have dabbled in every drug there is.

"But you probably already know that, right?" Hugo asks. "You two still keep up on social media?"

"Yeah," I lie. "We chat all the time."

And while the chatting part is correct, the keeping up part is not. My social media, like hers, only shows what I want others to see—a curated snapshot of what I want my life to be. Fun, happy, random. A series of photographs of the sun setting over San Pedro Bay, my sparkly painted toes in flip-flops dangling off my apartment balcony, my newest Starbucks iced coffee with a crowded sidewalk of people for a backdrop. My socials don't show the revolving door of men I "date" or the silent dinners where I ate alone in the apartment. Just like Gemma's socials show perfect selfies, most of which are in her backyard, no indication that her dad keeps her under lock and key.

Dinner goes by in a blur. Hugo easily keeps the conversation going, attempting to engage me in it, but my mind keeps slipping in other directions. It's not until we're pulling into the garage at his house that the fog clears.

Apprehension skitters through me knowing I'll have to face Spencer again and soon. I climb out of the car and take my backpack while Hugo grabs my suitcase. It's amusing to see a grown-ass man in a terribly expensive suit tugging a dented, hot pink suitcase on wheels behind him.

The house is exactly as I remember. Massive. Chilly. Decorated fit for a magazine spread. If I thought I'd felt out of place years ago, it's only made more obvious now that I'm a colorful, messy, tainted version of the girl I once was.

I follow Hugo down the hallway past Spencer's closed door to my old room. He abandons the handle of the suitcase to fish out the key that fits it. Once he unlocks it and pushes inside, a wave of familiar nostalgia hits me.

Oh, God.

"You kept the Harry Styles posters," I say, grimacing. "How sweet."

Hugo barks out a laugh. "What? He's not your boyfriend anymore? I didn't get the memo."

Crushing over Harry feels like a lifetime ago, especially since I actually slept with a musician who looked eerily like him. The guy's name was Wes and he was a dick who stayed high. I'd lost interest by the third time he couldn't keep his dick hard from being so stoned.

"Those posters have to go." I toss my backpack onto the bed and inhale the scent of oranges. "I can't believe you kept everything the same."

Hugo picks up my suitcase and sets it on the bed beside my bag. He saunters over to me until we're inches apart. I suck in a breath, expecting oranges, but am met with his expensive cologne—the same fragrant scent Spencer wears.

"I told you," Hugo rumbles, lifting a finger to stroke my cheek. "You're always welcome here. Somehow I knew you'd come back."

It's difficult not to melt into his delicate touch. But, if I have any hope of finding Mom and actually keeping this place to live, I'll not give in to my urges. It would be so easy to use my skills of luring a man into my bed on Hugo.

Then what?

With Hugo, the whole dynamic would be screwed up. He's my stepfather and I really care about him. I don't want him to resent me later, especially if Mom comes back home and they work it out. I'll be a dirty little secret.

I may be self-destructive and wild at times, but I protect my heart at all costs. Having it broken once in this lifetime was enough.

"Get settled in," Hugo says, hauling me into his arms for yet another comforting hug. "If you need anything, you come to me."

I cling to him, my palms greedily sliding over the prominent muscles in his back, and nod. "Thanks, Hugo."

"Anything for you, Love."

I've packed away the last of my things and am changing into my pajamas when the snick of the door opening has me whirling around. I expect to find Hugo coming to check on me but instead find Spencer.

In nothing but a low-slung pair of gray sweatpants, he saunters into my room like he owns the place. His sharp gaze is on me, raking down over my naked, exposed shoulders to where I clutch my nightshirt to my chest. He grins, calculating and predatory.

"Did I interrupt something, Aubby Loves Cock?"

Rolling my eyes, I turn my back to him and pull on the shirt. I can feel his stare still on me, so I make sure the shirt is pulled all the way down over my ass before discreetly shimmying out of my jean shorts. I drop them at my feet and step out of them, leaving them where they lie.

"That wasn't funny when I was sixteen. Still not funny," I say, turning to glower at him.

"Your mom had to have thought it was hilarious to name her kid Aubrey Love Cox. It's like she despised you from the second she pushed you out of her vagina."

I'd never thought my name was a problem until my beloved stepbrother twisted it into something that stuck—something that earned me ridicule from him after he randomly decided he hated me one day.

"Don't you have better things to do?" I ask, refusing to look at the deep curves of his abs that weren't there the last time I'd seen him shirtless. "Like organize your sock drawer?"

He doesn't flinch at my jab at his OCD. But he does glare

at my shorts on the floor like they've personally offended him. It pleases me to know I can get to him, even if just a little bit.

"My sock drawer is fine," he drawls out. "Besides, I have something better to obsess about."

Oh, if only he used his powers for good instead of evil. The lucky girl on the receiving end of his obsessive nature would be treated like a queen. But, since this is Spencer we're talking about, he'd rather fixate on torment and cruelty.

And *I'm* the lucky girl on the receiving end of *that*.

"You're different," Spencer says, intrigue coloring his voice. "It makes me want to know why. How. To uncover all these new parts of you barely hiding beneath the surface."

The last thing I want is Spencer digging into the person I've become in the past two years. As if he needs more ammunition against me.

"Is that all?" I give him a bitchy smile. "This conversation is boring and I'm ready for bed."

He stares at me for a long beat, unmoving and still like a panther about to pounce. A slow grin curls his lips up and he lets out a dark chuckle. "I guess it's time to up my game." He walks past me, bumping his shoulder into mine. "I'll come up with plenty to keep us both entertained, leech."

Asshole.

He scoops up my denim shorts and discarded shirt, tossing them into the hamper on his way out. When he reaches the door, he casts another glance over his shoulder, this one roaming over me in an appreciative way that makes my skin burn hot.

Two years ago, I might have swooned under that stare and stupidly hoped I was getting through to him. That we could be lovers, not enemies.

But it's not two years ago and I'm not that same girl.

His spell won't work on me anymore. I'm immune. To punctuate that thought, I flip him the bird. "Sweet dreams, big brother."

He adjusts his dick in his sweats and smirks. "Oh, it'll be fucking sweet."

The door closes behind him and I rush over to lock it. I'm no fool. Spencer Park is a snake. He'll bite when you least expect it, infecting you with his wicked venom.

Unlike when I was sixteen, this time I'll be ready for him.

This time, *I'll* win.

CHAPTER FIVE

Spencer

THE SMELL OF FRESHLY COOKED BACON, AS I WAKE, makes my stomach grumble. For half a second, in my head, I'm a kid again, spending the weekend at Dad's and cooking breakfast with him. Back then, despite my parents divorcing, I'd thought it was kind of cool.

Two houses.

Two bedrooms.

Two parents who took turns buying me whatever I wanted in an effort to distract me from the fact our family had been divided.

I used to love visiting Dad. Our weekends kept us busy with hikes, movies, and shopping trips. Dad always treated me like a man, even when I was little. And Mom was great... until she moved in with that dweeb, Guy Sellers, whom I later learned she cheated on Dad with.

All it took was one time of Guy telling me what to do like he was my damn father for me to lose my shit. I've been with Dad ever since.

I groan, unable to stay away from the savory bacon smell any longer. Quickly, I slide out of bed and neatly make it before grabbing a quick shower. As I soap down, I can't help but think back to last night when Aubrey changed right in fucking front of me. It was so ballsy and my dick perks at the reminder.

She's not the girl I remember.

It's like the innocence is gone, replaced by something fiery and passionate. I crave to pluck away at the feathers of her past, learning new things about her.

My slick, soapy hand brushes against my dick that's now hard as stone. It's probably fucked-up, but I don't care. I shamelessly take hold of my throbbing cock and fuck into my fist, pretending it's my pretty blond, newly tattooed step-sister instead.

I come within seconds like a two-pump chump.

Of fucking course.

Irritated, I rinse off and shut off the shower. Jacking off to the mental image of the girl I hate is a new low. I need to get laid for real, and not by her.

By the time I dress and make it to the kitchen, Aubrey is already up. Her laughter fills the air, reminding me of a time when we didn't hate each other. Back when she first moved in and I thought it was cool as shit to have a sister. Though I'd never admit it, I've always been jealous of Gemma and Dempsey's relationship. Even Dad loves and enjoys the company of his siblings.

But then everything changed.

And now we're here.

Aubrey's smile falters when our eyes connect. I smirk at her as I saunter in, choosing to sit right beside her. Early this morning, she smells like lotion, but it's different. Cheap. I bristle because I don't particularly care for this new scent on her.

"Glad you could join us, Son," Dad says in greeting. "I thought we could have a family meeting."

Dad sets a plate in front of me. Where Aubrey's plate is a mess of scrambled, cheesy eggs, bacon and toast crumbs, and jelly globs, my plate has a pile of flat, crispy bacon, perfectly round fried eggs, and a golden piece of toast with a slight sheen of butter over the top. My food doesn't touch and looks neat. I prefer it that way.

Even though Dad's sudden domestic air perturbs me, I don't let it be known. If he wants to pretend we're a happy little family, then I'll pretend. Aubrey will discover soon enough there's nothing happy about this house.

"Aubrey is going to be living with us," Dad states, shoulders stiffening as if he's ready for a fight.

I shrug as I pick up my toast. "So?"

Dad deflates, exhaling a sharp breath of air. "And I want you to treat her with respect."

"Does she deserve respect?" I snort out a laugh and cut my eyes her way. "Do you, leech?"

Her green eyes flash with a barely contained emotion—equal parts shame and fury.

What are you hiding, little sis?

"Spencer!" Dad growls. "Enough. If you can't follow the goddamn rules, you can get out." He points toward the front door, emphasizing his words. "I won't allow it this time."

This time.

But *last* time was okay?

I bore my gaze into Dad, not saying what's on my mind but letting him feel the impact anyway.

He shifts on his feet and clears his throat. "You will be nice to your sister. That's all I require from you. If not, you know where the door is."

Aubrey, who's been strangely quiet, finally pipes up, "I don't want to cause any trouble."

I roll my eyes as I tear through my breakfast. She's playing the docile, innocent girl she once was, but we both know she came back with claws, jaded, and harder than before. I'll soon peel back her layers and reveal just who she's become.

"You're no trouble at all, Love," Dad croons. "You're welcome here. This is your home."

Politician Papa is here now, saying all the right things to make everyone hang on every word he says and every smile he directs their way. But I've seen the real Hugo Park. He's a lot more like his disrespectful son than he realizes.

"Speaking of trouble," I add in a cheerful tone, cutting my gaze to Aubrey. "My car got keyed yesterday."

Aubrey freezes, fork poised at her luscious pink lips.

"What?" Dad crosses his arms over his chest, glowering down at us like we're two children misbehaving. "Where?"

"Right here at home," I say with a sneer. "What kind of ballsy asshole would come onto Park property and do such a thing?"

"Have you checked the cameras?" he demands, already grabbing for his phone to save the day.

I let Aubrey sweat it out for a beat before waving Dad's efforts off. "Nothing. Wi-Fi was conveniently down. It's fine. Pops is handling it."

Her exhale of relief is barely audible, but I hear it.

Dad nods in approval. "Good. This campaign puts a target on our family's back. Whoever would stoop to such childish levels should be punished."

"I imagine they'll get their punishment in due time," I say coolly. "Don't you think, little sis?"

Though it pains her to do so, she nods, smile tight. "Absolutely."

Satisfied, I push my plate away and rise to my feet. "As

much as I'm enjoying this chat, I have important errands to run."

Dad flashes me a grateful smile. Gullible fucker.

Aubrey, on the other hand, eyes me warily. She knows the kind of man I am. Awful and vindictive. She also knows we're not friends.

We're enemies.

She made sure of that a long fucking time ago.

This thing between us is a war I plan on winning.

Normally whenever I get laid, I'm satisfied. I'm able to go about my day and feel good about my life's choices. All is well in my world.

Not today.

After running my necessary errands, I took out my frustrations while fucking—hard, furious, and unapologetic—no doubt leaving behind bruises and teeth marks.

But am I satisfied?

Fuck no.

For some goddamn reason, I kept thinking about her. Aubrey Love. Little girl all grown up and transformed into this woman with secrets. Darkness lurks beneath her seductive green eyes. Her new tattoos and piercings seem to paint a picture of some of her past, though it's hard to decipher this early in the game.

I will figure her out, though.

Starting with what the fuck she's been up to for the past two years.

The house where Jude and my great-grandfather live is enormous and imposing. It sits nestled in the trees at the base of Park Mountain just up the road from where the rest of the family resides. Where we all have new, modern homes, Jude and Grandpa live in an old, dilapidated house that looks as though it's barely standing from the outside. But, on the inside, it has good bones and the décor is a little better maintained. I'm pretty sure the crotchety bastards keep the outside looking like shit to keep everyone away.

I rap on the door, waiting for one of the many house service people to answer. Jude and Grandpa rarely answer their own door. And if Jude does answer, it's to send you away because he can be an asshole like that. Seconds later, the door swings open and a tall, thin man answers. He's about as old as Grandpa but a lot friendlier.

"Anderson," I greet. "Looking good, man."

Anderson grins, his white mustache bouncing up comically on each corner of his mouth. "Miss Violet's been fattening me up with her world-famous pies. I could have her bring you a slice if you're hungry."

Pie would erase the taste of pussy from my mouth and I'm okay with that. "I'd like that. Where's Jude?"

Anderson chuckles. "Mr. Park is in Mission Control. World domination is a full-time job."

I smirk as I pass by him to enter the cold, dark home. They may keep the interior looking better than the exterior, but there's a certain chill that settles in your bones whenever you step foot into this house. When I was a kid, this place used to scare the shit out of me. Dempsey and Gemma once locked me in a closet when I was six or seven and I nearly hyperventilated until Pops rescued me.

My shoes echo on the wood floors as I make my way through the foyer to the stairwell. Grandpa is around somewhere. Usually, you can hear him before he shows up, the whine of his electric wheelchair an eerie warning. It's Jude who'll sneak up on you soundlessly and nearly make you piss your pants.

I take the steps two at a time, heading straight for Jude's massive office. I'm not sure what sort of work he does for the family, but I know it's important. His efforts bring in enormous amounts of cash that keeps the Parks perched on top of this town like the royalty we are.

The halls upstairs are dark, every door closed except for the one at the end. The glow of computer monitors casts light into the hallway. It's quiet aside from the hypnotic tapping of fingers on a keyboard. Slowly, I approach Jude's office. I know better than to assume I can sneak up on him. He's far too paranoid for that. Screens line every wall, pictures lit up of every angle of both the inside and outside of this monolith home. Hell, I'm surprised he doesn't have a camera feed in my house too.

"My favorite uncle," I state as I saunter in.

He grunts, not bothering to turn away from his screen. Jude is the biggest man in our family. Pops and Dad have told me stories about his stellar football career back in high school. How he could have gone off to not only play college ball but also have a place in the NFL as well. All that changed on the day of the fire that took his mother away from him.

"What're you working on?" I sit down on one of the armchairs in the room, sprawling my long legs out in front of me. "Besides spying on your staff and visitors."

Jude mashes a button on his keyboard with enough force I'm surprised he didn't Hulk smash all the way through the table, before spinning around in his chair to face me.

Another thing about this house that used to creep me the fuck out.

Uncle Jude.

Latex mask wearing, Freddy Kreuger slash Jason Voorhies wannabe Uncle Jude.

"Things your small mind can't begin to comprehend even if I explained them to you," he says icily, words slightly muffled behind his mask. "Are you here to shoot the shit or do you need something, Spencer?"

A soft tap on the door signals Violet's arrival. She's an old lady with wild white hair and a missing front tooth, but the woman can make the most fantastic pie in the world.

"Mr. Park," she says, setting the plate down on the end table next to me. "Still warm, hon. Hope you enjoy."

She scampers out of the room without another word. I pick up the plate and inhale the entire slice before answering Jude. Once the taste of pussy is gone, I set my plate aside to level my uncle with a firm glare.

"I need to find what Aubrey's been up to."

Jude doesn't react or move. He just sits there, staring at me from behind his white mask, frozen like some eerie wax sculpture in a museum. Even though he unnerves me, I don't bristle or fidget. I'm not six years old anymore. Jude's harmless as far as I'm concerned. A weird-ass freak, but harmless.

"Why?" he grunts out.

"She's back."

He nods as though he already knows that part. Go figure. Asshole probably has secret footage of her keying my car.

"I want her gone." I gesture at his many computer monitors. "Besides, she could be a liability."

A liability to my dick…

"A liability?" He leans forward, elbows on his knees, all of his menacing attention directed solely at me. "To whom?"

Mostly to me, but I'm not going to admit that.

"To Dad. She's hiding something and if it gets out before we get a handle on it, Dad's shot at attorney general will be over before it even started. Just check her socials and—"

"Already did."

I frown at him. "Are you telepathic now too?"

"When Neena disappeared, I picked through everyone's social media, looking for clues as to where she could've gone," he says with a grunt, "including Aubrey's. Nothing worth pursuing."

"What about her dad? Ex-boyfriends? Friends? Can you check into them too?"

Jude sighs. "I'll dig some more."

The tense muscles in my neck slowly begin releasing. He'll get me what I need to know. Jude always comes through for the family...and Aubrey's no longer a part of it. Time to clean house and kick our dirty little girl back to the curb where she belongs.

CHAPTER SIX

Hugo

I THOUGHT BY GETTING AUBREY BACK HOME, THINGS would slide into an old routine—one where she's my stepdaughter and I'm here to look after her. If only it were that simple. One look at her this morning with her big, trusting jade-colored eyes, pouty pink lips, and messy golden hair and I was gone for.

I didn't just want to provide for her—a home, a safe place, a loving environment. No, me being the sick bastard I am, had other ideas.

Safe in my bed, beneath me, with my dick deep inside her.

It took everything in me to keep my newly inappropriate desire for Aubrey at bay. No matter how much my dick thinks she's sexier than she has any right to be, I need to erase those toxic thoughts right away. She's younger than my son, for fuck's sake. Worse yet, she's my wife's daughter.

My mind is a mess as I let myself into my brother's house. Callum is prickly at times, but he's soft on the inside. Always was. That's why Dad taking his high school girlfriend fucked him up so bad. He'd still be living with the hurt and betrayal of what they did to him if it weren't for Willa. His new girl—and yes, she's a girl because she's not much older than Aubrey— fills him in a way I've never seen before.

"Cal?" I call out, craning my neck to listen for any sounds of life within the house. "Can we talk?"

It's then I hear the faraway sounds of two people having sex. Feral male grunts. Sweet, feminine moans. The soft thud of a bed hitting the wall over and over and over again.

Must be nice to be getting laid on the regular.

The only action my dick's seen is that of my right hand for months and months. I know things with me and Neena are over, but I still can't risk taking a woman to dinner or meeting someone through a dating app without it getting out to the media. I can see the headlines now:

Future Attorney General Cheats on Wife...Will Washington State be Next?

Feeling bitter about my entire goddamn situation, I help myself to Callum's liquor stash while he finishes his fuckfest with Willa. It's too early in the damn day to be cracking open a bottle of Cal's rare Stagg Jr bourbon, but I'm having a hell of a week and need something to get my mind out of the gutter.

Two fingers' worth of a glass—hints of licorice, fennel, and dried fruit—burns a delicious path down my throat and warms my stomach. The chill of my perverted thoughts of my stepdaughter dull right along with the edge I'd been sitting on since the moment I saw her yesterday.

She just caught me off guard, is all. By tomorrow, I'll have righted my brain and all this confusing shit will be behind me.

"What did my nephew do now?" Callum asks, sauntering into the kitchen wearing nothing but a pair of gray sweatpants and a hickey on his neck that has him looking about twenty years younger. "You're hitting the bottle early, which means he's being an evil little shit again."

For once, it's not my son.

Well, not completely.

I scrub a palm over my face before pouring another glass. Callum leans against the counter, crossing his arms over his chest, and patiently waits for me to get on with it. He's not just my brother, but he's my best friend. When there are problems, we always seek each other out for advice and support.

"Aubrey's back."

I knock back my glass, relishing the burn. My mind unwillingly drifts to her tattooed thigh. I'd wanted to trace each blue wave with my tongue.

Sick fuck.

Heat creeps up my neck to my cheeks and I clear my throat. Callum, always one to see past bullshit, lets out a snort.

"Asking about her mother?" he asks instead of poking at my obvious discomfort when mentioning Aubrey.

"Yep." My tone is clipped. I want to say more, though I'm unsure how. Callum isn't exactly one to judge, but it's still hard to admit such a dirty thing about yourself.

I find a barely legal woman—no, girl—hot as fuck. I'm going out of my mind with crazy fantasies of stripping her down and claiming her with my traitorous dick.

"Hmm." Callum abandons his perch to walk over to the coffee machine. "And what did you tell her?"

"The truth. That her mother is a manipulative bitch who likes making my life a living hell." Another glass of Stagg Jr. Another blissful burn. At this rate, his bottle will be half gone by noon.

"Harsh." He sets a mug in front of me, steaming and filled to the brim with black coffee. "Getting smashed isn't going to fix your problems, Hugo. Drink up."

Reluctantly, I relinquish my glass to my brother and take

the coffee instead. This burn doesn't feel as good going down, but I know he's right. Drinking until I can't walk anymore doesn't change the fact that Aubrey is back, looking hot as fuck, and needing me to take care of her.

"What else is bothering you?" Callum probes. "Is Spencer giving her a hard time again?"

If only it were that easy.

"Something like that," I grumble. "And…" When did she grow up?

"Let me guess. Neena's daughter no longer looks like a typical teenager but has turned into a spitting image of her mother." Callum cocks his head to the side, eyes narrowed as he studies me. No wonder his students hated his class. He makes *me* feel like I'm about to get detention. "She got hot."

I bristle, unable to meet his stare. "She was always beautiful."

"Of course she was. Neena's a knockout. I didn't say beautiful. I said hot. Took your old, horny ass by surprise?"

Squeezing my eyes shut, I can't help but remember how she strode into my office, all sexy and seducing me without even trying. My dick twitches at the reminder. Fuck.

"I'll get over it," I assure him. "Just wasn't expecting her to be so…"

"Fuckable?" Callum offers with an evil smirk.

Bile rises in my throat. I know I seem like the stereotypical old guy chubbing over some young thing with perky tits and silky thighs. It's not like that, though. Well, not completely. Seeing her went beyond physical attraction. Our past, with me being a parent to her, coupled with the need for me to once again take care of her, wove its way into how my cock took notice of her beauty and sex appeal. A deadly combination for a million different reasons.

"Are you going to fuck her?"

His question jerks me from my thoughts. Vehemently, I shake my head. "Hell no. It's Aubrey, for fuck's sake. My stepdaughter. Not to mention, man, I'm still married. To her mother."

I could use another drink, but Callum covertly hid the bottle while I was distracted. Settling for my coffee, I take another punishing hot swig before setting the mug down with a loud clink.

"You wouldn't be a Park if you didn't have a complicated love life," Callum says, features souring briefly.

"Oh, hey, Hugo." Willa walks into the kitchen, cheeks crimson and a sweet smile on her pretty face. "Didn't know you were coming over."

Callum's whole demeanor changes when he sees his girlfriend, losing the grumpy face and adopting a goofy grin instead. He tugs her to him, wrapping her up in his protective embrace. Bitterness claws at my stomach.

I'm jealous of my brother's happiness.

That makes me an asshole of epic proportions because he of all people deserves it after the hell he went through with Dad. And I want him to be happy. I truly do.

But it also reminds me that my love life has been less than stellar. My first true love and the mother of my child betrayed me. My second love was guarded, so when Neena started doing the same shitty things I'd been put through once before, it was easier to cut off my feelings.

I've never had such sweet love, though.

Not like Callum and Willa.

Aubrey's sweet…

I down the rest of my coffee before offering Willa my signature politician grin. It feels forced, but I've forced it enough over the years that I can make it appear natural.

"My stepdaughter's come to live with us," I say to Willa. "She's about your age. Doesn't know anyone aside from our family around here. Might be good for her to have a friend."

Willa's face lights up. "I'd love to meet her."

"Bring a suit. The pool will be nice this afternoon."

I manage not to stagger out of Callum's house despite my limbs feeling much looser thanks to the Stagg Jr. Since it's warm out this Saturday, I decide to go for a run. The house is quiet, so I quickly change into my running clothes.

I barely make it down the road toward Park Mountain, where several trails climb up the rough terrain through thick trees, when I realize running after nearly getting shitfaced isn't one of my best ideas. I'm drenched in sweat, dizzy, and about to puke before I even reach the first trail.

Ignoring the nausea, I push through, choosing to focus on both the campaign and some cases I'm knee-deep in. It's enough to distract me for nearly an hour. The run helped to sober me up, that's for damn sure.

Once back inside, I down two water bottles in a row, sweat pouring off me in buckets despite the chill of the air conditioning. I'm considering a third when I hear the sounds of bare feet padding across the floors and into the kitchen.

The empty bottle in my hand hits the floor with a noisy clatter. Meanwhile, all I can do is stare, my jaw slightly unhinged.

Aubrey in a tiny, barely-there black bikini, golden-blond

hair piled up loosely on top of her head, eyes hidden behind oversized sunglasses.

Don't look at her, pervert. Don't fucking do it.

Unable to stop, my gaze travels down her front, lingering at her full, round tits. Her nipples are hard, straining through the thin fabric, and her bellybutton ring shimmers in the sun. My mouth waters for a taste—just one tiny lick of one of her pebbled nipples would be enough to satisfy this monstrous craving I have for her.

"I could have gone running with you if you needed a partner," Aubrey says, voice chipper and seemingly unaffected by my blatant gawking.

"I, uh," I stammer. "Next time."

She grins at me as she saunters my way. Her scent invades my nostrils and I have to fist my hands to keep from grabbing onto her narrow waist to pull her to me.

"Is this for me?" She points at the third water bottle sitting on the countertop beside me.

All I can do is nod, fixating on her mouth so I don't check out her tits anymore. She leans forward, brushing said tits against my sweaty arm. A rough breath escapes me. I'm barely holding onto any shred of control around Aubrey. The temptation is fucking real.

"Thanks," she murmurs before stepping back. "I'm going for a swim. Care to join? You look as though you could use to cool off."

Is she flirting with me or am I just an old man with wishful thinking?

"Not done with my workout," I grunt. "Maybe later."

She shrugs and then turns on her heel, leaving me alone with my raging hard-on. I'm staring after her, eyes glued to her plump ass that's hardly covered by the black material, when I hear voices.

There's no hiding.

Especially since I'm frozen, caught in the act.

Caught by my son and baby brother.

While Dempsey is seemingly clueless, staring down at his phone, my son doesn't miss a thing. His eyes dart to my crotch, bounce over to where Aubrey can be seen beyond the glass windows as she dips a toe in the pool to test the temperature, and then back over to me.

His grin is vicious and calculating. "Seems like I missed all the fun."

"I'm going to lift some weights," I growl, rushing past them. "Be nice to your sister."

"I strive to be just as nice as you, Dad."

His taunting words hit their intended mark. He caught me ogling Aubrey and now he's going to be up to his usual fuckery.

I'm going to have to get a hold of my attraction for Aubrey or shit is about to get messy quickly.

CHAPTER SEVEN

Aubrey

O NE OF THESE DAYS, I'M GOING TO SELF-DESTRUCT. Blow up my already fragmented world because I don't know how to keep from chasing after things I don't need in my life, but also would feel incredible pain from.

Lusting after and flirting with Hugo is a recipe for disaster.

And yet…I still couldn't help prancing through the house in nothing but a bikini once I'd heard him return home. The thrill of the idea of him seeing me all grown up was too much to ignore.

I needed him to see me.

What I didn't count on was his reaction.

His blue eyes were blazing with barely controlled desire. Desire for me. I'd come into the kitchen hoping to get some sort of reaction from him, but what I got was more than I expected.

He wanted me in that moment.

Badly.

I can feel eyes on me as I sun myself on the poolside lounger. Hugo's gaze was hot and hungry, making me feel powerful. It's no longer Hugo watching me from inside the house, but his son instead. This feeling is one I recognize from him from two years ago.

Stripped down.

Powerless.

Gutted.

Cold.

I shiver despite the sun warming my flesh. I'm not the girl aching for her stepbrother and who thought she actually had a chance. That girl shriveled up long ago. My thoughts drift to the past against my will.

"Don't talk to Finch."

I look up from my paper, confused at Spencer's harsh tone. "What?"

His nostrils flare. He's pissed. And I have no idea why. Spencer stalks into my room, eyes filled with fury, not stopping until he looms over me at my desk.

"Don't. Talk. To. Finch."

"I heard you," I grumble, "but I guess the better question is why not?"

"Because I said so."

I scoff at his demand. Spencer isn't usually like this. Sure, I've seen him get pissy with his dad lots of times, and even Dempsey, but never at me. We're more than stepsiblings. We're friends. Sometimes I wish we were a lot more than either of those things.

"He's my lab partner. I kind of have to." I shrug, turning back to my schoolwork.

Clearly annoyed at my dismissal, Spencer swivels my desk chair around to face him. He grips the armrests, caging me in, and leans so close, I can smell his minty breath. I blink several times and swallow down the butterflies in my throat to attempt to keep my expression neutral.

Spencer Park cannot know I'm stupidly in love with him.

"Do what you have to for the class, but don't talk to him outside of class." His eyes narrow. "He wants to get in your pants and that's not fucking happening."

My heart stutters to a stop as I gape at him. "He does?"

And Spencer is angry about this?

The hope dancing in my chest is stupid, but I can't help but feel invigorated by it. I'd always thought my feelings for my stepbrother were one-sided and obviously completely forbidden, but now I'm wondering if maybe he feels the same way too.

"Is it just him I'm not supposed to talk to or every guy?" I ask, fishing for a little more from him. Spencer guards his emotions fiercely and it's difficult knowing how he truly feels about anything.

"You can date when you're in college," he says, eyebrow quirking as if daring me to challenge him. "No one here is good enough."

You are…

I try to convey my thoughts into my expression, letting him see that I don't want to date anyone. I want him. His lips on every part of me, his body in my bed, his heart holding mine. It's reckless and has the potential of tearing apart our family, but I can't stop the way I feel.

"Spencer," I murmur, voice unsteady. "I don't want to date anyone."

His features soften and his gaze drops to my lips. Unable to stop myself, I lick them. Heat unfurls in my belly at the sharp intake of his breath.

He feels it too.

He's not immune to this connection that always seems to zap and crackle between us.

Maybe this could finally be our moment.

I lean forward in my chair slightly, aching for his lips to come crashing to mine. Instead, all he offers me is a frustrated groan. *Defeated, I sink back into my chair, tearing my gaze from his so he won't see the way my eyes are starting to water.*

"Don't go there," he says softly. "We can't."

I know he's right. We'd be the town gossip. If there's one thing Spencer cares about, it's his family name and image in the community. Dating his stepsister would be catastrophic to the Park reputation, especially his.

Instead of answering, I clench my teeth, willing the tears to remain at bay. Then, his hand reaches up, gently gripping my jaw. He turns my head until our eyes once again meet.

"Trust me," he whispers. "I want. You have no idea just how much I want."

Is knowing his feelings are reciprocated enough? His thumb drags over my bottom lip, sending a shiver down my spine.

Yes.

It has to be enough.

The sound of girlish voices nearby pulls me from my memories. Thinking about Spencer before he turned into my monster is dangerous. Back then, he was so...different. I'd loved him. Helplessly loved him.

Until everything changed and I hated him.

"Aubrey!" Gemma's shriek as she enters through the side gate has me hopping up to greet her. "Oh my God! I haven't seen you in eighty-two years!"

I can't help but grin. "Someone's still dramatic as ever."

Gemma runs toward me, her sundress dancing up her thighs and perfect boobs bouncing. Last time I saw her, she had braces and an awkwardness that comes with being fifteen.

She's no longer that girl, though. Gemma Park is stunningly beautiful.

She launches herself into my waiting arms, nearly tackling me. Gemma smells like blackberries fresh from patches we'd find in the woods on Park Mountain. Fond memories of exploring with her, Dempsey, and Spencer as we ate the blackberries straight from the source have my heart warming, chasing off any lingering chill from Spencer's cold stare.

"I missed you," she whines. "You went and got all super-hot. Dad would legit trap me in my closet until the end of time if I even thought about getting a tattoo or piercing, which is totally unfair because Dempsey has lots of tattoos. Ugh, God, I want to be you, Aubs."

"Trust me," I mutter. "My life's not anything to be envious of."

She frowns, pulling back to study me. "Spencer being a dick to you again? I really thought after all this time he'd act like a normal human."

"Have you met him?" a female voice asks. "Spencer is anything but normal."

I glance over at the girl standing nearby. She's pretty in a way that's different than Gemma. Less Instagram-influencer-esque woman and more doe-eyed-innocent-unworldly girl.

"I'm Willa," the girl says. "You must be Aubrey."

There was a time when I was Gemma's best friend. But because I ran from this town with my tail between my legs, leaving every Park behind me, including her, it's evident she's moved on.

"Willa's going to be my sister-in-law," Gemma says, a wicked grin curling her lips up.

"Dempsey's getting married?" I gape at Gemma in

confusion. "Since when does he like a girl for more than two seconds? No offense, Willa."

Willa giggles. "None taken."

Gemma rolls her eyes in a dramatic way that tugs again at my warm memories of her. "Not Dempsey, Aubs. Callum."

It takes several long seconds for my brain to catch up. "Wait. You're marrying Callum? But he's…"

"Old?" Gemma offers with a cackle. "Right? But legit, they're so cute together. He's crazy obsessed with her. Like I'm surprised he even let her come over here with me."

I jerk my gaze over to the girl who Callum Park is *obsessed* over. Everything about her is so…simple and plain. And he's so sexy and broody and, yeah, old.

Hugo's older and you think he's hot…

Shaking my head to chase away that thought, I frown at Willa. "How old are you?"

"Barely legal," Gemma tattles, glee in her tone. "He got fired and everything."

"Wait, you're a student?" I gasp, shocked at this news.

"Was," Willa says, shooting Gemma an annoyed look. "I graduated in May. And we're not getting married yet."

Gemma laughs. "Try telling Callum that. He stares at you like he wants to eat you alive. I bet by the end of the summer he'll totally put a ring on you in a caveman-claiming move."

Willa's cheeks burn bright red and she chews on her bottom lip. "I mean, I wouldn't say no if he asked."

"Like I said," Gemma chirps, "my future sister-in-law." Gemma strips out of her dress, revealing an orange bikini that covers more of her body than mine, and then hastily pulls her long dark hair into a top knot. "Tell us everything about LA. We need to live vicariously through you."

As we settle onto our loungers, I find myself relaxing, fixating on the leaves and dead bugs floating on the pool's surface. Hearing Gemma prattle on while I enjoy the warm, summer day takes a load off my shoulders. I've been on edge since I got here between my mom being missing, Spencer being an asshole, and Hugo being flirty. Hanging out with Gemma like old times and getting to know the quiet girl who's charmed the prickly statistics teacher into obsession is just what I needed to feel more like myself again.

My good time is short-lived, though.

Not fifteen minutes into our conversation and the patio door opens. Dempsey saunters outside, looking more muscular and tattooed than I remember. Spencer prowls behind him, a sculpted beast and a calculating glint in his eyes.

"The pool's for swimming," Dempsey announces, taking off in a full sprint toward us. "Time to get wet!"

We all three screech as he attempts to drag us into the pool. Gemma gets easily wrenched from her lounger by her brother and in Willa's attempt to help her has all three of them splashing into the pool at once. I grip onto the edge of my lounger, glaring at Spencer.

He wouldn't dare.

I shriek when he grabs the end of the chair and then the other, picking up the entire thing with me in it. Before I have time to process, he drops us into the pool. Cold water shocks my system and forces air out of my lungs. Bubbles blind the water in front of me, confusing me on which way is up. I frantically try to kick away from the chair, but it presses into my ass as I'm dragged down to the bottom of the pool.

The panic bleeds into anger when I realize Spencer is holding on to the sides of the lounger, his back on the pool floor, trapping me. I hit his chest to no avail. His eyes are electric and evil. The anger is gone a second later as I start aching for a breath of air. Again, I try to untangle myself from Spencer's grip, but he's too strong. I shoot him a terrified look, pleading with my eyes.

He laughs, sending bubbles surging into my face, the sound muted beneath the water. My lungs burn with the desperation to breathe. I claw at his chest, hoping to hurt him enough to let go.

He doesn't.

A sob escapes me, the last of my breath released, and then it happens. I suck in water. There's no way to avoid it. The panic turns into full-on terror. I'm going to die. Spencer Park hates me so much he's going to drown me in his pool.

Everything turns black as I struggle for my life.

Then, he lets go of the lounger, hooks an arm around my waist, and then shoves up from the bottom of the pool. He brings us to the top where I choke for air. Water surges out of my throat and I gag. Tears of relief roll down my cheeks.

That was so close.

I choke out more water and am helpless to escape Spencer's hold. His lips find the shell of my ear.

"I rescued you, leech. Now you owe me."

"Fuck you," I rasp out, finally finding the strength to pull away from him. "I hate you."

He laughs as I awkwardly scramble out of the pool. I'm no longer interested in niceties or speaking to anyone. I yank up my towel, wrap it around me, and rush into the house, the need to escape Spencer overwhelming me. The door slams behind me, letting everyone know just how I feel about the whole near-drowning episode.

I bypass my room and burst into Hugo's, not realizing I've done so until I see him. He's bent over, a towel wrapped snugly around his waist, pulling a pair of boxers from his dresser when his head snaps my way.

I will not cry. I will not cry. I will not cry.

Something about my wrecked appearance and expression has him tensing. He strides over to me, concern etched on his handsome face. His hands grip my shoulders through my towel and he peers down at me.

"What's wrong, Love?"

I bite hard on my lip, so I don't burst into tears, instead leaning forward so he'll hold me to him. His hands slide from my shoulders to my back, drawing me to him in a comforting embrace.

"I accidentally got a lungful of water," I choke out, voice raspy from coughing. "It scared me."

I'm not sure why I don't just tell him it was Spencer. Maybe because it makes me feel weak. Like I'm no match for Spencer and need his dad to save me from him.

I don't.

I can handle Spencer myself.

And he'll pay for trying to drown me, joke or not.

"You're safe now," Hugo croons, stroking his fingers up and down my back. "See? I've got you, Love."

I nuzzle against his hard, bare chest, inhaling his manly scent. Our proximity is entirely too close for how nearly naked we are, but I don't even care. His dick is half-hard behind his towel, pressing into my stomach. It'd be so easy to drop my towel and then tug his away. To push him toward the bed, straddle his powerful body, and beg for more.

So easy.

Hugo clears his throat and then extricates himself from me. "Why don't you get dressed? I'll make you something hot to drink to warm you up."

Nothing he offers me to drink will ever heat me up the way his body pressed against mine does. Nothing.

But, because I'm trying to be a good girl, I nod obediently at him.

"Thanks for the, uh, hug. I do feel better now," I admit, voice shaking. "It just scared me more than anything."

And now that the fear has dissipated, I'm feeling the anger once again.

Spencer can try and intimidate me into leaving all he wants, but I'm not going anywhere. Especially since I know he wants me gone so desperately he'd try to nearly drown me.

I'm here for the long run.

I refuse to let Spencer Park run me off ever again.

CHAPTER EIGHT

Spencer

AUBREY IS DIFFERENT. A WHOLE NEW ANIMAL THAN I'm used to. A mysterious, mirrored fragment of the girl she once was with sharp edges that now has the potential to make me bleed.

Sure, I freaked her out for a minute when I'd held her under the water. It's not like I'd actually drown her. Dad would kill me. But I wanted to knock her off her lounger where she sat so regally—a queen in my kingdom.

And I'd won.

Sent her running into the house to sob into her pillow. Like old times.

That lasted a few hours, and then by dinner, she was back to invading my home unapologetically, laughing at all Dad's corny jokes and acting as if I were invisible.

Fuck. That.

Apparently, she's tougher than I gave her credit for. That LA life of hers hardened her until she's barely recognizable. She's still the girl who tried to ruin my life and I'm going to enjoy every second of paying her back.

I wait until it's past midnight before even attempting my next move. Long after the house has gone silent and the light from her bedroom doesn't peek through the cracks. When I turn the knob, it opens easily, inviting me into her space.

Using my phone flashlight, I scan her room. Beside her sleeping form, on the nightstand, her phone is plugged in and charging. I pick it up and it lights up, asking for a passcode since my face doesn't match. That's easily remedied.

I gently stroke away her silky hair from her face and stare down at her parted lips. There'd been a time—long ago—that I'd often fantasized about sex with Aubrey. Just a taste of the forbidden. A tease to get me by.

Forbidden fruit is poisonous, though.

Infects your every cell and decomposes your soul.

I'd barely survived her once, when I was young and fucking stupid. I'm not looking to almost die again.

Using her sleeping face to unlock her phone, I then walk over to her desk chair to sit. It creaks under my weight, but the rhythmic breathing coming from the bed tells me she wasn't disturbed by it.

Her most recent texts are from Gemma.

Gemma: Are you okay?

Gemma: Spencer and Dempsey were just being asses.

Gemma: Call me tomorrow when you're not upset.

Aubrey finally replied back to her this evening.

Aubrey: I'm good. Just sucked in water and felt like shit. Didn't need everyone seeing me puke. Talk tomorrow.

Gemma then went on to send her a million stupid emojis but nothing else of interest.

I scroll down to a couple of days ago to read the texts between her and her dad.

Tony: I'm so goddamn sick of the bullshit, Aubs.

Aubrey: It was a mistake.

Tony: A mistake? Are you for real right now?

Aubrey: Dad. Please. I didn't mean to. It was an accident.

Tony: YOU FUCKED MY BOSS. How in the hell was that an accident?

Aubrey stretches on the bed and then rolls over, the springs squeaking beneath her. I stare over at her, craning my neck and listening for any signal of her waking. When I'm sure she's still asleep, I turn my attention back to the soap opera that is her life.

Aubrey: I'm sorry, Dad! It just happened! I didn't think!

Tony: You NEVER think! First your teacher, then my best friend, but my boss? It's like you're trying to ruin my life! For fuck's sake, what did I ever do to you except give you a home when your mother wouldn't?

Holy shit.
Aubrey's a little whore.

Aubrey: Please don't be mad at me.

Tony: Mad? I'm beyond mad. I can't fucking look at you anymore. You're just like her. You and your mother are the same. Venomous and cruel.

Aubrey: I'm not like Mom. Dad, please.

Tony: There's nothing left to say, Aubrey, except get out. Get your shit and take your ass anywhere but here. You're eighteen now. Go be someone else's damn problem.

Aubrey: You're kicking me out?

Tony: Ben left his wife because of you! I had to deal with Kelly's tears and hatred. About what a monster I must be for raising a homewrecking daughter.

Aubrey: Why would he leave her? It was just sex, Dad.

Tony: You disgust me.

Aubrey: Dad, please don't do this. I'm sorry. I can do better. Everything's all messed up in my head since Wes.

Tony: You breaking up with your piece of shit boyfriend doesn't give you a free pass to destroy my life as part of your therapy.

She sends about ten more texts, all of which go unanswered.

I lean back in the chair, taking a moment to soak in the texts. She left a virgin. I'm a hundred percent certain of that. And somewhere in the past two years between leaving here and showing back up, she turned into a heartless slut who slept with everyone apparently.

Using my phone, I snap a few pics of the conversation between her and Tony before shooting them over to Jude with a request to look into these people. I want to know everything about them. How she got involved with her teacher, Tony's best friend, and his boss, Ben. I want to know about this ex, Wes, who she needs therapy over. I need to know everything.

I continue my scrolling until I find the last texts Aubrey sent to her mother not long after the fight.

Aubrey: I'm going to come back home so I can go to

college at PMU. Their business college is better than the ones out here in LA.

Aubrey: I know you're mad and avoiding me, but I'm still your daughter.

Aubrey: Mom, I need you.

Aubrey: We can talk when I get there. I want us to have a relationship again.

Not a shocker that she didn't tell her mother the real reason why she showed back up at Park Mountain. Her missing mother wasn't why she came back or the fact she wanted a relationship with her. Her promiscuous ways got her kicked out and sent back here. She had nowhere else to go. No one else wanted her.

Not Tony.

Not Wes or Ben.

No one.

And now she's back, begging for scraps.

Based on the way Dad looked like he was about to bust a nut when she was bouncing around in her bikini this afternoon, it appears she has her sights set on yet another older man. Another life to destroy. This time, *my* dad.

Not on my fucking watch.

Her little game ends now.

Ding-dong. Ding-dong. Ding-dong.

The incessant mashing of the doorbell wakes me up with a start—a cranky as fuck start. Growling, I hastily throw on some shorts and make my bed before storming to the front door. Why no one else in this damn house can be bothered to answer the door only adds to my irritation.

Aubrey's probably still asleep, dreams of fucking my dad dancing through her pretty little head.

I twist the lock on the front door and fling it open, ready to lay into whatever door-to-door salesman thinks 7:00 a.m. house calls are acceptable. Instead, I find her.

Tasha Portman.

Neena's best friend.

Like Neena, Tasha clings to her youth, paying out the nose for false lashes, hair extensions, and lip fillers. And, like Neena, Tasha easily turns the heads of every male with a working dick in a ten-mile radius. Though older, they're still beautiful women, even I can admit that.

Problem with Tasha is she's a nosy, meddling, catty witch.

"Mrs. Portman," I deadpan. "So lovely to see you this morning."

Her sharp green eyes narrow with suspicion, like she has the ability to peek inside my head, before she saunters into my house past me.

"Where's Neena?" she demands.

Her heels clack along our floors as she sweeps her gaze over the space. Neena's cold, impersonal decorating sense hasn't been touched since the last time she hired an overpriced designer to redo parts of the house.

"She's out," I say, apathy dripping from my words. "I'll tell her you stopped by."

She whirls on her heels, pointing a long, manicured claw at me, baring her teeth. "Like the last ten times? I'm not an idiot, Spencer. Something's happened to Neena. We never go this long without speaking."

"Not sure why it's my problem she's avoiding you." I shrug, shoving my hands into my shorts pockets. "You know how Neena gets. When she's pissed about something, she throws a tantrum like a child."

She sweeps her attention over to me again. "If she doesn't turn up soon, I'll know you two are hiding something."

I bristle at her insinuation. "What would we have to hide?"

"Where you…" Her voice cracks and her overly plumped lip wobbles. "Where you buried the body."

"You think we killed her?" A cruel laugh escapes me. "Someone's been watching a little too much Lifetime, Tash. What's wrong? Are Daddy Portman's deep pockets no longer enough to satisfy you? Are you a bored housewife now? Need something to take your mind off things?"

She hisses, fury whipping out of her like a category 5 hurricane. "You're such a child, Spencer. A bratty, taunting child. Where's Hugo?"

If anyone needs to deal with Tasha, it's me. Sure, Dad can soothe people better than I can, but he and Tasha have always disliked each other. His mere presence will send her into a screaming fit. I honestly don't know how that eighty-year-old husband of hers puts up with her psycho ass.

Glancing at the clock on the wall, I gesture toward the general direction of Park Mountain. "Out for a run just like every weekend morning."

"I'll wait," she snips. "And if he can't produce my best friend immediately, I'm going to call the police. Everyone in this damn town will know what you two have done." She sneers at me, flashing her veneers that aren't as sharp as her claws. "Your daddy's campaign will go bye-bye."

Anger bubbles up in my gut. I'm about to tell her to get the fuck out of our house when I sense another presence. I smell her before I see her—honeyed and sweet.

"Auntie Tasha?"

Tasha snaps out of her hateful pose to turn her attention to Aubrey. She lets out a gasp of shock before opening her arms. Aubrey runs over to her and they hug like long-lost family.

"She's not your aunt," I growl under my breath, irritated to now have them both teaming up against me.

"Are you okay?" Tasha asks, pulling back to inspect Aubrey. "I haven't seen you in two years, hon. Are you here looking for your mother?"

The sympathetic expression Tasha has on her face has me cracking my neck in anticipation, readying myself for their tag-team onslaught.

"Looking?" Aubrey cocks her head to the side, confusion marring her pretty, still sleepy face. "What do you mean?"

Tasha studies her for a beat before glancing my way. Then, she turns her attention back to Aubrey. "It's okay if you don't feel safe talking right now. We can have brunch and—"

"She's plenty safe here," I spit out. "Much safer than with her daddy."

Aubrey's flinch is slight. I like knowing what I know about her and her father's fight. Of course she doesn't know I know the details and that makes it much more sweeter. Making her squirm will be fun.

"Mom's just going through some stuff," Aubrey says, her voice light despite the heavy lie on her tongue. "Not much for anyone's company. Been spending a lot of time with her yoga instructor."

"Sawyer says he hasn't seen her in forever," Tasha accuses, voice rising several octaves. "What the hell is going on around here?"

Aubrey shakes her head. "Sawyer and her parted ways a while back. Did he not tell you?"

For the first time since her arrival, Tasha deflates. It's one thing to not believe me, but it's obviously more difficult for her not to believe her precious "niece."

"Sawyer talks a lot," Tasha says with a dismissive wave. "Sometimes it's hard to keep up with him."

Aubrey seems to relax at her words, shoulders losing their tension. "I can tell her you stopped by."

"And called," Tasha clips out, venom finding its way back into her tone. "Over and over and over again. Sure, we go spells without speaking, especially when me and Harold are traveling in Europe, but never this long."

"Maybe she's still mad at you," Aubrey says, fake wincing. "You know how Mom can be."

"I suppose we do go through our spats from time to time," Tasha allows, smoothing out the nonexistent wrinkles of her skirt. "We're practically sisters, you know."

Aubrey grins at her. "I know. That's why we love you. Maybe I can grab brunch with you another day here soon? It looks like I'll be staying awhile."

Satisfied by that, Tasha nods. "Of course, sweetie. We'll keep in touch."

They hug and then Tasha stalks out of the house without another word to me. Bye, bitch.

Aubrey closes the door behind her, resting against it. Her brows are furled as she chews on her bottom lip. She's hot as fuck with her messy hair and rumpled sleep clothes. I'm unable to stop myself from prowling over to her and crowding her against the door.

"Why?" I rumble, voice low and deadly. "Why would you lie for me?"

She goes to shove me away, but I'm unmovable. "For you? I've got nothing for you, Spencer. You're a monster."

My grin is wide and threatening. "You're just mad at a little horseplay in the pool, leech? Thought you were tougher than that. Besides, it was payback for fucking up my car."

Her chin lifts and she glowers at me. "Touch me again and I'll castrate you in your sleep."

If only she had the balls to even attempt such a thing.

"And for what it's worth," she says, voice dripping with contempt, "I wasn't protecting you. I was protecting Hugo."

I slam a palm against the door beside her, but to her credit, she doesn't flinch. "What's your end game, hmm? Going to try and fuck him like you fucked every man in LA?"

"Go to hell," she growls. "You don't know a thing about me."

Stepping back, I flash her a knowing grin. "I know you have a thing for older men. A very problematic 'thing' for them. Don't think I won't protect my father against people like you."

"People like me?" She glowers at me. "What's that supposed to mean?"

"Gold-digging whores."

She slaps me hard on the cheek. "Fuck off, Spencer."

I allow her to storm off…*this time.*

CHAPTER NINE

Hugo

"**G**O AWAY!"

I'd knocked on Aubrey's door after my run to see if she wanted to grab a bite to eat, but I am being met with animosity instead, which means only one thing.

Spencer.

He was gone when I got back, but obviously not before terrorizing Aubrey a bit. I swear to God, I'm going to kill him if he keeps that shit up. I put up with a lot from Spencer. A lot. Picking on Aubrey every chance he gets is tiring as hell and needs to stop.

Exhaling heavily, I say, "It's me, Love."

Seconds later, the door opens and her sweet scent envelops me. She hasn't been crying, which is good. However, her eyes flicker with an unnamed emotion—shame perhaps?—and her eyebrows are furled together.

"Oh, hey. Sorry."

I lean my shoulder against the doorjamb and study her for a beat. "Nothing to be sorry for. I know it's Spencer."

Panic contorts her features from frustrated to fearful. The pleading look in her eyes guts me. What the fuck did he do to her?

"What did he say?" she croaks out.

"Nothing," I say slowly. "I haven't seen him this morning. I just assumed. And, based on your reaction, I assumed correctly."

She exhales and her shoulders slump. "It's fine."

"It's not fine." I step away from the doorframe, crowding closer to her, unable to stop myself. "Tell me what happened."

She's quiet for a moment and then nibbles on her bottom lip. The vulnerable expression on her face reminds me of when she was sixteen, not her now legal age of eighteen. Fixating on her pink lip, I try like hell to keep all the blood from rushing to my overactive cock.

"Tasha came by. She was freaking out about Mom being missing." Her eyes water. "I lied to her."

"Why did you lie?" My own voice is slightly hoarse, already knowing the answer. "To protect my campaign."

She swallows and nods. "Well, to protect *you*. She didn't believe Spencer, but she believed me."

Unable to help myself, I cup her soft cheek, loving the warmth in the palm of my hand. Her eyes flutter closed and she leans into my touch. I marvel at her pretty face, intrigued by the nose ring she now wears and briefly wondering where else she's pierced. The fact that she seems to desperately need my affection has the protective, nurturing side of me flaring to life. I want to pull her to me and never let go, promising her the entire world—even her damn mother's appearance if I could.

"You don't have to protect me," I say gently. "You don't have to lie for me."

Her eyes pop open and she sears me with a heated gaze that burns straight to my cock. So much for trying to ward off an erection in her vicinity.

"You're so good to me, Hugo. I would do anything for you."

I'm not sure what I've done to receive such loyalty from her, but I greedily drink it up. I like that she's so willing to give it to me. I want to reward her. A hot, deep kiss is forefront on my mind. Of course I could never...

Instead, I settle for pressing a kiss to her forehead, lingering a few seconds longer than necessary. Finally, I pull away but don't step back. I'm still a hot-blooded male, for fuck's sake, and she's too much of a temptation to deny myself her nearness.

"Any news on Mom?" she asks, tilting her head to the side. "I feel like we should be doing something. Looking for her."

"Jude texted me this morning. It's nothing to get your hopes up about, but she used her card this morning at Sweet Holes & Coffee Co."

"The place right near the lodge?"

When I nod, she moves into action, grabbing a hair tie off her end table and tugging her silky strands into a messy top knot.

"We have to go there." She slides her feet into her sandals and grins at me. "This is a warm lead. If we talk to the donut shop workers, maybe one of them will remember something."

"Neena isn't exactly the type to discuss the specifics of her life as someone makes her a matcha green tea." I shrug, stifling a sigh. Her face falls, which has me rushing out, "But we can try."

Her smile is back as she snags her purse off the dresser. "Don't worry, Hugo, we're going to find her. I promise."

Does it make me an asshole if I'm not exactly eager to find my wife?

⊙

The drive to Sweet Holes & Coffee Co. takes longer than usual due to a fender bender involving four cars. An old woman with thick glasses and a toy poodle in her arms is nodding at an officer as he gestures to what must be her car at the beginning of the minor pileup. The rest of the people are in their Sunday's best, clearly rushing to church at the last minute, making them susceptible to an accident.

"Look," Aubrey says, pointing to the side of the road. "Baby ducks."

It's evident from my quick assessment that the old woman stopped in the middle of the road to keep from hitting the ducks and probably slammed on her brakes abruptly, causing the other three cars to ram into her from behind.

We eventually maneuver around the metal and debris scattered across the road and make our way to the donut shop. It's packed by the time we arrive. Parking is a bitch and we end up having to park next door in the Park Mountain Modern Christ Church lot.

This doesn't look promising.

We climb out of the vehicle and I have the urge to hold Aubrey's hand as we pass between two cars sitting in the drive-through. I somehow manage to refrain, instead choosing to palm her lower back, guiding her toward the building.

The "now hiring" sign in the window seems useless this late Sunday morning. They're severely understaffed and there are people everywhere. I'm itching to turn around to get the hell out of this place, but Aubrey's fierce, determined expression keeps my feet rooted in place.

I'll endure because of her.

"This doesn't really seem like Mom's kind of place," she says, turning to look at me. "Too much chaos."

I agree with her on that front, but she severely underestimates her mother's love for the matcha green tea they make. Neena wouldn't touch a donut hole to save her life, but that tea really turns her crank.

After a good twenty minutes of small talk, we finally make it to the register. The lanky guy with uneven facial fuzz offers me a tight, stressed smile.

"What can I get for you?" he asks, motioning toward the cases behind him. "All out of sausage rolls and pink sprinkled donuts, though. Always the first to go on Sundays."

"We're actually wondering if you can help us with something else," Aubrey says, finally drawing his attention to her.

His tired expression melts away to one of unmasked appreciation. I don't particularly like the way he devours her with just one look. Yes, based on the PMU hat he's wearing, he's a college kid and close to her age, but it doesn't mean I have to like it or approve of his blatant ogling.

I clear my throat, demanding his attention. "You remember a woman who came through here this morning? Probably ordered the matcha green tea. Blond, pretty, older. Looks just like her."

The guy eagerly darts his gaze back to Aubrey. "I think I'd remember a hottie like you."

"Think," I demand, voice edging past cordial, the irritation of his flirting with Aubrey bugging me. "It's important."

He shakes his head. "Nah, man. It's crazy busy every

Sunday. I barely have time to even take a break. This is the longest break I've had talking to you two." He chuckles and jokingly says, "Need a job?"

Aubrey shrugs. "I could take an application with me."

I think the fuck not.

"No," I clip out. "You're not working here." *With him.*

She snaps her head my way, brows bunching in confusion. "Why not? They're hiring. I need a job."

The cashier nods, grin wide and authentic this time. "I could put in a good word with the owner. Might get you started by tomorrow."

"I said no," I growl, pinning the guy with a hard stare. "She has a job."

"I do not—"

"You do too. I need another assistant."

Someone behind me taps on my shoulder. "If you're not going to order, kindly get out of line. I have two toddlers who are seconds from a meltdown if they don't get their pink sprinkled donuts."

Rather than tell the frazzled woman they're out of those particular donuts and a meltdown is imminent, I quickly thank the cashier before grabbing Aubrey's wrist to tug her out of the shop. Once outside, she pulls her hand free from my grip and frowns at me.

"What was all that about?" she demands. "You were rude. Like…"

Like Spencer.

Ouch. That hurts.

"Fuck, I'm sorry," I huff out. "I just…this place is too stressful. Too beneath you. Come work for me instead. The pay will be a hell of a lot better. That much I can assure you."

Hiring Aubrey to spend every hour of every day with me, all because I got a little jealous of some college dweeb checking her out, is high on my list of stupid decisions. But it's a decision I stand by nonetheless.

She's quiet as we get back into my car. I don't immediately start the engine, waiting for her to speak again. Finally, she turns her unsure gaze on me, fingers nervously picking at the frayed edges of her jean shorts.

"You seriously want me to work with you?"

Now that I've said it, it's exactly what I want.

Not what I need if I plan on keeping my dick in my pants around her, but it's what I want, that's for damn sure.

"Absolutely," I say with a genuine smile in an effort to warm her to the idea. "With this campaign, everything is a lot busier than usual. And I can't trust just anyone to fill in those gaps. I want you, Love."

Her cheeks pinken and she's unable to hold my stare. She's fucking adorable. I'd also be lying if I said my ego doesn't love how she seems to hang on my every word. It feels great even if it is the worst thing to be fixating on.

"I don't have anything appropriate to wear," she murmurs, gesturing at her bare, tattooed thighs. "All my clothes are like this."

I allow myself to linger my stare on her legs since she's pointing them out and clearly wants me to look. Casually, I rest my hand on my dick to hide the fact I'm getting harder by the second.

"We'll go shopping today." My voice is gruffer than usual. "I'll buy you whatever you need."

She perks up and grins at me. "Maybe by the end of the summer, I'll be making enough to buy a car."

I'll buy her a car, too, if that'll make her happy, but I'm not going to overwhelm her right now.

"Is that a yes you'll accept the job then?"

She nods and then leans over the console to hug me. "Yes. Thank you, Hugo. You really are the best man I know."

Unable to resist, I give her naked thigh a quick squeeze and kiss the top of her head. "I told you I'd take care of you, Love. You're my sweet girl who deserves everything good in this world."

Good, though, would be letting her work at the donut shop, free to date dorky PMU students who awkwardly flirt with her. Good would be removing my hand from her goddamn thigh. Good would be refraining from getting a hard-on every time I'm near her.

She thinks I'm the best man she knows…

Turns out, I'm actually the worst.

CHAPTER TEN

Aubrey

SPENCER'S STILL GONE BY THE TIME WE FINISH OUR shopping later that afternoon. The house isn't quieter without him, but it's something. Less tense. Empty.

I ignore the emptiness and peek into his room after depositing all my bags into mine. As soon as I crack the door, his masculine scent envelops me. It's annoying that monsters smell good, especially this one.

Though I'd come to his defense earlier when Tasha was here, I couldn't help but also feel unnerved by his behavior. I'd heard their heated voices and listened in a bit before I intervened.

She was scared.

For Mom.

Like she thought she was dead.

Sickness roils in my gut. Mom and I have had our differences and she's been less than motherly to me my entire life, but I'd never wish her to die.

Would Spencer have it in him to hurt my mother?

My mind drifts to the past. *After* the good times. *After* the best part. *After* getting caught.

THE TANGLE OF AWFUL

Something's changed.

Spencer is different.

Colder. Harder. Carved from impenetrable stone.

As if our kiss was all my fault. As if I seduced him.

We both know it was an inevitable coming together. We'd been dancing toward that kiss since the day we met, long before our parents were married.

And that kiss was everything.

The second our lips met, my heart collided with his and my world tilted on its axis. The kiss—my very first—was going to be the best one of my life. Surely nothing could ever top the way his soft lips pressed to mine or how his tongue tentatively slid into my mouth.

He was so sweet. So caring. So gentle.

A chill tingles up my spine, making the hairs on my arms stand on end. The kiss, though interrupted, was perfect.

So why is he acting like some emotionless statue?

I watch him as he strides into the kitchen, dressed impeccably for school. He avoids looking at me altogether, the same as every day this week since our kiss. The cut to my heart won't stop bleeding. I've kept quiet, trying to give him the space he needs, but I'm not sure I can take his ignoring me any longer.

"Spencer," I croak out, hating the way my voice quavers.

His shoulders tense as he pours his juice into a glass, but he doesn't respond. I swallow hard, watching him as he lifts the glass to his lips. He gulps down the orange juice quickly and then sets to rinsing the glass out.

"Spencer," I try again. "Why are you doing this?"

He sets the glass down into the sink with a loud clink before turning his angry stare toward me. "Doing what, leech?"

I flinch at his words. "Leech? What the hell, Spencer?"

His nostrils flare and a cruel smile curls his lips. It would be handsome if it didn't turn the blood in my veins to ice.

"You're a leech. Using me and my father. You disgust me."

I blink in confusion. "W-What are you talking about?"

"You almost had me there for a second," he snarls, as though the admission costs him part of his soul, "but I see you for who you are now."

Tears flood my eyes and I hastily swipe them away. "Why are you being like this?"

"This thing you thought you could make happen between us," he hisses, pointing at me and then at himself, "is over. I won't fuck up so stupidly ever again." He cocks his head to the side. "Stay out of my way. Don't fucking talk to me. And if you even think about ruining my family, I will hurt you in ways you will never mentally recover from."

With those awful words, he stalks away, leaving me with a broken heart and messy mind.

What happened?

His room is the same as it was all those years ago. Pristine. Seemingly untouched. I can almost hear my own soft mewls as we kissed on his bed. I remember the covers getting rumpled and it was the messiest I'd ever seen his room. Wrecking him in the best possible way felt like a win—like I was powerful enough to be a match for someone like Spencer Park.

Bitterness has me shuddering. That moment was so short-lived and was immediately followed by some of the worst days in my entire life. He was beyond cruel. My sweet, sexy step-brother mutated into a monster I didn't even recognize.

And he never transformed back.

With a heavy sigh, I make my way over to his dresser. I'm not sure what I'm doing in his room, but as soon as I open a drawer filled with neatly folded socks, a fire burns inside me.

His perfect, OCD room always felt like a mask hiding the real Spencer. When his lips were on mine, that mask was gone. I saw someone real. Someone I could love.

I close the drawer and open another one. I want to peel back every layer of his life and peek inside. Then, maybe I'll find answers as to why he suddenly treated me like a gold-digging whore. Like someone else's gum on the bottom of his shoe.

Each drawer is neat and perfect, nothing out of place. It emboldens me to keep looking—keep digging into the life of Spencer Park. After going through each of his dresser drawers, I make a beeline for his nightstand drawer. Inside is a bottle of lube and a strip of condoms. A flare of jealousy ignites in my chest. It's not like we're a couple or ever will be. Spencer is allowed to fuck whoever he wants.

But still…

With my memories of that kiss so fresh in my mind, it feels like a betrayal. Like he's cheated on me with all these nameless people. Broke my heart all over again.

I slam the drawer with enough force the lamp wobbles and nearly tumbles to the floor. I manage to catch it, saving myself from being busted for snooping in his room. I'm thinking about heading to the closet to investigate when I hear Spencer's voice.

He's close.

Crap!

If I'd heard him coming sooner, I could have slipped out of his room and into mine before he found me, but I didn't. He'll be here any second.

At the last moment, I drop to the floor and scoot under his bed. I've barely dragged myself under it when the door opens, his deep voice following it.

"Thanks, Pops. Bring it by tomorrow."

He ends the call with a hasty goodbye and then tosses the phone onto the bed with a soft thud. I can see his black shoes beneath the edge of the duvet. My heartbeat is roaring in my ears.

What will he do if he catches me under his bed?

I attempt to hold my breath, waiting him out. I'm not really in the mood of explaining why I'm in his room.

He strides away from the bed and into the bathroom. When the shower cuts on, relief floods through me. I just need to wait long enough for him to get in the shower and then I can make my escape.

He kicks off his shoes before picking them up and taking them into the closet. Nothing is ever out of place with Spencer. Not even a shoe or a rogue sock. He walks into his closet and remains in there for a long while. It shouldn't take long to grab clothes, but I can distinctly hear him rummaging around.

What's in his closet that would warrant digging before a shower?

I'm going to find out.

After what feels like an eternity, he slips out of the closet and then closes himself in the bathroom. As soon as the sounds of water splashing as someone washes up in the shower reach me, I hastily scrabble out from under the bed.

The smart thing to do would be to go back to my room.

When it comes to Spencer, I've never thought too clearly around him.

Instead of leaving, I make my way into his closet, keeping an ear out for the shower sounds. His closet, like everything else in his room, is sparse and incredibly neat. Even his shirts are hung from white all the way to black with every color on the spectrum in between in order of varying shade.

What was he doing in here?

At first glance, there's nothing amiss, but when I look up, I notice a gray plastic tub on the shelf above his hanging clothes. It's way out of reach for my short stature, but I'm determined.

Ensuring the shower is still going, I test the strength of the shoe organizer built into the wall. With its cutout shelves, I can use it as a ladder. If it'll hold, that is. But when it doesn't collapse after stepping on the first one, I'm emboldened to keep going.

I have to climb until my head brushes against the ceiling. Then, I'm able to reach over and tug at the lid of the box. Since I can't see inside of it, I have to settle for reaching my hand in. My fingers brush something and I'm able to make purchase. Carefully, I pull it from the box to take a closer peek.

It's a picture frame.

An old picture of me and Spencer. Before the kiss. When we were friends. Seeing the old picture has warmth spreading over me. He was so happy in that picture. We both were. I'm shocked he kept it.

I'm about to see what else I can dig out of the tub when

the shower faucets squeak as he turns off the water. My heart stumbles in my chest and I nearly drop the picture frame from my perch. I grip onto it and then slide it back into the box as fast as I can. Quickly, I shove the lid back over the top and hop to the carpet with a soft thud.

The hammering in my chest echoes in my eardrums, reminding me it's past time to get the hell out of here. I creep out of the closet, casting a brief look over everything to make sure it's as he left it, and then slip out.

I manage to make it back to my room unscathed and without getting caught, much to my relief. It still doesn't calm the questions bouncing around in my head.

Why does Spencer still have a picture of us?

Why was he just looking at it?

I mean, I suppose he could have been looking at whatever else was in that box, but something tells me he wasn't. Maybe the thing he's hiding has nothing to do with Mom and everything to do with me.

My heart aches at the thought of him being the same Spencer I fell for years ago. The boy who cared about me and made me laugh. Somehow, that's worse than all this hatred he has toward me.

It means I did do something, though probably not intentional, to hurt him.

Now if only I could figure out what.

CHAPTER ELEVEN

Spencer

SOMEONE'S BEEN IN MY ROOM.

Not our housekeeper who's well versed on how I keep my things. No, someone else. Someone who left her lingering honeyed scent that permeates the air.

Why was Aubrey in here?

I open my drawer for some boxers and note that the usual perfect lines seem to have been hastily straightened. She was looking in my drawer and tried to cover her tracks. Obviously, she doesn't know me as well as she thinks she does. The fact she's been in here is glaringly obvious. After throwing on a pair of black boxers and tidying the drawer to its usual look, I turn to inspect the rest of my room.

Nightstand drawer imperceptibly left unclosed.

Duvet slightly lifted on one corner of my bed.

Lamp askew, turned in a minor but maddening way.

Anger surges up inside of me. Knowing she was rummaging through my things has my hackles rising. I wonder if she found whatever it was she was looking for.

I make my way into my closet and pull on a pair of jeans. I'm reaching for a shirt hanging when I notice the lid of my box ajar.

There's no way she could reach that box.

Unless she climbed.

My gaze skims over to my shoe shelves, and sure enough, several pairs have been pushed aside as though she had to make room for her foot.

Unbelievable.

I storm out of my room on one mission. Find Aubrey. And I do find the sneaky weasel in her room, putting away mountains of clothes from shopping bags.

Total fucking gold digger.

She's manipulating Dad into giving her a place to stay and buying her all kinds of shit. Then, she has the audacity to go through my things. Who the hell does this girl think she is?

"What are you doing?" I hiss out, voice icy and sharp.

Aubrey gives a lazy shrug, back still turned to me. "Putting away clothes."

"No shit, Sherlock," I growl. "I'm talking about your snooping in my room."

"I have better uses of my time than to look through your serial killer bedroom," she sasses, unperturbed by my tone.

"Everything was ransacked."

She whirls on her feet, tossing a skirt onto the bed. Her brows furl as she studies me. I'm impressed at her ability to keep her eyes on mine instead of my naked chest.

"Ransacked? Seriously?"

"Maybe not to your sloppy standards," I snip, waving a hand at her bed that shopping bags vomited clothes all over. "Definitely rifled through. I know it was you, so stop the bullshit. The question is why?"

This time, her eyes drop as she avoids my gaze, but that puts them on my pectoral muscles. Pink stains her cheeks and she drags her eyes up to meet mine again.

"I was looking for a pair of scissors to cut these tags off," she lies, forcing a bitchy smile on her plump lips. "Happy?"

I grind my teeth together and shake my head, taking several long strides toward her until I'm towering over her. "You weren't looking for scissors in my underwear drawer, leech."

"Don't call me that," she spits out, lifting her chin. Fire blazes in her eyes.

"Maybe you'd prefer it if I called you Daddy's Little Whore—"

Smack!

It takes me half a second to realize she slapped me. The sting doesn't hurt but instead makes me want to return the swat. To her ass. My dick thickens at that thought. Annoyed at my body's reaction, I grip her jaw, hoping to gain the upper hand in the situation.

"Hit me again," I threaten, voice dripping in venom. "See what happens."

Her nostrils flare and her eyes flash as she raises her hand. Before she can smack me again, I do something I've been thinking about for two long years.

I kiss her.

My lips crash to hers, a violent promise of a war I'll undoubtedly win. The force of my unexpected kiss has her stumbling back a step, lips parting on a shocked gasp. I take the moment to plunge my tongue into her mouth, greedily seeking hers. A soft moan whispers up her throat as I command her mouth with mine.

I don't like or want Aubrey.

This kiss is a weapon to be used against her.

A reminder of who holds all the power.

Me.

I'm on to her slick games and duplicitous nature. Dad may be blind to what she's doing, but I sure as hell am not. I know she's been using men in LA, leaving a path of destruction along the way.

I won't let her burrow herself into our world and destroy us too.

"Ahh," she whimpers when my teeth tug a little too hard on her bottom lip.

Unable to stop myself, I soothe away the sting with my tongue and much softer kisses. My hand, of its own accord, slides away from her jaw and into her silky tresses. I grip her healthy ass cheek with my other, squeezing it to the point it might bruise. Another whimper—this one more pleasure-filled.

She hasn't put up a fight or any effort to end our kiss, which means she's used to her body being wielded as a weapon or tool.

I'm not like those brainless fucks in LA, though.

I know her true intentions.

"Spencer," she murmurs, a half-hearted attempt to put a stop to what we're doing. "We shouldn't—"

My tongue dominates hers, effectively swallowing any words she was trying to speak. I kiss her deeply and almost punishing. The craving to leave some sort of mark—mental or physical or emotional—drives me to keep inhaling and devouring her.

I'm hard in my jeans, cock straining against the denim and pressing into her stomach. It's not enough. I need more from her. I need *everything* from her.

Briefly, I pull away, breaking our kiss so that I can push her body down onto the pile of clothes on the bed. I'm lured in by her swollen, red lips that are parted and begging for more. For a moment, I lose sight of the purpose of this kiss and pounce on her, hungry for another taste.

With her pinned beneath me, I'm able to wrench her thigh aside and grind against her pussy through our clothes. Her gasp is a mixture of delight and horror, both of which serve to make me impossibly harder. I nip at her bottom lip, more gently than last time, and work my hips until I find the spot that makes her groan.

"You fucking like this," I mutter against her lips. "Me dry fucking you over your sugar daddy's gifts."

She grips at my damp hair, drawing me closer. "Shut up."

Grinning, I kiss away her annoyed words, drawing her deeper into the moment with me. I wait until she's gasping, close to climax before pulling my hips back.

"I could torture you like this forever."

Her lust-drunk eyes flutter at my words. "Stop talking. I like you better when you don't speak."

"Bitch," I say with a smirk and then trail kisses to her neck. "What's your game, leech?"

I suck softly just below her ear, letting my hot breath tickle over her flesh. When I reach a particularly sweet part of her neck, I put more force into the suction of my mouth. She moans, lost in the moment, allowing me to mark her like she's mine.

She *is* mine.

Mine to torment and tease and taunt.

This is my game and she's a player in it.

"You've been waiting two long years for me to fuck you, hmm?" I rumble, nipping at her slick skin. "You want me inside of you, don't you?"

She doesn't answer, once again tugging on my hair to bring my mouth to hers. As if she can turn off all conversation and just let our bodies do the talking.

My body says, "Let's fuck."

Her body says, "Now, please."

Unfortunately for both of our bodies, my mouth spits out other words.

"Your body might intrigue and confuse my dad, but make no mistake, leech, I'm well aware of what your plans are."

"I have no plans," she croaks out.

"Imbed yourself in our lives, bleed out what you can from us, put our nuts in your purse. You money-hungry females are all the same."

"I don't want your money," she growls, stiffening beneath me. "I don't even want you. Get off."

"Oh, I will." I smirk at her. "I'll get off all over your pretty face, leech."

She goes to smack me again, which is getting pretty fucking old if you ask me, but I anticipate the move, gripping her wrist and slamming it to the bed.

"Let me go," she commands, fire once again making her eyes glitter.

Watching her closely, I grind against her pussy. She gasps and tilts her head back, losing herself to the sensation.

"Nobody's stopping you. Go, leech. Let go."

Her lids flutter and she digs her heels into my ass. I continue to punish her with teasing circular motions of my body against hers, drawing her closer and closer to the edge of bliss.

"Are you close?" I murmur, mouth hovering over hers. "Tell me."

"Mmm." She nods sharply. "Fuck."

"Dirty mouth."

She's about to give in when I hear Dad's voice somewhere in the house, calling for her. As though she's been splashed with cold water, she freezes and her eyes grow wide. Panic has her swollen, just-kissed lips parting and her face blushing crimson.

"Spencer—"

I cover her mouth with my palm, effectively ending whatever she was going to say. We have a bit of a struggle as she attempts to escape my hold, but I easily overpower her, managing to grip both wrists in one of my hands and pinning them to the bed. Once more, I cover her mouth with my palm.

Dad's voice grows nearer, and I can hear footsteps beyond her open bedroom door. Since I've lived here all my life and know just how long it takes Dad to get to my room, I take advantage of the few precious seconds, grinding into her harder and faster.

She comes with a muffled moan, her entire body trembling. I don't give her time to finish riding the aftershocks before I'm off her and retreating to the dark bathroom. I've barely stepped out of sight when Dad enters the room.

"Love?"

Her face is bright red as she sits up and looks anywhere but at him. "What's up?"

"Are you okay?"

"Fine, uh, just fine. Was taking a break from putting away clothes." Her eyes dart toward the bathroom where I'm standing. "Did you need something?"

"Since it's our last bit of freedom before a long work week, I thought I'd see if you wanted to watch a movie or something."

She nods rapidly, guilt twisting her smile into one that's so obviously forced. "I'd love that. Give me, uh, just a few minutes to finish putting these clothes away so they don't wrinkle."

"I'll help," Dad offers, starting toward the closet. "I'll grab some hangers."

Her panicked eyes meet mine. I emerge from the dark bathroom and lazily stroll toward the open bedroom door, gaze searing into hers.

Blown pupils.

Messy hair.

Clothes askew.

Pink-tinged mouth from our making out.

It's so fucking obvious she's been wrecked by me. Dad, though, is oblivious. Just like he's oblivious to her true intentions.

I wink at her and slip back into my room, undetected as the perpetrator of our little forbidden romp.

Clearly, this is the way to cut open Aubrey and dig out all her nefarious objectives. I'll pull them out one by one, arranging them in neat little rows, and inspect why the fuck she wants to pick apart this family.

If I have to fuck her in the process, so be it.

Perk of the job.

We may be at war, but I'm a hedonist at heart. I'll take great pleasure in her body and emotional state until I've exposed her and no longer have use for her.

It won't take long.

And then little Aubrey Love can fuck off back to LA where the men there are ignorant to her slutty serpent ways.

CHAPTER TWELVE

Hugo

A UBREY IS ANYTHING BUT FINE.
When she lies, her eyes always shift away and her body tenses. Since she's open when it comes to worries over her mother, I'd bet her strange reaction is because of Spencer.

What did he do now?

There'd been a slight glimmer of terror shining in her eyes. Either he said something to her or he did something to her. I'll get it out of her eventually, and when I do, I'm going to have a come to Jesus meeting with my son.

I grab a handful of hangers and emerge from the closet. Aubrey is staring out the open door, a frown on her pretty face. My suspicions are confirmed. It's absolutely Spencer who's wound her up into this state.

"What did he do to you?" I ask, dropping the hangers onto the bed beside her with a clatter.

She jolts, jerking her head my way, eyes wide. "W-What do you mean?"

"I'm not blind, Love. You get this way when he's done something to you." I cock my head to the side. "Did he touch you?"

Her face burns bright red and she absently strokes her hair down one side of her neck as though to hide something.

"If he hurt you," I growl, "I'll—"

"He didn't," she rushes out breathily, rising to her feet. "He just annoys me sometimes."

She's being purposefully evasive, but I let it slide for now. Gently, I tug her into my arms, embracing her as if I can make everything better with a hug. A relieved sigh escapes her and she melts in my arms, nuzzling her cheek against my chest.

Fuck, it feels so damn right having her like this.

I can almost imagine Neena isn't my wife and isn't missing. That Aubrey is just some young, beautiful girl interested in a man in his forties. If she were truly mine, I'd take great pleasure in spoiling her. Shopping and spending time with her today was a testament to that. It stroked my ego knowing I could provide things for her and make her smile. I want to lavish her with praise and adoration, gifts, and my cock.

My thoughts drift away from simple caretaking to something far more sinister and forbidden. Her naked and writhing on my bed. Her tight pussy raw and red, leaking with my cum. Her sweet whimpers as I take her again and again until she loses her mind.

My dick is hard now, pressing into her. I clear my throat and pull away so I don't make a damn fool of myself.

"Let's get these clothes put away," I instruct, my voice gruff and commanding.

Her gaze drops to my cock, still straining behind the denim, and then she bites on her bottom lip. My cock jolts at that action and lust shoots through me like a lightning bolt.

"Aubrey," I growl. "Get to it."

Thank fuck she finally turns her attention to hanging clothes. I'm able to focus on the task as well, ignoring my dick long enough that it settles down, no longer a distraction for either of us.

I'm playing a dangerous game with Aubrey.

All this secret look-but-don't-touch shit I'm doing isn't going to last long. It'd be one thing if what I was feeling was one-sided and a simple attraction to a younger woman. But it's not. I'm somehow affecting her just as much as she is me. If we cross a line, there's no going back.

What happens when Neena finally decides to come back home?

Will she find me coupled up with her teenage daughter?

Furthermore, if I somehow convinced myself I could take a taste of what I wanted, it wouldn't be enough. I'd have to make her completely mine. That would be catastrophic to my entire world.

Neena would divorce me, which could look bad on my campaign.

Spencer might murder her since he clearly hates her.

Dad would have a fucking meltdown at me being the center of town gossip.

Cheating on my wife by fucking my teenage stepdaughter would define me for the rest of my life. I'd wear that scarlet letter until the day I died. It simply can't happen.

"All done," Aubrey says, a genuine smile gracing her lips. "Thanks for helping me."

I stupidly take her hand in mine and bring it to my lips, kissing one of her knuckles. "I like helping you, Love. It feels good."

Fuck. Fuck. Fuck.

So much for keeping my distance and avoiding tempting situations. Her grin is breathtakingly beautiful, which lights my soul on fire. Whatever discomfort she had moments before because of my son has been chased away. It's me who makes her happy—me who will continue to keep her happy.

I can keep my dick in my pants.

I have to.

Squeezing her hand in mine, I guide her out of her room and down the hall to the theater room. The faint scent of popcorn hangs in the air, making my mouth water. Aubrey lets go of my hand to busy herself making popcorn like when she was younger, and I set to getting a movie queued up on the screen.

Since I know she likes horror movies, I settle on something we've seen before and that feels familiar. Maybe that'll remind me she's my stepdaughter, not some woman I can fuck.

"Grab me a water too?" I ask, settling onto the sectional couch and grabbing a throw blanket.

"Of course."

It all feels so domestic and easy. But not at all familiar like I'd hoped. Something different crackles between us. Not a stepfather and stepdaughter spending quality time together watching a movie. Something far more twisted. An unspoken promise to take a forbidden journey with her.

We can't.

She sits down beside me, passes me a water bottle, and brings the bowl of popcorn into her lap. I chug the water, hoping to cool off all the heat burning through me. It's a fruitless endeavor because her nearness has me combusting from the inside out.

This doesn't feel like movie night with my stepdaughter.

This feels like a date with the sweetest, hottest, most tempting girl I know.

I force myself to think of my missing wife because

nothing kills a boner like Neena does. Where the hell is she anyway? Surely she's caught wind that Aubrey's back in town. You'd think that, even if she were punishing me, she'd want to see her daughter.

But that's assuming Neena is like Jamie. Jamie, despite screwing over my brother to have an affair with my dad, is actually a great mother. She loves the twins more than anything in this world. Jamie wouldn't abandon her daughter or even avoid her because her children always come first.

The only thing that's ever come first for Neena is Neena.

My phone buzzes. I pull it out to see I have a new message from my campaign manager, Vance.

> **Vance: Don't forget our meeting tomorrow morning. And show up happy because I have something I want to propose. I need you to say yes.**

> **Me: Don't be vague, V. Out with it.**

> **Vance: Though it wasn't my idea, and probably stems from nefarious intentions, I still think it could be great PR.**

> **Me: I'm already not liking the sound of it.**

> **Vance: Jeter wants to have dinner with you.**

I scowl at my phone. Scott Jeter is my opponent running for AG.

> **Me: Why the hell would I want to have dinner with that idiot?**

> **Vance: Because the press loves a juicy story. Jeter is a tool and you're the exact opposite. You wouldn't**

have to do anything but be you. He'll fuck things up and you'll be the media darling.

Me: Sounds too easy.

Vance: Here's where it gets tricky.

Me: Tricky?

Vance: You'll need to bring Neena. Is she done being mad at you?

Fuck.

I've evaded Vance thus far about media appearances with Neena because I admitted we were having marital problems. But I lied and said we were working through them. That by the time the election rolls around, we'll be fine. Nothing to worry about.

Here we are, though, late summer, and the election is on the horizon. Still no wife. I'm so fucked when the press gets wind I can't find my own goddamn wife. Sure, many people will assume she ran off and left me, speculating as to the whys. There will be a significant amount of people, however, who will assume foul play. They'll want to investigate her missing whereabouts. I don't need that shit in my life.

Me: She's still pissed, but I could bring my stepdaughter as my date.

I inwardly cringe at the word date, but I've already sent the text. Luckily, he doesn't read into it.

Vance: Father/daughter dinner. Even better. The press will love it. You're a smart man, Park.

Smart.
Yeah fucking right.

I'm an idiot. An idiot because I can already imagine Aubrey dressed in something beautiful, arm looped with mine, as I take her to a fancy restaurant.

"Everything okay?" Aubrey asks as I toss my phone away.

"Campaign stuff." I lean back against the cushions, staring up at the ceiling. "A dinner with the opponent."

"Ew. Why would you do that?" She sits up, turning toward me. "He'll probably try and bait you or get you to make a fool of yourself."

"That's what Vance, my campaign manager, is hoping. Well, for Jeter at least. There's just one problem."

"Mom," she says in a knowing tone. "Can we find her by then?"

I glance her way. "I've been trying to contact her for months, Love. Months. I'm not confident she'll suddenly show up when I need her."

"What will you do?" Her teeth worry over her bottom lip. "Can you deny his request for this dinner?"

It warms me knowing she's concerned on my behalf. I reach over, patting her bare thigh and then resting my palm there. It's inappropriate as fuck, but I can't help myself.

"I want to bring you," I admit, flashing her a smile. "That is, if you want to go schmooze with me."

"Hell yeah," she says, eyes glittering. "We'll show that asshole you're the better pick. We've got this."

Her faith in me—in us—has my heart squeezing in my chest. Of course the universe would give me what I want in a package I can't have.

She leans back on the couch, stretching her legs over my lap. We continue to watch the movie, neither of us keen on putting distance between us. No, it's as though Aubrey takes great pleasure in shifting and fidgeting, her calves rubbing over my cock any chance she gets. I pretend to be focused on the movie as my hand remains on her thigh, tracing over the tattooed designs with my thumb.

I can't fuck her, that much is for certain, but I can do this.

Cuddling with my stepdaughter isn't against the law. We're not making a big deal out of the way she makes my dick hard or how her skin is pebbled with goose bumps at my touch that strokes dangerously close to the hem of her shorts.

It's nothing.

Harmless.

Something we can quietly do that won't fuck up my world.

We haven't crossed any lines we can't come back from.

Problem is, it's not enough, goddammit. It's not enough and I wonder how long I can deny myself something I know will feel so fucking good.

CHAPTER THIRTEEN

Aubrey

T HE SOUND OF MY ALARM ROUSES ME FROM A DEEP, blissful sleep. I lie in bed for a moment, hanging on to the memories of last night that somehow worked themselves into my dream. Safe behind the veils of sleep, I was free to touch Hugo like I wanted, straddling him and fusing my lips to his.

My phone alarm continues to blare, disturbing my dangerous thoughts. I grumble as I reach over to turn it off. I'm wrapped in the blanket from the theater room. The soft chenille smells like Hugo and I inhale a deep breath of it. I have an overwhelming urge to touch myself and orgasm while I'm still saturated in all things Hugo.

But with thoughts of climaxing come thoughts of Spencer.

He dry-humped me last night until I came. It was exhilarating and horrible all at once. I didn't want it at all but also wanted it more than anything in that moment. His hold on me is still ever-present, which annoys me to no end. Why can't I just get over him once and for all?

As reality chases off the last dregs of sleepiness, a cold dread settles over me. I'm a terrible person. I already knew this because of my life back in LA, but I didn't expect it to carry over to Park Mountain. All too easily, I dragged my baggage a couple states north and right through the Parks' front door. My inability to use my moral compass has led me right to this moment.

I let my stepbrother dry fuck me and then, later, toyed with my stepfather, rubbing on him any chance I got.

I'm not innocent.

I'm a homewrecker.

I just never expected to be responsible for wrecking two of my homes. After this, I'll have nothing left.

Shoving all thoughts away, I focus on the day ahead as I shower and get ready. Today I'll be working with Hugo. I'm fortunate he wants to give me a job despite my inexperience. If I can keep from doing the unthinkable—fucking my step-dad—then this could be really good for me, especially since my grades aren't exactly great and college doesn't entice me a single bit.

Of all the outfits we purchased, my favorite is the burnt orange long lantern sleeve tie-waist dress that hits me about mid-thigh. It shows off my tattoo, which is probably unprofessional, but I like the way the inked waves always seem to catch Hugo's stares. I choose a pair of tan ankle boots to go with it and opt to wear no other jewelry aside from the over-sized gold hoops I also bought. I take extra time fixing my long hair into sexy waves that bounce when I walk. I'm just finishing up my makeup when my phone buzzes with a text.

Unknown: I miss you, gorgeous. Please talk to me.

A cold chill runs down my spine. It's Ben. I know it is. Dad's boss was the only one who called me gorgeous. At the time, it felt good. Now, all I feel is regret. I ruined too many lives by getting wrapped up with that man.

It was supposed to be just sex.

But then he took it too far.

I quickly block the number before shoving my phone into my purse. One last glance at my reflection and I'm certain I look good enough to work at a sleek law firm. Young and a little wild, but still presentable.

In the kitchen, I find Hugo fussing with the coffee machine. He's dressed in a navy suit that fits him perfectly, stretching over his broad back. His scent is everywhere in this house, but more potent wherever he is. I barely refrain from sucking the smell of him into my lungs like some sort of stalker freak.

"Smells good in here," I say in way of a greeting, alluding to the coffee that's now brewing and knowing damn well that's not what I'm referring to.

He swivels around, an easy smile on his handsome face. When his gaze drinks me in, the smile falls and his features harden. If I didn't know Hugo any better, I'd say he was pissed. But the intensity rolling off him isn't from anger.

It's heat.

I bite into my bottom lip with my teeth, resisting the urge to shift awkwardly. There's something about Hugo that makes me feel innocent—virginal even. Like I've never known what it feels like to truly be wanted and adored by a real man. Like every guy before him was a measly quiz, but he's the final exam.

He abandons his coffee mug to prowl toward me, jaw muscle ticking as he approaches. I don't back down, feigning confidence I don't have and offering him a playful grin.

"Is this outfit okay for work?" I ask, voice breathless. "I can change if it's not appropriate."

His body heat scorches my flesh as he stands too close. I have to crane my neck to look up at him. The urge to grab the lapels of his jacket is strong.

"You look…" He trails off, running his tongue along his lower lip. "Perfect. You look perfect, Love."

My skin burns at his praise. I wonder what he'd do if I stood on my toes and kissed his handsome mouth. Would he push me away? Would he deepen the kiss and fuck me in this dress over the kitchen table?

"Thank you," I murmur. "You look nice too."

He lifts his hands, curling them around my biceps like I might run off. I'm not going anywhere. His strong fingers slightly bite into me, but I don't mind because I like the proof of him barely containing his control.

All because of me.

I do this to him.

Shame rears her ugly head in the back of my mind. I quickly silence her, choosing instead to entertain sexy thoughts of the two of us together, naked and unbothered by anything in the world.

Hugo dips his head and for a moment, I wonder if he'll kiss me. I lick my lips in anticipation. A feral growl vibrates through him and he gives me a slight shake. My heart dances wildly in my chest, uncaring that he's no doubt leaving bruises from his claiming hold on me.

Kiss me.

Please kiss me.

I try to contain the needy whimper, but it escapes anyway. His eyes flicker in a dangerous way I've never seen before. It reminds me of Spencer, which surprisingly doesn't kill the mood like it should.

Kiss me, Hugo.

He leans in closer and I flutter my eyes closed. My lips are parted, waiting for his soft ones to touch mine. I'm practically drooling with the desire to taste him.

And then he kisses me.

Not on my mouth like I'm desperate for him to do.

No, he kisses me on the forehead.

The disappointment coursing through my entire body has my eyes snapping back open. He's already releasing me and stepping back. If it weren't for the inferno in his gaze and his thick erection straining against his expensive slacks, I'd have thought I dreamed up the entire fantasy of our heated connection.

I didn't dream it up, though.

He wants me so badly he can't stand it.

So why does he deny us what we both want?

Clearing his throat, he turns back to his coffee. "Grab a quick bite to eat and then we'll head out."

With those words, he strides past me, unable to look me in the eyes. I remain rooted in the same place he rocked my entire world only moments before. The wetness from his lips on my forehead remains. His scent lingers. The overwhelming fiery need he stoked earlier still rages on with no hope of quelling.

How do I have any hope of surviving an entire day working with him?

Karla hates me. I figured that out about three seconds after Hugo left me with her to go to his morning meeting with his campaign manager, Vance. Karla is his lovely assistant but wasn't too thrilled to learn he'd hired me as well. She feels threatened, that much is clear, and for good reason.

She loves him.

I'm not an idiot. I saw how her eyes lit up when we walked into the office. The look she gave him was one of barely hidden longing. Hugo was oblivious, but I picked up on it right away. Especially since he left me alone with her. I've been iced out ever since.

As she turns on her charm to take another call, I fidget in my chair beside her. When I'd chosen the dress I'm wearing, I'd only had Hugo in mind. But with every disdainful look Karla shoots my way when she gets an eyeful of my tattooed thigh, I'm beginning to think pants are a better work attire choice. I wish Hugo would get done with his meeting so she would at least pretend to be nice.

My phone buzzes, stealing my attention and causing my heart rate to skyrocket. I've received texts all morning, each one the same as the one before—all from new numbers, but all clearly from Ben.

Unknown: I miss you, gorgeous. Please talk to me.

One comforting thought is he's all the way in LA, near his job and family. He's not going to actually hop on a plane to come to harass me in person. Eventually, he'll get bored.

As soon as I block the newest number, my phone buzzes again. I let out a frustrated huff. But it's not Ben this time. It's him.

Spencer.

Heat creeps over my flesh, warming it and painting it crimson as I read his vulgar words.

Spencer: Did you confess to Dad that you had my tongue down your throat last night?

Flashes of his strong, firm body pressed against mine as he kissed me last night flood through me. I shift uncomfortably in my seat. At the time, it'd felt so good—so right. With him holding me down as he ravished me, it was easy to forget why I hate him.

"You shouldn't be on your phone," Karla snips, her cold voice cutting through some of the fire burning inside me. "Mr. Park would not be pleased if he were to walk in and see you."

Embarrassment at being chided has me swallowing hard and forcing a nod. I'm not too worried about Hugo. He loves me. Certainly isn't going to fire me for texting with his son. I don't need to argue that with his secret admirer, though. Before I can put away my phone, she takes another call. I use the moment to text Spencer back.

Me: I'm working. Leave me alone.

His response is immediate.

Spencer: Maybe I should tell him his precious "love" wants to fuck her stepbrother… Is that what you want, leech? Next time, there'll be no dry fucking. I want to feel how wet you get when you're being bad with me.

His words are crude and maddening.
Completely messed up.
And yet, I can't ignore the curl of heat deep in my core, aching for just that.
Sick, sick girl.
I don't understand him. He's been so hot and cold since

the day I've met him. Stupid me yearns for those warmer moments. As if I have the power to melt away the black ice over his heart.

Spencer: Are you wet right now? Does your pussy miss me?

The throbbing of my clit, a direct result of his texted words, is the only answer needed. Luckily for me, he can't see or feel the way he affects me. I'm thankful to be out of the house and far, far away from his tempting ways.

Me: I hate you.

Spencer: Hate makes for the best sex.

Is it wrong that I want to test his theory?

CHAPTER FOURTEEN

Spencer

"SHE'S IN PERFECT CONDITION AND SUCH quick turnaround," Pops says, smirking. "When I call in a favor, they move their asses. Or else."

I lift a brow at him. "You know you sound like you're with the mafia when you talk like that."

He chuckles, a dark, sinister quality threading through it, and shrugs off the statement. I know he isn't actually heading an organized crime family, but he likes to allude to it, even with me. It's one of the things I admire most about my pops. He's a powerful mystery, making things happen seemingly without effort—all for the ones bearing the Park last name.

"I overheard Gemma and Dempsey talking," Pops rumbles, voice growing cold. "Aubrey's back?"

Aubrey isn't the reason for his change in demeanor. No, Neena holds that title. However, since she's Neena's daughter, she's guilty by association.

"Unfortunately." I rub at the back of my neck, easing some of the tension there. Aubrey is the only person who can ruffle me. It's maddening.

"You're quite right. Misfortunate timing." Pops motions

for me to follow him next door to his house. "This is the last thing your father's campaign needs right now."

I fall into step beside him, shooting him a questioning look. "Aubrey's bad for Dad's campaign?"

He doesn't answer until we're standing on his porch. His lips thin out and his eyes narrow. He doesn't meet my stare as he says, "Not her per se. But it'll be a reminder about what happened to Neena."

What. Happened. To. Neena.

Pops clears his throat before stalking into his house. I follow after him, curious about his shifty behavior. If I didn't know any better, I'd think he was responsible for Neena's disappearance. I mean, Dad always has been his favorite son. It's obvious to everyone in the family. It's not a stretch to imagine him hiring a hitman to deal with his difficult daughter-in-law. His own wife conveniently died in a house fire while he was fucking his son's girlfriend.

But he's not the mafia.

"She covered for Dad," I admit as we walk into his home office and take a seat. "Maybe it's not the worst thing that she's back. Might actually make it appear as if everything is normal."

"I'm not a fool," Pops says, crossing his arms over his chest and leaning back in his chair. "You don't believe that. I can see it in your eyes that you can't stand that she's back. Is she the one who vandalized your car?"

You owe me, Aubrey...

"Nah," I lie easily. "It's just difficult sharing a space with her. We don't exactly get along or hang with the same kind of people."

Also a lie.

The only people I hang with on the regular are Gemma and Dempsey. Both of them like Aubrey, though Dempsey pretends not to for my benefit.

Pops shakes his head but thankfully moves on to other subjects like where he's taking Jamie and the twins for spring break vacation. He prattles on even though I've lost interest. My buzzing phone saves me from boring small talk.

Just who I was waiting on.

Jude: I have information.

Me: Be there in five.

"Sorry, Pops, but I need to head out."

"Keep your stepsister in line. This family depends on it."

My grin is wolfish. "I'll do whatever it takes."

Even if it means fucking her into submission.

Jude's nightmare house is no less imposing when I visit again. In a way, I like forcing myself to face the creepiness of it all. If I can handle his house, I can handle anything. The entryway smells like pie again, a temptation no doubt. I ignore the grumbling of my stomach and head for the stairwell.

The approaching whir of a motor echoes around me. A chill races down my spine. Sure enough, Grandpa's familiar wheeze can be heard seconds before he appears in a doorway. He has an oxygen tank but only uses it when he's damn near suffocating. One day, his stubbornness is going to literally suck the life out of him indefinitely.

"My," Grandpa rasps, "favorite." He sucks in a ragged breath. "Grandson."

He's never called me his favorite, which means he thinks I'm my father again.

"Came to see Jude," I grunt out.

Grandpa's body jerks as he waves a papery-thin, skin and bone hand toward the stairwell. "Jude." He wheezes again. "Avoids me."

"Jude avoids everyone," I assure him, plastering on a million-dollar grin that no doubt will further confuse him into thinking I'm Dad. "No hard feelings, Grandpa."

He nods, coughs roughly, and then starts patting around for the oxygen tube that's hanging around his neck. Once he pulls it around his head, situating it to rest at his nostrils, he fusses with the tank and then takes in a few better breaths.

"Keep your head," he says, pausing to cough again. "You'll become president one day, Hugo."

I barely refrain from rolling my eyes. Instead, I give him another smile and a clipped nod before stalking away from him. I don't have the patience for him right now. Normally, I take pity on the old man, but not today. I take the stairs two at a time to put distance between us before I get pulled into another conversation.

Jude's office is empty when I make my way into it. It's unusual not to find him in here, so I plop down in his desk chair, taking in the scene before me. If I didn't know any better, I'd think he was some computer hacker or worked in cyber security. Despite the obscene amount of monitors with everything from financials to stocks to video camera footage, it's a wonder how he knows what the fuck is going on.

The only thing on his desk, though, is a lined notebook with meticulous notes. Like a never-ending to-do list for stalker weirdos like my uncle. Each task carefully written out and checked off as he accomplishes prying into people's lives like it's a part of his job.

I suppose, for our family, it sort of is.

I'm pleased to see the most recent item crossed off on his list: Find more info out on Ben for Spencer.

"You shouldn't snoop," Jude growls in lieu of a greeting as he storms into the room like a charging bull. "Out of my chair, little shit."

I spin lazily in his chair a couple of times before getting up. He shoulders past me, nearly knocking me over, and then heaves himself into his seat with a creaking sound so loud it's a wonder it doesn't collapse beneath him. Jude is massive. Like NFL-tackle-anyone-and-everyone kind of massive. But he's a big scaredy cat, too afraid to see his own reflection in the mirror, instead hiding behind latex masks and walls of computer monitors.

"Don't you ever get hot wearing that thing?" I ask, unable to stop the words from tumbling out of my mouth. Not the wisest decision to piss off the guy who is helping me.

He cracks his neck and gives a sharp nod. "Yup."

I wait for him to elaborate, but of course he doesn't. Jude isn't exactly one for small talk. Shrugging it off, I lean against the edge of his desk and gesture for his notebook. "What'd you find?"

Jude mashes a few keys on the keyboard and a screen

pops up. A man, around Dad's age, with his arm around a woman who must be his wife, grins back at us.

"Owns an online party warehouse store. Twelve employees, including Aubrey's dad, Tony, who manages those employees." He pulls up a document and points a thick finger at it. "The wife just filed for divorce."

Jude pulls up another picture of the guy. He's decent-looking in the traditional sense—full head of hair, straight teeth, strong jawline. It's his eyes, though, that give him away as a smarmy fucker. I'm actually disgusted that Aubrey would let this douchebag put his dick inside her.

"That's not all," Jude says, pulling up another screen. "He recently bought a giant order of burner phones from China."

I lift a brow. "Burner phones? And how do you know this?"

Jude grunts, and it could almost be confused with a chuckle. But since he's not exactly the chuckling type, it can't be that. "I have his passwords to his bank accounts."

"Of course you do." I do chuckle, because I am that type, especially when we're discussing prying into douchebags' lives. "What do you think he's using them for?"

"I can't see where he's calling out to, but I had a hunch, so I worked backward."

Aubrey's text transcripts pull up on the screen from today. All similar in nature. Since she keeps receiving them, but from different numbers, it's obvious he's using the endless pile of burner phones he ordered to contact her. She blocks him and he's back with another.

"What a fucking stalker," I grumble. "What about her ex, Wes? Anything on him yet?"

My phone chirps a reminder at me. Irritation burns in my gut. I don't want to leave just when I'm getting good information, but duty calls.

"Still working on him. From what I can tell so far, he's a couch-surfing guitarist for a band trying to make it big, but aside from that, he's inconsistent on social media, never has money in his account, and doesn't have a job."

Aubrey really knows how to pick them.

"Thanks, man," I say with a sigh. "I appreciate the digging you're doing. Anything I can do to repay the favor?"

"Babysit Grandpa," he blurts out without missing a beat. I can almost imagine his smirk behind his mask, knowing that answer would rile me.

"Fuck no." I grin at him. "Anything but that."

"You could get my father off my ass."

"About?"

He's quiet for a long, uncomfortable few seconds. "He wants me to see a therapist."

Pops isn't wrong there. Jude is beyond screwed up. He wears a mask, for fuck's sake.

"About what?" I ask, deliberately playing dumb to see what he'll say.

He sighs heavily, the air swooshing under his mask and making a whistling sound. "Apparently, I'm 'wasting my potential' locking myself away like Beast when I could be out there finding my Belle."

"Pops wants you to get out there and fuck a librarian?"

He snorts. I don't have to see his mouth to know I earned a rare smile. "Something like that. Therapy will supposedly help."

"I'll see what I can do to get your dad off your back,"

I assure him. "Sorry to cut and run, but I have shit to do, unfortunately."

Jude's eyes narrow to slits from behind his mask, but I don't fidget under his scrutiny or this prick will peel apart my life too. I certainly don't need that shit right now.

He turns back to his computer, effectively dismissing me, and goes back to work. I bark out a quick bye and then text Dempsey on my way out of the freak house.

Me: We need to talk.

I used to look forward to my daily errands, but I'm beginning to resent them with my entire being. I can't exactly ignore them either, which means as much as I don't want to hear Dempsey's take, I need his help.

CHAPTER FIFTEEN

Hugo

SOMETIMES I HAVE GREAT IDEAS—IDEAS THAT MAKE my family a lot of money. Other times, my ideas are based solely on my dick's needs alone and nothing else being considered.

Hiring Aubrey was a terrible fucking idea.

Not because she sucks at her job or anything like that. If it were that simple, I'd just tell her she'd be better suited for the donut shop she considered applying at. No, this is completely out of her control.

It's not her fault she's sex on two of the hottest legs I've ever seen on this planet.

Thankfully, Vaughn distracted me most of the day, going over important campaign event dates, meetings, and media appearances we have planned for the next few months until voting day. I'd only lose my mind on the rare times I'd pop out of the conference room to take a piss or grab another cup of coffee.

"Hey, Hugo," Garrick, a junior attorney at our firm, says, grinning wolfishly at me as he joins me in the conference room now that Vaughn left for the day. "Are you trying to get me fired?"

I rub at the back of my neck, chasing away thoughts of Aubrey to focus on this doofus Dad hired. "What?"

He smirks as he saunters in. Garrick is about ten years younger than me, single, and is not shy about bragging about his sex life. My gut clenches, knowing I'm not going to like what comes out of this guy's mouth.

"The sexy little vixen out there greeting all our clients. Come on, man, anyone with a working dick can see she's hot as fuck."

Unease is chased away by indignation. "Excuse me?"

"Tell me you don't want to hit that," he says, laughing. "I mean, I know you're married and all but—"

"She's my stepdaughter," I snap, slamming my pen down on the table with enough force I'm surprised it didn't splatter ink everywhere.

His eyes widen comically and then he raises his palms like one would to a dog with sharp teeth that's snarling at them. "Oh. Holy shit. No disrespect, man."

I pinch the bridge of my nose and suck in a deep breath, forcing myself to calm down before I speak again. When I've composed myself, I level him with a firm glare. "She's off-limits, Garrick. You will not date my girl."

Mine.

My fucking girl.

He nods in agreement. "Of course not. She's just beautiful. That's all I meant."

"I understand," I say in a dismissive tone. "If you'll excuse me, I have a ton of work to catch up on in my office."

Garrick slinks out of my office, leaving me to gather my files. I attempt to keep my focus on my goal—get to my office without distraction—but I find myself slowing to a stop in front of Karla's desk.

Aubrey sits primly beside Karla as my assistant chatters

on the phone with someone. Aubrey's thighs are downright lickable, smooth and shiny, and my mouth waters for a forbidden taste.

Walk away, Hugo.

Walk the fuck away or everyone in this office is going to see how hard your stepdaughter makes your dick simply by existing.

I clear my throat and aim my attention at Aubrey's pretty, glossy lips. "Want to come tell me about your day so far?"

Her eyes light up and a grin spreads across her face. "Absolutely."

My dick chubs in my slacks. I turn on my heel, stalking into my office, so she doesn't take notice. I've barely sat down behind my desk when she walks in.

"Close the door," I say in a gruff tone. "Please."

She nods, her cheeks blooming pink like a rose, and shuts the door behind her. For a moment, we simply stare at one another. My mind is going a million miles per second, giving me illicit flash after flash of images—all of which have me shoving her skirt up her thighs, spreading her toned legs apart, and feasting on what I know would be the sweetest pussy in existence.

"I missed you today." My voice is hoarse with need. I roll back a little in my chair and pat my own thigh.

Fucking really, man? Your lap?

To my surprise, her smile twists from sweet into something deviant. My dick is eager, hard and forcing the fabric of my slacks to tighten around it. There's no hiding the fact I'm caging an erection in a sixteen-hundred-dollar pair of Tom Ford twill slacks.

She saunters my way, the unsure girliness gone and in

its place a sexually confident panther. I'm prey, caught in her grip, as she makes her way over to me. Her scent swirls around me and I ache to bury my face in her hair to inhale it straight from the source.

Turning in my chair to face her, I slightly part my thighs to give her room to sit. Her gaze settles on the obvious outline of my cock. The pink on her cheeks returns and the smile she offers me is private. A smile just for me. A knowing, pleased smile.

I'm in so much fucking trouble right now.

How do I stop?

She places her hand on my shoulder to steady herself as she sits on my thigh. Her leg brushes against my dick, sending explosive energy coursing through my entire body. I open my mouth to speak—to say anything to douse this charged moment in cold water—but nothing comes out. Her fingers tease along my neck and through the trimmed hair on my head. Unable to sit and do nothing, I give my hand permission to go where it wants.

A gasp escapes her as my hand meets her naked thigh. With her sitting, her skirt has ridden up, revealing more beautiful tattooed skin. I'm caught in a dangerous moment in time where we're on the precipice of something that could ruin my entire life. Anyone could walk in and make terrible conclusions—all of which would be true.

I want to fuck my stepdaughter.

And she sure as hell wants to fuck me.

Grabbing hold of her hip with my other hand, I pull her closer to me, loving the zing of pleasure that shoots to my balls at the touch of her body against my most sensitive part.

Her fingers slide deeper into my hair and she slightly tugs at the strands.

"Love…" The slight rasp is all I can manage. A weak attempt to ask her to move away before I do something regrettable.

"My day was good, but now it's even better," she murmurs, slightly parting her thighs as if to invite my hand closer.

I groan when she wriggles against me, sending more pleasure shooting through me. I grip her thigh hard enough to make her moan. The thought of leaving claiming bruises on her leg for all to see has me doing it again. I ache to leave more bruises on her, this time with my teeth and mouth.

We've crossed a line, but we're not too far gone yet.

I could stop this.

I *have* to stop this.

She grips my neck, pulling herself closer and bringing her ass over my cock. This time, I'm making the sound of pleasure. I need to tell her to stop, but it feels too damn good having her grind her ass against me.

My fingers have inched all the way beneath her skirt and I know this because I can feel the silky edge of her panties with my fingertip. The desire to pull it away and sink my fingers into her tight heat is maddening.

Fuck, I want her so goddamn badly.

Her efforts become more earnest, as though with every movement, she knows she's bringing me closer to coming. I'll ruin these slacks and my dry cleaner's image of me, but I can't find it in me to care at the moment. All I care about is coming with this sexy little thing on my lap.

But we can't.

We can't do this because there's no *un*doing it.

I'm about to tell her as much, to warn her off before the explosion, but she stops me dead in my tracks. In a surprisingly bold move, she leans closer, bringing her supple lips to mine.

The kiss is soft and sweet at first.

Almost…innocent.

Before I can process the perfection of it, she moans, a sound filled with pure need and longing. I gasp at the lovely sound. She takes the opportunity to tug at my bottom lip with her teeth.

Holy shit.

What the fuck are we doing right now?

My eyes roll back when she sucks on my lip. I can almost imagine her between my thighs, sucking on something bigger and harder. That image is too fucking hot for work.

Karla's loud laugh beyond my closed door is a shower of ice water on me. I stiffen as reality sets back in. I remove my hold on her thigh to then grip her throat, squeezing slightly as I push her away from my mouth.

"I can't do this with you," I rumble, voice thick with regret. "I can't, Love."

She blinks several times as though clearing away a daze and her brows furl. "Why not?"

"You know why." I release her neck, but not without stroking the column of her throat with my thumb first. "You're my stepdaughter. It's…wrong."

Her face burns crimson, a mixture of shame and anger warring over her features. I hiss as she slides off my lap, making sure to give my cock one last stroke of pleasure. Helplessly, I stare at her retreating form, hating myself for having to put a stop to this whole thing.

"I led you on," I mumble. "That's on me."

"Just stop," she snaps. "I don't want to talk about this ever again."

She slips out of my office quietly, but she may as well have slammed the door in my face with how I flinch. It fucking sucks seeing her disappointment and confusion—all of which I'm responsible for.

I'm an asshole.

A weak bastard who would allow his cock to lead the way into forbidden territory, just to have a sweet little taste.

And now, because of me, she's pissed and hurt.

I did that.

I fucking hurt her.

Facing that reality finally has my dick settling down. Sure, I could rub one out in the bathroom, lingering in the fantasy come to life just moments before, but it would be lacking in comparison. It'd feel cheap and not at all pleasurable.

My dick needs to stay in my pants and I need to start treating Aubrey like the beautiful, bright, brilliant woman she is.

This shit stops now.

CHAPTER SIXTEEN

Aubrey

HUMILIATED DOESN'T EVEN BEGIN TO DESCRIBE THE way I'm feeling right now. Sure, I'm embarrassed, but I'm also angry and devastated. I didn't misread the situation. Hugo was into everything we were doing. I'd felt how hard he was. There's no mistaking when you're sitting on a giant cock.

I'd read his signals—the pure, unfiltered want blazing in his eyes being the most telling. He wanted to touch me and I'd wanted it too.

What went wrong?

I think back to the way I'd sucked on his bottom lip, aching to do so much more. He'd gone still at that moment and didn't kiss me back.

Crap.

Did I mess up everything then?

I'd tried to get him to kiss me back, but he'd remained still, and then it was like he snapped out of a lust-filled haze, returning to reality without me.

He dismissed me so easily.

I'm so confused by the entire encounter.

This was different than with any man I've been with before. In LA, there weren't emotions or history involved. It was just following what felt good, uncaring of the consequences.

THE TANGLE OF AWFUL

With Hugo, there are consequences. And I broke my vow to leave him alone. I was never supposed to go there with him because he's not like those guys in California. He's different—better—someone special to me.

Shame has bile creeping up my throat. What's wrong with me? I go after these older men because it feels good to be seen and adored, but I'm destroying everyone's lives in the process.

I'm a broken girl.

The thought of riding in the car with Hugo after work makes my skin crawl. I can't deal with how awkward that will be. If I had a car of my own, I could just get in and drive far, far away from here. Away from the Parks, away from my past *again*, away from the baggage of my uncaring mother.

Before I can talk myself out of it, I order an Uber. Then, I escape my hiding spot in the women's restroom. Hugo's door is still closed, much to my relief, and I'm able to snatch up my purse without incident.

"Where are you going?" Karla asks, glancing at the clock on the wall behind me. "It's not five yet."

"Stomach bug," I hiss. "Hope you don't get it too."

Her face sours as she absently grabs for her hand sanitizer. "Feel better soon."

Not likely.

My stomach is in knots and is a complete mess, but until I can figure out how to stop sabotaging my own life, it'll probably be that way for a while yet.

I need a friend. Someone to talk to. A shoulder to cry on.

Spencer is not that friend. I know he's sitting in his giant

125

house, like the dark lord of everyone else's pain he is, waiting for me to come inside so he can further torment me. Not interested. Before I reach the front door, I turn on my heel, heading straight for Gemma's house.

The door opens, moments later, to my beautiful friend. Her dark brown hair is sleek and shiny, while her makeup is artfully applied. She's perfectly put together and I'm splitting apart from the inside out. The smile on her face falls immediately upon taking in my expression.

"Can we hang out?" I squeak out, hating how vulnerable and needy I sound. "Please."

Her sculpted eyebrows dip and scrunch together. "Of course. Come on."

I allow her to grab my hand, hauling me into her house. I'm thankful when she rushes me past her father's office where his voice booms beyond the door. We're not so lucky when we nearly crash into her mom, Jamie.

"Aubrey?" Jamie says, a huge grin on her face. "We missed you, girl."

I allow Gemma's mom to pull me into a motherly hug that has my eyes prickling. I'm envious of Gemma's life. She has two parents who adore her. Both of mine hate me and I'm on the fast track to getting my stepfamily to hate me too.

"Mom, you're smothering her," Gemma complains, saving me from an embarrassing crying spell.

"Missed you too," I manage to croak out as I pull away from Jamie.

Gemma takes my hand again, tugging me away from her mother and up the stairs. We pass by Dempsey's closed door. The bass is loud, making the pictures on the wall rattle. I'm glad we don't have to see him. Right now, I just want to be alone with Gemma. Once we're safely tucked away in her room that smells like sweet pea perfume, I sink onto the bed, dropping my purse at my feet.

"Spill," Gemma says, plopping down beside me. "You're scaring me. It's Spencer, isn't it? He hurt you."

The frown on her pretty face says she can't really believe it, but she'll try. For me. Her loyalty to our friendship makes me feel like the biggest bitch on the planet for ghosting her when I left.

Spencer is the least of my problems right now. I wonder if Gemma would still be so comforting if she knew I kissed her oldest brother at his office—my freaking stepfather. Would she be such a good friend then?

I chew on my bottom lip for a moment, trying not to think of the softness of Hugo's lips that didn't reciprocate my kiss.

"Aubrey," Gemma urges. "You're scaring me."

"I kissed Spencer," I say instead of telling her what's bothering me today. "That's why I left."

She gapes at me, eyes blinking almost comically. "What? You hate him."

I do now. Sort of.

"Back then it was different," I mutter, shrugging my shoulders. "We liked each other."

"So you kissed him and then he started hating you?"

"Something like that."

Gemma huffs. "That's stupid. Why would he get mad if he liked you too? It's not like you're actually related."

My mind drifts back to that day.

His lips are soft and wet. I wonder what they'll feel like on other parts of me. A soft moan escapes me. He responds with a groan—no, a growl, practically devouring me as if to chase away the sounds I'm making. I'm a captive to his expert, claiming kiss.

A gasp from the doorway has both of us stilling.

We're alone.

Right?

"What the hell are you doing?" Mom demands, voice equal parts shrill and furious.

Not alone.

Crap.

"M-Mom," I stammer out. "It's not what it looks like."

Isn't it, though?

I'm practically straddling my stepbrother in his bed, our tongues tangled only seconds before.

"Go to your room, young lady," Mom hisses. "Right now."

Tears of shame flood my eyes as I scramble off Spencer's lap. His full lips are swollen and red from our kiss. The lusty look in his eyes is shuttered away, an impassive expression contorting his features.

I want to tell him I'm sorry—that everything will be okay—but I can't. I don't know what's going to happen now that Mom knows.

Will I be grounded for making out with my stepbrother?

Doesn't seem like the end of the world.

"It's not his fault," I utter as I approach my mother. "It's all mine."

It's not.

We're both equally guilty.

But, while I can handle Mom's grounding, I'm not sure what Hugo would do to Spencer. Hugo isn't cruel, but I've never seen Spencer do anything like this before.

"Room. Now." Mom's nostrils flare and she regards me with obvious disgust. "I'll deal with you shortly."

I cast another look over my shoulder at Spencer. His spine is ramrod straight and the only tell he's affected by this entire ordeal is the way his jaw muscle ticks.

Mom shoos me the rest of the way out of his room and slams the door. Hard. She's about to lay into him like this was all his idea. I want to go back in there and argue more on his behalf, but I know it won't do any good. It's better to obey, listen to her pending lecture, and then accept my punishment.

As for me and Spencer, we'll be fine.

We'll go back to being friends or we'll be more.

This isn't the end of the world.

This isn't the end of us.

A shiver has me blinking away the past and bringing me back to the present. I was naïve to think everything would be fine. Whatever Mom said to him changed him. He was no longer the fun, flirty guy I lived with and eventually fell for. No, he transformed into a cold, callous, cruel stepbrother who made it his sole mission to torment me until I was forced to run to my father.

"Mom walked in on us. It got ugly." I sigh heavily. "After that, he hated me."

"And now?"

I could tell her everything. How I let Spencer pin me down yesterday or how I let Hugo run his hand up my thigh. I could confess that I'm a broken girl who likes breaking those around her also.

Instead, I lie.

It's what I'm good at, apparently.

"He's just an ass sometimes," I say, deflating. "Some days are harder than others."

Gemma begrudgingly accepts this answer and changes the subject. Listening to her babble on about her newest crush is refreshing. It does wonders to make me forget about this terrible day. When she moves on to shopping and a pair of sandals she wants, I dutifully listen, nodding where appropriate, giving her my entire attention. Before long, an hour has passed and I do feel better.

"Thanks for cheering me up." I hug her and then scoop up my purse. "Right now I just want to go home and get in my comfy clothes. Maybe next weekend we can go shopping together."

Gemma nods rapidly. "Duh. Plus, Willa needs new jeans. Don't tell anyone, but I think she's pregnant."

After that shocker of a statement, I follow her back downstairs. This time, when we pass her dad's office, the door is open. Nathan's eyes latch onto mine and narrow. I've never liked Nathan Park. Something about him is so...calculating. I suppress a shiver, hurrying past.

Thankfully, when I get back home, Hugo's still not there. I rush upstairs, eager to have a moment alone. Spencer's door is closed. Good. I can't deal with him either.

"Hey, leech."

My feeling of relief drains at my feet as cold dread seeps into my every pore. Why is he in my room? Butterflies flutter in my stomach as I think about the last time he was on my bed. He was such a dick yesterday, but there's no denying it felt good.

He rises to his feet, a predatory glint in his hard eyes. I remain frozen in the doorway, unable to retreat or make a hasty escape. It's almost as if, deep down, I want him to catch me. He approaches slowly, glowering at me in a way that feels both hungry and angry. Like he wants to nip at every piece of my flesh.

I drop my purse to my feet and my palms go up. To stop him? To grab onto him? In the end, I press them against his solid chest, intending on pushing him away from me.

However, I don't get that chance.

His mouth crashes to mine, starved and desperate. I'm caught off guard by the raw need rippling from him. He tastes sweet, such a far cry from his usual bitterness. I eagerly devour him right back. I'm not some helpless victim. I'm a co-conspirator in this crime of the flesh.

He thinks he's on the attack, winning this war against me, and I let him. My ego is bruised and bleeding. Having Spencer want me so undeniably, even if he sees it as a victory in this ruthless game he's playing, is exactly what I need in this moment.

This is dangerous.

It's like I'm handing the house keys over to a burglar and telling him to take whatever he wants. He'll take and take and take until there's nothing left but the walls around me, everything inside hollow and empty.

I try to drown in his kiss, losing myself in his scent, his raspy growls, and how his teeth feel razor-sharp as they nip at my lips.

It feels good, but it's also not enough.

He must sense my desperation because there's no preamble as he slips a hand between my thighs. Unlike earlier, with his dad, he doesn't tease at the edge of my panties. No,

Spencer is bolder and more reckless. His fingers easily find my clit and he rubs me over the material.

"Spencer," I cry out, breaking from our kiss to drop my head back.

His mouth hungrily finds my neck, nipping and sucking like I crave for him to do underneath my skirt.

"Feel good to have your brother's fingers on you, leech?"

I should shove him away for that question.

I don't.

I'm nodding instead, breathily begging, "I want more."

He sucks on my neck before latching on. The sting of it has me whimpering. "Bad girl," he croons. "Maybe Dad'll come after you with the belt for this."

Of course he'd ruin the moment with his stupid mouth. I want to shove him away and yell at him. To tell him I hate him and have since the day he started treating me like shit.

Again, I don't.

I cry out when his finger slides past my slick panties, rubbing over my sensitive flesh. He teases my clit and then firmly pushes into my body. I gasp at his intrusion, losing all sense of reality as he begins fingerfucking me.

This is it.

I've ruined everything now.

My stepbrother has his fingers inside me and it's consoling me over the fact they're not his father's instead.

Can this get any worse?

CHAPTER SEVENTEEN

Spencer

I WAS SUPPOSED TO WATCH HER UNRAVEL.

But not like this.

Not with my fingers inside her, marveling over how wet and tight and perfect she is.

I'm supposed to get off on her misery, not get off on *her* getting off. That's exactly what I'm doing, too. Grinding my hard as fuck dick against her body as I thrust deeper and deeper into her pussy with my fingers, wishing it were my cock instead.

She'd let me.

I have no doubt in my mind she'd let me peel off her panties, wrap her sexy legs around me, and fuck her into next week. I could come inside her, consequences be damned, and she'd let me.

The control I have over her is exhilarating. I'd assumed, at one time, she was the one wielding her spread legs like a weapon against all the men in her life, but it's not that way at all.

She needs the sex.

To feel wanted and desired.

It's more than an orgasm of her body, but an orgasm of her self-esteem.

It's empowering to know I can use her body to my

advantage. To play her like a fucking violin, rubbing over her strings in just the right way to make her moan music just for me.

The problem is, though, I'm beyond weaponizing her body against herself. I'm enjoying it too much. Not because I love to torment her, but because I like the way she tastes and feels and smells.

"What if Daddy comes in and finds us like this?" I murmur against her lips, unable to fight a grin when her pussy clenches around my fingers. "Would you be able to stop?"

She tangles her fingers in my hair, pulling me closer to her mouth. "Shut up."

"You'd beg him to join because you're a whore for older men, aren't you?"

"Spencer, shut up," she pants, no venom in her tone. "I'm close. Oh, God, I'm close."

I want to taunt her more, to refocus on my purpose with her, but once again, I lose myself in the moment. Her mouth is sweet and supple, her lips growing more swollen from our kiss with each passing second. I can tell when she's actually on the edge of bliss because her whole body tenses. Grabbing onto her thigh, I hike her leg as high as it'll go and plunge my fingers deep, making sure to massage the fuck out of her G-spot. It only takes a few seconds before she explodes.

"That's it, leech," I croon against her mouth, "make your pussy clench around my fingers like you're desperate for the cum out of my cock."

To my surprise, she obeys, her body squeezing tightly around my fingers even as she trembles and shakes. The vision of me inside her, filling her up, is too much to bear. If I don't get the fuck out of here, I'm going to come too like a god-damn chump. Then, she'll know she has some power over me.

That can't happen.

I don't wait for her to completely come down from her high before slipping my fingers out of her and pulling away. Not so gently, I release her leg. It drops heavily and she wobbles to regain her balance.

She's wrecked.

Positively wrecked.

Hair disheveled. Lips red and swollen. Skirt hitched up her thighs, revealing her askew panties.

I love her all messy and out of control.

A smile is forming, but I shut it down as soon as my lips begin twitching. Carefully, I shutter my expression and regard her with an impassive one.

"Should I tell Dad or should you?"

Her face flashes red hot, a mixture of shame, hurt, and embarrassment. Good. It's a reminder—to both of us—of what this thing is between us.

A game.

Nothing more than a game.

One I'm winning, too.

"You really should clean yourself up," I say as I push past her. "You're a mess, leech."

A hot, beautiful, sinfully sexy mess.

"Fuck you," she spits out, this time the venom burning like acid.

"Maybe tomorrow."

I shrug my shoulders and saunter out of her room. Her door slams hard behind me. I'm pleased with my little show for about three seconds. Once back in my room, alone, the façade falls away.

Why'd she have to go and fuck everything up back then?

Like the schmuck I am, I go into my closet and pull down the box—our box. The stupid box that holds all the good memories of me and Aubrey. Sitting on the floor, I pull out a stack of polaroids. Aubrey's dad sent her a dumb, cheap polaroid camera one year and we had fun taking pictures with it.

Back when I thought she was real.

A real friend. A real stepsister. A real person.

I have a hard time looking at the pair of grinning teenagers staring back at me from the photos. I'd been completely oblivious to her duplicitous ways.

She felt pretty real a short moment ago. Bringing my fingers to my nose, I inhale her sweet scent that remains. Still damp and sticky. Real. Fucking real.

My chest feels hollow. I'd had nefarious intentions when I'd gone in there earlier, but then the lines blurred.

What if I was wrong a couple of years ago?

What if I've been feasting on a lie?

"Spencer?"

Dad's deep voice startles me. It's not often he's been able to sneak up on me. Based on the mess at the bottom of my closet, I'd say I lost myself to memories for longer than I thought. Quickly, I start stacking up the pictures and throw them back into the box.

"In here," I finally say, giving away my location. "Just looking for a picture of Mom."

I hoist up the box and am sliding it into place when I sense his presence in the closet doorway.

"Okay," he drawls out, wisely choosing not to press as to why. He sighs heavily. "Can we talk?"

Sweeping my gaze over my father's impressive frame, I take stock of his appearance. His hair isn't styled anymore and hangs limply over his forehead. The tie that's usually perfectly knotted has been tugged loose. His eyebrows are furled and his lips are pressed into a tight line.

What's strange is his eyes don't meet mine.

Interesting.

"Yeah, Dad, what's up?"

He turns on his heel and stalks back into my bedroom. I notice the bedroom door has been closed. My curiosity is officially piqued.

"Is Aubrey okay?" His expression grows stormy and his nostrils flare.

I still my entire body, wondering if he somehow knows what I was just up to. Can he smell her sweet scent that's certainly invaded my nostrils?

"Seemed perfectly fine to me," I say slowly, narrowing my eyes. "Why?"

Dad glances at me briefly, a relieved glint in his eyes, before looking away again. He shrugs and turns away from me, choosing to walk over to my window.

"Just wondering."

It's then I realize what's wrong with him. Guilt. I've rarely seen my father looking guilty, because as far as men in this community go—and this family for that matter—he's one of the more morally stable.

"Did you upset her?" I probe, prowling closer to him.

He flinches at my question. "Maybe? Fuck." His fingers

spear into his hair and he tugs, giving away why his hair looks like shit today. "No, I did. I upset her."

Things begin to click into place quickly.

Aubrey's foul mood. Dad's shame. The evasiveness of both of them.

Something happened between them. My guess is she started it, he went along with it, and then his predictable morals started flashing warning signs at him. He probably freaked and embarrassed her.

What did they do?

Kiss. Oral. A quick fuck over his desk.

Anger boils in my gut, chasing away any fondness I'd been feeling minutes ago. Aubrey is exactly what I've always known—a broken girl who likes breaking families. She tried it once two years ago and now she's at it again. With her track record, especially since she just got done ruining her relationship with her father and his boss and family, it's quite obvious she's up to it again.

It's a part of her.

Ruination and destruction.

Awful, wretched, fucked-up girl.

Familiar bitterness poisons my veins and shrivels my heart. I'm so damn stupid when it comes to her. Always letting my guard down when I need to be applying war paint instead whenever she's around.

She fucked around with my dad. Then, she came home and let me fingerfuck her. Was his cum still inside her when I brought her to orgasm. The urge to scrub my hands is overwhelming. I curl my hand into a fist and crack my neck to release the growing tension.

Aubrey Love will not tear apart this family. I kept it from

happening once before and I'll do it again. In order to do that, I'm going to have to stop with the games and reveal how shamefully slutty she really is.

"Dad?" I say, adopting a soft, unsure tone. "I think I fucked up."

He turns away from the window, finally meeting my stare. The concern in his expression makes me feel like a dick, but it's necessary. "Everything's fixable, Spencer."

Not Aubrey.

She's a broken, ruined, used-up girl.

"Not this." I let my shoulders fall forward and crumple up my features. "I'm sorry, Dad."

Stalking over to me, he grabs both sides of my neck like he used to do when I was little. It still warms me and fills me with love. My dad might not be perfect, but he doesn't deserve to get sucked into Aubrey's whorish void. It makes me feel like an even bigger asshole that I'm going to have to poke him in order to get to her.

"What is it?" he says, eyes darting back and forth as if to assess me for invisible damage. "You know you can talk to me about anything."

"I kissed Aubrey," I blurt out. "Not long before you got home."

I also had my fingers in her pussy, but he doesn't need to know that. Yet.

The color drains from his face and his eyes widen comically. I've done some stupid shit over the years to earn this look of horror, but this one is especially satisfying knowing the pedestal she's on around him is about to be kicked out from under her feet.

"It won't happen again," I assure him, making my voice quaver. "I swear."

He closes his eyes and his jaw clenches. The shock is slipping away as anger floods in. I know he's pissed because his neck slowly turns crimson and his nostrils flare. The grip on my neck no longer feels like a loving father comforting his son, but more of a potential strangulation.

She did this to him.

Not me.

Aubrey.

"Please don't be mad," I croak out. "It just…it just happened."

"Fuck," he hisses under his breath. "Fuck, fuck, fuck."

"Dad?"

He releases my neck and points a finger hard into my chest. "It will *never* happen again. Are we clear? Never."

Under all the fury is jealousy. He's jealous of his own son.

"Don't take this out on her," I rush out. "She's so fragile with her mom missing and her dad kicking her out. Please, Dad."

His gaze softens. "I'm not going to punish her. Or you. In fact, I'd be happiest if we never discussed this again."

I nod and make a motion of zipping my lips with the fingers that still smell like Aubrey. "Not a word." I make a motion toward the house next door. "I'm going to go out with Dempsey. Maybe everything will be back to normal by the time I get back."

Unlikely, but I can pretend.

"Normal," Dad repeats, a pensive expression on his face. "Normal would be great." He walks over to the window again, back once more facing me, and grows quiet.

Good.

I've fixed Dad's little fixation by revealing how not-so-innocent his stepdaughter is.

He'll remember who she is and everything will go back to normal for him.

But for me and Aubrey?

Torment will soon be her new normal and I can't fucking wait to dole it out to her.

CHAPTER EIGHTEEN

Hugo

I T TAKES EVERYTHING IN ME TO HOLD MY COMPOSURE until I hear the faint hum of the garage door opening, signaling Spencer's departure.

Un-fucking-believable.

I'd been so wrapped up in my own shit with Aubrey that I'd completely been blind as to what was happening right under my nose—under my own roof—with my own son.

I thought they hated each other. And yet, the same day I had her in my lap with her lips on mine, she also had her tongue down my son's throat.

Bile creeps up my throat. The media would have a field day with this shit. Father and son secretly making out with the same goddamn girl. Worse yet, she's family. My stomach twists at the thought of everyone in Park Mountain a witness to our family drama.

That can't happen.

It'd cost me the election for sure.

And then they'd start asking questions about where Neena is. Conclusions would be drawn and suddenly, my ass would be in jail for the murder of my wife. I've seen enough crime TV to know the husband is always the suspect. Now, because of my dick, I'd have motive too.

She's not dead.

At least I hope not. I mean, I want to kill her because she takes such great satisfaction in ruining my life, but I know Neena. This is another stunt of hers.

What happens when she finds out her daughter was grinding against my cock this afternoon?

A shot of anger spikes through me again, this time directed at Aubrey. She seemed pretty fucking into me earlier. When I stopped what was happening, she was upset. I'd witnessed firsthand the hurt on her face. Longed for another taste of her pouty bottom lip.

She was pissed at me and decided to seek revenge by kissing Spencer?

I storm out of Spencer's room and head straight for hers. Twisting the knob, I send the door flinging against the wall with a loud bang. It would be smarter to cool off before addressing her, but I can't. I need to know what happened. More importantly, why.

Her figure appears in the doorway of her bathroom. She's wide-eyed and her lips are parted. The white towel wrapped around her body is snuggly tied, showing off her sexy curves. Her long blond hair is damp, dripping rivulets of water down her upper chest.

"Hugo?" she squeaks out. "Is everything okay?"

No.

Nothing is okay.

Everything is all fucked-up and has been ever since she walked back into our lives this week.

Stalking over to her, I feel a slight thrill when she backs away, fear glinting in her eyes. Good. I want her to be afraid.

Fucking around with us both is not okay. She needs to know that, even if I have to spank her ass to get the point across.

I grab onto her delicate jaw and push her against the doorframe. Her eyes grow huge, filled with confusion.

"Why?" I demand, fingers biting slightly into her skin. "Why did you do it?"

She swallows hard and frowns. "Why what?"

I crowd her further, letting her feel the strength and power emanating from me. My dick is hard as stone. There's no denying it. But I can keep that in check. My anger, however, is another beast altogether.

"Don't play stupid, Love. You kissed my son."

She flinches at my words and blinks furiously. My guess is she's combatting tears. I have this overwhelming urge to make her cry—to make her feel one iota of the pain I'm feeling right now. "Hugo—"

"So it's true?" I demand. "Did you fuck him too?"

Unfair. Un-fucking-fair.

Her pretty eyes flood with the tears I crave so badly, spilling over her crimson cheeks.

"I thought," I start, biting back a snarl of rage. "I thought you wanted me."

Oh, for fuck's sake. Don't go there, man.

She sniffles and her bottom lip trembles. "I did, but you said—"

"I didn't say you could fuck my son!" I roar, my voice booming so loud I'm sure I could rattle both our bones.

A sob catches in her throat, reminding me of when she was sixteen—a sweet-faced young kid who didn't hurt people. My girl. My Aubrey Love. Guilt comes smashing into me and the grip I have on her jaw loosens.

I should pull away and go drown myself in something expensive from my bar.

I don't.

That would be smart and apparently, with Aubrey, I'm pretty fucking stupid. The desire to erase my own goddamn son from her lips has me doing the unthinkable.

I kiss her.

Not sweetly or exploring in nature.

No, I kiss her like I ache to fuck her—claiming, brutally, savage. My groan of need pours out of me as I lash at her tongue with mine. Her mewl sends fire straight to my dick. I pin her against the doorframe with my hips, letting her feel just how hard I am for her.

I could claim her right here.

All it would take is ripping her plush towel away and sliding inside her tight heat. I could do it. It would satisfy every male craving inside me. I could finally get something I desperately want.

And then what?

Visions of the media circus are a cold shower on my need for her. I start to pull away, quickly retreating from this clusterfuck I'm all wrapped up in.

"Hugo," she whimpers. "Not again."

She can't take the rejection again.

I get it. I feel for her. I do. But it's something she's going to have to deal with because this can't happen. It just can't.

Her hand slides down and she boldly cups it over my dick. Fire burns through me at her eager touch. I let out an embarrassing moan as she rubs against me.

"I didn't fuck him." Her teeth capture her bottom lip

and her doe eyes implore me to believe her. "I don't want him. I want you."

Satisfaction purrs deep inside me.

The same sort of feeling surges through me whenever I win a case.

Triumph.

Which, again, is fucked-up. She's my stepdaughter. I'm not supposed to be pleased with the fact she wants me more than my son.

"Stop thinking so much," she breathes. "Just be here with me."

I'm unable to look away as she yanks away her towel while she expertly strokes my dick over my slacks. Every perfect inch of her is revealed to me.

She's naked.

Naked and mine for the taking.

I could. I so fucking could.

But I can't.

Her pert tits jiggle as she steps back. I'm fixated on her pink nipples that are hard, standing dutifully at attention. My mouth waters to spend an entire day tasting them—sucking and biting and bruising them.

A wicked glint in her eyes is my only warning before she kneels before me. Never in my wildest dreams did I ever think I'd have my sweet little stepdaughter kneeling in front of me, eager to put my cock in her mouth.

We can't come back from this.

If she does this, I can't undo it.

I grip her damp hair, expecting to pull her away. Her lashes bat prettily as she looks up at me, heat burning in her gaze. I don't want to tell her no. I want this. I fucking want this with every cell in my body.

With a slight nod, I urge her to continue, tightening my hold on her hair. For a moment, I'm able to pretend she's some random woman I'm interested in. Not my stepdaughter. Not my missing wife's little girl.

All too easily, she unzips my pants and seeks out my cock. Her hands are cold, chilling the heated stone-hard flesh of my cock.

"Fuck, Love," I growl, voice hoarse with need. "You're so goddamn beautiful."

Her smile is breathtaking and then she's taking my breath. She slides her luscious lips over the crown of my cock, licking at the bead of pre-cum there. I nearly collapse at the pure pleasure zinging through me.

Fuck, this feels good.

So fucking good.

"Holy shit," I hiss out as she takes me further. "You feel fucking amazing."

My words spur her on and she sucks my dick like she's been placed on the earth to do that and only that. With every lick of her tongue or hollowing of her cheeks as she sucks, I'm blasted with a high I've never known in all my life. It's like she's worshiping me—praying to me, her god, through my cock.

I grip her hair, unable to slightly push against the back of her throat with my dick. She relaxes some, breathing heavily through her nostrils, allowing me entry. Her throat swallows me down and I thrust hard against her.

"Fuuuuuuck." My head tips back and I groan. "Fuck. Fuck. Fuck."

She gags, throat constricting, and I pull back. Her fingers grip the meaty cheeks of my ass, urging me to do it again.

She likes it.

She likes having her pretty face fucked.

"You want me to make your throat nice and raw, Love?"

The hum in response is my undoing. I fuck rather harshly into her throat, oblivious to her slobber that's running down the front of my pants, until my balls tighten. Admittedly, it doesn't take long before I'm coming deep in her mouth and filling her belly with my cum.

"Good girl," I praise, voice raspy. "Good, good girl."

When I'm sure she's taken every drop, I pull out of her mouth so I can fully take in her wrecked appearance. I've never seen anything more beautiful in all my life.

Aubrey is perfect.

Her body is sexy-as-fuck, but it's her facial expressions that get me every time—so innocent but also somehow so naughty all at once. I love how her pouty lips are red and swollen from taking my dick. Lashes that are still wet with tears bat lazily against her cheeks, as if staying awake requires too much energy.

She gave me everything when she sucked my dick.

And now she's exhausted.

Quickly, I shove my still dripping dick back into my slacks and zip up before helping her to her feet. The hunger in her gaze has me wanting to scoop her into my arms, carry her to my room to spend the rest of the night.

That can't happen.

I need to process what happened a moment ago before I go jumping off into another stupid decision. Bending down, I snatch up her towel and then drape it over her shoulders. Her brows pinch together, worry flickering over her features.

"That was the best feeling in my entire life, Love," I murmur, briefly dipping down to kiss her supple lips again. "The. Best."

She smiles against my mouth. "We can do more."

Such a temptation.

More sounds like heaven with my devilish little girl.

"I can't," I grumble. "We can't."

"Hugo—"

"I said we can't, Love. Just take this as the stolen gift it was. A memory. A fucking great one. I won't ever forget it, but we can't do this. Nothing about this thing between us works. I'm married to your mother, for fuck's sake."

Tears well in her eyes again, but anger chases away any sadness. She shakes her head at me and starts for the bathroom. The towel barely covers her cute little ass.

"I love you," I remind her, my voice sounding fatherly and caring. "Don't ever forget."

She looks over her shoulder and glowers at me, even as tears stream down her cheeks like shimmery raindrops on a windowpane. "Your love is confusing and it hurts, Hugo. It really hurts."

I expect a door to slam, but again, she shuts me out with a soft click of a door closing.

Why do I keep hurting her? Over and over. It's like I have no control. Like I do it for fucking sport. Shame burns through my every vein, making my stomach twist violently.

It felt like a fantasy come to life while getting a blow-job from my sexy stepdaughter. Even now, my heart continues to race from the adrenaline rush of coming in her pretty mouth, but I'm sated in that way that always comes after good sex.

My head's a fucking mess, though.

Which is why I won't be doing that shit ever again.

Until my dick gets hard next time I see her mouth, remembering the way she sucked cock like she wanted a career in it...

What then?

My cock thickens in my slacks.

I guess I know my answer.

I'm a monster.

CHAPTER NINETEEN

Aubrey

PICK AT A PIECE OF LINT OFF MY NAVY PANTS. PANTS ARE safe. Pants are a barrier from your stepbrother's wandering hands.

Hugo had on pants yesterday and it didn't stop *my* wandering hands…

Heat licks at my neck and burns my cheeks. Work is not the place to be thinking of all the terrible, awful things that took place yesterday.

The thing with Spencer was almost…expected. He's rotten and for some reason, I keep letting him get away with it. But, with Spencer, I'm used to the way he is.

Hugo?

He absolutely confuses me because I thought he was better than his son. I waffle back and forth between being angry with him and being hurt by him.

Last night, in my room, Hugo came onto me. He kissed me. He led me on. I was justified in thinking we were doing this "thing"—whatever this thing was—together. He'd let me blow him. I'd seen the unmasked pleasure written all over his face. For a second, it felt great to be the reason for that look.

It was gone in a flash because right after, he was gone, telling me it couldn't ever happen again.

I was sure he'd break—that he'd bring it up this morning

on the way to work, but I was wrong. He kept the conversation light, babbling on about the campaign like I didn't just have his dick in my mouth the night before.

The sickness roiling in my gut only worsens as the day goes on. How can he pretend like nothing happened? I certainly can't turn it off, smiling at everyone I pass by. In fact, I feel perilously close to breaking. I'm fragile, brittle, and fractured.

I'm everything Dad said I was.

A woman who shamelessly uses her body to get a momentary high of attention regardless of the catastrophic consequences. The men take what they want because I allow it and then go about their merry little way. I'm not worth real love and commitment, that much is apparent. Every time I get myself in one of these situations, I'm left hollow and alone after. While it feels good in the moment, it feels awful once the moment has passed.

My stomach grumbles, signaling lunchtime. I glance up at the clock to confirm that Hugo has managed to avoid me successfully all morning.

What am I even doing here?

There's no alternative, though. I can't go back home to Dad. Mom certainly isn't showing her face. I'm eighteen, so I should just find my own place, but something tells me this black cloud I carry over me will follow me there too.

The clack of heels on hard floors draws my attention from the clock to the front door. Relief floods through me at seeing Tasha. Her smile is all for me as she saunters my way. Knowing someone actually cares about me and doesn't see me as some seductress is refreshing.

"Auntie Tasha!" I exclaim, grinning. "What are you doing here? How did you know I was here?"

Karla shoots me a dirty look, making sure to point in exaggeration at her phone. I refrain from giving her the middle finger and rush over to Tasha.

"I'm taking you to lunch," Tasha reveals. "We have so much to catch up on."

Of course Hugo decides to take that moment to open his office door. His eyes linger on me long enough to make my heart flutter before cutting them over to Tasha. He frowns, marring his handsome face.

"Tasha," Hugo greets, forcing a smile. "What a surprise."

Her genuine smile falls and she glares icily at him. "Is it? How's your wife?"

The flinch is slight, but I see it. As frustrated as I am with him at the moment, I don't want her to start dissecting his personal life in front of Karla and the entire office. Quickly, I scoop up my purse and stride over to her.

"We're grabbing lunch. That okay?" I meet his gaze briefly before stealing a glance at his lips that were parted so beautifully just last night as I sucked his cock.

He clears his throat and nods. "Take as long as you want."

Tasha barely holds back a sneer but doesn't say anything. I nod, offering him a grateful smile, and then loop an arm with Tasha's. I'm able to get her out of the office without her running her fingernails down the side of his face.

Her pearly white Maserati's engine purrs to life as she hits the fob. Tasha has long legs and practically sprints despite her sky-high heels. It's not until we're inside her car that smells of her familiar perfume that she finally explodes.

"I know he's your stepdaddy, but I hate him!" She beats

153

a fist against her steering wheel. "He's a snake. I can feel it. Whatever is going on with your mother, he's behind it. Mark my words."

"He's not a snake."

She huffs and shakes her head, making her earrings jingle. "You always were blind to the toxicity of that family. Your mother knew. Vented to me about it often, too."

The car grows silent. Eventually, she sniffs and waves off the awkwardness with a manicured hand.

"Let's have lunch at the country club today. I hear they have a new chef all the way from New York. My friend Marianna says the sea bass is to die for."

We chat about safe topics like Hugo's campaign and my new job. Eventually, once we're at the country club and seated in a quaint corner, Tasha drops the niceties.

"I'm so glad you're back here, honey, but why? Your mother said you and Spencer had a falling-out years ago that was irreparable. Why come back and live with that bratty child?"

I let out a heavy sigh. With Tasha, there really is no avoiding the topics she wants to discuss. She'll circle back relentlessly like a hawk with her eyes on prey. May as well make it easy for her.

"Dad kicked me out." I cringe at our last words together that involved a lot of screaming on his part and crying on my part. "I screwed up. Nowhere else to go but back here."

"Why on earth would he kick out my perfect girl?" she asks, lips puckering into a pout. "Tony always was a hothead with no sense. I'll never understand your mother's choice in men."

I understand why she fell for Hugo...

"I slept with his boss," I blurt out. "Not so perfect."

I have to bite down on my bottom lip hard to keep the tears at bay. My choices are always the wrong ones and they will continue to haunt me until the day I die. Reliving my fight with Dad only worsens how I feel since I'm up to my same shenanigans with the Park men. It's me. It's obviously always me who's the problem.

"You're perfect to me," Tasha says, giving me a kind smile. "Was he at least handsome?"

A laugh bubbles out of me, crazed and girly. "No! I mean, sort of. I think I just liked the attention he gave me. It was stupid."

"If I had a dollar for every time I made a stupid mistake, I'd be ten times richer than I am now," she sasses, arching a sculpted brow at me. "It's life, sweetie. It's what shapes us to be better people."

Behind Tasha's fillers and cosmetic surgery to preserve her youth is a woman I've always loved and looked up to. She was the fun aunt I never had. The one who treated me like kin, always available to take me out for a little retail therapy. Whenever Mom was cold to me, I used to pretend Tasha was my mother instead.

"I feel like a home-wrecking whore," I admit, stomach churning with guilt and self-loathing. "I know better and yet…"

She reaches across the table to pat my hand. "Don't take all the shame on yourself. That man was there too. And, I'm guessing he was older, which means he should have had the sense not to pursue you. I'm not saying you're blameless in the situation. But I also want you to know he's every bit as guilty of what went down. Did Tony lay into him too?"

"He still works there, so I doubt it." I shrug my shoulders. "Anyway, I packed up and came back here."

Thankfully, by the time our food arrives, we've moved on to her trip to Switzerland she's going on this winter. It takes the spotlight off myself and allows me to just listen to her. My mind travels, though. Not to Switzerland, but to Mom. I'd told Tasha there was nothing to worry over regarding Mom.

I sincerely hope that's the truth.

I'm finding it far too easy to slip into her place beside Hugo. It's sick that I secretly wish she'd stay away. Because if she showed up today and saw how I behaved with both Hugo and Spencer, my other parent would disown me too.

And that's enough to make me want to puke up sea bass.

Somehow, I made it through lunch and Tasha's interrogation. Then, after, I managed to avoid Hugo as well. Karla seemed to enjoy punishing me with grunt work. Little did she know, I was completely fine with burying my face in digging through files all day. When five o'clock hit, I bailed, jumping into my waiting Uber because I was not looking forward to awkwardness with Hugo, or worse yet, questioning as to what me and Tasha spoke about.

I'm distracted as I hop out of the Uber once home, head down, that I don't notice anything's amiss until the wind blows a photograph against my thigh. Confusion washes over me as I try to make sense of the picture.

It's me.

Naked.

Lips around a dick.

Oh my God.

Did Ben take this pic? Or Wes? I'm staring at it in horror, plucking it from my thigh, and dying a little inside when a fluttering sound pulls me from my shock.

There are more pictures.

Hundreds of them all scattered across Hugo's front lawn. No!

I shriek, dropping my purse to the ground, and begin frantically snatching up picture after picture. The wind blows, making them fly in a thousand different directions just like my panicked thoughts.

Who would do this?

Why would they do this?

I'm crawling on my hands and knees, ruining my new slacks with grass stains, as I attempt to grab all the pictures I can when I hear a voice.

"Aubrey?"

I look up to see Callum's girl, Willa, walking across the yard toward me. Oh God. She's going to see these photos. If I don't pick them all up, everyone will see them. Humiliation sours my stomach and I feel like puking up sea bass.

"It's fine," I choke out. "I've got it. Go away."

Tears burn at my eyes and I swallow down the rising emotion that's bordering on hysteria. Willa ignores my request for privacy and starts collecting pictures quickly. She doesn't seem to be judging me, only helping me. Even though I asked her to leave, I'm thankful for the help.

Soon another voice joins and the tears really do fall. Gemma has come out to also help. I can hear her and Willa whispering in hushed voices, but I can't worry about their judgment. I just need these pictures gone.

It takes us a good thirty minutes to chase down all the

photos. Several blew down into the other yards and into the copse of trees on the other side of the yard. Once we have them all, I shove them into my purse, my hands trembling wildly. The girls are silent behind me as I walk to the front door.

Things just keep getting worse.

SLUT.

The hastily carved word in the front door is no doubt meant for me.

"I'm going to kill Spencer!" Gemma hisses, pushing past me and through the front door. "Spencer! Where are you, asshole?"

I swipe at my wet cheeks, unable to stop her from going after him. It's not him, though. I know it isn't. This is just more of my own horrible decisions haunting me from LA.

Willa's voice is soft and reassuring, but I don't know what she's saying. My head is buzzing with a mixture of fear and shame. I feel violated in the worst possible way.

Shouting can be heard between Spencer and Gemma somewhere within the house and it breaks me out of my trance. I make my way into the kitchen on wobbly legs, worried my knees might give out at any moment. Willa follows behind me, trying to speak to me, but I'm not in a talking mood.

I want these photos gone.

I plug up the sink and toss all of the pictures into the basin. Snatching up one of them, I use the flame from the gas stove to light it on fire. Then, I toss it onto the pile in the sink, watching in sick satisfaction as they begin to burn.

Heat burns at my face as I stare at the growing flames. A different sort of heat swarms in on me from behind. Spencer's presence, for once, doesn't put me on edge. It reassures me. I allow him to gather me in his arms, hugging me from behind, and I relax into his comforting embrace.

"I didn't do this," Spencer growls, mouth near my ear. "You know that, don't you?"

More tears well, but I blink them away and nod. "I know."

He nuzzles his nose into my hair. The movement is gentle and protective. I want to wrap up in the feeling forever.

"I'm going to find out who did this," he assures me. "I'm going to make them pay."

His vow of revenge is a salve to my heart that's been burning in pain for two years. I'm reminded of why I fell in love with him in the first place. And, stupidly, I hope he remembers that he loved me once too.

CHAPTER TWENTY

Spencer

I KNOW I'VE DONE A LOT OF FUCKED-UP SHIT WHEN IT comes to Aubrey, but this isn't one of them.

Some asshole littered our yard with pictures of her sucking cock. I couldn't even appreciate the beauty of seeing her like that because I was livid. She's mine to torment and tease and do with as I please. Not only had they shamed her, but they did it on Park property. Vandalized our front door, too. All while I was in the goddamn house.

Whoever did this has some balls.

"Camera feed was cut about an hour ago," I gripe, tossing my phone onto the couch. "Unbelievable."

The girls went up to Aubrey's room a few minutes ago to console her. I'd wanted to be the one to do it, but Gemma was quick to tug her out of my arms and away from me. Gemma probably thinks she's rescuing her from my evil ways. She sure had no issue yelling at me and accusing me of being the monster who did this.

Dempsey, unruffled by my outburst, studies me for a beat. "Do you think it has anything to do with—"

"No," I snap, cutting him off. "It doesn't. This was clearly an attack against Aubrey for personal reasons."

He nods, eyes narrowing. I don't like being under his scrutiny. Now he knows more than I want him to. He took it surprisingly well. Only bitched a little about me being a "psycho" and then did what Dempsey always does—had my back. Still, he doesn't have to approve of my every decision and it's clear he doesn't. Right now, though, we have bigger shit to deal with.

"What are we going to do about it?" Dempsey asks. "Someone is fucking with our family."

Family.

A week ago, I'd have argued that Aubrey was family. Now, the lines of distinction between enemy and loved one are blurred. I want to hate her, but she makes it damn hard.

The front door flings open with enough force it knocks one of Neena's expensive art pieces on the wall crooked. Dad storms in predictably. I'd texted him right after Gemma finished chewing me a new asshole.

He's pissed. Just like I am. Because, whether I like to admit it or not, Aubrey belongs to the Parks.

"Who did this?" he demands. "Is she okay?"

I let out a heavy sigh and shrug. "She's with the girls. She'll be fine. I don't know who did this, but they were smart enough to knock out the camera feed. It went dark about an hour ago."

"I'll get Jude on checking the other cameras in Dad's yard and Callum's," Dad says in an authoritative tone that reminds me of Pops.

"Three steps ahead of you, bruh," Dempsey says, lifting his phone. "A white sedan is caught passing by our camera a couple of times before the cameras went out. Looks like a generic rental car."

Dad deflates, scowling. "This was someone trying to ruin my campaign."

"Not everything is about your campaign," I bite back. "Aubrey's not the little angel you think she is and someone is trying to take their vengeance."

Dad's cheeks turn pink and he looks away, ignoring my words. It's obvious he's thinking of her in devilish ways. Dirty bastard.

"Tasha?" He chances a glance my way again. "They went to lunch today. Could have been a distraction."

I roll my eyes. "As much as we hate that witch, it wasn't her. She'd rather burn our house down to get back at us than do something to Aubrey."

"Neena?"

Dempsey snorts and his eyes glitter. "Is her ghost capable of such things?"

Dad winces and I glower at Dempsey.

"You know it's not Neena," I spit out at the same time Dad says, "She's not dead, dammit."

Dempsey smirks my way. I have the urge to smack his head.

"It has to be an ex." I frown, trying to picture the face behind the dick Aubrey was sucking. "It was too personal to be anyone else."

"It could be you," Dempsey offers, stirring the shit pot. "Gemma sure as hell seems to think that."

Before I can answer, Dad shakes his head. "It's not Spencer. I know my son. If he's going to torment someone, he's going to want credit for it."

He's not wrong.

"I'm going to Dad's to talk to him about it," Dad says to us. "Keep an eye on her, please."

As soon as he's gone, Dempsey stands and motions down the hall. "Want me to grab the girls and bail?"

A minute ago, he was pissing me off, but I'm once again reminded why he's my best friend. He knows what I need. And right now, I need to be alone with her. Maybe I can get something out of her.

"Yeah, man," I grunt. "And thanks for earlier. I may need you a little more until we figure out this whole stalker shit."

It's hard handing over what's been such a vital part of my mental energy for so damn long, but there's no one I trust more than Dempsey.

He'll take care of my problem while I deal with Aubrey's.

As soon as the door closes behind the twins and Willa, I lock it and then head for Aubrey's room. Her door is ajar. Creeping up to it, I peek inside. She's no longer in her sexy work outfit but has long since changed into a pair of tiny cotton shorts that her plump ass cheeks hang out of and a white tank top. Sprawled out on the bed, she faces the window, hugging a pillow to her front.

I push the door open slowly and silently before prowling into her space. The scent is uniquely hers with a hint of the saltiness of her tears. I inhale the air, trapping it in my lungs.

Addictive.

"Who was it?" I demand, relishing in the way her body jolts in surprise. "Whose dick were you sucking in the picture?"

She rolls onto her back, mouth agape. "Excuse me?"

"Surely there weren't so many that you can't remember what they all looked like."

The sadness that saturated the room evaporates. Her features screw into a hateful scowl. It's unfair that she's so fucking hot, even when angry.

"Answer me, leech."

"I thought we were past this," she snaps. "Guess I was wrong."

I laugh as I kick off my shoes and crawl onto the bed beside her. "You know I'm the only one allowed to torment you."

"I hate you."

"You're not a victim, Aubrey. Don't start acting like one now. Where's the bitch who keyed my car?"

A smile curves the corners of her lips. "You deserved it."

"And you didn't deserve this?"

The smile falls and she averts her stare. "Maybe."

I lie down beside her and grip her jaw, turning her face toward mine. "Was it Ben?"

"I don't know," she admits, voice soft. "To be honest, I didn't stare at the picture long enough. I'm not exactly virginal in the bedroom. I like to be photographed in the heat of the moment. What I don't like is having it used against me later."

My dick can't help but twitch at the thought of taking hundreds of nude photos of her. If she notices my erection pressing into her side, she doesn't let on.

"You'd let me take pictures of you?" I murmur, teasing a finger along the column of her neck. "Kinky ones I can jerk off to later?"

Her lips part and her eyes darken. It's dangerous that she responds to my depravity. It's the only reason I can justify why I'm crashing my mouth to hers, needing to taste the desire on her lips.

Fuck, she always tastes so sweet.

I groan, delving my tongue into her mouth, desperate to have more of her. Her fingers find their way to my hair and she tugs, pulling me closer. My free hand roams to her ass and I squeeze one cheek hard enough to make her yelp.

"You're not some random slut," I rasp against her lips. "You're my slut, aren't you?"

I expect her to moan or dive deeper into this kinky fantasy, but the words are a cold splash on her and she freezes.

"It's true," she croaks. "I'm a slut."

"For me," I add, grinning evilly at her.

She shakes her head, frowning. "No, I, uh…" Her eyes begin to water again and her bottom lip wobbles. "I did something bad."

"Tell me," I demand.

Her eyes squeeze shut and a single tear races down her temple. "I blew your dad."

I laugh because she has to be joking. She's fucking joking. Right? The silence after that statement isn't filled with a teasing giggle. Just humiliated quiet.

"Seriously?" I bark out, glowering down at her. "You had my dad's dick down your throat? When?"

She swallows hard and peeks at me from behind wet lashes. "Last night."

"Before or—"

After. It was after I had my fingers inside her. Unbelievable.

I start to pull away, but she grabs my shirt. "Don't go, Spencer. Please. Something's wrong with me. I don't want to be this way. All I do is hurt people."

I'm not hurt, I'm pissed.

"What the hell do you expect me to do with that information? Huh? Give you a high fucking five?"

"No, I—"

"Is that what you want? To fuck your stepdaddy?"

What about me?

"No, I mean, I don't know. Spencer," she says with a choked sob. "I want…I think you should punish me."

I lift a brow at her. "You think I can spank the sluttiness right out of you?"

I'm pissed and yet my cock is leaking with pre-cum. The desire to whip her for fucking around with my dad is overwhelming.

"Make it hurt," she breathes, voice soft and filled with need. "I deserve it."

I'm hit with the vision of her bent over, ass up, and waiting for me to strike. Before she can change her mind, I give her a clipped nod and then slide off the bed. She yelps when I roughly flip her onto her stomach and drag her to the edge of the bed. Her body shudders as I palm her ass over her shorts.

I bet she's fucking drenched between her thighs, needy for a little pain.

Hooking my fingers into her shorts, I pull them down but leave her thong on. If I took those off too, I'd be doing a lot more than spanking. My dick would find its way inside her and I'm not ready for that. Everything in my head is zinging all over the place. Fucking her could get ugly quickly, especially if my anger takes over.

"I'm going to use my belt," I threaten, giving her ass a quick smack. "You'll cry."

"Do it."

Her moaned taunt flips a switch inside me. I can't get my belt off fast enough, eager to hear the leather strike against her skin. I fold the belt in half and then rub it down the crack of her ass. Without warning, I raise my arm back and then swing it down.

Crack!

Her surprised shriek makes my dick twitch. The red welt that begins forming on her ass cheek is fucking beautiful.

Swing. Strike. Crack.

Swing. Strike. Crack.

Over and over and over again, I swat her pretty ass, fixated on the crimson stripes painting her flesh. The sounds coming from her are a mix of moans and pained sobs. Her fingers dig into the bedspread, pulling the material into her fists and squeezing.

Time becomes a blur. I'm so damn turned on punishing her like this. Her body is responsive and she doesn't try to run away despite her manic squirming.

"Please, stop," she croaks out. "I can't take any more."

The belt whistles through the air, but I stop it right before it reaches her ass. Her whole body flinches, readying for the strike. I toss it aside and begin undoing my jeans, eager to free my cock. Once it bobs heavily in front of me, I lean forward, placing my hand in front of her mouth.

"Get it wet," I order. "I'm going to come all over this pretty, ruined ass."

Her breath is hot against my flesh. I expect her to deny me of this moment, but she doesn't. A groan rasps out of me the second her tongue meets my palm.

"Lick it like you licked Dad's cock."

She sucks two of my fingers into her mouth without hesitation, moaning around them. I nearly shoot my load right then, high from the sounds she's making. Once she's gotten my hand good and wet, I yank it away and curl it around my dick.

Having her saliva as my lube while staring at her ass that looks like an exquisite piece of art is blissfully maddening. I fuck into my fist, wondering how it'll feel when I'm finally inside her. That day is coming soon. I want her a helluva lot more than I hate her. I bet she fucks wild and will allow me the freedom to do whatever I want to her. It doesn't take much more of those thoughts before I'm coming with a groan. Thick ropes of cum shoot out, splattering over her reddened ass cheeks.

Hot.

So fucking hot.

I wring my cock dry and then smear my cum all over her sore cheeks. Her body becomes boneless and she relaxes, also spent from our devious activity.

"You look good wearing my cum, leech." I lean forward, pressing my still-hard dick against her ass crack. "I think you'd look even better with my cum running out of your pussy."

She lets loose a ragged breath. "Don't call me leech."

I inhale her sweet scent, rubbing my nose into her hair, and then find her ear with my mouth. "I'll call you whatever I want because you're mine."

"Yours?"

"Yes. That means only I get to touch you. Not Dad. You touch him again and…"

"And what?"

"Next time it'll be a worse punishment. Maybe I'll make you wear a butt plug while I whip you. Maybe I'll gag you so you can't tell me to stop."

Another moan.

Fuck, why does she get off on this shit?

Why do I get off on this shit?

She grows quiet and I know she's thinking about that image of what I'll do to her.

"You're going to disobey me, aren't you?"

The door to the house opens, echoing down the hall and into Aubrey's room. Dad calls for me and I can hear his footsteps pounding on the floors. She scrambles to pull her shorts up over her cum-soaked ass while I quickly tuck my cock back in my jeans. We share a heated look before she pulls the covers over her body. Her eyes turn to the doorway, anticipation— at seeing *him*—glinting in them.

She's going to disobey me.

And, because I'm a sick motherfucker, I kind of hope she does.

CHAPTER TWENTY-ONE

Hugo

EVERYTHING IS ALL FUCKED-UP.

I can't stop thinking about what happened yesterday afternoon. Some prick printed hundreds of photos of Aubrey and scattered them all over the yard. Then, they had the audacity to carve the word "slut" into my front door.

I'd wanted to call the cops, but when I spoke to Dad, he strongly advised against it since Neena is still in hiding. If I didn't know any better, I'd say Dad knows something about Neena. Imagining the man I've looked up to all my life having something to do with my wife's disappearance is a box I'm not keen on opening.

What if this isn't just about Aubrey?

What if whoever did this is just using her to get to me and our family?

My thoughts drift back to yesterday when I'd gone to check on her again. Spencer was there, stance protective, and it rubbed me wrong. As much as I want her to be comforted and for them to repair the friendship they once had, I wanted to be the one to console her.

Had I not let her suck my dick, maybe I could have been that person for her.

Frustration eats at my insides. I can't think straight now that Aubrey is back in our lives. I'm supposed to be focusing on the campaign and finding Neena. Instead, all I can think about is my stepdaughter.

Beautiful. Young. Tempting.

I need her in ways I can't even explain. Every second of every day now my mind is on her. The memory of her supple lips wrapped around my cock is engraved in my head. It's on a loop and I replay it over and over and over again.

Get it together, man.

She was attacked yesterday by some coward prick and it's my duty as her stepfather to get to the bottom of it. I'm supposed to protect and care for her. Not think about all the ways I can get her lips on me. If I can't physically comfort her because I can't trust myself, I can help in other ways.

I glance at my inbox and groan at the massive amounts of emails I haven't even gotten to this morning. Karla's already been in three times trying to get me to call people back. The only person I feel like calling right now is Tony.

Aubrey's dad.

How would he feel if he knew I let her suck my dick?

He's a gym rat with a tendency toward 'roid rage. Knowing him, he'd probably drive all the way up here to kick my ass.

It's never going to happen again, so it's pointless for him to know. Not like I'd ever tell him anyway.

I grab my cell phone and locate his contact before I can change my mind. This is what a stepfather should do.

"Who'd she fuck now?"

It takes me a second to replay his greeting and make sense of it.

"Excuse me?" I clip out. "Tony?"

He sighs heavily, making the line sound raspy. "What do you want?"

I've never cared much for the guy but have met him a few times because of Aubrey. Now, I want to reach through the phone and strangle his thick neck for talking about his own goddamn daughter with such vicious disdain.

"I know you've disowned your daughter, but for fuck's sake, man, give it a rest for five minutes. She's been the target of harassment."

"Did she deserve it?"

My fingers curl around the phone much like the way I'd like to wring his neck. "No, she didn't deserve it. She's just a kid."

A kid who sucked my dick.

My dick twitches in my slacks, remembering fondly just how good she worked her pretty lips.

"No, Hugo, she's not. She's a grown-ass woman who's on the fast track to becoming her snake of a mother. How is Neena these days? Usually, she's rubbing her wealth in my face on social media. I warned her Aubrey was coming but never got a response."

"This isn't about Neena," I growl, wanting to change the subject from his missing ex-wife before he actually discovers she's missing. "It's about your daughter. Someone is harassing her. Scattered nude pictures of her all over the yard and carved profanity into our front door."

"Let me guess," he sneers. "Was the word 'homewrecker'?"

I seriously want to punch this guy.

"Slut," I spit out.

He laughs. "Close enough."

"She's your daughter. How can you be so fucking callous?"

"She ruined my life," he snarls, the humor long gone. "I barely make ends meet as it is, but she had to go and fuck with my job. You want to know who is harassing her? Could be anyone. Anyone, man. The girl couldn't keep her legs closed since she came back home."

"Don't talk about her like that." I grit my teeth together, swallowing down the rage. "Regardless of her sex life, she doesn't deserve to be tormented. Think, Tony. Were there any disgruntled exes? Anyone who would travel all the way up here and seek revenge on her?"

"Like I said, it could be anyone. Maybe it's my boss's wife. Maybe she wants Aubrey to know she ruined her life too." He huffs. "I don't know, but I've got to get back to work. Have fun keeping a leash on her. She's wild and it'll only be a matter of time before she's wrecking your life too."

He hangs up without another word.

Asshole.

I rise from my desk and toss the phone on top of it before striding toward my closed door. Opening it, I dart my attention to Karla's desk where Aubrey is. There's no indication that she was crying and upset like she was yesterday afternoon. No, today she's perfectly put together in a black knee-length pencil skirt and tucked in white top. Her blond hair is in shiny waves, catching each glint of light and illuminating like spun gold.

How that motherfucker can be so cruel is beyond me.

"Aubrey," I bark out. "My office, please."

She jerks her head my way, a frown tugging at her pink glossy lips. Karla's brow lifts at my abrupt tone and she smirks.

I want to tell her she's not in trouble, but that's not true. Her life is messy just like mine is right now. We're all in trouble.

Aubrey stands up and smooths out her skirt with her palms. I dart my gaze down the silky material that clings to her pert breasts. I've seen those breasts naked and jiggling as she sucked my cock down her tight throat.

My dick thickens uncomfortably in my slacks. Since I don't want Karla to see my raging erection, I pivot on my heels and stride back into my office. A few seconds later, I can sense Aubrey's presence by the way the hair on my arms prickles up and then her sweet perfumed scent finds its way to me, flooding my nostrils and filling my lungs.

The door clicks shut, sealing us inside. I'm not sure why I've called her in here, only that I needed to see her. To offer the comfort I'm craving to give her. To show her fatherly love since her own goddamned father won't.

When I turn back around, she's standing in front of the closed door, frowning at me. Fear glints in her eyes. Is she afraid I'll kick her out and turn on her too? People have a habit of doing that to her.

"Lock the door." My order is gruff and laced with the need thrumming through me. "Please, Love."

She visibly relaxes at the endearment and nods. The click of the lock is like a gift of permission. Permission of what?

"We'll find who did this to you," I assure her, taking several long strides toward her. "I'll ruin them."

Her long lashes bat against her cheeks as she stares up at me. I've invaded her space, so near to her that I can feel the brush of her breasts against my suit jacket. My dick has fully awoken, straining against my pants, desperate for more of her lovely mouth.

To keep from putting my mouth on her slender, soft neck, I lift my hand and grip it instead. Firm but gentle. It feels as though I'm claiming her as mine. She is mine. My stepdaughter.

Her tongue flicks out and she runs it along her bottom lip, heat flaring in her gaze. "What are you doing?"

"Comforting you," I rumble, stroking my thumb along her flesh. "Apologizing."

"Apologizing for what?" she murmurs.

"For leading you on and then avoiding you. Had I acted like a real man and taken you home myself, you wouldn't have had to deal with that shit on your own."

Her eyebrows furl together. "I had Spencer."

My son's name on her lips chases off the rest of my sanity. I don't think or obsess or analyze. All I do is lean forward and take. I take a kiss that doesn't belong to me. I steal it.

She tastes minty like she's been sucking on a peppermint. I want to nibble on her tongue and lips for hours, discovering new ways to make her whimper. As though tuned into my thoughts, she groans against my mouth. The sound is fucking beautiful and gasoline to the fire raging inside me. I slide a palm to her ass, squeezing it hard.

"Ow," she yelps. "Fuck."

I pull back so I can look her in the eyes. "Did I hurt you?"

Her face burns bright red. "Uh, no. It's nothing."

I'm a lawyer and have a good sense of when someone is evading some hidden truth they don't want discovered. Testing her, I squeeze her ass again, gentler this time. She winces, shooting me a panicked look.

"What happened?" I demand. "Did you fall? Did someone hurt you?"

"Hugo," she mewls. "Please don't be mad."

Rage ignites deep in my gut, churning with jealousy. I know what's happened and she doesn't even need to tell me. He did this. My son.

What the fuck?

Homewrecker.

Tony's choice of word slams into me. I'm unable to keep my anger in check. I glower down at her and demand, "What happened?"

Her throat bobs as she swallows. "He spanked me."

"He did what?" I growl, voice rising several octaves.

"I asked him to," she breathes. "I'm fucked-up. I'm so sorry."

Sorry?

She's sorry for asking my son to whip her ass?

I should be angry with Spencer, but he's an eighteen-year-old kid. If a beautiful girl—even if she is his sister—begs to be punished, he'd have to be a saint to deny her. Especially after how vulnerable she was yesterday.

"You think because some asshole calls you a slut that you have to be punished?" I ask, scowling at her. "That it's your fault you're being harassed?"

"I deserved it," she whispers, eyes filling with tears.

One tear races down her cheek. I can't help but run my nose along the wetness and then press a kiss there.

"You're a good girl," I murmur against her flesh. "You deserve to be praised and adored."

"I don't, though," she argues. "I needed his belt."

I pull away and give my head a violent shake. She yelps when I grab onto her wrist, jerking her toward my desk. Her eyes flare with heat, anticipation dancing in them.

"Are you going to spank me too?"

I smirk as I slide my palms down the sides of her thighs until I reach the hem. Then, I drag the material back up her thighs, loving the hitch of her breath. I tug it up over her ass and bunch it up at her waist. Stepping back, I take a second to appreciate the angel before me.

She doesn't deserve to be punished.

She deserves to be worshipped.

I lift her by her waist and gently sit her on the edge of my desk, taking care not to hurt her sore ass.

"Lie back, Love. Let me show you how good I think you are."

Her teeth bite into her bottom lip as she obeys me. She bores her gaze into me, tense with anticipation of what happens next.

What happens next is I pray to this gorgeous goddess.

I worship at her feet.

She gasps when I kneel down. The thin, lacy piece of fabric barely constitutes for underwear because it's see-through. A pink slit peeks at me beyond the lace, shaved smooth and begging to be tasted.

"I don't like these. They're in my way." I take great pleasure in the ripping sound the cheap lace makes. Her own sound of shock only heightens the pleasure of this moment. Once I've divested her of the offending material and shoved it into my pocket, I grin at her. "There. Better."

She matches my smile with one of her own. I may be completely fucked in the head for doing this with her, but it feels right. Ever since she got back, something inside of me clicked and I can't turn it off.

I grasp onto her knees and slowly spread her apart. The

folds of her pussy open up like a blooming rose, revealing her bud of a clit. Her scent here is less perfumed and more her. A natural honeyed scent that I need on my tongue and coating my dick.

"I'm going to treat you, Love. Relax and enjoy what I'm desperate to give you."

She nods but refuses to take her eyes off me. While maintaining eye contact, I flatten out my tongue and lick her from asshole to clit.

Fuuuuck.

She tastes better than she smells. She tastes like peaches and heaven and temptation all in one delicious treat. Unable to quell the ravenous hunger inside me, I begin feasting on her like a starved man whose only sustenance is slippery young cunt.

"Hugo," she gasps. "Oh God."

I grunt against her and slide my tongue into her tight hole. This magical golden pussy of hers should be used as a weapon. It's perfect and I don't fault her for using it to get what she wants. Right now, she wants me and I'll give it to her freely. My nose rubs against her clit as I attempt to suffocate on her slick heat. I want to drown in her pussy.

Her fingers fly to my hair and her back arches up off the desk. Knowing I'm driving her wild is a high I've never known before. I want to pleasure her all day every day until the end of time. I suck on her pussy lips and clit and then spear her again with my tongue. When it doesn't feel like enough, I slick up my fingers and push those into her hot, quivering body.

All the sounds coming from her are stifled as she attempts to be quiet. If anyone knew what we were up to, I could kiss my campaign goodbye. The whole town would hate me for eating this teenager's pussy while still being married to her mother. It's fucked-up beyond reason and yet I can't stop.

It's not enough.

I need her.

I need inside her.

My fingers brush against her G-spot and it works like a live wire of electricity. She yelps and squeezes around my fingers. Since I know she loves it, I tease her into a frenzy. Her entire body tightens as her orgasm seizes her. She slaps a hand over her mouth, muffling her cries of pleasure.

Like a madman who can only see one thing—her—I rise to my feet and begin working at my belt. I need inside her. I need to fuck her until she's full of my cum. I want it running out of her as she sits at her desk or whenever she walks. I just fucking need her.

Knock-knock-knock-knock!

We both freeze, eyes slamming onto each other's.

"Yes?" I call out, affecting an irritated tone. Truth is, I'm not at all irritated. My tongue tingles with her sweet taste.

"Mr. Park, Vance is on the line. He said he's been trying to reach your cell and it's important," Karla says through the door.

"Put him on hold. I'll take the call."

I buckle my belt up and then grab Aubrey's hands to pull her back into a sitting position. Her hair is slightly messy, eyes are glazed over, and bottom lip swollen from all her biting. She's a fucking vision.

"We'll finish this later, Love," I promise and actually mean it this time. "You okay?"

She nods, a smile teasing at her lips. "Never felt better. Seriously, never."

I help her to her feet and then push her skirt back down into place. Where she once sat is a smear of wetness—a mixture of her arousal and my saliva. I'll never look at that spot on my desk the same way again. Using the inside of my jacket, I dab at my damp face and then capture her jaw in my hand.

"You seem happy," she says, hope glinting in her eyes.

"I am."

Crashing my lips to hers, I kiss her fast and hard, making sure to slide my tongue over every part of her mouth to let her taste herself. Once I'm sure she'll have the reminder of what we did imprinted on her for the rest of the day, I give her a soft, teasing kiss and then pull away.

Her eyes are hooded and she wears the most serene expression. I can't wait to have her beneath me, naked, and looking at me that way while I drive my dick into her sweet body.

It will happen.

Fuck, I'll die if it doesn't.

She starts to pull away, but I grasp onto her wrist, stopping her. Her head turns my way, a frown of confusion crossing over her features. "What?"

My smile falls. "Stay away from Spencer, Love. He'll never treat you how you deserve."

Her lips press together in a thin line and she nods. I want to believe she heard me and she'll obey, but something tells me things are beyond complicated and it won't be that simple.

He's my son and lives across the hall from her.

She might try and stay away from him, but there's no way in hell he'll stay away from her.

Fuck.

CHAPTER TWENTY-TWO

Aubrey

NOTHING IS MORE AWKWARD THAN A SILENT CAR ride with Karla, who hates me and loves Hugo, while wearing no panties. I'm probably being self-conscious, but I'm pretty sure I can smell pussy—my pussy—when trapped inside her car.

Hugo refused to let me Uber home after the drama from yesterday. But since Vance showed up for a meeting late in the day, Hugo kindly forced Karla to be my personal driver. She only thinks she hates me now. If she knew I was spreading my legs on the clock for our boss, she'd probably stab me in the eye with her keys.

My heart flutters at the memory from earlier. After he ate me out, I was boneless and flying high. None of Karla's usual snippiness bothered me. I daydreamed about what more we could do when we were home and alone.

"We're here," Karla says, voice tight with irritation. "See you tomorrow."

I jerk my head up and scan the yard, relieved when I realize it's not littered with my own personal porn. Small victories. Aside from Ben texting me all day long with his usual crap, it's been a great day.

"Thanks for the ride."

She forces a smile my way. "Happy to help Hugo."

I refrain from rolling my eyes. Sorry, lady, but he's not into you. Grabbing my purse, I climb out of her SUV and quickly make it to the garage door. I'm not keen on seeing the word "slut" on the door again.

After mashing in the door code, I step inside and close it after me. I'm too spooked after yesterday to take any chances. My phone buzzes in my purse.

Spencer: I saw you walking across the yard, leech, like a little girl whose ass still hurts.

Though I'm happy the cameras seem to be working, I'm annoyed at his text.

Me: Don't call me leech, asshole.

He sends me a bunch of emojis of a hand and a peach. It makes me smile even though I don't want to. Damn him.

I make it inside the house and head for my room. It's eerily quiet without Spencer here. At least he knows I'm home and checked in on me in his own obnoxious way. My phone buzzes again with an incoming text.

Unknown Number: I miss you so much, gorgeous. I'm leaving my wife. She's nothing to me. Stop blocking me and tell me where I can come pick you up. Everything will be so much better when we're back together.

I shudder at the thought of seeing Ben again. If I told Hugo about this, he'd change my number in a heartbeat to protect me. But it's just another glaring fact that I'm the "slut" I've been proving myself to be.

Spencer: Aww, but you're MY leech.

I reply back with eye roll emojis as I walk back into my room. Kicking off my shoes, I stop just inside the doorway, waiting for him to reply.

And then I hear it.

Rattling.

A mixture of dread and horror runs through my veins as I dart my head to the source of the sound. I'm frozen, unable to comprehend what I'm seeing.

My phone hits the floor as I let out a blood-curdling scream.

There's a rattlesnake coiled in the center of my bed, staring straight at me.

Run!

I turn on my heel, racing barefoot down the hallway and out of the house. In my head, the snake is slithering after me, ready to take a venomous bite of my ankle. Blinded by tears, I run as fast as my legs will carry me until I'm next door. I beat on the door, screaming for help. Seconds later, Callum yanks open the door, intense eyes assessing me.

"Are you hurt?" he demands.

Willa rushes up behind him, concern in her big eyes.

"Th-there's a s-snake in my b-bed," I stammer out, choking on a terrified sob.

"A snake?" Callum and Willa both blurt out at once.

"Please get it out of there," I beg. "I don't know if there are more. Please help me."

"Come inside," Callum orders. "I'll take care of it."

Willa grabs hold of my arm, tugging me inside while Callum heads for his garage. He returns with a shovel that doesn't look like it's ever been used and pushes past us out of the house. Willa guides me over to their sofa and encourages me to sit. Then, she starts rapid-fire texting someone.

"I'm sure it just came in from the woods across the street," Willa offers, though she sounds doubtful. "Spencer is on his way. He was at the lodge, so he'll be here in ten minutes or so."

I try to distract myself from the terrifying snake and re-member back to the days Spencer would bring me to parties at his pops' brother's lodge. Back when we were friends on the verge of more. It feels like we might get back to that point one day. I'd rather hope for something like that than think about why there's a rattlesnake in my bed.

Time seems to crawl by, and then, finally, Spencer bursts through the front door. He yanks me up and into his arms, hugging me to him. I cling to him, choking on a sob.

"I was so scared," I admit tearfully. "I've never been so scared in my entire life."

"Shh," he croons, rubbing my back. "You're safe. I'm here now."

I allow myself to be comforted by him. It feels good to not think and just feel. But the feelings grow sour when I hear another voice.

"I came as quickly as I could," Hugo booms upon enter-ing Callum's house. "I needed to make sure you were okay."

Shame chases away the lingering fear icing my veins as I pull away from Spencer's hold. Hugo is watching us, eyes tight and mouth pressed into a hard line. Unable to bear the look any longer, I rush over to him, letting him scoop me into a comforting hug.

This is sick.

I want them both to hold me and promise me everything

will be okay because I'm a sick girl who clearly enjoys wreaking havoc on everyone else's lives.

"Callum just texted that it's dead and we need to get over there now," Spencer barks out, voice clipped with anger.

I wither a little inside, knowing he's pissed at me for leaving his arms to go to his father's. And Hugo is probably pissed at me for seeking comfort in Spencer's arms. Everything about this is a mess and I'm solely responsible for it.

Willa takes my hand and I gratefully allow her to lead me out of their house. Hugo and Spencer stride ahead of us.

"It's okay," Willa assures me. "Everything will be okay. You're safe now."

I nod, hating that more tears are welling. I'm not usually this fragile or emotional. Park Mountain, Washington, has that effect on me. At least in LA, I felt with my body, not my heart. Here, I can't stop feeling everywhere.

We follow the men inside the house and into my room. In the center of my bed is a now severed snake, blood all over my bedspread. Bile creeps up my throat. Gross. I'll never be able to sleep there again.

"How did a snake get into the house?" Hugo demands, clearly stunned and confused.

"Someone put it here," Callum says through gritted teeth.

My blood runs cold. I'd thought, deep down, something was off. There was something menacing and purposeful to that snake being in my bed. Someone did this to me. Someone wants to hurt me.

"How the hell do you know that?" Hugo takes several steps forward.

Callum points with the bloody shovel to the snake carcass. "They left a note."

Spencer walks over to it, shoves the dead snake aside, and picks up two pictures and a note.

"What's it say?" I croak out.

Spencer turns to look at me, features hard with fury. "Snake? Slut? Or both?"

"Can you and Willa take care of this?" Hugo barks out, waving a hand at his brother. "Please. We need a moment alone with Aubrey."

Callum nods and then makes quick work of wrapping up the dead snake in the bedding. He passes the shovel to Willa and then they both exit, somber expressions on their faces. I stare at the center of the bed. The mattress is perfectly white. No blood droplets or any indication that a snake was just killed on it.

"Dad, look," Spencer grinds out. "Fuck."

I drag my gaze from the bed to the photographs in his hand. The one on top is a picture of me and Hugo cozied up on the couch when we watched a movie in the theater room. He moves it and replaces it with the other picture. It's of Spencer hugging me from behind yesterday in the kitchen.

There are cameras in the house.

Oh my God.

The world spins and I grow alarmingly dizzy. Panic claws up my throat. I cry out, falling to my knees, and grip my neck as I gasp for air.

I can't breathe.

I can't breathe! I can't breathe! I can't breathe!

I'm going to pass out.

Everything turns black.

Aubrey.

Aubrey.

Aubrey.

The voice finally breaks through the darkness and light comes rushing in along with air. I gulp several times in an attempt to fill my lungs. Both Hugo and Spencer are kneeling beside me, matching concerned expressions on their faces.

They are father and son, but in this moment, they could be twin brothers they look so much alike.

"That's better," Hugo croons. "I think you were having a panic attack."

I reach for his hand, needing to ground myself to something. His fingers thread through mine, giving me the comfort I need almost as much as the air.

"How did this monster get a snake into our house?" I croak, staring up at Hugo. "Why would they do this?"

His lips thin out and he scowls. Spencer holds up his phone and answers for him.

"It's someone we know. Has to be. The code was disabled while I was gone." Spencer's jaw tightens and he spears his fingers through his hair, messing it up. "Fuck."

Hugo's grip tightens around my hand. "Why weren't you here, Spencer?"

Spencer shrugs, evading his gaze. "I had shit to do."

"What shit? You don't have a job and college hasn't even started yet!"

"I'm not your goddamn house sitter," Spencer snaps back. "Lay off."

"Stop," I cry out. "Stop fighting. It doesn't matter. I just want the cameras gone."

Spencer hops to his feet and stalks out of the room. Hugo helps me up and then motions for my bathroom.

"Want to take a bath while we deal with this?"

The thought of someone watching me while I bathe makes me want to puke. Hell no.

"Can I go over to Gemma's until they're all gone?"

He cups my cheeks and kisses the top of my head. "Of course, Love. Whatever you want to do. We're going to deal with this. Once I discover who's fucking with my family, I'm going to destroy them. You trust me?"

"I always trust you."

"Good girl. I won't let you down."

CHAPTER TWENTY-THREE

Spencer

THIS THING WITH AUBREY IS CHANGING. IT'S morphing into something I can't control. While I hate that, I also welcome the refreshing change. I've been chained to my monotonous life that I resented with every part of my being for nearly a year.

Yes, I want to fuck with her, but I also want to *fuck* her.

It's like I have this invested claim over her. She's mine. Though she maddens me and pisses me off, I still want her. I don't want to share her with anyone, especially my fucking dad.

Dad is the least of my problems, however. Someone is stalking and harassing Aubrey. They're not just messing with her, though, they're messing with the Parks. We own this mountain, this town, and all the people in it. Whoever is doing this has balls—balls that we'll eventually crush in our powerful fists.

The cameras Dad and I found earlier were in plain sight. Cheap stick-on shit. It makes me want to throttle our housekeeper for not mentioning them. One could even suspect she was the culprit since she has the alarm code, but she's old as fuck and has no motive to terrorize our family.

Then who?

I rack my brain for who would have some vendetta

against her, no fear of us, and access to our home. We Parks are pretty close-knit and don't let many outsiders in, so it's frustrating to be clueless. Even Jude, a man of many means when it comes to uncovering information, has come up short.

Once I'm sure Dad has gone to bed, I make my way back into Aubrey's room. Earlier, once we cleared the house of cameras, Gemma and Jamie put new bedding on her bed and tried to cheer her up. Everyone left and it's been fairly quiet. I've been biding my time.

I twist the doorknob and push into her room. The bed is still perfectly made and there's no one in it. Aubrey sits in her desk chair, hugging her knees to her chest, staring blankly at the bed. A flare of fury ignites in my belly. Someone is breaking her.

She's mine to break.

Mine to piece back together.

Mine. Mine. Fucking mine.

Stalking over to her, I clear my throat and speak with authority, "Up. Come on."

Slowly, she turns her head to look at me. The blank expression is haunting and I don't like it. I peel her arms away from her legs and draw her into a standing position.

"Where are we going?" she croaks out, confusion lacing her tone, attempting to tug her hand from mine.

"My room." I grip her hand tighter. "You're not sleeping in here."

All resistance evaporates and she lets me lead her out of her room. We go back into mine. I shut the door behind her before bringing her over to the bed.

"Get in," I instruct, releasing her to pull back the covers. "Now, leech."

She rolls her eyes, the first sign of the sassy brat I've been obsessed with ever since she returned. Despite the flash of sass, she obeys and climbs in. I'm about to join her when she looks past me at the closet.

"What's in the box?"

My muscles tighten and I follow her gaze to the box that holds secrets I like to keep hidden away. It's pointless to hide from them now. She's no longer the girl I was trying so hard to forget. She's different and has burrowed herself inside of me. With a sigh of resignation, I retrieve the box and bring it back to the bed.

"I snooped in your room," she says, flashing me a daring look. "I was trying to find clues to where Mom was. Like a murder weapon."

I snort out a laugh. "Okay, Sherlock. I'm guessing you didn't find what you were looking for."

"You came back and I had to hide. You know your bedroom is serial-killer clean. I mean, what conclusions was I supposed to draw from that?"

Chuckling, I grab the lid and move it to the bed. She leans forward, peering inside. Nothing exciting like murder weapons or tokens from my supposed kills.

"Oh," she breathes, picking up a movie ticket.

"We didn't see that movie," I remind her. "We snuck into that gory R-rated one. You were terrified the whole time. I was pretty sure you were going to piss your pants."

She shoves at my shoulder, a grin finally tugging at her lips. "You were the one who yelled in the theater."

"I don't like jump scares," I grumble. "It startled me."

We sit, looking through pictures, laughing and

reminiscing. This was all before. Before she revealed her true nature and broke my heart.

"I used to think you were so cool," Aubrey admits, holding up one of the first pictures of us together. It was the first summer after our parents married. "Then I learned you were just a big dork."

The picture makes my chest ache. We're sitting on Pops' boat, both wearing sunglasses and matching grins. Back then, I was just a skinny twerp and she hadn't turned into this curvaceous woman with tattoos and sexy tits. We were happy— thrilled to no longer be only children.

"Why the sudden change, Spencer?" she asks, dropping a picture into the box and pinning me with a penetrative stare. "What did I do that made you so angry? Was it the kiss? I thought you wanted it too."

Ignoring her, I toss the pictures back into the box and replace the lid. She sighs heavily as I carry it back to its rightful place in the closet. When I return, she's back to regarding me with a sad, broken expression.

She can't be this good.

She really is confused.

"Spencer," she murmurs. "Why?"

I tug off my T-shirt and then pull off my jeans, placing them neatly in the hamper before approaching in nothing but my boxers. Her eyes remain locked on mine, though I can tell she aches to check me out.

"I don't want to talk about it, Aubrey. It doesn't matter."

She lies back, a small smile forming.

"What?" I demand, sprawling out beside her and resting on my elbow.

"You called me Aubrey."

I shake my head and bark out a laugh. "Don't get used to it, leech."

She sticks out her tongue and I'm reminded of when we were younger. How playful we used to be. How I lived for her smiles and teasing. Dipping down, I capture her mouth in a sweet kiss. Her whole body seems to melt and it encourages me. My tongue teases hers and I want to swallow the sweet moan that escapes her. We kiss for several moments, losing ourselves to the moment and living in a pre-messy past where it was good. Always so good.

Sliding my hand beneath her tank top, I'm pleased to find her breast naked and bra-less. Her tit feels perfect in my palm. I squeeze it and then thumb her nipple that's hardened like a small stone. The urge to taste her nipple is maddening. I sit up and pull away her shirt before finding her mouth again with mine. When I can no longer wait, I pull away from our kiss and trail my tongue in teasing kisses down her neck and to her chest. I let my tongue run a lazy circle around her nipple.

"Oh," she says, gasping. "That feels good."

I suck the nub into my mouth, nibbling until she's squirming. Her fingers thread into my hair, tugging and guiding me just the way she likes it. Eventually, she's had enough of that nipple and pushes me to the other one. I give this nipple just as much attention.

My hand travels over her taut stomach to the waistband of her cotton shorts. Her hand leaves my hair to clutch my wrist.

"We can't," she whispers.

"Sure we can." I bore my gaze into hers. "I'm taking your shorts off, Aubrey."

Again, she melts like butter at hearing her name. Her hips

lift, giving me silent permission. I pull the shorts and under-wear away, eager to see her fully naked. Of course she's hot as fuck. My dick is granite as I appreciate her perfect form.

"I can't have sex with you, Spencer. I can't."

I arch a brow at her as I press a thumb against her clit. Her legs part and she bites down on her bottom lip. Circle after circle, I tease her right into an orgasm. The whimpers coming from her are a siren calling me to the rocky shore. I need to be right there with her.

"Spencer, we can't," she says, eyes wild with lust.

I pull down my boxers and kick out of them before crawl-ing over her spread body. My cock rests against her clit, but I don't make any moves to enter her. She gasps, fingers find-ing my hair, tugging me to her for a kiss. I kiss her hard and claiming, slowly rocking my hips to tease her sensitive clit. Her legs find their way around my hips, heels digging into my ass.

"We can't fuck," I taunt. "Remember? Your stupid rule."

"We can't," she echoes, lifting her hips. "We can't."

"But I want to feel you, baby. I want to know how it feels to be inside the girl I've loved for years."

"Spencer."

"Beg me, baby. Beg me to fuck you."

"Please," she chokes out. "Please...don't."

I start to pull away, but she digs in harder. Reaching be-tween us, I grip my dick, teasing at her slick opening. She nods once and then flutters her eyes closed. Agonizingly slow, I glide into her. Her cunt is tight, sucking me in like a throat swallowing a dick.

"You're letting me fuck you because you know you're mine," I croon against her lips. "You always have been."

All talk is silenced as I lose myself to her lips and body.

My hips piston wildly as I drive forward, needing to make my mark on her—to claim her once and for all. Her fingernails claw at my arms as her body tightens. A scream is on her lips and I smack my hand over her mouth, fucking harder and faster. Our eyes meet—hers wild and mine determined. I thrust into her like a madman long after her body stops shuddering from another orgasm and until mine chases after hers.

I come inside of her.

Spurt after spurt.

Mine. Fucking mine.

She doesn't stop me or ruin the moment with talk of condoms. Her body clenches around my cock, milking me for every drop. This girl wants all I have to give.

"Time for bed, leech." I grin at her. "I'm still going to call you leech."

She smiles back. "I secretly like it."

I pull back, fascinated by the way cum runs out of her red, swollen pussy, leaving a puddle below her. So fucking hot.

Climbing out of bed, I head for the bathroom for a warm washcloth to clean her up. When I return, she's droopy-eyed and half asleep, still sprawled out and spent from our fucking. I quickly clean her up and the spot beneath her. After gathering her pajamas and the cloth, I deposit them in the hamper, turn off the lights, and then rejoin her.

She allows me to pull her naked body against my side and she snuggles into me. I absently stroke her shoulder in the dark, eyes wide-open as I replay the entire encounter.

It was fucking amazing.

Just as I always knew it would be.

I don't know what the future holds for us, but in this moment, I'm pretty damn content.

If I could somehow make it where the outside world didn't touch us, I could live the rest of my life happy with her in my arms. We could stay in this room forever just the two of us.

Unfortunately, life isn't that easy.

The complications stacked against us are bigger than Park Mountain itself.

I have to figure out a way to change that indefinitely no matter who or what becomes a casualty.

I have to.

CHAPTER TWENTY-FOUR

Hugo

I THOUGHT I KNEW STRESS...BEFORE.

When Neena would play her games and torment me with her threats. With her, it was a daily bout of nerves always wondering what she had up her sleeve in an effort to manipulate me into getting what she wanted.

Like the time she reminded me she slept with my brother, Callum, long before our marriage and threatened to "accidentally" send a sex video to the whole goddamn parent contact list at Park Mountain High.

Why the threat?

Because she wanted her nose done and I told her it was a waste of money.

I didn't want Callum dragged into my psychotic marital problems, so I happily funded her cosmetic surgery.

Always eggshells with Neena. Always. It worsened when Aubrey left. For a few short years there, we almost behaved like a family. Neena wasn't such an unstable, conniving bitch.

The stress now stems from her daughter.

Aubrey is a different kind of game. One she and I play together. Spencer's on the board too if I'm being honest. Everything's all fucked-up. I can't even attempt to be the father figure here because some dipshit is harassing her, so I'm always in protective mode when it comes to her, which certainly doesn't help me keep my distance.

On the outside, to everyone around me, I'm a picture of control. A pillar of the community. A family man who's built a solid career representing many of the townspeople.

Inside, I'm unraveling.

The thread of my sanity has long been pulled. By my son, by my wife, by my stepdaughter, and by whoever is hell-bent on terrorizing us.

My inner brooding is interrupted by a text.

Vance: Can you do dinner on Friday night?

Me: THE dinner?

Vance: Yes. THE dinner. It'll be conveniently photographed and leaked to the press. All you have to do is be you, Hugo. People will eat it up.

I groan and scrub my palm over my face. The only highlight of this dinner is getting to bring Aubrey. Seeing her all dressed up and hanging off my arm like she's my date is enough to have me agreeing to Vance.

A knock on my office door has me setting my phone down and calling out for the person to enter.

Aubrey saunters in looking unflappable and hot in a sexy navy-blue dress. It's professional and demure, but it makes my mouth water. Her cheeks turn pink and she avoids my gaze.

My stomach twists at her avoidance. Is she regretting what we did yesterday? Or is she wishing it were Spencer instead? Irritation claws at me.

"Your dad is here to see you," she says, still unable to look at me. "Want me to send him in?"

"Yeah, Love, send him in."

She doesn't respond and hurries out of the office. I don't like the fact she seems to be avoiding me. I'm over here remembering how fucking perfect she was coming while my mouth was on her and it seems as though she's trying hard to forget.

God, I'm such an idiot.

I don't have time to ponder this new development because Dad strides in carrying with him an air of authority. Callum hates Dad and avoids him as much as possible, but it's not like that for me. Dad has always been my hero. He's brilliant and fearless and protective over his family. I've always admired him and wanted to be like him.

He walks over to my desk and then sits, making himself comfortable. "So, any news?"

"Nothing new. Aubrey is doing okay today. We cleared out the cameras and I changed the code. Only me, Aubrey, and Spencer know it now. Feels safer that way."

Dad nods, crossing his arms over his chest. His brow dips as he considers me. "I feel like Aubrey is a smokescreen. It's obviously an attack on our family because of your political aspirations."

"Nah, I don't think so," I argue. "It all started happening when Aubrey arrived."

I shift uncomfortably in my chair. Dad knows about the snake and cameras, but I left out the part about the note and the pictures. This all started happening when me and Spencer both started our involvement with Aubrey.

"I think it's an ex. She was involved with Tony's boss back in LA. I'm inclined to believe it could be him." I let out a harsh laugh. "Hell, it's probably Neena."

Dad dismisses the latter statement too quickly with a sharp wave of his hand. "It's not Neena."

"Because she's such a great mom who wouldn't hurt her own daughter?"

"Neena would happily take the credit for something that violated your family. I don't see her around rubbing it in your face." He diverts his gaze. "Neena isn't a problem anymore."

A cold rain tickles over my flesh. It's not the first time my problem-solving father has been on my radar for my suspicions about Neena's whereabouts. I don't think he'd have it in him to kill her, but I'm not so sure he wouldn't pay someone to do it for him.

"Anymore?"

Dad leans forward, resting his elbows on his knees, eyes finally meeting mine. "She wouldn't be caught dead touching a snake. No, this is someone more ruthless."

"More ruthless than my wife?" I ask in astonishment.

"She was your wife. She's nothing to you now."

Was?

"We're still married," I say slowly.

"Only because she's unavailable for a divorce," Dad growls. "We both know you have papers sitting locked away in your desk just waiting for her signature."

He's not wrong.

"You need a protection detail," Dad continues. "I can have someone watch the house twenty-four seven."

The last thing we need is someone watching us. Our family secrets would be even more vulnerable to public scrutiny than they are now. Not everyone on Dad's payroll is perfectly loyal to him. He may be naive enough to believe that, but I don't think for a second we can trust some security guy.

"It's fine," I assure him, flashing him my politician smile that soothes people because it exudes confidence. "The code is changed and cameras are gone. We're going to make sure Aubrey isn't ever alone outside of the house until we figure out who's doing this. We don't need security. We need a private investigator looking out, not in."

Dad studies me for a bit and nods. "I'll get someone on it. Jude can pass on anything he's found. We'd get further if your brother ever left his goddamn house."

Dad and Callum don't get along because Dad stole his girlfriend when he was a teenager.

The reason Dad doesn't get along with Jude is because he wants Jude to snap out of the trauma that shaped him into the recluse he is. Nearly every time they see each other, Dad suggests a therapist.

Dempsey is the rebel who's always getting in trouble and Gemma is a doll he must protect at all costs.

I'm the only child of his that he doesn't fight with, need to fix, or protect. The golden son. The favorite.

Would I retain that status if he knew I had my tongue in my teenage stepdaughter's pussy?

"I'll leave you to get back to it," Dad says, rising to his feet. "Don't worry. We'll figure this out and then you can focus on what's important. Becoming attorney general. Love you, Son."

I tip my head at him. "Love you too, Dad. Can you send Aubrey back in?"

He leaves and then a few seconds later, Aubrey reappears. She remains standing in the doorway, arms folded over her perky tits and a guarded expression on her pretty face.

"Come in," I instruct, voice firm. "Close the door."

She remains rooted in place and lifts her chin. "I'm kind of busy. Can it wait?"

"No. Please shut the door and come here. I want to talk with you."

Her shoulders drop and she lets out a sigh. Slowly, she closes the door but stays close to it. "What do you want to talk about?"

I study her, taking in every slight twitch of her face muscles. She's hiding something from me. My gut tells me it's about Spencer.

"What happened?" I demand, a flash of anger popping like a firecracker in my chest.

"What? Nothing happened." Her eyes dart to the floor. "Don't worry about it."

I rise to my feet and stalk over to her. Gently, I grip her jaw and tilt her head up so I can see her eyes when she lies to me. "What. Happened?"

She tries to look away, but my grip tightens, forcing her to hold my gaze. "You don't want to know, Hugo. You don't. Just drop it."

"I want to know, Love. I need to know." Anger swells up inside of me. "Tell me."

I slide my free hand to her pussy. Her eyes glimmer. Slowly, I rub at her through her clothes. Her breath hitches and her nostrils flare.

"Did he touch what's mine?"

Her eyebrows pinch together. "Hugo..."

"Goddammit, Aubrey, fucking tell me."

She blinks several times, shocked at my harsh tone. Then, her face takes on that cruel expression that reminds me of her mother. "I had sex with Spencer. Are you happy?"

My blood runs cold at her words.

She fucked my son?

I reach behind her, lock the door, and then guide her over to my desk with my firm grip on her jaw. She whimpers, stumbling over her heels, trying to keep up with my pace.

"You promised," I snarl, nose close to hers. "What the fuck?"

"I didn't promise anything," she snaps back. "I can't help it that everything's so confusing!"

I gape at her. "What's so confusing, Love? I ate you out. We were secretly giving this thing between us a go." Releasing her jaw, I drop my arm and glower at her. "But then you fuck my son behind my back? Is it because he's a dick to you? That it? Like for a man to push you around and take what he wants?"

My voice is rising, but I'm beyond controlling it. Truth is, I'm pissed and fucking hurt. Yesterday, I'd thought something was happening between us and it was worth the risk.

"You're being an asshole," she accuses, tears in her eyes. "And loud. Someone could hear."

"You like assholes," I throw back. "You like being hurt. Tell me, did my son beat on you while he fucked you? Is that what you want?"

She smacks me hard on the cheek. "Fuck you, Hugo."

I crash my mouth to hers, expecting her to fight, but she relents, allowing me to kiss her. It's brutal and harsh, both of us nipping at each other's tongues and lips. She whimpers when I roughly lift her dress and start wrenching down her panties.

This is wrong and all kinds of fucked-up, but I'm beyond stopping now. All I can think about is erasing his presence inside her. I need it to be me. I need her to remember how good it was between us yesterday and that it can be that good again.

"Did he even know how to make you come?" I demand, breath hot against her mouth as my fingers find her clit. "Did you wish it were me instead?"

She doesn't answer, just kisses me again, losing herself in the moment. I easily bring her to orgasm with a few expert strokes of my fingers. Before she's done coming, I flip her around, place my palm on her back, and push her over the edge of the desk.

Yesterday, I worshipped her.

Today, I'm punishing her.

Showing her the difference between gentle and rough. How she may think she wants it to hurt, but she doesn't. She needs to know the fucking difference.

I take a brief moment to admire her ass poking in the air before quickly unfastening my slacks to pull out my cock. Spitting into my hand, I then stroke over my dick to wet it, and then I'm pressing against her slit.

A low groan rumbles from her. I reach forward, slapping a hand around her mouth to keep her from making a sound, and then slam into her slippery, tight body, finally taking what I've dreamed about for what feels like an eternity. Her cunt grips me in a way that makes me see stars. Without waiting for her to adjust to my thickness or incredible length, I quickly pull back and drive in so hard the slap of our flesh echoes in the room.

Fuck. Fuck. Fuck.

Over and over, I thrust into her perfect body, not trying to make it sweet or make it last. I want this to be quick and a brutal reminder. The next time we fuck, I'll make love to her like she deserves. Right now, I need her to feel my anger and hurt.

She sniffles, a sob moaning out of her. I release my hand to make sure it's not too much, waiting for some verbal command to quit. Nothing. Moans and slight squeezes of her pussy around my dick.

"Feel how good it is to have me inside you?" I murmur, squeezing her bruised ass cheek. "Feel it, Love?"

She nods. Good girl. It emboldens me to fuck with less vigor and longer strokes, hitting her in the right spots inside. Her fingers grip the desk as she quietly pants. A few more thrusts and then I'm on the precipice. I grip her hips, lifting her slightly, and then aim for her G-spot. Another groan of pleasure escapes her.

Fuck. Fuck. Fuck.

I'm sweating underneath all my clothes, but I don't stop. I keep going until her body explodes. Shudders start from her core, quivering around my cock, and then ripple outward making all of her limbs quake. My nuts tighten and I lose it. I start to pull out and then think better of it. Grinding deeper into her, I hiss as cum jets out of me, filling her deeper than my damn son could ever go. Knowing I'm spilling cum over his attempt to claim her is a surge to my ego.

He's a teenager. A boy.

I'm a fucking man.

And I just fucked her like one.

Once my dick stops throbbing, I pull out and watch in sick fascination as cum runs out of her like a faucet, leaking down her legs and dripping onto the floor. Seeing her used up and spent, sprawled out on my desk, is a turn-on like I've never known before.

"He was sweet." Her soft voice is barely audible.

I freeze, confused by her words. "What?"

"Spencer was sweet. He made love to me."

Turning from her, I drag my fingers through my hair and swallow down the panic. What the fuck did I just do? I snatch some tissues from a box and quickly clean off my dick.

"Fuck, Love," I mutter, disposing of the tissues and then tucking my dick away. "Are you okay?"

She still hasn't moved. As much as I want to admire her ass, used pussy, and the puddle of my cum on the floor, I can't. Guilt is swelling like a tide, coming in quickly and threatening to drown me. I grab more tissue and begin cleaning up my messy girl. She's boneless and allows me to drag her panties up her thighs. I pull her dress into place and yet she still doesn't move.

Fuck.

I fucked her up. Us up. Everything up.

Hooking an arm under her, I lift her up and then manhandle her over to my desk chair. I pull her into my lap, curling her legs up close to me. I hold her like she's a little girl and I'm her father. I want to fix all her pain even though I'm the one who caused it.

"Shh," I whisper, kissing the top of her head. "Let me hold you, Love. My sweet, beautiful girl."

Then, like a dam being smashed through, she starts to cry. Soft, sad sobs. I feel like the worst asshole on the planet. I hurt her. No one to blame but me. Tears sting my own eyes, but I don't let them actually form, choosing to blink fast and hard. I hug her tighter, whispering praise over and over again.

"I'm sorry," I choke out. "I'm so sorry. I just lost control. I love you, Aubrey. I love you so fucking much."

She snuggles closer, relaxing in my arms. Her crying subsides and she tilts her head up, lips finding my neck. "Love you too, Hugo. I…I'm glad it happened. Us, I mean. I always wondered…"

Guilt drags me under again.

I want to punch myself in my own face.

"It can be better," I whisper. "I promise. That was fucked-up. Next time let me love you right. In a bed and so sweet. Just us."

"It was good," she rushes out. "I didn't say I liked it any better or worse than with Spencer. It's my emotions that are wrecked. My heart hurts."

"Because of me?"

"Because of both of you."

"You can't fuck us both," I spit out. "It has to be me and me only."

She sits up, pinning me with her teary eyes. "I…I can't give him up. Not now. Not after last night."

Pain slices down the middle of my chest and the world tilts.

"Y-You're choosing him over me? Because I fucked up and hurt you? Goddamn, Love, please don't choose him over me. I love you and I need you."

She presses a soft kiss to my lips. "I'm not choosing him over you. I'm just stating I can't give him up." I tense up and she gives me another kiss. "I can't give either of you up. I need you both."

This is beyond messy and fucked-up.

It's a colossal nightmare all three of us are starring in.

I'm jealous of my son because he also gets to fuck my stepdaughter.

And yet…

It's just Spencer. Not some stranger. Not some ex from LA. My son. That's better than the alternative. If I had to share her with anyone, it'd be him.

This twisted entanglement of ours is awful.

So fucking awful.

I don't know what to do about it either. I'm sure as hell not about to stop anytime soon.

CHAPTER TWENTY-FIVE

Aubrey

MY MIND IS IN A MILLION DIFFERENT PLACES, BUT I need to reel it in and focus. Tonight is a performance, according to Hugo, where the media will see him having dinner with his campaign opponent. I'll need to play the good stepdaughter who supports her stepfather by taking her mother's place since she couldn't come.

I bounce back and forth between looking forward to my date with Hugo and dreading filling my mother's spot, knowing she's still missing. Pretending to know where she is will be difficult. I'm hoping Hugo will steer us away from any uncomfortable territories because I would hate to be the reason his campaign goes south over a verbal misstep on my part.

I stare at my full-length bedroom mirror, smoothing out my dress that hits just below the knees. It's a black, floral print ZHIVAGO with a single cutout on my left ribs. Elegant but also sexy.

There's no denying I look good. Knowing Hugo will appreciate my appearance sends a thrill down my spine. Knowing Spencer will peel me out of this dress sends another one down my spine.

What is wrong with me?

It's been days since Hugo first rudely fucked me in his

office and my handling of this situation hasn't improved. Thankfully, there's been no more harassment from my stalker. I've been able to settle into this new rhythm.

At night, I'm in Spencer's bed. We talk, have sex, and then cuddle.

Then, at work, Hugo pins me in his office, fucking me like he can erase Spencer's scent.

It's insane. I shouldn't be having sex with both of them. It's wrong. Seriously fucked-up. If anyone knew what I was up to, I'd be shamed and probably shunned.

They're practically family.

But I want them. Both. They're like an addiction I crave more than my next breath. I don't understand how it can continue without coming to a brutal head. Does it stop me? Do I even try to stop? No. I keep falling back and forth into their arms, unable to keep from unraveling their relationship.

"You ready?"

Hugo's deep voice rumbles into my room and vibrates my bones. I turn to see him leaning up against the doorframe in a black suit, watching me with unmasked desire. My heart catches in my throat and sexual energy buzzes through my veins. We had sex hours ago against his office wall and I could go for round two right now.

"Yep," I say, lifting my chin. "How about you?"

He straightens and then strides over to me. "I'd rather stay here with you. Alone. You're so fucking beautiful right now, Love, it's taking every ounce of self-control I have not to tear this sexy dress off you."

I grin at him and touch his cheek. "I'd rather do that too, but you have a media appearance to pull off. You've got this. I'm going to make sure this goes well for you."

His eyes shine with pride. I flutter my lids closed as his mouth drops to mine. Spencer is out with Dempsey, so I don't feel guilty about stealing this moment with Hugo. For one night, I can pretend I'm a normal girl going on a normal date with a man she loves.

Hugo groans, hand sliding into my curled hair, and tightens his grip. His tongue spears into my mouth, owning me with every swipe of it. I'll have to reapply my lipstick, but it's worth it. I love how Hugo always devours me like I'm something rare and he must greedily consume it or it'll disappear forever. It's nice to be so treasured and adored.

He pulls away all too soon and peers down at me, eyes burning with heat. "We have to leave or I'm going to mess up all your hard work. Fuck, Love, you drive me insane."

"Likewise," I say, grinning at him. "Let me reapply my lipstick and we can go. Try to keep your hands off me during dinner."

He smirks at my flirting. "What about the car ride there and back?"

"Hmm," I tease, "I guess we'll see."

His hand reaches for mine. "I guess we will."

Turns out, having Hugo's hand on my thigh while he drove us to the restaurant was torment for both of us. He'd been so hard by the time we arrived, I thought he was going to need to get off before getting out of the car. But he'd seen Scott Jeter, his opponent, and his wife, Sarah, walking into the restaurant, which killed all sexual tension.

Now he's just tense.

Sure, he's wearing a bright, fake smile as he guides me

into the restaurant with a gentle hand on the small of my back, but I see through it. The last thing he wants to do is spend time with Scott. The feeling is mutual. I wish it were just me and Hugo.

"Hugo Park," Scott booms from a nearby table where they've already been seated. "My nemesis." He cackles, waving us over.

Hugo's fingers brush over the cutout opening on my dress at my ribs, making my skin break out in goose bumps. He leads us over to the table where our party is waiting.

Scott is probably in his fifties or so and a far cry from Hugo's handsome good looks. Thinning hair slicked back in an attempt to make it look fuller, pudgy around the middle, and a condescending grin on his face, Scott reminds me of Ben. Past his prime but still wanting to play like he's young.

"Hugo, this is Sarah. Sarah, this is the guy I'm going to beat," Scott says, laughing at his own joke. "And who's this gorgeous little thing?"

Hugo shakes both their hands and then introduces me. "This is my stepdaughter, Aubrey. Since Neena couldn't make it, I asked her to come along."

Scott winks at him. "I'd let her fill in anytime for Sarah."

Sarah, also a woman in her fifties but with a whole lot less fillers and plastic surgery than the other women in this town, elbows her husband. "Oh, stop. You're a dirty old man and you're making the child uncomfortable."

Child.

Hugo tenses but plays it off well, changing the subject to the wine selection at the restaurant. I sit between him and Sarah, heart thudding hard in my chest. This is a lot more awkward than I anticipated what with Sarah pointing out my youth and her husband's pervy comments.

While the men jokingly razz each other about the campaign, Sarah asks me about school. She also waves away the waiter when he attempts to pour me wine. I want Hugo to save me from her mother henning, but he's in politician mode.

I just have to make it through this dinner.

Sarah bores me with stories of a charity gala she's doing in the spring and how her children are all involved. One of her daughters is around my age and still in high school. It grates on me that she keeps pointing out my age.

Can she sense more is going on between me and Hugo?

Does she know his knee is pressed against mine beneath the table and my blood is running hot from the small but illicit touch?

"How's the boy?" Scott asks, piquing my interest. "Must be difficult for a young man to share a home with such a beautiful temptation."

I cringe at his insinuation. Mostly, because it's true.

"Ew," I blurt out, feigning disgust. "He's my stepbrother."

"Good girl," Sarah purrs, patting my arm. "Boys are dumb. Focus on school like my Leah. She's going to be a doctor. What are you going to be when you grow up, sweetie?"

When I grow up.

Hugo moves his leg away.

My stomach twists itself into a knot. The steak I'm staring at doesn't seem so appetizing despite the fact it's so expensive it doesn't even have a listed price on the menu.

"I don't know," I admit, shrugging my shoulders. "Haven't thought about it much."

Sarah drains her third glass of wine and narrows her eyes

at me. "What teenager hasn't thought about her future by your age?"

"The Park family tends to take a gap year off," Hugo interjects smoothly. "Though, if she and Spencer want to go to PMU this fall, we can easily enroll them with a quick call. There's really no rush, though. Aubrey has time to figure out her life."

His words, though meant to defend me, poke holes in me, shining light into the dark secrets I'm actively hiding from the outside world. Does he think a year off from college will help me choose between him and his son?

I grow quiet as the men discuss more of their campaigns, dancing jovially around the specifics so as not to give each other an edge. Sarah keeps sucking down wine like it's her job and barely touches her meal.

"What does your mother think about all this?" Sarah asks, waving a hand in the air, nearly knocking over her empty glass. "She approves of you having date night with Daddy?"

"Mom doesn't care," I snap, unable to keep up the polite façade.

It's the truest statement I've made all night.

Hugo, sensing my distress, places a hand on my upper back and studies me intently. The warmth of his touch is comforting. I feel stupid for my outburst.

"You two make a cute couple," Scott says, wagging his brows at Hugo. "Keep it in the family."

"Scott Jeter," Sarah snarls, slurring her words. "Apologize to the girl." She waves a manicured hand toward another table. "All of social media will see you behaving like a horndog."

Scott follows her gesture to a guy holding his phone up,

recording our dinner. He holds up his fourth or fifth glass of wine in a toast to the onlooker. "Vote for Jeter, AG!"

Sarah, clearly annoyed with his behavior and shitfaced herself, rises unsteadily to her feet. She points a finger at him and wags it. "You always do this. You're an embarrassment."

"Sarah," Scott bellows. "Sit back down and maybe lay off the wine."

She scoffs and storms off, bumping into a waiter. The guy's tray wobbles and he nearly loses several hundred dollars' worth of steaks to the floor. As soon as she's gone, Scott shrugs.

"Don't ever get married," Scott says to me. "Stay single and fuck whoever you want. I sure as hell wish I had." His gaze drops to my tits and he grins in a salacious way that makes my skin crawl.

"That's enough," Hugo clips out. "I believe that's our cue to leave."

"Oh, come on," Scott complains. "I'm just ribbing you, man. I can behave. Promise."

Hugo is already rising to his feet and tossing his napkin onto the plate. He holds out a hand for me to take, which I happily do. Once I'm also standing, he wraps a possessive arm around my waist. I want to remind him we're being watched, but he doesn't seem concerned.

"You can get this dinner," Hugo says with a fake polite smile. "I'll get the next one. Goodbye, Scott."

Relief floods out of me as we walk through the restaurant. Eyes are on us, but Hugo doesn't seem to care. When we finally make it outside, I'm able to breathe again. We spy Sarah leaning against a Mercedes while on her cell phone, chain-smoking. She sees us but doesn't wave. Fuck you too, lady. Fuck you and your husband.

Hugo opens my car door and helps me in. He's once again behaving like a gentleman on a date. At the restaurant, I began to feel like his stepdaughter and honestly it sucked. He climbs into the driver's seat and then reaches over to take my hand.

"I'm sorry, Love. That was a fucking disaster."

"Yeah. They're both obnoxious. You know you're going to win, right? That guy probably gives everyone the creeps. No one will vote for him."

His smile is handsome as he regards me in the dark car. "You're always so loyal and supportive. Another thing I love about you. What do you say we go someplace else? Somewhere discreet. I'll sneak you some wine. A real date."

It sounds lovely aside from the whole sneaking me wine because I'm so obviously under the legal drinking age.

"Yeah, sure," I say with false cheer.

As much as I want to spend time with Hugo, I also ache to just end the night in Spencer's cozy bed, laughing and listening to him tell me crazy stories about the twins.

Hugo backs out of the parking spot and heads down the road, palm resting comfortably on my thigh. My phone buzzes in my clutch. I pull it out, hoping to see a text from Spencer. It's not.

Unknown Number: I know you're fucking them both, whore. Keep at it and you'll be next...

My blood freezes in my veins. This doesn't feel like the usual needy text from Ben. This one bleeds with animosity and hatred much like the carved "slut" on the front door, the scattering of my private photos, the snake in my bed and the accompanying note. It's my stalker.

I'm about to block the number when a picture comes through.

It's a wrecked car, folded around a tree like it's made of aluminum instead of steel. The car looks familiar. Oh my God.

"Aunt Tasha!" I croak out in horror.

I immediately dial her phone number. It rings and rings. A man answers, voice haggard and raw.

"Aubrey?"

"Mr. Portman?"

"Call me Harold," he says softly. "Listen, there's something you should know…"

"Where's Aunt Tasha?" I whisper, tears flooding my eyes.

He sighs heavily, voice tight with emotion. "She was in an accident earlier this evening. Tasha is a mess." He chokes on a sob. "Been in surgery and we're not out of the woods yet."

The tears roll down my cheeks in an endless waterfall. I can hear Hugo asking me something, but my ears are ringing too badly to comprehend.

"I'm on my way," I manage to garble out despite the rising hysteria.

"Be prepared to talk to the cops," Harold says, voice taking on a sinister edge. "They're here at the hospital."

"The cops?"

My stalker did this. Sent me a threatening text telling me so. Oh God. This is all my fault.

"They think it was foul play. From what they can tell, she never braked, which could mean they were cut." He growls. "Whoever tried to kill my wife will pay. I'll exhaust every resource to find who did this to her."

The horror of the entire situation consumes me the second we hang up. I drop the phone into my lap and bury my face in my hands. A pained sob wrenches from me, echoing in the car.

I did this.

I'm the whore my stalker claims me to be and they're not just hurting me, but they're hurting the ones I love now too.

Is that what happened to Mom?

"Aubrey, Love, you're scaring me," Hugo murmurs. "What's going on?"

"Aunt Tasha was in a terrible car accident."

"Fuck. I'm so sorry. Is she okay?"

No. She's not okay. Nothing is okay.

Nothing will ever be okay.

CHAPTER TWENTY-SIX

Spencer

I'M EAGER TO WAKE AUBREY UP THIS MORNING. LAST night, super late, she came back home and locked herself in her room. Dad explained Tasha had been in an accident, and from what Aubrey told him, her stalker seemed to be taking credit for it.

It's the first night I haven't had her in my bed all week and it was too damn lonely. I lay in bed all night staring up at the ceiling, trying to understand my relationship with Aubrey. It's confusing and entirely fucked-up. Me and Dad are both sleeping with her.

Yeah, I know all about their daily office fucking because she told me. And, as pissed as it made me, I didn't want to give up my nights with her. We kept on like it didn't matter.

But it does matter.

It's Saturday, which means they won't be leaving for the office. I want to be with her. How will Dad feel about that? This shit doesn't look so neat and tidy now. I can't watch them fawn all over each other and wait to have her in my arms tonight. That's not happening.

Speaking of tidy, I make quick work of making my bed and straightening all the hung clothes in my closet. This week, despite my obsession with neatness, I wasn't all that bothered by seeing Aubrey's clothes on my floor. If that's the tradeoff for having her in my bed, I'll take it.

It's still early, but I can't wait to see her any longer. I may hate Tasha, but for some reason Aubrey loves her, so I know she was destroyed that Tasha was in an accident—one that might be connected to her stalker.

I rap on her door fast and hard. "Wake up, leech. Time to cuddle."

A drawer slams shut in her room. I try the knob. Still locked.

"Don't make me break in," I warn. "Open this damn door."

Footsteps thud over to the door and then it swings open. I'd expected to see her in her pajamas, bedraggled from sleep. She's fully dressed in a tempting pair of jean cut-off shorts and white tank top that reveals the tops of her juicy tits. God, she's so fucking hot.

"Where are you going?" I demand, sweeping my gaze back over her delectable body. When I notice the suitcase at her feet, all heat turns to ice. "Aubrey. What the actual fuck?"

"I'm leaving," she says, lifting her chin in defiance.

I'm confused. Leaving where? "With Dad?"

Her eyes, red from crying all night, narrow. "What? No. I'm leaving Park Mountain."

"By yourself."

She nods, crossing her arms over her chest. Her nostrils flare, the nose ring glinting in the light, reminding me of a bull ready to charge. "Yep."

"No, you're not." I bark out a harsh laugh. "Unpack your damn suitcase, leech. You belong here." I stab a finger toward my room. "Actually, you belong in there. Stop fucking around."

"I'm not fucking around!" Her voice is shrill and her eyes manic. "I'm a liability to everyone around me! Look at what happened with Aunt Tasha!"

I gape at her, stunned at how she thinks leaving will magically make all this shit disappear. "You can't leave, dumbass," I growl. "You're safest here with me and Dad."

"Until that freak hurts you too," she chokes out. "I can't let that happen. What if…What if he did something to Mom?"

Stalking over to her, I then shove the suitcase over on its side with my foot before grabbing onto her bare biceps. "That motherfucker won't get a chance."

"Let go of me, Spencer. I've made up my mind." Bitterness in her tone makes her face screw up into a sour expression. "It's done."

"Fuck you, leech. It's not done. This is bullshit!"

She struggles against my hold. "Don't make me scream for Hugo!"

"You think he's going to let you walk right out of here? You really are dumb." I let out a harsh laugh. "Nah, Dad's going to side with me on this one."

Her face burns red-hot with fury and she tries to fucking bite me. Vicious brat.

"Dad!" I bellow. "Dad!"

"Stop," she wails. "Just stop!"

I can hear Dad's sneakers pounding the floors as he runs from his room to hers.

"What the hell is going on here?" Dad demands. "Spencer, let her go."

"No," I growl, turning so I can see him and manhandling her with me. "She's trying to leave us."

Dad frowns. "What? Where are you going? To see Tasha?"

"It's not safe having me here," she says, chin wobbling. "I need to leave to keep you both safe."

"Not happening," I grind out. "Sorry, leech. You're stuck with us."

She glowers at me and then turns her puppy dog eyes on Dad. He usually melts under that particular gaze, but not this time. His body straightens and he steps forward, crowding us.

"You're not leaving," he says, voice firm and unyielding. "End of discussion, young lady."

I laugh because Dad trying to be fatherly right now is pretty fucking comical.

"Excuse me? You're not my dad!" Aubrey yells, going back into psycho mode. "I'm eighteen. I can do whatever I want."

Dad grabs her jaw, forcing her to look up at him. Her eyes are wide, nearly bugging out of her head. "I said you're not leaving. We're done talking about this."

"You can't hold me captive!" she shrieks, wriggling in our hold.

"The hell I can't," Dad growls. "You'll stay here where it's safe. Where we can protect you."

She freezes and then tries a different tactic. "Oh yeah? Gonna tie me to your bed, Hugo?" Her head jerks out of his grip and she pins me with a hard glare. "Or will I be taken to yours, Spencer? Exactly who do I belong to? Who's my warden?"

The room goes quiet as she waits. She's trying to trip us up—playing chicken until we release her. I peel my stare from hers and look my dad right in the eye.

"I'm going to put my dick in her smart mouth, Dad, until she stops fucking talking about leaving." I grin evilly at him. "Any objections?"

His jaw clenches and I can see the moral battle flickering in his eyes. Then, much to my surprise and a testament to his equal obsession with her, he shakes his head. "I'm rather tired of this conversation too. Do what you need to do, Spencer."

"You're just going to walk away and let him face fuck me?" Aubrey screeches. "Fuck you, Hugo. I thought you loved me."

He chuckles, dark and sinister. "Who said I was walking away?" He hooks his finger into her tank top and bra strap, slowly tugging it down over her shoulder. "I'm staying right here."

She gasps as his mouth meets her bare shoulder. This is totally fucked-up, but I'm here for it. Honestly, I want to see if Dad will really go through with it. Sharing a girl with your son has to be a mindfuck.

"Take her shorts off," Dad orders. "She can't go anywhere without shorts on."

I rip off my T-shirt and then reach for the button on her shorts. She doesn't try to stop me. In fact, her hand slides to my hair, fingers ruffling through it like she does at night before she falls asleep. I can hear Dad messily kissing her shoulder and neck as I pull her shorts down. Her panties come down next. Before I can touch her, Dad's hand cups her pussy and then his finger slips inside of her.

"Oh," she breathes.

I want to shove his hand away, but it's fucking hot watching him fingerfuck her.

"Get on the bed and watch her come," Dad growls between kisses on her neck.

I'm hard as stone, which makes taking my jeans and boxers off a little complicated. When I'm fully nude, I climb onto her bed and grip my dick.

"Take your shirt off, Love. I'm tired of looking at it. Bra too."

She trembles with need but dutifully obeys him now, ridding herself of the last of her clothing. Dad dips down to suck on her tit, tongue laving over the nipple and making her groan. I fuck my hand harder and faster, enjoying this fucked-up show.

"Look at your stepbrother," Dad rumbles. "Would you rather be over there sucking his cock or with my fingers inside you?"

"B-Both," she whines. "I need you both."

Pre-cum leaks from my slit, rolling down the crown of my dick, begging to be licked.

"Come suck my dick," I murmur. "Come here, baby."

Her hooded eyes meet mine and she gently pushes Dad's hand away from her pussy. She saunters over to me, tits jiggling with each step. I'm entranced by how goddamn sexy she is. Like some sort of lethal panther, she prowls onto the bed, finding her way to my dick. I stare at her, fixated on her supple lips and rosy cheeks.

From the corner of my eye, Dad removes his clothes and then walks over to the edge of the bed. Her tongue licks up the pre-cum on my dick and then she's yanked away from me. Her nails rake down my abs and she cries out. Without preamble, Dad grips his own dick and then thrusts into her.

Seeing her staring up at me, inches from my dick while

my dad fucks her is the single most erotic thing I've ever encountered. I grab hold of her hair, jerking her closer to me. Her mouth eagerly tries to suck my cock into her mouth. Again, Dad yanks her back, slamming into her roughly.

She moans, eyes fluttering in ecstasy. She fucking loves this.

I use my elbows to scoot closer to her so she won't be ripped away from me again. Her plump lips slide down over my dick and she takes me until she gags.

Fuck.

This feels insanely good.

So fucking good.

Dad begins a fast, brutal pace, driving into her like it's the last opportunity he'll get. I'm about to black out from sheer bliss as she sloppily sucks and gobbles my cock. Her saliva is making a big fucking mess and I don't give a shit because it's hot.

His hand strikes her ass and then he squeezes it until she cries out around my dick. He fucks her like a madman and then growls. Her resounding moan must mean he's coming. As much as that turns me on, I don't release yet. I watch in awe until his movement slows.

"Fuck," he hisses. "Holy fuck."

He pulls out and then flops onto the bed beside me, staring up at the ceiling. I grip the sides of Aubrey's head and draw her off my dick and to my mouth. Our kiss is desperate and starved. I devour her mouth that tastes like my salty semen.

Her wet pussy that drips with Dad's cum rubs against my length as we kiss. I reach down, grab hold of it, and then guide it inside of her hot body. She moans at the intrusion. It's extra lubricated from all the cum. She rocks her hips, taking from me what she needs while I suck on her tongue and lips.

Dad's hand is suddenly between us, cupping her tit and squeezing. This must be the extra bit of sensation she needs because she cries out, coming with her head thrown back. I piston my hips hard, quickly finding my release. Knowing I'm filling her up just like my dad did has my heart hammering in my chest.

Ours.

She's fucking ours.

Her body collapses onto mine, boneless and sated. We're quiet for a moment and then I can sense Dad's distress from beside me. He curses under his breath and slides off the bed to throw on clothes.

"I'm going for a run," he barks out.

And then he's gone.

Reality probably just slapped him in the fucking face. He slept with his stepdaughter and then watched her have sex with his son. Total mindfuck.

I hug Aubrey to me and kiss her head. We stay there for a good fifteen minutes, long after the front door slams, signaling Dad's exit for his run.

"I love you, leech. I guess I always have." I sigh heavily, irritation threading its way into my words. "I'm pissed about it too."

She finally slides off my flaccid cock and sits up. "Why would you be pissed?"

I climb off the bed to fetch a wet washcloth. I clean off the sticky cum and then hand her the cloth to take care of herself while I dress.

"That's a dumb question. Really? Because I've spent the last two years hating you, remember?"

She throws on her clothes and then walks over to me, eyebrows knitted together. "But why, Spencer? Why did you change?"

Anger swells up inside of me, hot and out of control. The memory of that time feels like razor blades slicing through my heart over and over again until it's a useless pile of meaty ribbons.

"Neena told me everything," I growl, waiting for her eyes to flicker with recognition of her crimes. "All of it."

She studies me for a long beat. "Told you what? I have no idea why you turned on me."

"Turned on you?" I spit out, voice laced with venom. "She told me your plan to get back at her!"

The more she stares at me with a dumbfounded expression, the more I begin to doubt myself. I didn't make this up, though. I didn't imagine it. Neena told me.

"It wasn't a secret you two were having issues," I remind her. "You confessed to me all the time how you could barely stand her and if it weren't for me and Dad, you'd have left to go back to LA long before."

"She was intolerable," Aubrey admits, stepping closer to me, "but I wasn't really going to leave."

I take a step back, not letting her distract me. This shit was bound to come to a head eventually. Might as well be now so we can move past it. Hurt shines in her eyes at my putting distance between us.

"No, if you left, it would have foiled your plan." I cross my arms over my chest and lift a brow. "I'm still not sure if this is a mindfuck game of yours."

"What plan are you even talking about? Whatever Mom told you wasn't true."

Unease settles in my gut. Something doesn't feel right. "You threatened her. Said you were going to ruin her life by fucking me."

"What?" she hisses. "I most certainly did not."

"Then how do you explain the text messages?" I bellow. "She showed me her phone where you said these things. That you were going to secretly record us and then share them with the school to humiliate her. Newsflash, Aubrey, if you did that, it was going to ruin our family, not just her."

"Did it ever occur to you that I didn't write those texts?" She shakes her head in disgust. "How could you even believe her over me?"

"I saw the texts," I say again weakly. "I saw them."

Everything begins to unravel in my mind. I'd been on the precipice of doing something with Aubrey that had the power to change the dynamics of my family and put the Park name under scrutiny. I was already hesitant because of that. But then her lips were on mine and it felt fucking right.

Getting caught, though, by Neena, and then discovering Aubrey's true motives had me backpedaling so fast. I was no longer in defense mode but had to switch to offense. I put distance between us, tormented her with my cruelty, and spread vicious rumors. She couldn't destroy our family because I was too busy destroying her.

Her hand cups my face as she looks me directly in the eye. "Spencer, you were wrong. I don't know how, but she lied to you. I swear on everything. I loved you. I still love you. Even after everything. The last thing I'd ever want to do is hurt you."

Before I can process her words that don't feel like a

lie—not anymore—the doorbell rings. I push away her hand, turning on my heel to see who's at our door. She follows behind me, huffing at my dismissal. I fling open the door, expecting to see Dempsey, but instead, I see that douchebag from my researching into Aubrey's past.

"Ben?" Aubrey chokes out, shock in her tone. "How did you find me?"

Ben smiles, relief at seeing her, and takes a step forward. I block the doorway, giving him a menacing glare.

"Get the fuck off my property, dude," I snarl. "Now before I call the police."

"Back off, kid," Ben bites out. "This is between me and my girl."

A red cloud of fury rolls in, blinding me with rage. "She's not your fucking girl."

"Gorgeous, come out here so we can talk. Alone. Please. I've missed you. I drove all this way to find you. I love you, Aubrey."

I shove him and then again, harder. He falls into the yard on his ass. "Get off my property!"

Ben climbs to his feet, shaking his head, and bellows at me. "Not until I have my girlfriend!"

Aubrey is screaming at both of us, but I'm focused on this asshole. I'm about to punch him in the fucking face when a figure charges for us. Dempsey tackles him to the ground and starts beating him.

"You could have killed her with that rattlesnake, you fucking prick!" Dempsey roars, slamming his fist into the loser's face over and over again. "I'm going to ruin you!"

"You're going to break his nose," Aubrey yells. "Stop, Dempsey! It wasn't him!"

I let Dempsey get a few more nasty punches on him before I yank him away. As much as I'm enjoying seeing this fucker bleed for assuming Aubrey is anything to him, I know she's right.

This dude's a pussy.

Whoever planted the snake and caused Tasha's accident is far deadlier.

CHAPTER TWENTY-SEVEN

Hugo

DON'T THINK.

Run.

My feet slam against the pine needles on the worn path through the woods that makes up the base of Park Mountain. I've been running this same path since I hit puberty, needing an escape from the pressures of my life, if only for an hour or two. It's warm already this morning, but the cover of trees keeps the temperature bearable.

Unlike earlier when I thought I'd melt from the inside out…

Don't think.

Run.

I force the images from this morning out of my mind. There's no logical explanation for me to grasp onto that says what happened was okay in any way, shape, or form. I mean, for fuck's sake, it was bad enough defiling my sweet stepdaughter. But to tag team her with my own flesh and blood?

Bile creeps up my throat, forcing me to stop. I bend over, elbows on my knees, and breathe heavily, trying to keep from vomiting on the trail.

I could have stopped it.

I could have, at the very least, sent Spencer away or carried Aubrey to my room.

That didn't happen, though. I was so goddamn alive with

the need to prove she was mine to my own son. Apparently, he felt that same need. It was a battle of wills—an immoral competition—between me and my kid to have the girl we've both been obsessing over.

My feet begin moving again, driving me faster along the trail.

What we did can't happen again. It just can't. If she wants to fuck Spencer when I'm not around, it'll suck knowing she doesn't want just me, but I'll deal with it. Then, when I'm alone with her, I'll be able to do whatever the hell I want with her without this sick, gnawing feeling in my gut.

If she'll stay...

I can't believe she packed up and was fully prepared to leave us. She thinks Tasha's accident was her fault. Spencer and I both know that's bullshit. This stalker of hers is terrorizing her at every turn, but that's in no way her fault.

It was on the tip of my tongue to blurt out what'd been happening with her to the police last night. They suspected foul play and were trying to gather any information to help on their case until their primary witness was out of surgery. I could have told them about Aubrey's text or the snake.

Then what?

They'd be no closer to finding out who did this and then more of our business would be spread to the world. This shit that's going on between the three of us does not need to get out.

I stumble over a root that's always been on my path. Even when I was a kid, I'd jump over it at the exact moment. Today, I nearly face-plant. Trotting to a halt, I run my fingers through my sweaty hair and bark out a harsh laugh.

I'm considering running back up the mountain trail again

when I see a squad car rolling up our road and parking in front of the house.

What the fuck?

I take off in a sprint, racing across Callum's yard and into my own. By the time I reach it, I'm confused by the scene in front of me.

Aubrey is standing between some guy on the grass and Dempsey, who's red-faced and pissed based on his pacing. Spencer, arms folded over his chest, stands in front of them, waiting for the cop to make her way across the yard.

"What happened?" I demand, eyes on Aubrey as I speak to my son.

Don't think about watching Aubrey fuck him earlier. Don't fucking think about it.

"Aubrey's boyfriend came to visit. Dempsey lost his shit."

Sloane, with her blond hair tied neatly in a bun and fully dressed in uniform, walks up to us. "You guys want to tell me why there's a bloody man in your front yard?" She cuts her hard, no-nonsense eyes to me. "For a man running for office, this is terrible timing, Hugo."

"Which is why we called you, Officer Killjoy," Spencer says in a droll tone.

I shoot him a sharp look that could get him to behave when he was a kid. Now, he's out of control and a goddamn adult. My looks won't do shit.

He smirks, a devious knowing glint in his eyes. I'm forced to look away, choosing instead to glance over at Aubrey and then at the bloody asshole on the ground.

"That guy right there is the reason Tony kicked Aubrey out," Spencer explains. "Tony got pissed when she fucked his

233

boss. Say hi to Ben the Trespasser." He waves at the groaning guy who doesn't wave back.

"Is this the guy who put a snake in her bed?" I ask, anger igniting in my gut.

Before Spencer can answer, Sloane steps forward. "A snake? What the hell, Hugo?"

The last thing I want to do is involve the police, even Jamie's best friend, Sloane, but I'm at my wits' end with this whole situation. At least I know she'll be discreet.

I quickly fill her in on all the shit that's been happening lately, making sure to leave off the part with the pictures of both me and my son each with Aubrey.

Sloane's eyes widen when I tell her about Tasha. Everyone in this town knows Harold and Tasha Portman. They're influential and have money just like the Parks. Difference is, we own most of the real estate here, making it *our* town in which they live in.

At some point in my story, Callum, Willa, Gemma, Jamie, and Dad all come out of their houses to see what all the commotion is about. The girls go over to be with Aubrey and Callum steps over to talk to Dempsey while warily eyeing Ben the Trespasser, who's still groaning on the ground. Dad joins our trio, just out of earshot of everyone else, intently listening to everything.

"I'm going to need help on this case," Sloane says slowly. "Someone is actively threatening your family. Aubrey could have been bitten by a rattlesnake. And Tasha's in ICU over this person." She glances over at Ben. "You sure it's not that guy? Someone seems to think he's responsible for something."

Dempsey rubs his hand with the bloody knuckles while glaring at Ben.

"This case," Dad clips out, "is a family matter and requires extreme discretion. Don't fail our family now, Sloane. Don't fail Jamie."

Spencer smirks. He always admired his pops' ruthless, no-bullshit attitude. "Guilt trip much, Pops?"

Nathan winks at him, a rare show of playfulness and affection, reserved for his only grandson.

"I'll have to haul him in," Sloane says with a resigned sigh. "I can arrest him for trespassing and attempted breaking and entering, but he'll be able to post bail."

"Unless he's also there for questioning for the possible hit and run from Tasha's accident," Dad supplies, sneering Ben's way. "You can hold him a little longer for that. It'll give us time to look into the real culprit."

Sloane shakes her head. "Nathan, you're not the mafia or some vigilante. You can't run your own criminal investigation. Then what? You going to hand him over in cuffs for me? The law doesn't work that way!"

Dad steps closer, pointing a finger in her face. "I am the law around here, goddammit!"

Dempsey, like some emo avenging angel, charges our way and shoulders his way into our circle, turning his wrath on our father. "Do not speak to her like that. She's trying to help us."

Spencer's grin is devious. I'm no idiot. I see it too. Dempsey's sweet on his mom's best friend. As if we need any more drama in this family right now.

Always the peacekeeper, I hold up both hands and say, "Everyone cool down. Sloane always has our best interest at heart. She'll do what she can on her end and we'll do what we can on ours. No one is going to jeopardize the integrity of our family name in the process."

Sloane nods, shooting me a thankful smile, and then strides over to Ben. She reads him his rights while helping him to his feet and cuffing him. The pathetic excuse for a man sobs and attempts to speak to Aubrey, but Sloane roughly guides him back to her squad car.

"A little heads-up you called Sloane would have been nice," Dad says, frowning at me. "It's much easier to clean up you kids' messes if I can stay ahead of the spill."

"Sorry, Dad," I say with a sigh. "It's been a shitshow."

He claps me on the back. "It'll be fine. Go back inside and enjoy your day."

The group disperses. Spencer and Dempsey take off to do God only knows what nor do I care, finally leaving me alone with Aubrey. She follows me into the house, quiet and forlorn.

"I need a shower," I grunt out, taking her hand. "As do you."

I'm eager to wash away the debauchery that took place this morning. To replace the scent and semen of my son with my own. Thankfully, she allows me to tug her along without a fight. Once we're alone in my room with the door closed, I strip us both out of our clothes and head for the shower.

I try not to think about this shower being a place where I fucked her mother before. Back when Neena wasn't such a conniving witch. My dick is semi-erect and thinking about my cruel wife does nothing to help harden it.

"You okay?" I ask when the water gets hot and steamy.

She nods as we step under the spray. "It was shocking to see him here, but I shouldn't be surprised." Her eyes close and her lips purse. "He's been texting me a lot from different numbers saying he misses me and wants to get back together. We were never together, Hugo. It was just sex."

If I thought I wanted to erase Spencer from her body, that was mild in comparison to how I feel about Ben touching her. Grabbing a bar of soap, I start slicking it over her body. She stands still as I wash every part of her, gently cleansing her pussy and ass crack. Once we're both clean and no longer stinking of our wicked morning, I crash my lips to hers.

Our hands are frantic, both of us needing the other. I devour each needy moan until I'm dying to be back inside her. She clutches onto my neck as I lift her. Her sexy legs wrap around me and then I'm pushing into her hot body. A pained hiss escapes her, reminding me she's sore from both me and my son fucking her this morning.

"I'll be gentle," I murmur, kissing her sweetly. "Nice and slow for you, Love."

"I love you, Hugo," she breathes. "I didn't want to leave."

I smile against her mouth. "Didn't plan on letting you leave."

We fuck until she's crying out in pleasure. I release inside her, not as much cum as before since I'm getting older. The water starts to run cold, so I quickly shut it off and dry us off. Naked but dry, we crawl into my bed so I can hold her close. She stares at me, stroking my cheek.

I don't know what I was thinking this morning, but it was truly fucked-up. I don't want what happened to ever happen again. I just want this. Me and her. Alone.

Her lids start to droop. I kiss her forehead and allow myself to drift off as well.

I wake some time later, the late morning sun warming my flesh through the window, to the sound of my phone buzzing where it's charging on my nightstand. Untangling myself from Aubrey, I roll over and grab it.

Jude: We need to talk. On my way.

If Jude's coming to visit, it's serious. We barely get him out of his house for family dinners. Fuck. This can't be good.

Me: About what?

The three dots move.

Jude: It's about Neena. You're not going to like this.

CHAPTER TWENTY--EIGHT

Aubrey

I KNOW THEY'RE TWO DIFFERENT PEOPLE, BUT STRANGELY, their beds smell the same. It's another added layer to why this thing between me, Hugo, and Spencer is so complicated and confusing.

Rolling over, I stretch to touch Hugo. The bed is cold and empty. My heart is full, though, and my body is deliciously sore.

I can't believe I had sex with both of them at the same time. It all just sort of happened. With Hugo being the older, wiser father figure, I'd expected resistance. He didn't resist. He was an active participant.

So wild.

Although he bailed pretty quickly after, it was fine. Something settled in my chest after we'd had sex. Completion. I finally felt complete.

Maybe the crap that happened with me and Spencer two years ago was meant to happen. We were just kids then. I could have had him had my mother not intervened, but then it would mean not having Hugo.

I can't imagine being with Spencer only.

That feels incomplete.

I'm not ready to thank Mom or anything. In fact, when she finally resurfaces, I'm going to have a long discussion with her. How could she pit her stepson against her own daughter? What was her motive for making me out to be some villainous gold-digging toxic girl? I'm still upset that Spencer would actually believe her.

Those texts weren't mine, which means Mom used my phone to create this false narrative to present to Spencer. But why?

Dad hates me and I deserve that for humiliating him.

Mom's animosity toward me has always been confounding. I've never understood the distance between us or the walls she put around herself. All I wanted was for my mother to love me unconditionally. Truth is, I'd have preferred Tasha for a mother, or even Jamie next door. Too bad you can't choose your parents.

Thoughts of my parents have me thinking back to Dad. Did he give Ben my address up here in Washington? Or was Ben resourceful in finding me? I'm not exactly hiding, so it wouldn't be difficult for someone really trying. It's still super creepy that he came all this way up here to profess his love to me.

Gross.

What did I ever see in him?

Nothing. Ben was a distraction. Something daring and rebellious to entangle myself in. A way to feel past the numbness that had grown like a fungus all over my entire being since the day I left Park Mountain. It seemed as if I was in a fog at the time, doing the bad things because I could, not caring who I hurt in the process. Now that I feel awake to my life, and the fog has lifted, I realize how lost I truly was.

I'm not a whore.

I'm just a broken girl looking for love in all the wrong places.

Deep voices can be heard rumbling from beyond Hugo's closed door. If Hugo and Spencer are having some sort of discussion, I feel like I need to be a part of it. Sliding off the bed, I head straight to Hugo's closet for something to wear.

Mom's perfumed scent still lingers, though she hasn't been here in close to a year. I force my gaze away from her rows of expensive, tailored clothing and endless amounts of shoes to Hugo's side. Grabbing an old, white PMU T-shirt that's probably been around since the late '90s or early 2000s, I throw it on and then head out to find them.

I round the corner, locking eyes with Hugo, who's sitting in an armchair, his elbows resting on his knees.

"Did we wake you from your nap, Love?" Hugo asks, plastering on a false cheerful smile.

It's then I realize it's not Spencer he's speaking to, but instead, Jude. All the warmth I'd felt on seeing Hugo gives way to a sudden chill. I'm barely clothed and it's obvious with me wearing Hugo's shirt where I've come from.

Jude sits on the sofa, thick, muscular thighs spread, somehow taking up all the air in the living room. His white mask is in place, hiding his mysterious face from me, but his eyes are sharp and calculating. It's always weirded me out that his family accepts that he hides behind a costume.

I can feel Hugo's stare on my legs, probably secretly imploring me to go change. But I feel as though something's going on and I'll miss out if I leave. Instead, I make my way over to Hugo's chair and sit on the arm. The shirt hem rides up my thighs, showing off my colorful tattoo, but Jude's stare doesn't move from my eyes.

God, he is so creepy.

"Maybe you should get dressed for the day?" Hugo asks, voice tight and slightly pissy.

It takes me a half second to catch on that he's angry at Jude seeing me like this. Warmth blooms inside my chest. I like the way his jealousy feels burning through my veins.

"What did I miss?" Ignoring Hugo's suggestion, I glance over at Jude. "You guys were whispering. Either you were being quiet because I was napping or you were talking about me. If you were talking about me, I'd like to know what was being said."

Jude's eyes are still boring a hole into me like he's trying to pick apart my brain and learn everything there is to know about me. It's not pretty beneath the blond hair. It's a dark, shameful place.

I might be wearing Hugo's shirt and scantily dressed, but Jude's gaze doesn't wander. Hugo's jealousy is misplaced.

Jude's in love with his demons. There's no room for anyone else.

"We weren't talking about you," Hugo says with a resigned sigh, moving past the worry of my lack of clothing. He, like me, must sense Jude's complete and utter disinterest. "We were talking about your mother."

I straighten, whipping my head down to look at Hugo. When he's not in his suits and casual in a pair of gray sweatpants, he's still sexier than just about any man alive, rivaling only that of his son.

"Not just Neena." Jude's muffled voice draws my attention back over to him. "Spencer too."

My stomach hollows out and a wave of nausea passes

over me. Based on the whispers and the tension in the air, I have a feeling I'm not going to like this.

Spencer, what did you do?

"What about them?" I croak out.

Jude leans forward, iPad in his fire-scarred hand, to show me a video still. It's Spencer. At a hair salon. Big deal. I don't understand what's so dramatic about this.

"Swipe," Jude instructs, relinquishing the iPad to me. "You'll see."

Spencer again and again and again. All over town in businesses and restaurants. The dates on some of these are as recent as this week.

"So he has a shopping addiction?" I laugh weakly and completely humorless. "What does this have to do with Mom?"

Hugo squeezes my naked thigh in an effort to comfort me. "Those purchases being made are from her debit card."

My head begins to throb as I process this information. "Why would Spencer be using Mom's card to buy things?"

"I don't know," Hugo admits, "but we're going to find out."

Where is he right now? Is he off buying more stuff to pretend to be her? This doesn't make any sense. The only reason he'd do something like this is to hide the fact she's truly missing.

Where is she?

"When he gets home, we'll demand to know what he's been doing," I rush out. "Because there's no reason to go to such great lengths unless..."

Unless he hurt my mother.

In a permanent, irreversible way.

"What if...Hugo, what if he killed her?" I manage to squeak out. "Oh God. Oh God."

Hugo's arm slides around my waist and he pulls me into his lap right in front of his brother. I can feel Jude's intense stare, but I'm more worried about the bomb Hugo just dropped on me. The last thing I care about is if Jude can see how intimate me and Hugo are being.

"Hey," Hugo croons, rubbing my thigh. "We're not going to jump to conclusions, okay? Jude's going to track his car and phone to see exactly what he gets up to each day."

"Why can't we just ask him?" I set the iPad down on the arm of the chair, curling into Hugo's solid, safe chest. "There's no reason to go to all these lengths."

I can ask him. To look at his eyes to see if he can lie to my face.

"He's my son," Hugo rumbles. "I'm not going to accuse him of something without having more to go on. We'll see what Jude uncovers and then I'll confront him. But he needs time to do that. Can you please let me handle this, Love?"

I nod, squeezing my eyes shut. "Yeah. I can do that."

For now.

"Good girl."

Is Spencer capable of murder?

A shiver dances down my spine. He's not exactly nice. I've been on the receiving end of his cruelty and it's not pretty. It's painful and devastating. Could he have turned that wrath on my mother?

Maybe he's behind the other stuff too. Is he capable of planting a snake in my room? Definitely. Would he? Doubtful.

The pictures and cameras, though? That's more his speed. It's suspicious that the cameras were planted by someone who has the code to their home. Spencer could have easily done that.

I'm sitting cross-legged in the center of his bed, waiting for him to return home. His room is so perfectly neat. It's a total serial killer room. Maybe Mom is one of many. What if I'm next?

My phone buzzes with an incoming text.

Harold: The doctor thinks we'll get moved from ICU to a regular room soon. Tasha is awake but in a lot of pain and can't really speak. I'll let you know when she's in a room so you can visit. Be safe, Aubrey.

Guilt grabs my ankles and drags me into a deep, dark pool of despair. Spencer hates Tasha. If he killed Mom, she'd be a loose end to clean up. She'd been pretty nasty toward him the other day.

Would he do such a thing?

An ache in my chest begs me to disagree. It's Spencer. The same Spencer who'd been so upset when telling me his reasoning behind why he started hating me two years ago and the utter confusion on his face when he learned he might've gotten it all wrong. He's not some evil mastermind. Just passionate and sometimes angry.

He loves me.

He wouldn't try to kill the ones I love.

I'm lost in my torturous thoughts when Spencer's door opens and he saunters in. At first, he doesn't see me, but then, when he does, he flashes me a flirty grin that makes my stomach tighten.

That's not the face of a monster.

"What's Jude doing here?" Spencer asks, sitting down on the edge of the bed. "And why are you wearing Dad's favorite shirt?"

I'd like to clear the air right now. To demand to know what he's been doing with Mom's card and to make sure he hasn't done something with her. Everything would get straightened out in a flash.

Or, it could blow up in my face.

Maybe I'm blinded by him.

Maybe he is capable of such things and I could be jeopardizing a real opportunity to learn what's happened to my mother.

"Hey, leech. I know you want to suck my dick, but I'd like to have a little small talk first. Sometimes I think you use me for my dick and body heat at night."

Playful Spencer makes my heart weep.

I can't say anything about the card, but I could try a different tactic. Go another direction to see if I can get a read on him.

"I don't know," I finally rasp out. "Harold says Tasha is awake."

He blinks at me, features impassive. "Cool."

Cool?

I know he hates her but for real. Cool?!

"Don't be an asshole," I snap, shoving his shoulder. "She almost died."

"What's your problem?" He scowls at me, no longer in a teasing mood. "Did you fuck my freak uncle while I was gone? Did Dad participate?"

I gape at him in disgust. "How can you turn on me so quickly?"

He scrubs a palm over his face and shrugs. "Sorry. I've had a shit morning. Was looking forward to getting back here with you, but the second I get back you start bitching me out."

"Because you're being a prick!" I poke a finger at his bicep. "You cut her brakes, didn't you?"

Spencer blinks at me, a brow arched. "What?"

"That's why you don't care! You cut her brakes and tried to kill her!"

Striking like a snake, he grabs my jaw and tackles me to the bed. Before I can scream out for Hugo, he slaps a hand over my mouth and rests his heavy body on mine, trapping me on his bed. My heart thunders wildly in my chest and terror creeps its way through my every cell.

Am I going to be next on his psycho hit list?

CHAPTER TWENTY-NINE

Spencer

WILD EYES STARE UP AT ME—A VIOLENT STORM OF hatred and love and betrayal and lust. She doesn't really believe I sabotaged Tasha's car and tried to kill her, but she's looking for someone to blame. I'm the easy way out. The one she's blamed for all her heartache for the past two years.

"You're in love with a killer," I taunt, voice a low growl. "I bet you're wet imagining I'll take you by force before I kill you too."

She narrows her gaze, fury burning hot in her eyes. Aubrey is beautiful when she's angry. I love the way her cheeks turn pink, her nostrils flare, and her mouth lashes out. Only now, she can't say a peep.

Testing my theory, I slide a hand down her front, roughly handling each of her breasts through my dad's thin shirt before making it down to her naked pussy. She weakly attempts to struggle, which tells me all I need to know.

She wants this.

She wants me.

Killer or not.

Even if I were the one responsible for causing Tasha's accident, she'd want to fuck me anyway. My girl is depraved just like me. What other type of person carries on a sexual relationship with both her stepbrother and much, much older stepfather at the same time?

"Admit it," I rumble, bringing my nose close to hers. "You thrive on the thrill of doing bad things. Of being with bad people." I brush my fingertip over her pussy, delighting in the shiver that racks through her. "You get off on it."

I can tell she wants to speak—probably to argue—but I don't let her. My finger slides along her slit, teasing at her clit. A muffled mewl crawls out of her throat and her eyes flutter.

"Oh, leech, you're so fucking needy for all the bad shit I have to offer." I slip a finger farther down and rub at her opening. Slick and hot. "You're so wet, you're leaking. Or is that my daddy's cum?"

She moans as I push a finger inside her. Slowly, in a tortuous manner, I fingerfuck her, letting her hear the juicy sounds her body makes. There's no faking me out. Her body needs this—she craves this. Deep down, she knows I love her and she fucking loves me. She's just looking for someone to blame. An easy way out.

There's nothing easy about us.

And I'm certainly never giving her an out.

I take my time, bringing her closer and closer to ecstasy, only to pull back before tipping her over the edge. Her hands have long since found my shoulders, holding on to me rather than pushing me away. Each time she's about to come, her breathing hitches and her lashes flutter.

Finally, I take her to heaven despite being the devil, one expert stroke at a time. Her whole body tenses and then quivers wildly as she comes. Before she can fully relax, I finally move my hand from her mouth and bring my other one to her lips.

Our eyes remain locked as I paint her bottom lip with her own arousal. The tip of her tongue peeks out, licking at my finger, sending fire straight to my cock.

"I didn't fuck with Tasha," I rumble. "I may hate that witch, but I didn't try to kill her. Someone very real is out there trying to hurt you. I will find them and hurt them back."

I crash my lips to hers and kiss her hard. I can tell from her eager kiss, she's no longer suspicious of me. It's annoying she'd even jump to that conclusion. Since my cock is hard and achy, I reach down to free it. My fingers are still wet and sticky from her arousal, which makes for just enough lube to get the job done. It doesn't take but a few strokes before I'm coming as we kiss. Cum spurts out of my cock, soaking the front of Dad's shirt.

Good.

I like the idea of her wearing my mark.

When I'm spent, I break our kiss, rolling away from her. I expect her to cuddle, but she's off the bed before I can stop her.

"That was a real dick move," she snaps, cheeks still flushed from her orgasm.

"Coming all over Daddy's shirt?"

Her eyes roll hard. "Saying all that shit, Spencer. It was mean."

"See how you like being accused of murder."

She flips me off and then storms out of my room. Irritation itches under my skin. I know she's running to tattle on me. He'll scoop her into his arms, stroke her hair, and apologize that his son is a fucking asshole.

That's what really pisses me off.

I have to share her. That's exactly what we're doing. Sharing. I've been an only child until Aubrey showed up a few years ago, so sharing was never something I cared to do. Sharing with Dad sucks. Why can't he find some old-ass woman to stick his cock into? Why does it have to be the girl I've loved since day one?

I'm still stewing as I clean myself up and right my clothes, anger growing and the need to take it on someone becoming almost unbearable. I grab my phone and shoot Dempsey a text.

Me: Work your magic with your mom's bestie and get us access to Ben.

⊙

"You really don't think this dude was responsible for the snake?" Dempsey asks, rubbing at his bruised knuckles. "You heard him. He's fucking obsessed with Aubrey."

I shut off the engine of my car and shake my head. "Nah. He's a pussy. The guy doesn't have the balls for that."

"He had enough balls to show up on your doorstep professing his love to her."

"Yeah, but he's from LA. The chances of him wrangling a rattlesnake out in the woods and sneaking into our alarm-armed house is slim to none. It's someone else."

Dempsey lifts a brow at me. "Then why are we here, man?"

"Just because he didn't try to hurt her doesn't mean he won't need a warning to stay the fuck away." I shove open my car door and climb out. Dempsey follows suit. "He needs to know where he is and who the hell he's messing with."

Dempsey flexes his hand. "I'm pretty sure I left a literal impression of that on his face."

"And now I'm going to beat it into his thick skull so he doesn't forget."

Dempsey chuckles as we make it around to the back door of the police station. Our town isn't huge, so our police force is pretty pathetic. Dad and Pops are pretty influential as well and have managed to keep the police at bay anytime we're involved in anything remotely shady. It helps Sloane is on the force because she always does Pops' bidding, even though I think she low-key despises him, only putting up with him because of Jamie being his wife.

I rap on the door and it opens a few seconds later. Sloane, though super-hot for her age, has dark circles under her eyes and wears a frown. This job must drain her soul.

"You," Sloane says, pointing at Dempsey as she hands me a key, "can sit in my office. You're lucky you aren't sharing a cell with that guy after what you did to his face."

Dempsey's face hardens. "I thought he put a snake in my brother's house. What the hell was I supposed to do?"

Sloane shakes her head and sighs. "Not that. Seriously, Dempsey. You're almost eighteen. What happens if I'm not around to clean up your messes? Every time I turn around, you're in a fight. First with Callum's girl's stepbrother and now this out-of-towner. One day, I won't be able to rescue you."

"I don't need saving," Dempsey growls.

I walk away, leaving them to sort out their shit alone. I'm interested in talking to this douchebag before Sloane decides to change her mind over something dumb like morals or ethics. Right now, she's distracted by Dempsey, which works out better for me.

The key unlocks the door to where there are a few holding cells but unfortunately doesn't gain me access to the actual cell. Luckily, though, the other cells are empty, leaving me privacy to chat with this motherfucker.

Ben sits on the metal bench, back against the wall, staring straight ahead. His nose is bruised and swollen, eyes are turning black near his nose, and blood stains his shirt. Dempsey fucked him up. He deserved it, too.

"You didn't really think she'd throw herself into your arms, did you?" I say, approaching the cell and standing right in front of him. "I mean, she's her and you're you. Have you looked at your receding hairline in the mirror lately? Have you noticed that pudge in your midsection?"

Ben stands and scowls at me. "Fuck off, kid."

"This kid has more money in his trust fund than you'll ever have in your lifetime. I think you meant to call me sir." I smirk and shrug. "Seriously, man. Do you think she would want some loser when she literally could have anyone on the planet?"

"I love her," he growls, fisting his puny hands. "I love her and she loves me."

I grip the bars and lean forward, face between them. "That's where you've got it all fucked-up. She doesn't care about you, dumbass. You caught her at a vulnerable moment where she needed comfort and release. But even though you're old as fuck, you couldn't fully service her daddy issues."

"Leave me alone."

"Not until you answer some questions first." I lift a brow. "Did you fuck with Aubrey's aunt's brakes?"

His eyes narrow. "What?"

"Have you been threatening Aubrey with snakes and pictures and letters?"

"No," he snaps. "And if someone is, they'll have to answer

to me. I'll take care of her. As soon as I get out of here, I'll make her see. We can run away together and be happy."

"Actually," I snarl, voice dripping with hatred, "you won't ever talk to her again."

He scoffs. "Try and stop me."

"Oh, I *will* stop you," I warn. "Indefinitely."

His eyes flash with uncertainty and he darts his gaze over to the door as if he could manifest someone to walk through it and save him.

No one is saving him.

"You can't do shit," he says weakly, retreating back to his seat on the bench.

"As soon as you post bail and get out of here, you'll take your ass back to LA and to your wife. If you don't, I'll send you back through UPS in a body bag to her."

"Something tells me murder isn't something you're capable of." He swallows but squares his shoulders in false bravado. "I'm not listening to some spoiled rich kid."

"I'm not some spoiled rich kid," I say with venom. "I'm protective over what belongs to me. You, Ben, are a fucking threat to someone I love. If you want to test me, try it. You'll learn that I'll exhaust every ounce of energy and money into ruining you."

"My life is already ruined," he spits back. "My wife is leaving me. My employees hate me. What have I got to lose?"

"Your life, dipshit. You will lose your life." I crack my neck, eyes burning into him. "If I have to buy a farm full of pigs to eat you alive, I will. If I have to borrow someone's woodchipper to grind you into pathetic hunks to bury you in my yard, I will. If I have to sneak into your hotel room or home and stab you through the goddamn eyeballs while you sleep, I will."

He blinks at me, fear gleaming in his eyes.

"You even speak to her again and I will make good on my promises. I'm not like Dempsey. I don't typically use my fists to get even. My ways are much darker and sinister." I chuckle at him. "Want to know the best part?"

"What?" he croaks out.

"My family will help me. Every single one of them will have my back. See, you're not just pissing me off, you're pissing off every Park alive." I tap the bar with the key. "Tell me what I want to hear, Ben. Tell me and I'll walk away. You'll never have to see or speak to me again. Your life will go on as normal. Aubrey will be a memory of that one time you got super fucking lucky to get someone like her in your bed."

The clock on the wall ticks audibly in our silence. Finally, he rushes out a deep breath.

"Fine, man. I'll leave. It's obvious she's fucking you anyway. I don't want to get in the middle of your shit."

I don't agree or disagree with his statement.

"Remember our little talk, Ben. This includes phones, emails, text, social media, what-the-fuck-ever. Zero contact."

"Yeah, psycho. I got the memo."

I stalk away without another word. If he truly loved her, he'd have fought harder against me. All he cared about was getting his dick wet with someone half his age. At least with Dad, he loves her too—like really loves her. Dad wouldn't have let me throw down that threat and push him away from her.

When I reach Sloane's office, she's picking up papers off the floor. I toss the key and it skitters over to her. She scowls at me but doesn't say anything to me.

Dempsey is waiting by my car, smoking a cigarette when I get outside.

"You and Officer Boob Job have a fight?" I ask, smirking at him.

He exhales a plume of smoke and then flicks his cigarette into the back of a truck that's parked beside us. "Don't call her that."

"Didn't she and your mom get their tits done at the same time five or six years ago?"

"Don't talk about my mom's tits."

"You're in a pissy mood."

"Fuck off, Spence. Where're we headed next?"

"The lodge."

"Drop me off at home on your way. I'm not in the mood to deal with all your bullshit today."

Well, fuck you too, asshole.

CHAPTER THIRTY

Hugo

"HE LEFT AGAIN," JUDE SAYS, HOLDING UP HIS iPad. "Looks like he dropped Dempsey off."

We've moved from the living room to my home office. I'd gone to check on Aubrey earlier, after Spencer left, and she'd hopped in the shower. Since she hasn't come back out, I'm imagining she needs her space from the both of us. Me and Spencer, that is.

How could she not?

We both used her this morning like she was our own personal whore.

First, together. Then, individually.

Fuck.

I'm not sure what to do about this whole thing. Stupidly, earlier, when we were alone, I'd thought maybe it could just be the two of us. But, while completely oblivious to Jude, I knew they were alone together in Spencer's room. I'm not an idiot. They were being intimate.

Goddamn, this is maddening.

"Hugo." Jude's deep, muffled voice draws me from my inner thoughts. "He's headed to the lodge now."

I give my head a slight shake and take the iPad from him. Sure enough, Spencer is traveling up to my uncle Theo's lodge on Park Mountain. It's not uncommon for Spencer to hang out there. I've had to ground him a few times for parties he threw there that got out of hand enough that I was called to come intervene.

It's the afternoon, though.

Usually, when he goes off to party, it's at night.

"I was able to access the records of his traveling and he goes to the lodge every day without fail."

I stew on that statement for several minutes. I should call Theo to see what's going on.

"He's on the payroll," Jude reveals, already two steps ahead of me.

"What?" I snap my attention to my brother. "Why wouldn't he tell me he was working for Theo?"

Jude lifts one muscular shoulder. "He didn't tell me either."

Rising to my feet, I hand him his iPad back. "Can you stay a little while to look after Aubrey? I'm going to have a talk with my little brother about what he knows about Spencer."

Jude grunts and I slip out of the office.

I listen for Aubrey and can hear her music playing beyond her closed door. I want to go to her but know now's not the time. As much as I'd rather stay in our love bubble, there's a reality I can't ignore: Someone is still stalking her.

At Dad's house, I can hear him and Jamie talking in the kitchen. I catch a glimpse of them holding each other tight. A pang of jealousy twists my stomach into a knot. Dad's been happy ever since he got with Jamie. They've always had this fiery, intense, passionate love that I never knew.

Until Aubrey.

Unlike Dad and Jamie, though, I can't love Aubrey for

all to see. For one, she's my stepdaughter, and two, I'm sharing her with my fucking son.

I pass by them without greeting and head up the stairs to Dempsey's room. The thumping of the bass gets louder with every step closer to his space. I don't bother knocking and let myself in. Dempsey is sprawled out on his unmade bed, shirtless, and staring up at the ceiling. Tattoos litter his chest. I'm surprised Dad condoned that shit. There would have been no way in hell I'd have been allowed to get *one* tattoo at seventeen, much less a whole shit ton of them like Dempsey has.

Storming over to his Marshall Bluetooth speaker, I flip the switch to turn off the loud rock music. This earns Dempsey's attention. He sits up on his elbows and glowers at me.

"What the fuck, Hugo?"

Scowling, I cross my arms over my chest and pin him with a hard glare. "I want to know everything."

His brow deepens. "What are you talking about?"

"The lodge," I growl. "I know you and Spencer go there. I know he's there right now. Question is, why?"

Dempsey's face doesn't twitch or give anything away, which probably is what gets him out of so much shit with Dad. He can turn on the innocent look, just like his twin Gemma can, and pretend he's a perfect little angel.

My gut, though, doesn't deceive me.

He's hiding something.

Dempsey cuts his eyes away from my penetrating ones. "He got a job there."

This I knew as well because of Jude, but something about the way he says it is off. It sounds a little too rehearsed.

"What does my trust fund son, who essentially never has

to work a day in his life if he so chose to do, have any business working at a lodge?"

Dempsey stands up and throws his hands in the air. "I don't fucking know, Hugo. Maybe he wants to get away from your suffocating presence. Ever consider that?"

I don't take the bait. Aside from the time since Aubrey returned, me and Spencer have always gotten along just fine. He's never once indicated to me that he feels smothered by me. It's bullshit and I can see it a mile away.

"Enough with the crap, Demps," I growl, stepping toward Dempsey until we're nearly nose to nose. "I know you both went to the police station and I know you know all about whatever it is Spencer is up to."

"Are you tracking us?" He pokes me hard in the chest. "Back the fuck off, bruh, or I'll knock your ass out. Today is not the day to be messing with me."

Footsteps thunder our way and seconds later, Dad strides in, concern etched on his distinguished face. We both shut our mouths, turning away from each other to face Dad. As much as I want to knock my little brother on his ass, I refrain. Barely. Dad's disapproving frown reminds me of when I was a teenager and me and Callum would pick on Jude. I haven't felt this judged by him in a long time.

"What's going on, boys?"

I nearly cringe at being called a boy.

"Just having a chat with Dempsey, but we're working it out," I grind out, forcing a reassuring expression on my face. "Right, bro?" I clap him on the shoulder and squeeze.

Dempsey shoots me a scathing glare, but to my surprise, nods. "You can leave the belt on, Dad."

I roll my eyes. Dad has never, not once, whipped his children. Not even the shit starter baby boy.

Dad nods and strides into the room. He bypasses us and walks over to the window. His body is tense as he stares down at the pool. "Has your or Callum's pool been cleaned lately?"

With all that's been going on lately, I honestly can't remember.

"Probably. The guy comes like clockwork. I haven't noticed, actually."

Dad turns from the window. "Hmm."

Whenever Dad takes that tone, it means someone is about to get destroyed. At the very least, a seriously vicious verbal lashing. Dad may never have spanked us, but he does enjoy figuratively whipping everyone who wrongs us Parks. Even if the wrong is skipping a pool cleaning week.

"The girls can't even swim until we get this straightened out," Dad grumbles. "Unbelievable."

I let out a heavy sigh. "I'll clean them until you find someone new."

"Jamie's gone over to your house with Gemma. They wanted to cheer her up after what happened this morning and to get her out of the house. Start with your pool."

I nod, leaving my dad and brother alone. I'm barely out Dempsey's door before Dad starts bitching him out about something. Of all Dad's children, Dempsey acts out the worst, therefore gets griped out the most.

Spencer still isn't home when I get back. Still at the lodge "working." Whatever the fuck that means. He'll be explaining that shit later when he gets home.

Laughter can be heard outside. I stride over to the back door and peer out. Jamie, Gemma, Willa, and Aubrey are all outside, making themselves comfortable on the poolside lounge chairs. My focus homes in on Aubrey in her tiny orange bikini. Fuck, she looks hot. Her damp, blond hair is piled up high on her head and her sunglasses are oversized. The triangles over her breasts barely cover her nipples, revealing the roundness of her firm, young tits. Even her bellybutton ring looks lickable. Thank God it's only women out there because a man, no matter who it is, wouldn't be able to keep their eyes off her beautiful body. I know I sure as hell can't.

Bugs and debris coat the top of the pool, and it looks like it might be trying to turn green soon. I'll change into my own swimsuit so I can clean the pool as I promised my father and sneak a few peeks at my sexy girl in the process. The trouble will be hiding my fucking boner from my stepmother, sister, and my brother's woman.

I pass by my office and the lights are out. Of course Jude would bail the second I left. He's not diagnosed with anything yet, but I'm certain a therapist would have a field day uncovering all the psychological conditions he's developed over the years because of his trauma. He probably ran his ass all the way home and locked himself away in a dark room, having "peopled" enough for one day.

On the way to my room, I stop in front of Spencer's room. As per usual, it's immaculate. I don't think he's ever left his bed unmade. Ever. It pains me to know he's working with Theo and didn't even bother to tell me. What else hasn't he told me? I'd always thought I'd done right by my son, parenting him the best I could, but I've fucked it all up since Aubrey returned. I'm not a good dad. If I think Jude has issues, Spencer is going to be worse by the time I'm done with him.

Fuck.

THE TANGLE OF AWFUL

I bounce back between being angry at my son and feeling sorry for him. It's not right. And yet, I don't know how to undo any of this. There's no fucking way I can give up Aubrey. Not now, not ever. My son, so much like me, won't give her up either. Nothing about our situation will improve or ever be okay. It'll keep going deeper and deeper into this twisted sinkhole until we lose ourselves completely to the darkness. After that, I don't know what life will look like.

I'm just pulling my swim trunks on when I hear a scream. It's not unusual to hear Gemma yelling at Dempsey for throwing her in the pool. But this scream is different. It's not hers. It's Willa.

I tie the drawstrings as I start for the bedroom door, a swell of unease rising up in me. Gemma's scream follows Willa's—not a pissed scream at being dunked in dirty pool water, but straight terror. Fear.

Goddammit!

I take off running through the halls and am making it through the kitchen when I hear another scream. This one, Jamie. She's screaming Dad's name.

Snakes?

I anticipate Aubrey's scream, but there's silence where she's concerned. Dread claws at my throat and I choke for air as I yank the back door open. My eyes land on her pool lounger. Empty. Fuck. I dart my eyes to Jamie, Gemma, and then Willa.

They're all panicked and sobbing.

What the fuck?

"Where's Aubrey?" I demand, voice hoarse with fear.

"S-She's gone," Jamie stammers, eyes wild, pointing

toward the house. "He just came out of n-nowhere." She hugs her middle and tears well in her eyes. "He had a gun!"

The world spins, but I take off running around the side of the house to the gate. It stands wide-open. Screeching of tires on asphalt can be heard as I run across the grass and out the gate.

I pray she'll be standing on the driveway, a pretty smile on her face, ready to tease me for falling for their prank.

Except, this isn't a prank.

It's horrific and my reality.

A white sedan hauls ass down our road and then peels out onto the main road.

Keys.

I need my keys.

Bolting back inside, I scramble to find where I dropped my keys last. Where the fuck are they? Panic swells inside me, seeping into every cell of my body. I can hear the girls yelling and talking over each other as they make their way into the house. I also hear Dad's voice and Dempsey's.

I'm focused on one thing.

Getting my girl back.

CHAPTER THIRTY-ONE

Aubrey

DON'T PANIC. DON'T PANIC. DON'T PANIC.

I rub at my head where some guy pistol-whipped me in front of his open trunk. I'd blacked out for what felt like an eternity and am just coming to. My body rolls hard, slamming against one side of the trunk as the guy takes a turn too fast.

Bile rises up in my throat and I gag. Between the painful hit to the head, the terror of my situation, and the nauseating scent of chemicals, I'm seconds from puking.

Why does it smell this way?

Bleach?

My kidnapper is a serial killer who uses bleach to wash away his victims' blood. I'm never going home. I'm in the captivity of a professional.

Is this random or orchestrated by my father?

I can't help the dreadful feeling in my gut that Dad hates me so much he hired someone to kill me. How horrible would that be?

At least it's not Spencer.

A sob breaks free as I slam into the other side of the trunk. I'd been so eager to blame someone for all the terrible things that have been happening that Spencer made the perfect target. It was easier to see him as responsible for all the pain in my life.

God, I'm so stupid.

Spencer loves me. Yes, he loves to torment me, but he was never truly evil. Not like this monster who's taken me.

Tears spill out and I hastily swipe them away. I don't have time to feel sorry for myself. My captor didn't bind my hands or feet—just coldcocked me and tossed me in his trunk. I need to be ready to fight the second he opens the trunk. I feel around, looking for some sort of weapon. Nothing but dusty crumbles of what's responsible for the scent.

I give up on my weapon search and start looking for a way to pull the carpet away from the back panel. I'd seen on TikTok once how to escape being trapped in the back of a trunk. I thought it was silly at the time and seemed so easy to bust out the back taillight in order to wave to other drivers.

TikTok didn't tell me you had to be strong or in a certain model car.

I sob in frustration, yanking and tugging on the edges of the carpet that seems superglued into place. Since I can't bust out the taillight, I try placing my bare feet on the top of the trunk and pushing. I even try taking turns beating my feet against the metal. It doesn't budge.

"Think, Aubrey," I say shakily. "Think."

I start to fumble around the part of the trunk that leads to the car. In Dad's car, back in LA, it had a hidey-hole that offered access to the trunk. If this car had one, I could shimmy through and escape through the back door.

Of course, this model doesn't have such a hidden door.

"No!" I scream in frustration.

I'm completely drenched in sweat now because of my

efforts and the airless trunk. I start to gasp for air that doesn't exist.

I'm going to suffocate.

Oh my God, I'm going to die from lack of oxygen long before this psycho gets to carry out his perverse deeds.

My breaths are coming out and back in, sharp and laborious. I am becoming dizzier with each passing second. I gag and gag again.

"I can't breathe!" I bellow. "Please help me!"

It's not like my captor can hear me as he's too busy driving like a bat out of hell.

Hugo will catch up. He has to. He's not going to let this monster get away with taking me. And when Spencer finds out what happened, he'll turn the entire town upside down to find me.

They're coming for me.

They won't leave me.

But your mother went missing, too, and they don't seem to care...

I shove away those toxic thoughts. Thinking they'll abandon me will only make my situation worse. I have to believe they'll be here to save me soon.

I can't breathe.

I'm going to pass out.

Oh God.

After what feels like an eternity of reckless driving, I slam again against the back of the trunk as we turn. The car bounces and groans as we travel over a long gravel drive. It finally rolls to a stop and the engine shuts off.

Fear weighs my body down and a wave of dizziness washes over me again. I get my hands ready, bared like claws, and bring my knees to my chest so I can kick out the second I can.

Gravel crunches beneath his feet as he steps out of the vehicle and then the car door slams. The footsteps make it closer. A fob beep resounds and then the trunk unlatches. Sunlight pours in as he lifts the trunk. I don't waste a second, kicking forward and landing a loud crack on his jaw. It sends him stumbling away and just as he's turned away from me, I scramble out.

On wobbly legs, shaking with terror and adrenaline, I take off running down the gravel driveway. Rocks stab at my bare feet and I cry out in pain. Veering off the road, I step onto the overgrown grass, picking up speed once my feet are no longer being battered.

Where am I?

There aren't any houses around. Only trees.

"Get back here," the man bellows, charging after me.

I screech because he feels too close, running faster than I've ever run in my entire life. My tears blur my vision. I blink them back, needing to focus on my surroundings so I don't—

Slam!

I fall face first on the grass, my ankle screaming in protest, as my foot gets tangled up in an exposed tree root. My teeth bite into my tongue and the metallic taste of blood fills my mouth.

Get up!

I scrabble back to my feet, wincing when I put weight on my sore ankle. I'm about to take off again when my head smarts in pain, making me black out.

"Let go!" I bellow, clawing at the man's hand that's gripping my hair and yanking. "Ow! Stop!"

He drags me by my hair toward him and then easily hefts me over his shoulder, just as he did when he took me from my own backyard. Through my sobs, I beat my fist against his kidneys and claw at whatever skin I can get ahold of. He grunts and smacks the back of my thigh hard.

"Feisty like your mother."

My blood runs cold. He knows Mom?

He walks past his vehicle and onto a wooden porch that's flaking with paint. When he opens a door and steps through the threshold, I grab onto the frame, trying to keep him from taking me into his serial killer lair.

Since he's bigger and stronger, he muscles his way ahead and my arms burn when I'm forced to let go.

"Please," I choke out. "Let me go. I won't tell a soul about this."

His chuckle is dark and manic. "Oh, I want people to know. I want them to know what I'm capable of. That I'll destroy you in whatever means possible unless they give me what I need."

"You want money? Hugo is loaded. They all are. Name your price. They'll pay it," I rush out. "Just let me go."

He ignores me and proceeds to carry me into a bedroom of the small house. I'm tossed onto the mattress, but before I can escape, the man pounces, shoving a knee against my chest. I can't breathe with the pressure he's putting on me and everything turns black.

My eyes flutter back open what must only be seconds later to discover my wrist is zip tied to one corner of the bed. He has my other wrist and is forcefully also zip-tying it, this time to the other corner.

I'm trapped.

Completely at the mercy of a monster.

My hair has come loose from the hair tie and sticks to my sweaty face. From beneath the curtain, I can see him as he walks over to the end of the bed. Testing my restraints, I try to pull my hands to me only to be met with searing pain biting into the flesh of my wrists.

"Let me go," I screech. "Let me go! Let me go! Let me go!"

"Stop being a fucking brat or I'll gag you."

More tears well and flood out. I bite down on my bottom lip, finally taking in the man before me. He's tall and muscular—the kind of guy who spends more time at the gym than anywhere else. His skin is a sun-kissed golden hue and his blond hair that's longish and curling over his ears shimmers in the light.

My monster looks like an angel.

He's older than me and Spencer, but definitely younger than Hugo by at least a decade. The man's green eyes are nearly glowing with some evil emotion I'm completely terrified of.

"You thought you could ignore me?"

I scowl at him, again yanking on the restraints even though it's pointless. "I don't know who the hell you are!"

It's true. I don't know him and I hate how it seems like he knows me. My blood turns cold. Is it someone from LA? Someone I slept with and ghosted on?

"This is all your fault, you know," the man says, ignoring my outburst. "Everything was fine. We were going to be together."

"Who?"

He narrows his eyes at me and purses his Cupid lips. "Me and your mother. Keep up, bitch."

I recoil at his nasty words. "You slept with my mother?"

"I did more than sleep with her," he growls. "I fucking loved her!"

My eyes dart to the bedroom door as though I can make Spencer and Hugo materialize out of sheer will alone. No one appears.

"Mom's married," I say weakly.

His lip curls up and he sneers at me. "Because the sanctity of marriage matters so much to you? You're a manipulator and I liar, Aubrey. I've been observing you for a long-ass time."

A chill races down my spine. This stalker/kidnapper/psycho/serial killer has been "observing" me.

"You're not making any sense." My voice wobbles. "I just want to go home."

He grabs my sore ankle and squeezes it, making me yelp in pain. Then, he produces another zip tie from his pocket. I'm too hurt to fight him, easily giving him access to tie my other ankle to another bedpost corner.

"You may as well get comfortable. You're not going home anytime soon. Hell, you may not go home ever."

Despair coils in my gut.

The reality of my situation hits me harder than the gun to my skull did.

I'm not getting out of here.

Different tactic. Try talking to him.

"I'm sorry," I whisper. "Tell me why I'm here."

His anger melts away and his eyes darken as he rakes his stare over my body. It's then I realize my swimsuit top is askew, brazenly revealing one of my nipples. He runs his tongue over his bottom lip and then grins. "You look just fucking like her. Even your nipples are the same."

My heart races in my chest. I don't like the salacious look on his face. But sex is something I can do. If it keeps him from killing me, I'll seduce him if that's what it takes.

"How do you know my mother?"

He rests a knee on the end of the bed between my spread legs. "We go way back."

"How far back?"

"I've known her since I was seventeen and started my own business. I'd given her my business card and she hired me on the spot." He brings another knee onto the bed and crawls over my body, inspecting every hair and beauty mark along the way. "She has a freckle like this one in almost the same spot, too."

I whimper as his thumb brushes along my lower stomach at the edge of my swimsuit bottoms. The zip ties are cutting into my flesh. A blood rivulet runs down my arm, tickling me along its path.

"We were off and on for years," he explains, fingers trailing up over my ribs. "I fell madly in love with her." He freezes and pain twists his features. "Imagine my heartbreak when she told me she was marrying Hugo fucking Park. Some rich asshole who couldn't love her like I could. It was wrong!"

I flinch at his outburst toward the end but don't say a word, waiting for him to continue.

"She promised me, though, we could still see each other. She said, 'Drew, baby, it'll always be you and me. We need him for the money, but I need you for everything else.' I may have cleaned her pool, but I was more than that."

Drew is his name. And he's the pool cleaner? Never in my years of living with Hugo and Spencer did I ever notice the pool guy. Ever.

"I promised her I'd make us a shit ton of money one day so she could leave him and be with me. Everything was going smoothly until you took things too far and ruined my life."

I gape at him in confusion. "What did I do? I don't even know you."

He hooks a finger under the fabric between my two breasts and pulls hard. I can feel the strings biting painfully into my back and ribs. Squirming, I attempt to roll away from his abuse to no avail. A ripping sound echoes loudly as he finally tears my swimsuit top away, leaving my breasts naked to him.

"Don't touch me," I snap, shooting him a nasty glare. "Do not fucking touch me."

He scoffs, grabbing a handful of one of my tits. "These are real. Your mother's are perfect and symmetrical and expensive. God, I miss her tits." His softer tone when speaking about her changes on a dime and he snarls at me. "When you got it through your slutty head that you wanted to fuck your stepbrother, my world imploded. Neena started behaving differently."

I squirm, attempting to wriggle away from his wandering palm. "I didn't try to fuck him. We just kissed!"

He smacks my tit so hard I see stars. "Shut the fuck up. I know what a whore you are. When your mother put distance between us to 'work on her family,' I lost my shit. You eventually moved away and I thought it was over. That me and Neena could be something again."

I blink at the tears that are forming from the pain of being hit. This guy is a complete nutjob. Delusional. Insane. And I'm his captive. Lovely.

"But she stayed distant. Sure, we still fucked, but her

mind was always elsewhere. I figured she felt guilty about you leaving or something." He grabs a nipple and twists until I'm sobbing. "On one of Neena's and my many breaks, I drove my ass to LA. God, you were such a slut in LA."

Shame burns hot across my skin. How does he know what I did in LA?

"I would go visit several times a year to check up on you. Always fucking and sucking dick." He clucks his tongue. "And I was the only one who knew just what a whore you were. I even tried to tell Neena so she'd let go of the guilt. So we could go back to being a secret couple."

His rough palm roams over my hip and then tugs at a bikini string there. I whimper as he unties the bottoms and fully removes them. I'm naked and at his mercy.

"W-What happened next?" I choke out, eager to keep him talking and not touching.

"Time passed and then Neena stopped taking my calls." He scowls at me. "I thought she was pissed at me again. I fucking left." He chokes, tears welling in his green eyes. "I fucking left and lost myself to the Seattle scene for a bit this past winter. Even told myself I was quitting her for good, and that when summer hit, I just wouldn't go back and clean any of the Parks' pools. That I'd be done with her." One of his tears rolls out and splashes onto my breast. "Which is why I didn't know she was gone until I overheard Tasha bitching about it a few weeks ago."

I shudder as Drew runs his thumb over the wetness of his tear, circling my nipple almost reverently.

"Gone?"

"Missing. And those motherfuckers had something to do with it."

My stomach churns. "Are you sure you didn't kidnap her too? Is she dead and buried in your backyard?"

His hand curls into a fist and he strikes my stomach. Exploding pain sears through me, making me gag. I've never been punched before and it hurts like a bitch.

"Don't speak so callously of your mother," he growls. "She was a queen that had no one to worship her. I was that man but all this other bullshit was in the way!"

The bullshit being her family.

Us.

Me.

"I'm the one who told your dad about you fucking your boss. When I learned Neena was missing and no one fucking cared, I had to do something. Stir up the hornets' nest. I started with your dad and it created a chain of events that drew you back here." He grabs my jaw, fingers biting into me. "I thought I could torment you and those Park fuckers to reveal what they did to her. I could get her back. I knew I could convince her to leave with me, but I had to find her first."

He lets go of my jaw to sit up on his knees, straddling my naked thighs. "Despite my efforts, you were too busy fucking them both to worry about your mother. It's like you forgot about her. You forgot about the love of my fucking life, you selfish cunt!"

I cry out when he strikes me again, this time, the blow landing painfully on my ribs. A howl screeches out of me. I'm going to die. Right here. Right now.

"You look just like her," Drew rumbles. "I'm going to fuck you because you owe it to me for taking her away from me. And then, I'm going to send pictures to everyone you love until someone gives in and tells me where the fuck my woman is." He unhooks his belt and then unfastens his jeans. "I will beat you and fuck you and beat you and fuck you until you're unrecognizable. We'll see how much those Parks care about their favorite toy."

"Please," I beg, choking on a sob. "Please don't do this."

He hits me again, this time glancing across my jaw. I black out again for a dangerous few seconds. When I blink my eyes back open, he's pulling his dick out, a manic, sinister grin on his lips. Fear of what's to come has my body losing control of my faculties. The strong scent of urine fills the air and the bed grows hot and wet beneath me.

"Sick bitch!"

His hands find my throat and he squeezes so tight I'm sure he's crushing my windpipe. I writhe and choke as I attempt to suck in air.

Nothing.

Just the quick blanket of darkness that steals me away.

This time for good.

CHAPTER THIRTY-TWO

Spencer

I HATE THIS PLACE.

I hate it. I hate it. I hate it.

Coming to the lodge every day has become the bane of my existence. I resent it with everything in me. It's a fucking job I didn't plan to take, but once I did, there was no getting out of it.

It can't go on much longer.

Maybe a week?

Less?

Then what?

I can't think past that.

My phone buzzes in my pocket as I exit the lodge and tip my head at my buddy, Davey, who works there. I pull out my phone and groan to see that it's Dad. This has been a day from hell. I can't deal with him right now. I decline the call.

A text pops up immediately after.

Dad: Aubrey was taken at gunpoint. We're at Jude's trying to figure out where the hell he took her.

I gape at my phone, confused by his text. Taken. Aubrey was taken. Fuck!

My feet take off before my brain catches up and I sprint toward my car. I climb in and peel out of the parking lot like my ass is on fire. The limits of my BMW are tested as I swerve around people, going as fast as possible down the mountainside.

Less than ten minutes later, I'm screeching to a halt in front of Jude's house behind several other cars. I fly out of the car, barely remembering to slam the door shut. Not waiting for an invitation, I burst into the house, startling Grandpa, who sits in his wheelchair at the bottom of the stairs.

I take the steps two at a time until I'm in Jude's now-crowded office. From the look and sound of it, everyone is here. Pushing past Gemma and Jamie, I force my way over to where Dad stands behind Jude's desk. Jude is flying through screens of video surveillance recordings of our backyard.

"Who the fuck took her?" I demand, panting heavily from exertion.

Dad spears a hand through his hair and tugs. "We don't know. The guy had a hoodie pulled over his head and was wearing sunglasses. The girls didn't recognize him."

I'm just now realizing Dad is wearing nothing but swim trunks. Willa, Gemma, and Jamie are all wearing coverups over swimsuits. Callum, at least, seems to be dressed like someone ready to chase after a kidnapper in jeans and a T-shirt.

"You all were having a pool party while Aubrey got kidnapped?" I snarl in disgust. "Why didn't you stop him?" This question is aimed at my father.

"I tried," Dad growls. "I was too late."

"Spencer," Pops says from the other side of the office. "Breathe. We're going to find her."

I can't breathe.

Not when some psychopath has *my* girl and is doing fuck knows what to her.

"You recognize this vehicle?" Jude's muffled voice rings out, pointing to the screen.

The camera angle only captures just a section of a white fender on a small sedan. Could be anyone.

"No," I grumble. "Have you looked beyond today? Like this week?"

"I have a program that can search through recordings based on certain criteria," Jude explains. "I'm searching for white vehicles across all the cameras on our road."

Four hundred and seventeen possible matches.

Fucking great.

"This is a waste of time," I snap. "We should be out there looking."

"I'll go with you and we can look," Dempsey offers, revealing himself from a chair in the corner. "I can't sit here idly either."

"Call me if you find anything and we'll investigate," I rush out, turning on my heel.

Dad's hand cups the back of my neck and he squeezes. "We'll find her, Spence. I fucking swear it."

His reassurance matters even though this whole situation feels hopeless. Dad always had the confidence that everything would work out. When he divorced Mom, he assured me everything would be fine and it was. When I accidentally ran over Callum's mailbox at age fifteen, he told me it would be okay. Or that time me and the twins trampled over a wasp nest and we all got stung. He always promised things would be okay and they were. I have to believe him.

I give him a quick nod and then tear out of the office with Dempsey.

"Did ya find the girl?" Grandpa asks as we tromp down the stairs.

"Not yet, but we will," I bite out.

Grandpa gives us a small wave. "No one wrongs our family and gets away with it."

Once we're in the car and barreling down the driveway, I glance over at Dempsey. He's buzzing with energy, sitting up and scanning everything while I drive.

"Dad said he saw the car turn right." He points east. "Head that way first."

I peel out and gun it. This highway weaves in and out of thick areas of trees. There are a few turnoffs along the way. They could be anywhere. It's going to be like searching for a needle in a haystack. Fucking impossible. Still beats sitting back at Jude's twiddling my thumbs.

"Start there," Dempsey says, pointing at the first road on the right. "We'll explore each one of these side roads one at a time."

Since it's impossible to look everywhere at once, I go with his instruction, turning so fast, he has to grab onto the "oh shit" bar to keep from landing in my lap.

This is a damn nightmare.

Where is she?

What's the sadistic fuck doing to her?

If he was brazen enough to kidnap her in broad daylight in front of friends and family, there's no telling what he'd do. Dark images of blood and violence and rape make it to where I can hardly see to drive. Rage boils up inside me. When I find this fucker, I'm going to destroy him. He'll regret the day he ever laid eyes on Aubrey.

The next three roads we go up and down produce nothing. Just old houses and no cars matching the description.

This time when Dad calls, I answer on the first ring. "What?"

"You're not going to believe this," Dad rumbles. "There's footage of Neena climbing into a waiting white sedan over a year ago." He coughs and clears his throat. "You think this bastard took Neena and..." He trails off. "What if he does the same to Aubrey?"

"What's the make and model, Dad?" I demand, bringing him back to the most important thing. Finding Aubrey.

"2018 Chevy Malibu. Your pops has Sloane on the phone. Looking for anyone with a registered vehicle in town matching that make and model." He pauses for a moment. "Anything?" he calls out to Pops. He sighs and then says, "She's looking. Jude is trying to hack into the DMV."

Jude's voice can be heard next. "Five vehicles matching that description. Edna Johnson. Lindsay Wallace. Frank Gotti. Thea Montgomery. Andrew Porterfield."

My blood runs cold. "Drew? As in frat boy wannabe, pool cleaning Drew?"

"Who?" Dad asks.

"Put me on speaker," I bark out.

"You're on."

"Jude, get me Drew's address. Now. The accountant might have it since he's our goddamn pool boy."

Pops curses in the background. Seconds later, Jude rattles out the address.

Less than two miles away.

"We're going to get her," I growl out, peeling out onto the main highway again. "She's close."

"Spencer, don't do anything rash. We're sending Sloane out—"

I end the call and step on the gas.

There's no time for this bullshit.

All that matters is getting to Aubrey.

CHAPTER THIRTY-THREE

Aubrey

EVERYTHING HURTS.

Why does everything hurt?

I've been kidnapped by my mother's old lover. It's all coming back to me—the kidnapping, being bound to his bed, the abuse.

I slowly come to, too afraid to open my eyes, taking stock of my injuries. My hands are completely numb due to lack of circulation, my ankle is throbbing, the zip ties cutting into me no longer hurt compared to the nauseating pain in my ribs. Maybe, if I pretend to be asleep, he'll leave me alone.

My breathing has picked up despite my effort to keep it even. Tears burn at my eyes, but I manage to keep them safely dammed behind my eyelids. I'm parched and my throat hurts something fierce, but I don't dare ask for water.

The bed is still wet where I peed. From sheer terror. One good thing about wetting myself is he was so disgusted that he stopped his efforts to rape me.

What happens when he knows I'm awake?

I desperately keep the whine that's lodged in my throat at bay.

"You want her back?" Drew growls. "Then give me what I want. Tell me where the fuck my girlfriend's body is. I know you crazy motherfuckers had her killed."

Panic claws at my chest.

Stay quiet.

Don't move.

As much as I wish to cry out, begging whoever is on the other line to save me, I can't take that chance. If he's recording a video and not a live call, I'll compromise myself.

"I'll hack her to pieces and send you a body part each day," Drew threatens. "And then I'll take out each and every one of you one by one just like I did Tasha." He chuckles, dark and cruel. "But that bitch just wouldn't die, would she? There's always time. Later."

My body shudders so hard the bed squeaks. Dumb girl. Dumb, dumb girl. Get a hold of yourself.

Something cold and metal presses against my pussy. I shriek in surprise. No!

"Ahh, the little princess has awakened. Were you trying to trick me, bitch? Open your goddamn eyes!"

I sob as my eyes open. Drew comes into view. His face is maniacal, gaze darting all over, pupils so tiny they've nearly disappeared. There's no escaping this monster. He could pull the trigger at any second and I'd bleed out through my pussy of all places.

I gag and then I gag again.

I'm going to be sick.

Vomit rushes up and I'm helpless to stop it. It projectiles across my torso against my will. I'm going to die like this. What a horrible way to die.

"Nasty fucking bitch," Drew snaps, pulling back and slamming the gun down on the dresser. "You're ruining my fucking sheets!"

He pulls a knife out of his jeans pocket and flips it open.

The sadistic glint in his eyes has me howling in terror. I cry out when he grabs my sore ankle.

He's going to chop me up just like he said.

Loud, hysterical sobs wrench out of me. I'm trapped and alone and going to die.

Snap!

Drew cuts through the zip tie and starts working on the other one. "Your filthy ass is going in the shower before I fucking touch you. How the hell am I supposed to get and keep my dick hard when you're pissing and puking?"

He removes the zip tie at my wrist and manages to saw through the other one quickly. My muscles are burning and stiff from being stuck in the same position. I try to move my limbs to me, but they tremble violently, the muscles twitching of their own accord.

I'd thought I could fight him off if I ever got free, but I can't move. Oh God. I can't move. I attempt to roll away to no avail.

Shouts.

Two male voices.

I think hope is playing tricks on me.

"Fuck," Drew snarls, grabbing hold of my hair and pulling me to my knees. "How the fuck did they find me?"

It's not a trick.

It's real.

Someone is here to save me.

Thundering footsteps head our way. I want to cry out in joy, but Drew digs the tip of the knife into my neck just deep enough to break the skin but not tear through muscle and veins.

Then, my saviors reveal themselves. Spencer and

Dempsey. I'm so happy to see them I don't even care that I'm naked, dripping in pee and vomit, or that snot coats my upper lip.

Spencer's normally antagonistic face is twisted into one of pure fear. Fear for me. The expression on his face makes him appear as though he's a child having a nightmare.

"You've been caught, pool boy," Spencer grinds out, voice shaking. "Might as well give up now. The cops are on the way."

"After years of cleaning your goddamn pool, you finally connect me?" Drew bellows. "I fucking loved Neena and saw her every chance I could. You Parks have your heads so far up your asses, you don't even see what's happening around you!"

He drags the knife tip through my skin, tearing the top layer. I cry out in pain, shooting Spencer a panicked, pleading look through teary eyes.

"We saw you," Spencer taunts, finding his arrogant tone I love so much. "You just didn't matter. You're unimportant."

"Not to Neena!" Drew roars. "I was her everything!"

Spencer sneers. "Funny. She never mentioned fucking the pool boy. Aww. Did you think she was going to run away with you? Give up her million-dollar life to shack it up in a shithole like this?" He gestures wide, indicating Drew's house, his fingertips coming close to the gun sitting on the dresser. "Keep fucking dreaming, dude. Neena's a spoiled brat who used you for your dick."

"*Was* a spoiled brat," Drew hisses. "But you took care of that, didn't you? I know you motherfuckers killed my woman! Where the fuck did you drop her body? You're all going down!"

At that exact moment, Dempsey darts to my left, distracting Drew. My eyes are on Spencer and I watch as he swiftly picks up the gun. I let my head lol to the side and clench my eyes closed.

Pop!

The loud gun firing so close to my head is too much. Drew lets go of me and I flop uselessly to the messy bed.

"You shot my fucking ear off!" Drew screams.

Pop! Pop!

Thud.

I think it's gone silent, but the ringing in my ears over-shadows all else. Hands grab onto me, roughly yanking me up.

"N-No," I choke out, trying to escape Drew's grasp.

But it's not Drew.

I recognize these smooth hands. Fingers that have been on me and inside me.

"I've got you, leech. I've got you now."

He pulls me to his chest, hugging me to him, and rains kisses down on my head. I've never felt such complete and utter relief.

I'm alive.

They got here in time and saved me.

"I hear sirens," Dempsey barks out. "Wrap her up in this while I wipe your prints."

A sheet is thrown at us and Spencer dutifully obeys, wrapping the thin material around me to shield me from onlookers.

"Wait," Spencer rasps out. "Why are you wiping my prints from the gun?"

"Because, dumbass, you're eighteen. I'm still underage. Plus, Dad can get me out of this much easier than my brother can get you out of it. Hugo's under scrutiny with the campaign and they're going to start asking questions about Neena. It'll spread quicker and we won't be able to contain it."

"Fuck," Spencer mutters. "You're right. They're also going to want to know this guy's motive."

"He stalked her," Dempsey supplies. "Saw her while cleaning your pool, wanted her, and then kidnapped her. That's it. No need to bring in his connection with Neena."

Dempsey fires off another shot into Drew's body, this time in the chest. I'm no expert, but I've seen enough crime shows to know they're covering their tracks, making sure Dempsey will have gunshot residue on his hands, solidifying their coverup.

"We're going with that story, understood?" Spencer asks me. "It'll be the safest and quickest way to get us cleared of all this. When Dad gets here, he'll follow our lead."

I nod even though it hurts my sore neck to do so. I don't care what Spencer and Dempsey tell the cops. I just want this day to be over and done with. My whole body hurts and I feel disgusting.

"I want to go home," I whisper, more tears spilling. "The only thing I need is you and Hugo."

He hugs me tighter. "You have us. No one can hurt you ever again. I promise."

With my abduction, Drew managed to get inside my head. Something *else* happened to Mom. Something no one wants to fess up to. Eventually, I'll press the issue, but right now I'm just thankful to be alive and in the arms of one of the men I love.

"Is he dead?" I croak out.

"A bullet to the ear, face, and neck. Yeah, he's dead."

"I want to see."

Spencer groans. "That's a terrible idea."

"He hurt me. I want to see his body."

He lets out a resigned sigh before shifting me in his lap. I peer down at Drew's unmoving form. It's gruesome to see so much blood. There's a gaping hole on the side of his neck and a smaller hole that went in his face just above his eye and below his eyebrow.

He's dead.

This man can't torment me ever again. No more snakes or kidnappings or beatings. He's dead. How could my mother even care for someone as twisted as him?

"Spencer! Aubrey!"

Hugo's voice booming as he enters the house has me crying out with joy. He storms into the room, curses, and then steps over Drew's body to sit on the other side of me. His hand grips my jaw that's smeared with vomit and he turns me to look at him.

I know I'm a mess.

But he looks at me like I'm the most precious and beautiful thing he's ever seen.

"So happy you're alive, Love," Hugo murmurs, leaning his forehead against mine. "So fucking happy."

"I threw up," I say, beginning to notice the smells coming from my body.

"Pissed all over the place too," Spencer adds, burrowing his face in my hair. "You smell fucking awful, leech."

I cry with happiness because despite his mean words, he's holding me like I might vanish. His lips are kissing me near my ear.

"You know we love you," Hugo assures me. "Even when you're messy. *Especially* when you're messy."

He dips forward, kissing the corner of my mouth that I hope is dry of vomit, completely forgetting we have an audience.

"Well, fuck me," Dempsey mutters. "I am *not* seeing this shit."

Hugo stiffens and Spencer laughs.

There's no time for an explanation because seconds later, the tiny home of a monster fills with policemen and police-women, Sloane leading the fray.

I'm bloody and bruised and sore beyond belief. I'm covered in bodily fluids and wearing splatters of another man's blood. My body won't stop shivering and my mind is a mess.

But I'm safe.

My guys came for me and I'm safe.

This nightmare is finally over.

CHAPTER THIRTY-FOUR

Hugo
Two weeks later…

THE BRUISING HAS FADED ON HER BODY AND THE stitches on her neck are gone. It's her eyes that still carry the pain from that horrible day. She'll need to see a therapist and soon. Unfortunately, because of our name, we have to find someone discreet—someone who will take heaps of money to keep their mouth shut. I'm afraid that when the therapist opens Pandora's box with Aubrey, she's going to let spill a whole lot of shit that involves both me and my son.

It's selfish and wrong to deny her the help she needs until we find the right therapist, but I'm not just protecting her. I'm protecting my son too. Hell, I'm protecting the whole family.

Aubrey's not in her room. She houses all of her things there, but she rarely steps foot in there unless to grab clothes or a quick shower. As far as sleeping, she does that in Spencer's bed or mine. Thankfully, she takes turns, allowing us each our time with her. Every night she's with me, she wakes in a panic, gasping for breath and sobbing. I need to sort out this therapist and quick because she needs something to help her sleep.

While I wait on Dad's text, I turn the knob to Spencer's room and peek in on them. Spencer isn't wearing a shirt and the sheets barely cover his waist. Aubrey is wearing one of my

T-shirts. Her body is glued to his side, head buried in his neck and leg thrown over his thighs. It's the same way she sleeps when in my bed, except she's usually wearing his T-shirts.

I shut the bedroom door and head toward my home office. Dad calls rather than text. I answer on the first ring.

"Hey, Dad."

"Son." Papers shuffle in the background. "How is Aubrey? The girls are asking after her."

"Gets a little better each day," I admit, "but she has nightmares every night. We have to get her some help."

"I think I found the perfect person. He can't keep a job at any of the centers. Keeps getting fired."

I make a beeline for the coffee maker in the kitchen, needing to shake away the dregs of sleep because this isn't making a lick of sense.

"Why do we want to hire someone who can't stay employed?"

Dad chuckles. "Because, despite not being able to keep his job anywhere, Tate Prince is educated, lacks family, not a local, and is drowning in debt. He'll accept considerable pay for his discretion."

My stomach tightens, not liking how deep Dad has dived into this for Aubrey, whom I'm certain he doesn't even like all that much. I know it's not just to make me happy. Dad is a great father, but there's always an ulterior motive to everything.

"Dad…"

"Hear me out," he says, a grin in his voice. "Mr. Prince would be paid to be our primary mental health care provider. Live on the premises and be available to everyone."

And here comes the ulterior motive.

"Aubrey's the only one needing it at the moment," I

mumble. "This seems like a lot of effort and money for a guy to listen to her a few times a week and prescribe sleeping meds."

"We all know Dempsey's out of control and could use someone to talk to," Dad grunts, humor evaporating from his voice. "Callum's had his fair share of heartache and trauma."

That you caused…

I don't say that out loud, of course.

"And Jude," I say with a sigh. "He won't do therapy. You know that."

"Perhaps not directly, but if we can ease Mr. Prince into our family dynamics, it's possible for him to help Jude inadvertently."

"Jude rarely leaves his cave."

"Which is why Mr. Prince will be taking up residence in that cavernous house alongside my father and your brother."

"This is going to go over like a lead balloon."

"Jude is suffering," Dad says with a sigh, "but he's not heartless. He loves his family. He knows what Aubrey went through and isn't going to disturb that. Like I said, we'll ease him into it."

I try to imagine a day when my brother pulls the mask off. The fire that killed Mom destroyed my brother both inside and out because he couldn't save her. Taking off the mask means showing the rest of us the pain and scars that were left behind.

"Yeah, okay," I say with a sigh. "Aubrey can't wait any longer. How quickly can you make this happen?"

"I'm working on it as we speak. I may not be able to talk Mr. Prince into uprooting his entire life right away, but at the very least, I'll make contact with him and get the ball rolling."

We hang up and I stare at the coffee machine. I don't

need coffee. I need to run. It's the only thing that clears my head and resets my focus.

I quickly change into my running clothes and then slip out the back door. The pool sparkles now, but that's because of me. After the whole Drew debacle, I'm hesitant to let anyone who isn't family onto my property. I jog through Callum's backyard and then turn left, toward the street. The pavement echoes the rhythmic sounds back at me as I pick up my pace. When I reach the end of the road where Jude and Grandpa live, I try to see the monstrous home from an outsider's point of view.

Old. Dilapidated. Haunted by the ghosts of those who are no longer with us.

Dad's going to have a helluva time getting anyone who isn't family to step foot into that place. I crack my neck and sprint past it toward my trail.

My mind drifts to the day of Aubrey's kidnapping. The anger of what happened and fear of losing her is what fuels me to run at an incredibly taxing speed. Burning in my hamstrings and calves feels better than the agony I'd felt when I imagined her death at the hands of that psychopath.

It's really fucked-up to know Neena was screwing the pool boy. Who else was she screwing while we were married? I know about the yoga instructor and some asshole she went to college with. I'm sure there are more. For some reason, I kept enduring and staying with her. Now, after all that's happened, I won't hesitate to slap the divorce papers in her face the next time I see her.

If I see her.

If Drew came after Aubrey because he hasn't been able to locate his lover, then that means something really has happened to Neena. I've spent nearly a year being pissed at her for leaving me high and dry, but never really considered her death.

Was this one of Dad's "fixes" for our family? He'd go to great lengths to protect us.

Or was it Spencer? He's certainly doing something suspicious because he continues to run around using her card every day to keep up appearances.

Dad and Spencer are close. Maybe they concocted something together.

I slow to a stop at a huge boulder in the woods. It's covered in black sharpie writing from the years. We've all made our mark here. The most recent ones belong to Dempsey—skull drawings, curse words, and Spencer's number to "call for a good time."

Dempsey has now taken the rap for both Callum and Spencer. I don't know what gave him this martyr complex, but we have to stop letting him take the fall, because if we don't he will end up with more than a slap on the wrist. He might permanently find himself behind bars.

The birds chirp and the wind blows gently through the trees. Is her body buried out here? I wouldn't put it past Dempsey and Spencer burying her right under the path I run on all the time.

Could my son really kill my wife?

He shot Drew without hesitation. Three times, in fact. He shot him because he was protecting someone he loved. Would killing Neena be his way of protecting me and our family?

My gut churns. If he did, it's my responsibility to keep him protected from the outside world. Damn. Dad's right. This whole family needs therapy and with someone we can trust. Spencer has had a helluva few years. Ever since Aubrey left when they were both sixteen, he's been harder, sharper around the edges, chronically angry.

I can't have Spencer continue to cover up her death all on his own. That's what he's doing after all. My son is smart and using her card to purchase all the things she always loved was brilliant at keeping eyes off the situation. He was protecting me one hundred percent. When I get back home, I'll need to see if Jude can help me create a new trail that shows Neena traveling up to Canada and disappearing from our lives for good. Spencer will finally be off the hook and we can put this behind us.

"Goodbye, Neena," I say to the trees. "I hope it was painless."

I don't want to think of how she was killed because then I'll need therapy too. With a heavy sigh, I start my jog back home.

The shower is hot, but I can't escape the chill that's settled in my bones. My family has always had our secrets, but whatever happened to Neena feels like the biggest one of all. I want to sit my family in a giant circle and demand everyone's involvement. Because if Spencer murdered Neena, he had help.

Dempsey. Dad. Theo. Jude.

I shut off the water and quickly towel off. I'm walking into my bedroom when I discover Aubrey is in it. She's no longer wearing my shirt and the sheet exposes her breasts. Yellow bruises still color her ribs and the pink scar on her neck will forever be visible. But she's safe and alive.

"Good morning, Love. What are you up to?"

I head for my dresser, but she sits up, shaking her head. "I need you."

"What do you need?"

"*You*," she says in exasperation. "No one will touch me. Not after…" She trails off and her bottom lip wobbles. "Drew didn't rape me. I'm not ruined."

"No one said you are ruined," I growl, tossing the towel to the floor and prowling toward the bed. "We're just letting you heal."

We.

As in my son hasn't had sex with her either.

My heart thunders with pride. Sometimes he behaves like an evil shit, but he's good deep down. He loves Aubrey and wants to protect her, same as me.

"This is how I heal," she clips out. "Until then, I'll be trapped on his bed, with his gun pressing down on my pussy, with his grimy hands stripping my clothes away."

"Where's Spencer?" I ask as I crawl over her body.

"Running errands. Again." She looks away from me, frowning. "He left not long after you went on your run. I tried to get him to touch me, but he blew me off."

Her hurt is palpable. By us trying to give her the space to heal, we've made her feel unwanted and unloved. That changes today.

I bring my lips to hers, kissing her softly at first, and then dive deeper, thrashing my tongue against her own. She moans and I devour that too. My hips settle against her, the thin sheet the only thing between us, and I rub my hard dick against her.

Her legs slide out from under the sheet, hooking around my waist. It feels good to be intimate like this with her again.

The fire that rages between us is always so uncontrollable, burning everything, including my morals, in its path.

I start kissing down her chin and to her neck on a path to her pussy when I sense a presence.

My son.

"I deny you my dick and you run to Daddy. Classic move, leech."

"Spencer," I warn. "Knock it off."

"Nah, Dad," Spencer growls. "I think I'll join instead."

CHAPTER THIRTY-FIVE

Aubrey

FINALLY.

For two full weeks, I've felt like a leper. Like Drew had tainted me in some way that kept Hugo and Spencer from ever wanting me again. It was a horrifying thought—one that kept me up for hours every night.

But that changes now.

Hugo's mouth is on my breast, sucking and teasing with his tongue. Spencer has quickly shed his clothes and is sliding onto the bed beside us. He tugs away the sheet and tosses it off the bed.

"She likes to be fingerfucked, Dad," Spencer says, slipping a hand between us. "Watch how she comes undone."

Hugo stiffens and then relaxes, eyes moving up to meet mine. He sucks on my nipple hard. Spencer's finger finds my clit that's finally no longer sore from how Drew shoved his gun against it. My eyes slam shut.

I feel the cold metal.

Images of blood.

"It's us," Hugo rumbles, breath hot on my breast. "You're here. With us."

His voice is a rope and I grab onto it, allowing him to pull me out of the dark abyss. Spencer's soft fingertip expertly rubs me in just the right way.

This feels good.

They feel good.

"Oh," I croak out and then bite down on my bottom lip.

Spencer rubs me straight into my first orgasm since the incident. As soon as I cry out, leaping over the edge of bliss, he slips two fingers inside me. He's right. I love getting finger-fucked. I also love how Spencer tests the limits of my body, adding more fingers, stretching me more than going deep.

It's almost like he's been preparing for something.

Images assault me again, but these are forbidden and fiery hot. I wonder if they'd ever try to take me at once.

"Dad," Spencer rumbles. "Feel inside of her. She likes this."

Hugo groans and sits up on his knees. His eyes are lava as he draws them to where Spencer is still fucking me with four fingers.

"Get the lube," he instructs Spencer. "I don't want to hurt her."

I whine at the loss of Spencer's hand. I'm so empty now. I need them to fill me.

I'm transfixed by the way Spencer coats his fingers with lube and then grabs his dad's hand, spreading it over his fingers as well. Their fingers thread together, making sure to get the lube on every inch of their digits. They pull their hands apart and then Spencer's fingers are back inside, easily sliding in. Hugo lies down beside me, mouth close to mine, and slips a finger in with Spencer's.

Five fingers total.

Still not as thick as either of their dicks.

"More," I whimper.

Hugo's mouth seals over mine and then I feel the

delicious burn as my body stretches to accommodate more of his fingers. Spencer's tongue finds my other breast and he nips at the flesh. Neither of them stops moving their hands, stretching and reaching deep and rubbing all the sweet spots.

It's too much.

It's not enough.

"I need," I rasp out. "Oh, fuck, I need more."

Spencer slips his hand out and rolls onto his back. "Get on my dick, leech."

Hugo pulls his hand away and then smacks my pussy. "Listen like a good girl, Love."

With shaky limbs, I scramble over to Spencer. My mouth falls to his, kissing him eagerly as I rub my pussy against his body until I'm sliding over his cock.

"Guide her in, Dad," Spencer rumbles.

I feel Hugo's hand between us, helping Spencer's cock to push inside me. Then, Hugo's fingers are also pushing inside. It's wild and crazily delicious.

"You want us both fucking you, Love, don't you? Need us both inside your pretty pussy, owning every inch of you?"

I whimper and moan. "Y-Yes. Oh God."

Hugo's fingers slip out as he gets on his knees. His palms find my hips as he straddles us both. I gasp when I feel the head of his thick cock, rubbing against my pussy lip. Spencer's movements are shallow but steady.

"Is this possible?" I croak out. "Will I break?"

Spencer chuckles. "Nothing could ever break you, baby. You're a Park."

Not really. Not legally. But in spirit? Hell yeah.

"Hugo," I beg. "I need to feel you too."

He grabs for the lube and starts pouring generous

amounts down my ass crack. Spencer hisses when Hugo coats not only my pussy lips but also his dick. Then, Hugo grunts. Slurping sounds can be heard as he slicks up his own cock.

"If you cry," Spencer murmurs, "it'll just turn me on more. I'll lick up the tears you make from letting a father and son tag team you."

"I won't cry." I nip at his lip. "I want this."

Hugo takes that as permission to proceed. He starts working the head of his cock into the same hole his son is deep inside. It burns like nothing else I've felt. Tears fill my eyes, but I don't want to stop. I don't care if they rip me in two. I need this. I need to feel them. I need to take this sensation everywhere I go, long after this moment is over.

Hugo's crown teases in and out, slowly. It's torture, but I understand the need to take his time. A woman isn't designed to fit two dicks inside her at once.

If a woman can have a baby, surely she can take two large cocks.

A vagina was meant to stretch and change shape.

"Fuck," Hugo hisses. "Fuck, this is intense."

Spencer growls beneath me, biting my jaw and then my ear. It must feel good for him too, another slick cock rubbing up against his.

Droplets of sweat from Hugo drip onto my back. His hold on my hip is painful. Bruising. I'll have another reminder of this moment. A grin tugs at my lips even as Spencer bites at my bottom one.

Pain burns hot as my body slowly stretches. Hugo pours more and more lube all over us, making everything slick. His other hand presses down onto my back, forcing me against Spencer, sandwiched between them.

And then he thrusts.

Shallow at first, but it's enough to make me scream.

From pain? Pleasure? Both?

He doesn't stop. He goes deeper. Harder. And then they're both moving—in and out, going opposite ways as the other. It's painful and also the most incredible thing I've ever felt.

"Fuck, you're perfect, Love," Hugo snarls, hips relentlessly ramming forward now that he's found his way inside. "Taking two big dicks at once. Fucking amazing."

"Our sexy little slut," Spencer rumbles. "Not satisfied unless her cunt is stuffed by her daddy and brother."

Their words are dizzying. Wrong but oh-so-right.

I'm lost to the sensation of them. It's more than I ever could have imagined for myself. I don't want it to end. I want to stay with them forever. Just like this.

"C-Come inside me," I choke out. "I want to feel you both coming."

Hugo thrusts harder, as does Spencer. We're all sweaty and moaning and panting. It's messy and beautiful. And then I feel it. Pulsing. Throbbing. Wet heat flooding inside me. I'm not sure who came first, but both dicks are vibrating, releasing spurt after spurt of cum. Something about the forbidden feeling coupled with the sensation sends another wave of ecstasy rippling through me.

I'm not sure if it's an orgasm of the body or the soul.

Regardless, I tremble and quake, long after they both pull out of me. Long after I'm cleaned up with a towel. Long after I'm wearing both their sweaty arms across my chest as I stare up at the ceiling.

I may tremble forever.

Hugo's lips find my scar and he kisses it. "No one can ever know about this, Love. You hear me, Spencer? No one."

"Not going to tell everyone I had a threesome with my dad," Spencer grumbles.

Hugo winces and I laugh. A river of cum runs out of me, soaking the towel that's been placed beneath me.

"Not even Dempsey," Hugo says. "I know he suspects something, but it doesn't mean he needs details or even confirmation. Understood? No one can know what we three get up to behind closed doors."

"So this wasn't a one-time thing?" Spencer taunts.

Hugo sits up and arches a brow at him. "I don't know how we could possibly stop at this point."

I run my fingers through Hugo's hair and then my other through Spencer's. "We can't. I refuse to. I'll take this secret to my grave if I have to, but I won't ever give you two up."

They both relax at my sides.

They won't give me up either.

Days pass by in a blur. I've had more sex in the past few days than I've had all month. Hugo and Spencer are insatiable. Sometimes they fuck me individually—at night in Spencer's bed or behind Hugo's closed office door while at work. Most often, they corner me after dinner, the three of us coming together in a way absolutely no one would approve of. I'm raw and sore between my legs, but my heart has never felt so healed and full.

The movie we're watching is a dumb sci-fi flick with bad CGI. I'm not here for the movie, though. I'm curled up in Hugo's lap, lazily playing with the hair at his nape while

Spencer rubs my feet. Together, like this, I'm the happiest. It feels complete.

My phone buzzes and I look down at it.

Tasha: Harold is threatening everyone's jobs again.

I smirk, thinking about Aunt Tasha still all bandaged up and laid up in a hospital bed. I've been by just about every day to see her. Now that she's stable and healing, she's been her usual demanding self. And Harold, her doting old man husband, has been valiantly fighting her battles for her. For everyone who said she married him for his money, they don't know the real Harold and Tasha. Those two love each other immensely.

Me: I'm surprised Harold hasn't bought the hospital just to fire everyone on the spot for grins and giggles.

Tasha: Don't tempt him. I'll be able to go home soon, though. The hospital should be safe.

I send her a bunch of heart eye emojis. She'll need plastic surgery once her face heals, but at least she's alive. She knows I was abducted and hurt, but she doesn't know it was Mom's ex-boyfriend. Some secrets have to stay secret.

The doorbell rings and Hugo groans. Spencer huffs, pushing my feet out of his lap and standing. If it were a family member, it's likely they'd let themselves in, hence why we don't do anything in the living room for fear of being caught. If someone is at the door, it's someone else.

A few seconds later, Spencer yells at us, "Dad! The police are here!"

Hugo and I bound to our feet. He races ahead of me. We

make it to the front door where Spencer is glaring out the window beside the door.

"What do they want?" I ask, voice tight with fear. The last time I saw the cops, I'd been naked and a victim. The memory physically hurts and sends terror surging through my veins.

"I don't know," Hugo rumbles. "Let me do the talking."

He pushes Spencer aside and unlocks the door. When he opens it, four officers are standing on the porch. The lights from two squad cars are illuminating the darkness with flashes of red and blue.

"Can I help you?" Hugo says, squaring his shoulders. "Is everything okay?"

"It's about your missing wife," one of the officers says, voice tight. "I'm so sorry, sir."

She's dead.

They found her body.

Oh God.

Bile creeps up my throat. I'd been perfectly content hoping she'd just bailed, leaving this town to go after her own desires. When Drew took me, though, I'd had real stirrings of doubt about my wishful thinking. Everything pointed to her death. I was too eager to step into her place and pretend it wasn't true.

"Why are you sorry?" Hugo asks, voice husky.

"She was found at the lodge," the officer reveals.

Spencer curses and kicks the wall beside the door. The officer's hand goes to his gun. Panic rises up inside me. I clutch onto Spencer's arm, attempting to calm him down. He seems angry, not upset or shocked.

"I'm sorry, Mr. Park, but we have to do this. We're placing your son under arrest."

Hugo gasps. "W-What? No. You can't do that. He didn't kill anyone. My son's not a murderer."

Except he *did* kill someone.

He killed Drew.

"Murder?" the officer snaps. "No, sir. We're arresting him for the kidnapping and unlawful imprisonment of your wife."

What?

"She's alive?" I croak out, the world around me spinning and closing in.

The officer smiles at me. "They're taking her to the hospital now, but she's alive."

I fall to my knees as the gravity of his words sinks in. Mom's alive. She's alive, but Spencer's been keeping her in captivity and now he's going to jail because of it.

She'll come back to her husband.

My lover.

Oh God.

CHAPTER THIRTY-SIX

Hugo

SPENCER OPENS HIS MOUTH TO SPEAK TO ME, EYES burning with shame and regret.

"Don't say anything, Spence," I bark out as they cuff my son. "Pops will be there soon." Then, I turn to Aubrey, who's pale and sitting on her knees. "Get my father on the phone, Love. Now."

She scrambles to her feet and pulls her phone from her pocket. Her hands shake as she makes the call.

"What happened?" I demand to the officer whose name tag reads Knowles. "I need you to tell me everything."

Knowles steps out of the way to let two of the officers guide Spencer out of the house and toward one of the waiting squad cars. The other officer, Jimenez, stands beside Knowles, arms crossed over his beefy chest.

"Apparently, there's a wedding happening soon, and the lodge was booked to capacity. A couple just checked into their room and were talking when they heard Mrs. Park's cries for help through the wall. They contacted the front desk. One of the lodge staffers opened the room up and found your wife being held captive." He frowns. "They called the station and she told us who was responsible."

I scrub a palm over my face. "And you believed her?"

Knowles exchanges a confused look with Jimenez. "She

was shackled by her ankle and a chain that was anchored to the bed frame." His brow furls. "Mrs. Park was hysterical and in a lot of pain, but she was quite clear about who did that to her. It was your son, Mr. Park. I'm sorry."

"He's on his way," Aubrey blurts out behind me. "Nathan is on his way."

Knowles tenses at the mention of Dad. Despite the obvious evidence against my son, no one wants to have to deal with Dad.

"I understand you want to protect your son," Knowles says gently, "but your wife needs you right now. Would you like an escort to the hospital, Mr. Park? I know this is a lot to take in."

Before I can answer, a news van pulls up, and then two more are on its trail. Fuck. Dad trots our way, face stern.

"Come on," I say to Aubrey. "Let's get to the hospital before this turns into a shitshow."

"I'll handle it," Dad assures me, waving me off. "Let me speak with these officers and then I'll head up to the station."

I can't believe this is happening.

My son has just been hauled away in cuffs and I'm about to see my wife for the first time in what feels like an eternity. And this relationship with Aubrey... What happens next?

Everything in my life is blowing up in my goddamn face.

I want to grab Aubrey's hand and squeeze it, promising everything will be okay, but I can't lie to her. I have no idea what the hell is going to happen. All I know is we're striding through the hospital, eyes on us both, the subject of a lot of hushed whispers.

Word travels fast in this town.

"I'm here to see, uh, my wife," I grunt to a receptionist, hating how I cringe at the statement. "They brought her here by ambulance."

The woman, whom I don't know but who clearly knows me, nods and taps on her computer. "Ah, Mr. Park, they're still in the ER, getting her prepped for surgery."

Surgery?

Spencer, Son, what did you do?

Aubrey sways on her feet beside me. I grab her shoulder and pull her to my side. I'm just a stepfather comforting his stepdaughter. Nothing to see here, folks.

"Is she going to be okay?" Aubrey asks, voice trembling. "Will she live?"

The receptionist frowns at her. "I should hope so, dear. Women deliver babies all the time and survive. Cesareans are common. I'm sure everything will be okay."

Blood rushes to my ears.

"What did you say?" I grind out.

"Oh," the receptionist whispers. "I assumed this was her daughter. Should I have not said anything? I didn't realize."

The poor woman looks like she might cry.

I'm not going to fucking sue her.

"Take us there," I demand.

She nods. "I can escort you, Mr. Park, since you're the husband, but they'll only allow one person back during the surgery. Again, I'm so sorry."

"G-Go," Aubrey hisses. "Hugo, just go. Mom needs you."

I give her a long look, hating how broken she is right now. We'd just gotten her to a good place after everything that happened with Drew and now this.

"I'll call Callum or Dempsey to come sit with you," I tell her and press a kiss to her forehead. "Everything's going to be okay, Love. I promise."

Her eyes are watery, but she nods, putting on a brave face. I leave her without another word. The aftertaste of my lie on my tongue is bitter.

How will this be okay?

The next few minutes are a blur as I'm ushered into a room where I change into scrubs and wash up. Then, I'm pointed to the doors that lead to the surgery room—to the first time I'll see my wife in nearly a year.

I stare past the bustling of nurses and doctors at the body on the table, stomach swollen and bare. Fuck. It's really her. It's really Neena. Pregnant. With my child.

It all makes sense now.

She probably got pregnant and said or did something that freaked Spencer out. He did this to protect me.

I walk around where the sheets are tied up and latch onto the cold eyes of Neena Park. Her blond hair is nice and silky, clearly not the hair of a horribly kept captive. She's even wearing makeup. Flawless as per usual. Her plump lips twist into an ugly sneer.

"Get this baby out of me," she hisses. "I hate these people. This family. I don't want this thing inside me!"

I drop into the seat beside her and take her hand, the one that is adorned with the massive diamond ring I bought her years ago. Her nails are painted and pretty. Not her usual acrylics but beautiful nonetheless.

Spencer took care of her. All the places he shopped at were to bring her the things she was used to and loved. My son isn't a complete monster.

"Don't touch me," she snarls. "Your family is poison."

"Neena—"

"When I finally get this baby out of me, I'm going to wring its neck, Hugo. I'm going to kill it." She glowers at me. "They're destroying my body!"

"Neena," I growl, squeezing her hand. "You're talking crazy."

"Crazy? Your son kept me captive and forced me to have this child!"

"Stop. Just stop."

Her eyes sparkle with familiar cruelty. "I'll make you watch as I kill it."

"Neena, you would never hurt a baby. I know you think you mean it, but you don't."

A hand touches my back. It's the doctor. "I'm going to give her a little something to relax her, Mr. Park. Sometimes women lash out and don't know what they're saying."

Neena bellows and within seconds it turns into murmurs. Her eyes flutter closed.

My mind reels at her words. So vicious and nasty. I suppose if I were held captive for as long as she was, I'd be pissed too.

We'll deal with her anger later. Right now, getting our baby out of her is the most important thing. The rest will get dealt with in due time.

"It's a boy," the doctor says cheerfully, jerking me from my inner thoughts. "A healthy big boy."

I tear my stare from Neena's closed eyes to the bloody, squawking baby in one of the nurse's hands. Holy shit. Holy fucking shit. I'm reminded back to when Spencer was born. When my entire world shifted on its axis. Another son.

They wrap the baby in a blanket and hand him over to me. I gape at the squirming infant, shocked at how this day took a turn in a way I never expected.

I have another son.

"Hey there, little man," I murmur, blinking back a wave of emotion. "Were you playing hide-n-seek from Daddy?"

The baby wails.

What do we name him?

Does Neena have something picked out?

I don't know what's happening with my life right now, but I do know one thing for sure. No matter what, this baby will be loved and taken care of. This baby is a Park.

I'm holding a bottle, feeding the little man, when Callum and Aubrey walk through the door of a family room I've been assigned to. The relief at seeing them is crushing. I nearly collapse beneath it.

"You're here," I rasp out.

Callum's brows are arched high on his forehead. Aubrey's eyes are swollen red from crying. I want to hold her in my arms, but the baby is our priority right now. This baby needs us.

"Where's Mom?" Aubrey asks, voice raspy.

"On psychiatric watch," I say with a sigh. "She was spewing nonsense about…" I swallow hard. "Hurting this little guy."

"Guy?" Aubrey whispers. "I have a brother?"

Yes, Love, this is your half-brother.

And I'm still your stepdad.

"I can't believe this," Callum says, pacing the room. "This is so fucked-up, man."

I snort in agreement. "You're telling me." And he doesn't even know half of it. "Have you talked to Dad? How's my other son?"

"Dad was meeting with his buddy, Joseph, the hospital administrator." He drops down into a chair across from me. "Doing what Dad does best. Damage control."

"And Spencer?"

Aubrey slowly approaches, eyes locked on the bundle in my arms. "Dempsey talked to Sloane. He's in a holding cell and in decent spirits all things considered."

"Want to hold your brother?" I ask, pulling the bottle away from the little guy's mouth. "You can finish feeding him."

She frowns but nods and sits down on the sofa. I stand and walk over to her. Gently, I move the baby from my arms into hers. Her eyes widen as she looks at him.

"Looks just like Spencer did when he was a baby," I say with a nostalgic laugh. "Park genes run strong."

"Let's hope this one doesn't turn into a little shit like his brother," Callum grunts, smirking at me.

I sit back down beside Aubrey, curling an arm around her. I need her to know that despite this baby shocking the shit out of us and Spencer going to jail and her mom reappearing, that everything's going to be okay. She's tense but relaxes, leaning into me. If my brother wasn't watching us like a hawk, I'd kiss her pretty mouth and assure her I'll handle everything.

"Dad is going to have to call in all the favors for this one," Callum says. "There's no keeping this under wraps."

This is a clusterfuck of epic proportions, but if anyone can get our family out of this mess, it'd be Dad. He's the backbone of this town—the mastermind puppeteer holding all the strings.

"Have you thought of a name yet?" Aubrey asks.

"I wanted to talk to your mom first. See if she's already picked one out."

Her face sours and she looks away. Then, she passes the baby back to me. "I'm not feeling so hot. Can I go home?"

My heart breaks for her. This whole thing is mindfucking all of us. I can only imagine what's going through Spencer's mind right now as he stews alone in a jail cell. I'll fix this. I have to.

"Yeah, Love, go on home. I'll see you soon."

"Mr. Park," a nurse named Dani chirps, peeking her head in through the door. "They've moved Mrs. Park to a room. We thought it would be good for her to see the baby now that the sedation has worn off."

I hug Baby Park, as the handwritten name on the portable crib boasts, and try to squash down the rising panic. "I don't want her alone with him."

Dani presses her lips together and nods. "I know. You can walk him down there yourself."

I rise to my feet and settle him in the crib. Then, I start pushing it, following after her. We get a few curious stares along the way, but they quickly avert their eyes. I'm sure they've all been threatened with termination and personal lawsuits if they speak a word of any of this. Dad is thorough if nothing else.

Dani knocks on a door and then announces herself before motioning me in. Neena is still a picture of perfection, sitting up in a hospital bed. The hatred burning in her eyes is powerful enough to have me falter on my feet.

"Mrs. Park, do you want to hold your baby?" Dani asks, voice light and friendly. "I know he's eager to meet his momma."

Neena glowers at her. "I'd like a moment with my husband. Alone."

Dani shoots me a questioning look and I nod. As soon as she's gone, I brace myself for whatever Neena has to say.

"You want to hold him?"

Her lip curls up when I scoop our baby into my arms. "No, I don't want to hold him. Are you insane?"

Anger burns hot in my gut. This woman has been nothing but a thorn in my side since she took my last name. I should have divorced her after Aubrey left because she became unbearable to live with.

"What did you want to name him?" I ask, ignoring her nasty words. "Surely you had a name picked out."

"You think I was sitting around thinking of a name for that abomination?" she snaps, making the baby jump at the harsh tone. "Fuck no, Hugo. I plotted how I would ruin you in divorce. God, there are so many ways."

"Neena—"

"Don't Neena me. I had the paperwork drawn up. Me and Drew were going to go to New York on your dime, Hugo. We were going to drain you for every penny you had." She winces and gently touches her stomach. "But your goddamn son lured me to that room and trapped me there. He took my life away from me and now I've been butchered."

My heart hammers in my chest. "What did you say to him to make him lure you away? Were you spouting that same shit about killing our baby? Or taking all our money? Spencer was only trying to protect me."

"You live with blinders on, dearest husband. I was fucking our pool boy right under your nose and you didn't care. I did a lot right under your nose. And your precious Spencer? Do you honestly believe he was some angel?"

Spencer is a lot of things but definitely not an angel.

"I need to get a hold of Drew. I refuse to go back to our house. Not with that monster living there."

"And your daughter," I snap out. "You haven't even asked about her. She's back. Did you know that?"

She rolls her eyes. "Of course I know. Who do you think had to console your son when she first came back?"

A trickle of unease drags its way through my veins.

"Console? I thought he was your captor. Neena, you're not making any sense." I kiss the baby's fuzzy dark head. "I think all the drugs have gotten into your head."

"Oh," she sneers, eyes glittering evilly. "He was a lot more than my captor. Aubrey broke his little heart and he freaked when she came back. Aubrey has never liked me and the feeling is mutual." She snaps her head toward the door. "I want to see Drew. Find me Drew, so help me, or I'll call every reporter on this side of the Pacific and tell them just how fucked-up the Park family is."

"Neena." I grit my teeth and look away from her. "There's something you should know."

The room goes quiet except for the suckling sounds of my son as he tries to suck on his fist.

"What?" she whispers, voice cracking with emotion. Then she starts to cry. "No. No, no, no. No!"

Her outburst causes the baby to start to cry. I gently bounce him, trying to comfort him. My eyes find hers that have filled with fat tears.

"Drew is dead, Neena. He was killed after the kidnapping and attempted rape of your fucking daughter."

A strangled howl—one mixed with pain and betrayal—belts out of her. Our entire marriage she was an icy bitch and yet she breaks over the birth of her son and then again at the knowledge of the death of her lover.

"He hurt her," I croak out, hating the memories that assault me from that day. "He hurt her so fucking bad."

The baby continues to cry and I try to calm him. "It's okay, little guy. Daddy's got you."

Her wails stop abruptly, and her features transform into something monstrous and cruel. She points a manicured finger at me and flashes me a vicious smile. "Stop calling that baby your son. He's your *grandson*, Hugo. That abomination is the seed of the devil himself—your son."

CHAPTER THIRTY-SEVEN

Spencer

SHE HAD THE BABY.

I knew this day would come and that it'd blow the fuck up in my face.

It did.

The explosion was spectacular, far more impressive than I could have imagined.

"You okay?" Pops asks as we pull into his driveway. "You've been awfully quiet."

I rub at the achy muscles in my neck at having spent a night in a concrete cell. Knowing Sloane didn't get me any special treatment either. I was left to stew over the realization of what my life has become.

A disaster.

A fucking disaster.

But I'm still a Park, which is why I'm home and not left to rot in that cell. Pops has been hard at work, ensuring the fallout of this mess is dealt with.

"Come on," he grunts. "Let's get you inside."

I climb out of his vehicle and together we walk from his driveway over into our yard. The lights are on inside. Knowing Aubrey is probably crushed at discovering I'd kept her mother captive and also at her mother having a baby, has my heart sinking.

We push inside. Callum and Willa are seated on the sofa. Aubrey is nowhere to be found.

"Where's Aubrey?" I demand, shooting a glare at Callum.

"Sick. I think the emotions of all this caught up to her."

All this being the shit storm *I* created.

"I've got calls in to several people who can make this go away," Pops assures me. "Neena can be bought, that much I do know. I've got plenty of money to do that with. All you need to worry about, Spence, is resting."

A car door slams outside and then Dad bursts through the door. At first, I think he's happy to see me, but then I take in the absolute fury twisting his features.

"You raped my wife!"

Dad lunges at me, tackling me to the living room floor. He grabs my shirt and shakes me hard.

"Why, Spencer?!" Dad roars, spittle landing on my face. "How could you do this to me?!"

I try to push him away, but in his anger and having the upper hand, he's stronger. "Dad, get off!"

Dad is suddenly wrenched off of me by Callum. Pops' face is red. He's pissed, too. It's then I see Aubrey standing in the doorway, horror causing her mouth to part and her chin to tremble.

"I didn't rape her," I snap, rising to my feet. "Fuck, Dad. I'm not some sicko."

Well, aside from the whole fucking my stepsister with my dad. But that's consensual. We want that shit.

"Enough with the shouting," Pops growls. "We're going to get to the bottom of this together. Calmly." He nods at Dad. "Go on."

"Make it make sense, Spencer. So help me. Talk fast,"

Dad bites out, hurt shining behind all the anger. "Tell me how we got here."

My stomach twists at seeing his expression.

Goddammit.

I didn't want to have to deal with this shit, but I guess we're going there.

"You asked," I spit out, shrugging. I straighten my shirt, stealing a glance over at Aubrey. "She caught us. Neena caught me and Aubrey kissing."

The room is quiet aside from Dad's heavy breathing, everyone waiting for me to continue.

"Once she walked in on us, she sent Aubrey to her room. Immediately, she started in on how I had to be careful with Aubrey. That she had ulterior motives. That Aubrey was dangerous to the Park name." I scrub a palm over my oily face, aching for a shower I won't get yet. "I was shocked at first. Didn't believe it."

"And then she showed him texts from me," Aubrey chimes in. "Texts I didn't write."

Shame slicks over me and I sigh. "It felt so real. All of it. I was sixteen and just got my heart broken by my stepsister. It was a mindfuck."

Dad huffs. "This entire ordeal is a mindfuck."

"Every day Neena came to me with more evidence of Aubrey's intent to ruin us. Neena spoon-fed me her lies, feeding my anger. I wanted to make Aubrey pay. I fucking terrorized her." Guilt swarms in my belly, stinging over and over again. "And then she'd had enough. She left. I thought I could move past it."

"And then," Dad encourages, voice returning to the calm, fatherly one I recognize. "What happened next?"

"Dad," I mutter. "It just happened."

"What happened, Spence?"

"We had sex."

Pops curses under his breath. "You were sixteen."

"I knew what I was doing," I blurt out.

Dad's face grows stony. "It continued after that?"

"Yeah. Neena had a way of getting inside my head. Of pissing me off and making me feel worthless, but then she'd get sweet and nurturing. I wanted her to fix my pain."

"So you two slept together under my roof—under my nose—when you were a child?" Dad clarifies, nostrils flaring.

"Dad, I was sixteen. I had a working dick. Hardly a child."

"Spencer," Pops warns. "Don't be flip."

"Neena preyed on you," Dad growls. "She preyed on my fucking son and used him like a toy."

Aubrey sniffles and hugs herself. I wish I were the one hugging her. My words are stabbing her and I hate that.

"Neena was always sneaking off and I knew she was fucking someone else. I was jealous. I hated her for making me care for her. I was betraying my own dad for her." I pinch the bridge of my nose. "Now I know it was Drew. Fuck."

"How did she end up at the lodge?" Callum asks.

Both he and Willa are watching me with wide, shocked stares.

"She got pregnant. Bitched me out because I didn't use a condom."

"So you locked her up for bitching you out?" Pops frowns at me. "I don't follow."

"No," Dad bites out. "She threatened to terminate it."

I wince at his cold words and nod. "I panicked. It was my

baby. I didn't even want a fucking baby, but I certainly didn't want it to die. I begged her not to, but she wouldn't listen."

My eyes find Aubrey and I try to let her see how much I hate how this all turned out. I wish I could rewind back to that kiss. To tell Neena to fuck off. To take a chance with Aubrey and not assume the worst.

"I was freaking out," I admit. "I managed to get her into my car and took her to the lodge so we could discuss it more. I thought if I could calm her down for a bit, I could change her mind."

Everyone stares at me like they're seeing me for the first time. I did what I had to do. I couldn't let her kill my baby.

"I thought I loved her." My voice is hoarse. "She'd fucked with my head for such a long time by that point. I thought I could get her to see we could raise the baby together." I scoff bitterly. "But she wouldn't let up. I knew I'd be keeping her under until she gave birth."

Pops paces the living room. "Why didn't you come to me? I could have dealt with this a lot sooner."

"I freaked out, Pops. Dad had his campaign. She was pregnant with my baby. I didn't even tell Dempsey until a few weeks ago because I needed someone to help me check on her."

"Did my brother know about this?" Pops asks, scowling.

"No," I grumble. "I rented out the rooms above, below, and beside the room I had her in. I told him I wanted them to take girls there for privacy since Dad was knee-deep in his campaign. He agreed that it was a good idea to keep my promiscuity hidden under the guise of visiting the lodge. Theo even hired me. I sometimes would work on his website and shit."

"Did you sleep with my mom the whole time?" Aubrey asks, voice a whisper.

I shake my head violently. "Not the whole time. She always tried to manipulate me when I'd bring her supplies and food. I was a teenager with a working dick, thinking he was in love with his stepmom. I'd almost released her a few times. She wasn't some prisoner. I fucking spoiled her. I was the prisoner, forced to check on her several times a day." I drop down into an armchair, exhaustion taking over me. "And then Aubrey came back. It's like Neena's fog over me had been lifted. I wanted to punish Aubrey for what she'd done but…"

"You learned Aubrey was innocent and you'd been played," Dad supplies. "Fuck."

"Once Aubrey came back, I never saw Neena like that again. I talked to Neena about Aubrey's return and even tried to be intimate with her, but something was different. It felt cheap and dirty." I groan, imploring with my eyes for my dad to understand. "You have to believe me, Dad. I didn't rape her. I was just keeping her until she gave me my baby. Then, I was going to come to you and Pops. Tell you everything. I had to make sure my baby survived."

Dad storms over to me and for a moment I think he's going to throw me around again. He yanks me up by my shoulders onto my feet, then crushes me to his chest in a bear hug.

"I'm going to deal with Neena," he vows. "She's going to walk away from our lives, giving up the rights to your son. I swear to God, Spencer, that woman will leave this state and never come back."

I cling to my dad, needing him more than I ever have. "It's a boy?"

Dad releases me and pulls back to grin. "He looks just like you, Spence. He's beautiful."

"A boy," I mutter, a grin tugging at my lips. "What's his name?"

Dad rests his forehead against mine. "Just waiting on you to pick one, Son."

I have a baby.

A baby boy.

After months and months of psychological torture, I managed to make it to the finish line. My baby lived and he's waiting to be named. By me.

"When can I see him?" I ask huskily. "I want to hold him."

"Soon," Dad vows. "He'll come home soon. I'll make sure of it. This shit is over, Spencer. It's over."

Finally.

Fucking finally.

CHAPTER THIRTY-EIGHT

Aubrey

I'M IN SHOCK.

Still.

It'd been one thing to learn Spencer had kidnapped my mother and lied to my face. Sure, that hurt and was hard to comprehend. But then, the shockers kept piling on.

Mom was pregnant.

Was.

She delivered a baby—Spencer's baby.

I have a brother. A real one.

The biggest shocker of all was how she'd weaseled her way between me and Spencer, manipulating him from the second she caught us kissing. I feel like I've been played by the person who was supposed to love me the most. My mother. Now, all I feel is disgust and betrayal. It's nauseating.

Everyone left a few moments ago, but me and Spencer remained. He's been sitting in the same chair as earlier, face buried in his hands. I've been staring at him, trapped between wanting to cry for the crumbling of our lives and laugh joyfully at the idea of having a baby brother.

My emotions are a mess.

How could Mom do this to me—to us? I never understood her attitude toward me. When she and Dad divorced and he would take me places or buy me nice things, she would get so jealous. Often, she would forbid me from seeing him for long stretches. It wasn't until I hit puberty that she really let her dislike for me shine openly for all to see.

I had been so elated when she'd found Hugo. He was nice and brilliant. Plus, he had a son. I finally felt like I wouldn't be in a constant battle with a mother, who hated me. That I'd have people on my side day in and day out.

Well, she took care of that too.

Made sure to make Spencer hate me the first chance she got.

"It should be me up there," Spencer says, voice muffled by his hands. "I should be with my son."

Nathan managed to get him out of jail, but it doesn't mean he's out of the clear yet. Going up to the hospital to visit the woman he "allegedly" kidnapped is just asking for the media to fuel the sensational story. Hugo and Nathan both thought it was best for Spencer to lie low.

Plus, he looks completely and utterly exhausted.

His hair is disheveled and limp. His clothes are wrinkled. And his shoulders hunch inwardly. I'm not sure I've ever seen Spencer—preppy, arrogant Spencer—so not put together.

"Come on," I say, rising unsteadily to my feet. "You need a shower."

Spencer may have lied about my mother, but he was acting on behalf of the baby. He was protecting him just like he protected me by killing Drew. Now, it's my time to offer comfort and protection.

He offers me his hand and I pull him up. I don't let go of it, guiding him through the house to his bedroom. We make our way into the bathroom where I start the shower. I quickly undress and then glance over at him as steam fills the room. He stands there, dazed and frowning.

"Let me help," I murmur. "It's okay."

His eyes lock onto mine, heat and love burning in their depths. He remains still as I undress him piece by piece. Once he's naked too, I draw him into the hot shower with me.

"I let her use me," he croaks out, perfect lips pulling down. "I don't know how or why, just that it happened."

Grabbing his biceps, I gently push him under the spray. "Manipulators are good at that sort of thing." I run my fingers through his hair and then stand on my toes to kiss his lips. "You were her victim."

His eyes flutter closed. "I was just trying to save the baby."

I pour shampoo into my hands and then start lathering up his hair. "You saved him. He's alive and safe because of you."

He allows me to rinse his hair and then wash his body. Once I've cleaned myself, I wrap him up in a hug. His strong arms crush me to him.

"We could have had all this way back when we were sixteen," he rumbles, regret lacing his tone. "I'm sorry, Aubrey. I'm so fucking sorry."

"Hey," I murmur, cupping his face in my hands. "None of that. This is the direction our lives took. We're all going to be okay."

His hands slide to my ass and he lifts me. My emotions take a quick turn from sad about what could have been to fiery need. I reach between us, guiding his wet cock to my opening. He glides deep inside me without much warning.

"Ahh," I cry out, dropping my head back against the tile wall.

"Fuck, leech, you feel so goddamn good. You fix my fucked-up head every time."

I smile as his mouth attacks mine. This is the first time since he's come home that I feel like I have my Spencer back. Earlier, he seemed so young and vulnerable. His strength flows through me, scorching and thick like lava.

He fucks me tenderly but with the occasional wild thrust that has me screaming out in pleasure. All too soon, I'm quaking with an orgasm. His teeth sink into my neck as his dick swells. I gasp as cum shoots inside of me.

We eventually break apart and clean up again. The two of us remain under the spray until the water goes from hot to warm to icy.

It's not until we're dried off, naked, and cuddled under his covers that I finally relax. The anxiety of my mother missing had been weighing heavily on me. That coupled with the trauma I'd endured with Drew, I wasn't at my best.

But even though some pretty awful events transpired over the past twenty-four hours, I'm relieved. All the terrible stuff feels as though it's over. We can move forward now with nothing else holding us back.

With that thought, I fall asleep in the arms of one of the men I love, heart full and soul happy.

Crash.

Slam.

Bang.

I blink open my eyes, trying to make sense of the noises. Is Hugo back?

Crash.

The sound is most definitely coming from Hugo's room. I slide out of Spencer's bed, leaving him sleeping, and grab one of his T-shirts out of a drawer. Once I've stolen some of his boxers too, I tiptoe out of his room, closing the door behind me.

Hugo's bedroom door is open and the light is on. The sounds are coming from the closet. He's not one to throw things around, so I'm worried about who I'm going to find.

"Mom?"

I gape at the woman hastily throwing clothes into a suitcase. She's still wearing a hospital gown and wincing in pain.

"Mom, you should be at the hospital. You had a baby yesterday."

She turns her vicious glare on me. "They butchered me, Aubrey. My body is ruined now."

"That's why you should be in the hospital." I hold both palms up in a placating nature. "Let me drive you back."

She zips up the suitcase and with a lot of cursing, manages to stand back up. "Where are my car keys? I'll be damned if I ride in another Uber."

"Where are you going?"

"I'm getting the hell out of this town," she bites out. "If you knew what was good for you, you would too."

Not a chance in the world.

I stare at my mother as she slowly hobbles out of the closet. Tears wet her lashes. She's in pain, obviously, but she doesn't appear to be ready to rest anytime soon.

"I don't think you're supposed to drive," I say softly. "Please, Mom, let me help you."

"They were going to put me in the psyche ward." Her eyes slice right through me. "I don't want a baby and I'm a monster.

Look what happened the last time I had a baby." She waves a dismissive hand at me. "Disappointment."

Her words are whips lashing at my skin. I don't recoil because she obviously needs help. Getting my feelings hurt won't get us anywhere.

"Where will you go?" I ask instead of giving in to my emotions.

"I guess New York's out of the question since that monster murdered my boyfriend." A sob racks through her and her hand tenderly touches her belly. She hastily wipes the tears away. "I'm going back to LA. Back home to where normal people live." She gestures to her belly. "And the second this heals, I'm getting a tummy tuck so I can put this entire ordeal behind me."

"Mom…"

"I'm no one's mother. I'm Neena. Just Neena."

This time, her words hit their mark. My heart aches from the abuse she's striking it with. Her bloodshot eyes light up with delight. Hurting those around her is her favorite pastime.

"He has my keys, doesn't he?" Mom demands, pointing toward Spencer's room.

I don't say anything and follow her as she slowly hobbles out of Hugo's room. She makes it to Spencer's room and leaves the suitcase at the door. All I can do is trail after her. Spencer is still sleeping, features boyish and innocent.

She took advantage of him when he was a kid.

Anger chases away the hurt.

I watch her with narrowed eyes as she makes it into his closet, yanking sweats and a shirt off the hangers. The hairs on my arms stand on end. I don't like how she is taking clothes from him like she owns them—owns him. I stand between the bed and the closet, creating a barrier between them.

She carefully tugs away the gown. Her stomach is bandaged up and her breasts are leaking milk. And still, despite the teary, unhinged expression, she's beautiful.

Yet, she's so ugly inside.

It takes some cursing and whimpering, but she manages to dress in Spencer's clothes. She even takes a pair of his flip-flops. Then, she goes straight to his end table. Now that I've gotten to know him well, I know he always puts his keys in there since he doesn't like clutter. It pains me to know that she also knows this.

She knew Spencer as intimately as I do.

Once she has the keys, she limps into the bathroom. I can hear the sink turn on and the splashing sound of water. She returns, a sneer on her still dripping pretty face.

"Your clothes are in Hugo's room and also in Spencer's. You really are a whore."

Hearing the nasty words and the hatred being spewed my way cracks my heart the rest of the way. She's not my mother. She's my nemesis. She always was, but I never allowed myself to see it.

I see it now.

"Get out," I say lowly. "Now."

Her head cocks to the side and her nostrils flare. "Did someone find her backbone?"

"Out!" I shout, no longer worried about waking Spencer. "Get the fuck out of my house, bitch."

My words don't strike her like I want. If anything, she seems pleased by them based on the slow grin that spreads across her face. Her eyes glitter with pride. It's a look I've ached for my entire life. Now that I have it, I don't want it. She's proud of me for losing my shit. Like her.

I am nothing like her.

"There's hope for you yet, baby girl. See you in LA when you get bored of this Park bullshit."

With those words, she walks out of the room, less wobbly and more self-assured. There's no denying the woman is made of fire and titanium.

I remain rooted in place, hands curled into fists, long after the front door slams and I hear tires peeling out of the driveway. Spencer, as exhausted as he is, still quietly snores peacefully.

My phone rings from somewhere. I find it still in the pocket of my discarded jeans on the bathroom floor. The battery is almost dead. I don't answer it in time, but I notice Hugo has called several times. I rush into my room and plug it into the charger before calling him back.

"Hugo? Is the baby okay?"

"Yeah, Love, the baby is fine. I called to warn you." He sighs heavily. "Neena broke out of the hospital. I don't know how the hell she got out of here without help. But I wanted to warn you guys. She might go home."

I sit down on the edge of my bed, hugging an arm to my stomach and suppressing a shiver. "Yeah, she came home."

"Is everything okay?"

"She packed a bag, left me with some choice words, and then took the keys to her car. She's gone, Hugo. I don't think she's ever coming back."

He sucks in a sharp breath and then a relieved laugh escapes him. "Thank fuck."

"My thoughts exactly," I say with a slightly crazed giggle. "When are you coming home?"

"Soon, Love. I'll be home soon. Everything is going to be okay."

Finally, I actually believe that it will.

CHAPTER THIRTY-NINE

Hugo

"DO YOU REMEMBER WHAT TO DO?" JAMIE ASKS, grinning at me. "It's been a long time, old man."

I casually flip her off before going back to figuring out the buttons on the onesie she brought. Thank God for Jamie. I was so completely unprepared for this baby. She showed up today with a car seat, diaper bag jammed with supplies, and a backpack full of outfits. I certainly don't remember Spencer needing all this shit just to go home.

But that was nearly two decades ago.

Fuck, I am old.

The green onesie has a big T-Rex on the front that says "rawr" in cutesy writing. I'd just grabbed the first outfit on the pile, much to Jamie's dismay.

I'll be glad when Spencer names this baby. I've literally been calling him "baby." The nurses don't hide their annoyance with me either. They're probably worried about the well-being of a baby who was born from a mother who escaped the hospital after threatening to kill it and a "father" who can't even think up a name for him.

Baby Park squawks, kicking one of his skinny legs out. I pull on the matching pants that go with it and then add green socks and a green hat. There. I did it. I dressed a newborn infant without my stepmother jumping in to rescue me.

"Did they give you any trouble about taking the baby home?" Jamie asks, features turning serious.

"How could they? I'm the father."

We share a pointed look. I'm not the father, but until Spencer decides what he wants to do, I need to play it this way. I'm not taking any chances when it comes to Neena. Aubrey said she showed up at the house after she fled the hospital, packed a suitcase, and disappeared again.

I'll find her this time.

And when I do, she'll be met with divorce papers, an NDA, and some other necessary documents to ensure Spencer doesn't have any of this shit follow him or go on his record. I'll also give her an opportunity to be in the baby's life if she has a change of heart.

There will never be shared custody.

Ever.

That woman made her choices and shattered my family in the process. I'll be damned if I let her wreak any more havoc. Best-case scenario is she'll sign the papers—because she's selfish and will want to rid herself of us—and move along with her life. It won't take long before she's cozied up to some mega-rich chump wherever it is she lands.

Good riddance.

"You're all set to go," Dani, our primary nurse, says with a smile. "Looks like the little man is all ready."

I pick up the tiny thing and carefully set him in the car seat. It takes some finagling, but I manage to get his squirming arms through the straps and buckle him in.

Jamie picks up the backpack and my own overnight bag I'd packed to stay with him until he was released. I shoulder the diaper bag and then pick up the car seat. Jamie scoops up the blanket lying in a chair and drapes it over the baby.

"I'm ready," I say, letting a long breath escape.

And I am.

Ready to move on from the ugly Neena chapter of my life.

$$\odot$$

Jamie opens the door and sets the bags just inside. "I'll check in on you later. We'll give you all some privacy to get acclimated and to name that precious angel."

"Thanks," I say, giving her a side hug. "I couldn't make it through all this shit without you all."

Once she's gone, I close the door behind me. I can hear voices down the hall in Spencer's room where the door is closed. I want to burst in, but something holds me back. I gently knock.

"We're home."

"They're home!" Aubrey squeaks and then wrenches open the door.

Standing behind her is my son, eyes wide and slightly terrified. He's too young to be a father, but it doesn't change the fact that he is one. I supposed if he can kill a man and kidnap a woman, he can take care of an infant.

I walk into his bedroom and set the car seat on the floor. Aubrey holds her hands to her mouth, darting her gaze from Spencer to the baby and then back again. He remains frozen, entranced by the sleeping baby at his feet.

"You can get him out," I urge. "He won't bite."

Spencer gives a slight shake of his head as if to clear his mind and then sits cross-legged in front of the car seat. Ever so gently, as though he's opening a gift, he unwraps the blanket and tugs it away.

"Holy shit," he whispers. "He's so little."

"Same weight and length you were when you were born."

Spencer flashes me a quick, boyish grin before turning his attention back to his son. Slowly, he unbuckles the latch and then assesses how to take the baby out of the car seat. Carefully, he moves his arms through the holes and then slides his hands beneath him.

"Support his head," I remind him, though that's pretty much common sense.

My son nods, not at all put off by the suggestion. Then, he pulls him out, bringing him close to his face.

"You're so cute," Spencer coos, awe in his voice. "We knew you would be."

Aubrey playfully nudges him with her toe. "Don't teach him to be a brat."

"If he's anything like his daddy, he'll teach himself," I say in a teasing tone.

Spencer continues to admire his baby and then says, "rawr," when he sees the writing on the onesie. "T-Rex? You like dinosaurs, little buddy?"

The baby yawns wide and makes a cute little roaring sound. This makes Spencer laugh. He turns to me and says, "Rex. I want to name him Rex Nathan Park."

My chest swells with pride for my son.

"I like that," I encourage. "It's a fitting name. Your pops will be pleased with the middle name choice."

Spencer stands with his child—Rex—in his arms and hugs him to his chest. I'm in awe of my son's unfiltered delight. Sure, he's young, but parenthood already suits him well.

I suppose I'm a grandfather now, huh?

Although, I don't know what the rules are when the mother is my wife.

"You don't have to decide now, but how we proceed from here on out is up to you. We can tell the world Rex is your son, but until we sort shit out with Neena and make sure she won't retaliate, it'll be rocky." I walk over to Spencer and drop a kiss on Rex's head. "There are other options. Ways to make this smoother for everyone."

Spencer's gaze bores into me. "People think Rex is your son already, huh?"

"They do, but that can change. All it takes is a press release."

"It's going to fuck up your campaign even more than it already is because of me."

"You did what you thought was right to protect Rex," I assure him. "You didn't fuck anything up. I can fix this."

"What if you don't and you lose?" Spencer challenges.

"Do you think I give a rat's ass? I don't. I want what's best for my son and grandson. Politics are a nonissue for me."

Spencer's shoulders relax. "Maybe, for now, we let things stay the way they are. If you're his 'dad,' then it'd be harder for Neena to come back and take him away. I can be his brother in public." He kisses Rex's soft head. "At home, I can be Daddy."

I let out a quiet breath of relief. I really don't care about the campaign, but this will be the easiest for me to manage, especially with all the Neena stuff and legal implications. Later, we can make changes as necessary, but for now, we have a plan of action.

"Why don't we let you two get acquainted," I say and

then turn to Aubrey. "I'm beat and need a nap. You coming with, Love?"

"I'm right behind you," she murmurs and then walks over to give Rex and Spencer a kiss. "Be good for your daddy, Rexxy."

Spencer laughs quietly at the Rexxy remark. "Go away, leech. I've had enough of you. I have a new toy to play with."

She rolls her eyes, but she's grinning. I take her hand and guide her out of Spencer's room. We walk into my room and I shed clothes until I'm in my boxers. I wasn't lying. I am beat. The past several days have been intense as fuck. I could probably sleep for days. And, luckily, I'm the grandpa, not the father, which means Spencer's on the hook for late-night feedings.

"I can't believe I'm in a relationship with a grandpa," Aubrey sasses as we lie down beside each other.

I smirk, pulling her to me, under my arm and against the side of my chest where she fits perfectly. Her scent envelops me, filling my every thought with her. Exactly what I need. It relaxes me to the point my eyelids droop heavily.

"You have a smart mouth," I grumble, though I'm still smiling. "When Gramps gets his energy back, he's going to pay you back for that comment."

"Gramps?" She giggles. "You really do sound old referring to yourself as Gramps."

I reach over, giving her round ass a playful swat. "Hush, Love."

Her fingers draw absently over my naked chest. I'm pretty sure she's making lots and lots of hearts. It fills my own heart and spills over.

This life I have now is messy as fuck.

A tangle of awful.

Forbidden and wrong.

But it's also perfect.

I'm happier right here in this moment than I ever have been in my entire life. Spencer is a father—and a good one from what I can already tell. Aubrey is in a home where she's loved by everyone in it, free of conditions. And we have Rex. Sweet, perfect Rex.

The best part of all: Neena isn't dead. I never wished death on her, but I did want her gone from my life. Now that I know what she did with my son, I'm determined to make it so that she stays gone from our lives.

I'm not sure what the future looks like with me having a three-way relationship with my son and stepdaughter or being the grandfather of my wife and son's baby, but I have the confidence that it'll all work out in the end.

It always does.

We're Parks after all.

EPILOGUE

Aubrey
A few months later…

THIS IS THE LONGEST NIGHT OF MY ENTIRE LIFE. AND that's saying something considering we just made it through months of helping take care of my baby brother, who doesn't think nighttime is for sleeping.

Spencer should have named him Owl, not Rex.

I've started buying him owlish clothes and blankets to make my point despite my bedroom having been turned into a T-Rex-themed nursery.

"My face hurts from smiling," Gemma complains, flashing me her media-friendly grin. "Seriously, I think it's going to stick this way."

"It can't go on forever," I point out. "He won."

I scan the crowded hotel conference room that's brimming with well-dressed people on this cold November evening, looking for the man of the hour.

When our eyes lock, his grow soft and he gives me a wink that never ceases to make my blood run hot. I playfully stick out my tongue at him. His eyes darken, warning me of a delicious punishment later.

Hugo looks good surrounded by his admirers and voters. Despite the hell our family has been publicly put through, he's persevered and managed to swing the election in his favor.

I'm proud of him. He's a heck of a lot better than his opponent we went to dinner with months ago. Hugo is a good man. *My* man.

Rex hollers, his loud voice carrying over the many voices all talking at once in celebration. I see my brother, now awake from his nap, waving his tiny fist and his face screwing into a pout. Spencer has him strapped into a carrier on his chest, which looks funny considering he's wearing an immaculate Tom Ford suit.

Spencer's gaze finds mine and his is a lot more salacious than Hugo's was. Where Hugo tried to rein in his need for me, Spencer boldly shows me how much he wants me with a seductive lick over his bottom lip.

My thighs clench thinking about that mouth earlier this morning. While Rex slept, Spencer ate me out like it was his last meal. And he was ravenous. I still have the bite marks on my thighs to remember it by.

But because I've been surrounded by people all day, I haven't had a second to myself.

I need a minute.

Just one.

"I'm running to the restroom," I tell Gemma, holding my clutch to me. "Keep an eye on my little brother. I don't put it past Spencer to try and feed him cake."

The whole family is here, even Wyatt, Hugo's grandfather. Well, everyone except for Jude for obvious reasons.

Gemma laughs and then makes her way over to where Spencer is now intently listening to Dempsey as he gestures wildly, eyes wide and grin even wider amidst his vibrant storytelling. Because of Nathan's influence in this town, and my statement against Drew, the police saw Dempsey's killing as a matter of defending an innocent. Sloane was instrumental in making sure the case was open and shut, heralding Dempsey as a hero rather than a villain.

It pays to be a Park.

I make my way through the throngs of excited people and into the restroom. There's a line and I'm about to wet myself by the time I make it into a stall that reeks of old lady perfume. Finally, I rip the box out of my clutch and open it.

It's probably negative.

I only forgot my birth control a few times last month.

But I had sex. *A lot*. Sometimes with both of them when Rex was asleep, but more often than not, with each of them individually. We steal the moments when they come and it just works. We're happy.

Awkwardly, I lift my dress and attempt to pee on the test. Once finished, I clean off the pee and set it on the edge of the toilet paper holder. I finish up and then stand, waiting on the results. There are people out there, probably about to piss themselves as they wait for an open stall, but they're not getting this one. Not yet.

Time seems to tick slowly by despite the rapid hammering of my heart.

A baby—another one—would be a complication we don't need. Hugo has been incredibly busy with work, and me and Spencer started school in late August, with Spencer taking night classes at PMU to be home with Rex during the day while me and Hugo are out.

Another baby means more juggling.

More sleepless nights.

And more love.

THE TANGLE OF AWFUL

Tears well as I read the results of the stick. *Pregnant*. I knew it. Deep down, I just knew. Now it's been confirmed.

As much as I want to run into that crowded room to tell them both, I know now's not the time. I'll tell both Hugo and Spencer soon. One day when all three of us are cuddled together after lovemaking that requires each part of our unique tripod.

That's when I'll tell them.

They're daddies.

Both of them will be the daddies. *Again*.

Speaking of daddies. I'm not sure what to do about mine. For some reason, he's been reaching out and trying to make amends. All his texts go unanswered. His last one said:

Dad: You'll be happy to know I quit working for Ben. No matter how pissed I was, he wasn't faultless. I unfairly blamed you for everything.

It wasn't the apology I'd wanted, but it was something. A start in the right direction at repairing our relationship. I also learned via his texts Ben was working things out with his wife.

Maybe one day me and Dad can reconcile our differences. He's going to be a grandfather after all.

I deposit the pregnancy test into the trash receptacle and then exit the stall. All these things can wait. Right now, I need to get out there and support Hugo on his big day.

Sunday dinners at Nathan and Jamie's house are going to require a new table soon to fit everyone. This family is growing rapidly.

I can't take my eyes off Willa. She's glowing. Her apple

cheeks are brighter than usual and her big eyes are round, gleaming with happiness. Callum's arm is draped possessively over the back of her chair and he's watching her with rapt attention.

"We have some news to share," Willa says softly, not at all letting her voice carry.

Callum's features flash with anger and then he barks out in his teacher voice that still comes in handy, "Listen up, dammit!"

The table grows quiet, everyone's eyes on them.

Willa holds up a sonogram picture. "We're having a baby and just learned it's a girl."

Gemma squeals with excitement and everyone starts chattering all at once. Even Jude, stiff and slightly terrifying with his white mask on has angled his head, seemingly pleased based on the way his eyes shine beyond the two holes. I still haven't told my guys we're having a baby. I'm certainly not going to do it today and rain on Willa's parade.

This is her moment to shine.

And, boy, does she shine.

She gets up to show everyone the picture. Even Nathan is smiling, pride rippling from him. Jamie hugs Callum. They've had an incredibly rocky past, but I think they're finally finding peace.

Willa will obviously deliver her child first, but not too long before me. It means Rex and our kids will grow up together. Being that I was an only child, until Rex came along, I know how important that will be to those kids.

My mind is filled with future playdates and birthday parties.

A lifetime of happiness with the Parks.

Rex starts to cry in Spencer's arms from beside me. I take my baby brother, attempt to comfort him, and then pass him to my right. Hugo holds him in a special way that he seems to love because he settles down.

Spencer squeezes my thigh under the table and flashes me a wolfish grin. "Wanna sneak out and go make a baby?"

His teasing makes my heart skip a few beats. There are a few family members, like Dempsey, who know the truth of our secret threesome, but it's not exactly discussed openly. I'm not ready to have that conversation with anyone right now. Maybe not ever. This family protects each other, so it's not like we'd be in any sort of trouble. It doesn't mean I want everyone knowing, though. Deep down, I know Spencer also feels this way, but he just likes to taunt me to watch me squirm.

"Behave," I say, narrowing my eyes. "You're at a family dinner."

He smirks. "Yeah, leech, but our family is a little fucked-up."

I bump his shoulder with mine, totally ignoring his silly request, and get pulled into a conversation with Gemma on the other side of Spencer.

This family might be a little fucked-up, but they're my family.

And I'll never let them go.

I hope you enjoyed Hugo, Spencer, and Aubrey's story!
Want to read about the mysterious Jude Park?
The Heart of Smoke is next!

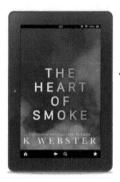

UP NEXT!

Thank you for reading!

He is a mystery, a madman,
and a masked villain...

THE HEART OF SMOKE

If you're curious about Callum and Willa's story, check out
The Teacher of Nothing!

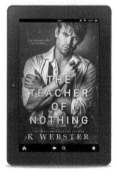

CALLUM AND WILLA'S BOOK

Thank you for reading!

*I'm obsessed with
my student..*

THE TEACHER OF NOTHING

ABOUT THE AUTHOR

K Webster is a *USA Today* Bestselling author. Her titles have claimed many bestseller tags in numerous categories, are translated in multiple languages, and have been adapted into audiobooks. She lives in "Tornado Alley" with her husband, two children, and her baby dog named Blue. When she's not writing, she's reading, drinking copious amounts of coffee, and researching aliens.

To see the full list of K Webster's books, visit authorkwebster.com/all-books.

THESE PLUS MORE...
FREE SHORT STORIES
DOWNLOAD HERE

Happy Reading!

JOIN MY NEWSLETTER
at authorkwebster.com/newsletter

JOIN MY PRIVATE GROUP
at www.facebook.com/groups/krazyforkwebstersbooks

Follow K Webster here!

Facebook: www.facebook.com/authorkwebster

Readers Group:
www.facebook.com/groups/krazyforkwebstersbooks

Patreon: patreon.com/authorkwebster

Twitter: twitter.com/KristiWebster

Goodreads:
www.goodreads.com/author/show/7741564.K_Webster

Instagram: www.instagram.com/authorkwebster

BookBub: www.bookbub.com/authors/k-webster

Wattpad: www.wattpad.com/user/kwebster-wildromance

TikTok: www.tiktok.com/@authorkwebster

Pinterest: www.pinterest.com/kwebsterwildromance

LinkedIn: www.linkedin.com/in/k-webster-396b7021

Excerpt from
The Heart of Smoke

Tate

FIRED. *AGAIN.*

It's not that I'm not good at my job. In fact, I'm great at my job. I worked my ass off in school to climb out of the cesspool I came from. To be something better than what I was expected to be.

To become *someone.*

Only problem is, with a last name like Prince, you're bound to attract a bunch of frogs. In my case, my most recent frog has made it his mission in life to destroy me.

I shudder at remembering the look of disgust on my last employer's face. She called me a delinquent. A damn heathen. I wish I could say I was surprised, but since this crap keeps happening on repeat, I calmly gathered my things, not at all shocked, went back to my lonely apartment, and then cried all of my woes to my cat, Funky.

But things are changing.

Well, one particular phone call was the catalyst of change.

A wealthy man named Nathan Park wanted to hire me— *me!*—to be the private therapist for his entire family on some huge compound they all live on. Apparently, they've all got issues and I'm their magical solution.

Me.

Tatum Oliver Prince.

Dread consumes me as I follow my GPS, making my turn down the road that will take me to my destination.

How long until I'm fired from this job too?

Nathan promised to be discreet and to pay me under the table. Not to mention, I'll be given free room and board. My apartment will sit empty like a tomb, cold and welcoming for frogs, but free of me.

God.

Freedom is so close I can taste it.

So why the underlying panic?

Why the dread that's consuming me?

Anytime something felt easy in my life, I was immediately proved wrong. And yet, I still keep believing my life will take a turn for the better. That I can be free of the chains of my past and actually find happiness.

I pass by three really nice houses, wondering which one I'm supposed to be living at. But none of them boast of the address I'm looking for. I continue down the road until a monstrous, dilapidated home comes into view, sitting at the bottom of Park Mountain like some grumpy gargoyle.

My heart rate picks up.

Of course I'd have to live in the one that looks haunted.

"Funky, we're home," I say, voice tight. "I promise we'll be safe here."

Lies.

Poor Funky.

He's used to my lies.

I put my car in park and then step out, taking in the massive home. Dark paint is peeling from the wood and it appears that half the porch is leaning slightly to one side. With my luck, it'll probably collapse the moment I step on it.

Not that I'm anywhere remotely big.

Shrimp. Baby. Little Pussy.

For someone who helps people get past their traumas, I have a heck of a time getting past mine.

Funky meows loudly and I fetch his carrier from the back seat. His golden eyes are wide, assessing our new home with suspicion.

"It's fine," I chirp, voice high and not at all reassuring to either of us. "Everything's fine."

Meow.

Funky is apprehensive. Understandably so. It's not the first time I've said this phrase seconds before my life blows up.

"This time is different," I hiss.

Meow.

In kitty-speak, he means to say, "No, it won't be, Tate."

I have to believe this is the turning point, though.

Ever so gracefully, I climb the steps, leery of weak boards, and make my way over to the front door. I swallow down my unease and then force myself to take a few steadying breaths.

Breathe, Tate.

You got this, man.

Knock. Knock. Knock.

Heavy footsteps thud through the house. Nathan mentioned I'd be helping the whole family but that I'd be staying with his son, who needs me the most. He didn't elaborate, but he said his son lost his mother tragically and hasn't taken it well. That was nearly two decades ago. There's going to be a lot of trauma to unpack.

Thunk.

The sound of a deadbolt unengaging echoes loudly and then the door opens. I'm not sure what I expect, but it certainly wasn't the Boogieman.

Funky hisses in terror.

I freeze, mouth agape.

The man—no, the monster—who towers above me is straight from nightmare territory. He wears a white latex mask, sporting all black.

"I, uh, I'm Tate Prince. Your dad hired me. I'm the therapist who—"

"No."

I blink at him, shocked at him cutting me off so rudely. The muffled word barely constituted as a word and was more of an animalistic grunt.

A shudder runs down my spine and I visibly shiver.

Don't get me wrong, I've had my fair share of patients who've gotten nasty with me, but I've always handled those situations with professional ease.

This feels different.

They were in my office seeking help.

But now, I'm in *his* territory. I'm on *his* doorstep with my cat. I'm an intruder. A trespasser. I clearly don't belong here.

He starts to close the door in my face, but my foot kicks out, stopping it with my shoe. Funky hisses again.

I should leave.

I really should.

But I can't. I can't go back to that apartment. I can't keep hunting for job after job only to have it taken away the second I get comfortable. This job was supposed to be my way out. And I'll be damned if I let some Halloween freakshow send me packing.

I lift my chin, giving the beast before me as much attitude as I can muster. "Your dad hired me. I'm not going anywhere."

He's silent for a beat and then he leans down, bringing his masked face close to mine. I'm forced to stare into his icy blue eyes that peer out beyond the eyeholes. His eyes are cracking open my head and raping my thoughts against my will.

I feel exposed.

Seen.

Fileted and molested.

"You're fired," he snarls through his mask. "Now go before I break your foot."

I squeak in horror, jerking my foot back. As promised, he slams the door hard in my face. If I'd left my foot there, I'd probably be missing a few toes by now.

"What now, Funky?" I ask, voice shaking and heart beating a million miles a minute. "What do we do now?"

Funky meows.

It's kitty-speak for, "Whatever it takes, Tate, because we're quickly running out of options."

The Heart of Smoke is coming...

Milton Keynes UK
Ingram Content Group UK Ltd.
UKHW020811150823
426904UK00018B/908